## PRAISE FOR *Undiscovered*

"As West Texas native Bob Buckel well knows, small towns in the Lone Star State, even those 'growing more tumbleweeds than kids,' keep their secrets close. In *Undiscovered,* two old friends, reunited after years apart, discover that they just can't let one particular small-town secret lie unresolved among the dust and decay of yesteryear. The reader is happy to tag along as the witty and likeable couple—think Nick and Nora Charles with just a hint of Texas twang—delve ever more deeply into an intriguing mystery, one that turns out to be a bit more dangerous than they bargained for."

— JOE HOLLEY, Pulitzer Prize-winning editorial writer and author of six books, including *Hometown Texas,* a collection of his weekly "Native Texan" columns; *Hurricane Season: The Unforgettable Story of the Houston Astros and the Resilience of a City*; and *Sutherland Springs: God, Guns and a Small Texas Town,* recipient of the 2021 Carr P. Collins Award from the Texas Institute of Letters as the year's best work of nonfiction.

"Like the West Texas winds, Bob Buckel's novel is full of grit and lays bare small-town secrets hidden by the ages. *Undiscovered* is a rare find these days: a hard-hitting story told with a gentleman's touch."

— TRAVIS BURKETT, author of *An American Band,* 2024 Elmer Kelton Award winner

"A decades-spanning tale of intrigue that sends childhood friends, now reunited as adults, on the trail of a twisty mystery. Readers will find a variety of interesting characters, vistas from West Texas to Canada, and intrigue that genre fans will consume with glee as Buckel keeps the tale zipping along to its dramatic conclusion. This is an excellent read."

—MARK K. CAMPBELL, author of *Sense Vs. Soul, The Snake in the Dishwasher,* and *Fat Chance, Indeed.*

I0894181

# UNDISCOVERED

Library of Congress Cataloging-in-Publication Data

Names: Buckel, Bob author
Title: Undiscovered : a novel / by Bob Buckel.
Description: Fort Worth, Texas : TCU Press, [2026] | Includes bibliographical references.
Identifiers: LCCN 2026022111 (print) | LCCN 2026022112 (ebook) | ISBN 9780875659824 paperback | ISBN 9780875659831 ebook
Subjects: LCSH: Women--Crimes against | Auctions | Texas, West | LCGFT: Novels | Detective and mystery fiction | Fiction
Classification: LCC PS3602.U2634 U53 2026 (print) | LCC PS3602.U2634 (ebook)
LC record available at https://lccn.loc.gov/2026022111
LC ebook record available at https://lccn.loc.gov/2026022112

Cover design and illustration
by Karina Rodriguez-Alcorta

TCU PRESS

TCU Box 298300
Fort Worth, Texas 76129
www.tcupress.com

# UNDISCOVERED

A NOVEL BY BOB BUCKEL

TCU PRESS
Fort Worth, Texas

## DEDICATION

This book is dedicated to my beloved wife, Krisan, for her unfailing encouragement and support, not just in its writing and editing, but throughout our years together. She has been a loving critic who has not only made me a better writer, but a better man, as we continue to discover each other.

. . . All that tread
The globe are but a handful to the tribes
That slumber in its bosom.

"Thanatopsis"

WILLIAM CULLEN BRYANT, 1817

**Thurston, Texas: 1969**

Evelyn leaned against the door of the dark basement, playing a flashlight on her son's hands as he slid the last brick into place.

"Level it up," she said, her voice raspy as sandpaper in the cool night air. "That's it. And don't forget to dress that mortar. It's got to look just like the original."

"I couldn't find a jointer," he said, panting.

"Use your finger!" she whispered. "Round it in."

"That hurts, Ma! It's bleeding already!"

He worked on without sympathy, sniffing back tears amid the dust that drifted like smoke through the beams of furtive light. Finally, the last brick went in. He tucked the mortar above it with raw fingers and winced as he scraped the joint one last time. He reached down, picked up blobs of mortar drying into rocks on the floor, and dropped them into the bucket.

"Now, take that broom and smooth the dirt out," Evelyn said. "No footprints. No trace we were ever down here."

"Ain't nobody gonna look down here, Ma," he said.

"We don't know that, boy!" she barked. "What if they come straight here? First thing?"

She glared at him, her eyes sharp with anger.

"Ma," he said, his voice breaking. "You know it was a accident. I just—"

"You were an accident!" she spat into the dark, empty space. Tears welled in her eyes at her sudden venom. She closed them and hugged him from behind, her head against his broad, damp back. Rain continued to pour down outside. Her voice softened.

"You ought to . . . join the army," she said, patting him on the shoulder. "Maybe they'll send you to Viet Nam. . ." She paused. "Wouldn't that be something?"

"I'm sorry, Ma!"

"Me too, son," she said, pushing him away with one hand, wiping her eyes with the other. "I'm sorry about a lot of stuff. Now, get on out of here. Tonight."

She reached into the pocket of her apron, grabbed a roll of bills and placed them in his hand. He took it, raised the door, and stepped out into the rain without a word. Before he could turn around to say goodbye, she rolled it down with a bang, and he was alone.

He trudged through the rain to open the truck's door.

"Ain't nobody ever comin' down here," he whispered to no one.

**Fort Worth, Texas: 2015**

It was Monday. Henry stood in the lobby of the Worthington National Bank, waiting for the elevator, clutching his overpriced coffee. As usual, he thought about walking up, elevating that heart rate, tightening those quads. As usual, he didn't. He did, however, glance to his left.

There was Ella.

She stood in the middle of the small crowd, tall and well-dressed, staring straight ahead. She looked professional, formidable, unapproachable. He thought about not speaking. But how could he not? It had been, what, more than twenty years? They were childhood friends. He *had* to speak. His pulse shot up, as if he was indeed climbing the stairs.

He was afraid she wouldn't recognize him, terrified she would. But fear had always been his best motivator. He heard his voice say her name.

"Ella?"

She turned and looked at him, blank for a second, a little annoyed. Then her eyebrows shot up and her face came to life.

"Henry? Henry!" she said, smiling. "Oh, I was hoping I'd run into you!"

She spread her arms wide, almost splashing a bystander's coffee. He stepped over and awkwardly offered a side-hug. She wasn't having it. She locked him in a head-on embrace. He felt squished. It was, perhaps, the best moment of his life.

The elevator doors opened, and people crowded past them, filling the box. She linked her arm through his and guided him to the side, out of the flow.

"Wow! It's *you!*" she said. "Henry! Baby! I knew you worked here, but I didn't think I'd see you this soon!" She pushed him away and looked him up and down. He was thin but not frail, sandy haired, bookish but not nerdy. A little shorter than she was, but not too short, not excessively handsome but what most Texas women would call "cute."

"You look great!" she said and hugged him again. "Oh, it is *so* good to see you!"

Her greeting was much more enthusiastic than he would have expected, if he'd had expectations. The sight of her, her smell, sparked a cascade of memories—the time they'd sneaked into the drive-in theater in the trunk of Barry's car, and he was so scared of Barry he crawled all the way to the back of the trunk, so he didn't touch her. And the choir trip when they played spades all the way to Monahans.

Henry was almost forty, but at the sight of Ella, he was a sophomore again. The cool girl was talking to him. He loved it and couldn't stand it at the same time. He took a deep breath.

"Ella, what in the world are you doing here?"

"You work here, right?" she asked, ignoring his question. "What's it like?"

"I asked you first," he insisted. "What are you doing here? Are you suing someone? Us?"

"No!" she said, laughing. "I moved to Fort Worth. I got a job at this big architect firm—"

"Penwell?"

"Yes!"

"That's who I work for!"

"I know! I found you on the website!" She linked her arm through his and pulled him over to a marble bench. *She touches a lot,* he thought, as if every nerve in his body wasn't already standing at attention. He kept having to remind himself to breathe.

"I was just ready to get out of Lubbock, you know?" she said as they sat down. "My son is at Tech and my daughter's coming to North Texas. Fort Worth seemed like a good place, close but not too close.

I saw this job on a law website, looked into it, went to the company's site, and just randomly going through the directory, I found you. I got the job! Here I am!"

"You didn't call me?" he asked.

She shrugged. "Babe, I don't have your number."

He quickly forgave her, melted by her brown eyes. "Yeah, I guess I don't have yours, either."

"I figured we would just bump into each other." She laughed. "I didn't know it would be at the elevator, my very first day."

Her eyes locked on his. "But Henry, I'm *so* glad to see you, really."

He was still processing. His feet were tapping, fingers drumming, eyes darting all around her, still crawling away from her in Barry's trunk.

"So, tell me . . . what is it you do here?" she asked. "Last I heard, you were some kind of newspaper guy, over in East Texas."

"Yeah, well, that was a long time ago," he said with a shrug. "The job was fine, but I was engaged to the boss's daughter. When we broke up, it . . . you know."

"Oh, yeah." She grimaced, then continued. "Yeah. That would be awkward, I guess. Sorry. So, you're still single?"

"Yeah," he said, almost apologetically. "I may just be too weird . . ."

She reached out and touched his shoulder, a sad, tender gesture. "Hey, don't say that. You're a great guy. That girl . . ."

"Rhonda."

"She doesn't know what she missed!"

"Hah," he half-laughed. "I think she's probably okay with it. She married her old high school boyfriend, and they've got a couple of kids."

"Well, I hope she doesn't think a high school boyfriend and a couple of kids is any kind of guarantee. It took Barry and me nearly twenty years to figure that one out."

He touched her shoulder. "Yeah, I couldn't believe . . . you and Barry. I'm sorry."

She looked down with a half-smile, then looked away for a moment and shook her head, like she was clearing away a mild concussion. Her eyes went a little wonky. When they came back to his, a page had turned. He would come to cherish this habit.

"But hey, that's life," she said. "You move on, don't you?"

"Yep," he said. "You do what you've got to do."

She took his hand and held it between both of hers, and they sat and looked at each other. *She touches a lot,* he thought again. *And wow, she's still beautiful.* But it was a matter-of-fact beauty, like it just happened, not high-maintenance like so many Texas women.

As he scanned her face, another snapshot came back. After her and Barry's wedding, the reception, the dancing, the standing around, just before the car door slammed and they drove away. Henry was in the crowd outside the church, clutching his bag of birdseed, and she looked up at him, and all of a sudden there was nothing but her face: lost, scared, frozen. That look haunted him for years. He'd only seen her a couple of times since then.

"So," she asked. "What does a newspaper guy do for an architect?"

He wagged his head from side to side.

"Well, I write about architecture—our architecture, the stuff we build. I help put together presentations, meet with clients, basically tell them what geniuses our people are," he said. "There's a language. If I do a good job, they hire us and we get a bunch of money. It's a lot like newspaper work, except for the 'bunch of money' part."

She laughed, then began to pepper him with questions, probing for details, taking nothing at face value. *She would have made a terrific reporter,* he thought.

"So, I know you did some construction in college, but, did you . . . study architecture?"

"No . . ."

"Building?"

"Nope."

"Landscaping? Interior design? Anything related to . . ."

"No!" He shook his head. "I was an English major. Am I on trial?"

"Maybe . . ." she said, giving him a stern-but-skeptical look.

"Hey, English is the most useful degree you can have," he said defensively. "Just make sure you learn enough words to convince someone to give you a job. But I've always had a thing about buildings. This one, for example, the Burk Burnett building . . ."

He looked up, waved his arm as if he were showing the place to a potential buyer. "Twelve stories, built in 1914, tallest building in Fort Worth at the time. Samuel Burk Burnett, the rancher, didn't build it—he bought it, in 1915, when the bank that built it went belly-up—"

"Wow, that's a lot of alliteration, even for an English major," she said, laughing. He continued, unfazed.

"Ella, I've loved architecture all my life—Frank Lloyd Wright, Frank Gehry, I. M. Pei, Louis Kahn, Phillip Johnson." "The water gardens, the Stockyards, the art-deco at Will Rogers—we've got all this great stuff here. At the *Star-Telegram*, I actually got to interview Tadeo Ando through a translator after he was picked to design the Modern."

"You worked at the *Star-Telegram*?" she asked.

"Yeah, ten years. But eventually, I got laid off, took a buyout. I was knocking around, doing some freelancing, writing high school football games, when this job came up. I got an interview and put the old sales pitch on 'em. They went for it."

"Ten years?" She looked at him mournfully. "You did something for ten years and I didn't even know about it? How did we get so out of touch? We were friends!"

"I know!" he said. "But there was always Barry . . ."

She took his hand. "But *we* were friends, Henry."

"I know," he said with a gulp. Again with the touching.

Being close to her for this long was intoxicating. He blushed, then turned his own page.

"So, that's what I do. What about you? Why does the company I work for need a hot-shot criminal lawyer? Is there something I should know?"

She leaned back and sighed, playing the big-shot lawyer. She wasn't afraid to act goofy. It was another endearing quality.

"Oh, Henry, baby," she said, smiling. "You know how it is. They needed an in-house lawyer to write contracts, respond to lawsuits—all that crap. It's not exciting, and it doesn't build any buildings, but it's my job. I did some criminal, some corporate, it's just . . ."

"Just what?"

"Just something to help me put a couple of kids through college," she said, again with that head shake and a tone of finality. "And I'm about to be late. On my first day." She stood up.

"What floor are you on?" he asked. "We have the top two."

"Oh, man!" She started leafing frantically through her case. "I think I'm up with the grand poo-bahs, wherever that is . . ."

"That would be twelve," he said. "The view is awesome."

He gently took her arm and guided her onto the elevator while she kept flipping through papers. The doors opened and they stepped in. Just as they closed, she found what she was looking for, holding it up like a prize.

"Yeah! Twelve! I'm meeting with Mr. Penwell at 9:15! I have plenty of time."

"You obviously haven't ridden these elevators," he said ominously. "So, old Mr. Penwell or young Mr. Penwell?"

"Henry, how would I know?" She deadpanned. "Do you think they put that on there?"

He smiled. "I'm sure it's old Mr. Penwell, but I'll bet Junior invites himself."

The elevator stopped at eleven, the doors opened, and he stepped out. She started to follow, but he held up his hand to stop her.

"No, this is where *I* get off, with the worker bees," he said. "You go on up and enjoy your meeting. Lunch?"

"Uh . . ." she stammered as the doors began to close. "I don't think I can, I—"

"I'll find you," he yelled. And she was gone.

He stood there and basked for a moment. That was the longest conversation they'd had since they were kids. His voice hadn't cracked, he didn't fall down, and as far as he knew, he hadn't grown any new zits.

"Hmmm," he said to himself as he turned. "This could get interesting."

* * *

Ella didn't move to Fort Worth because of Henry, but she was happy he was here. She'd known him most of her life, and that was reassuring. She'd always been a little intrigued by him, a voice in her head whispering that maybe instead of going for the big handsome jock, she should have focused on the cute, insecure, quirky, brainy guy.

It would be good to have an old friend around. Everything else in her life was new.

She and Barry had been "Cutest Couple" in the yearbook. Ella had captured other honors, including the killer combination of "Most Beautiful" and "Funniest." If there'd been a category for "Least Likely to Get Married Right Out of High School," she'd have won that, too. She was articulate and independent, with college and career and success written all over her. But Barry bought a ring, took a knee, and proposed to her in front of the entire football team. How could she say no?

As soon as they got their diplomas, it all seemed silly. But she had a ring on her finger, the weight of expectation on her shoulders—and a baby on the way.

After graduation, wedding arrangements took on a momentum of their own, powered by their mothers, both eager to get it done and get them out of town before her condition was visible. Ella, who had never been passive about anything, was a mere passenger on the train taking her life in a direction she had not chosen. Amid a blur of showers, flowers, and pastel dresses, opening gifts and oohing and aahing, she remembered thinking that if anyone could come up with an idea to save her, it might be Henry. She'd wanted to ask him for help, right up to the moment the car door slammed, and it was too late.

Henry's lost, sad face was the last one she remembered seeing that day.

The elevator dinged, and the doors opened. A young woman at the reception desk looked up expectantly. "Hi," she said. "Can I help you?"

"I'm Ella Franklin." "I have a 9:15 with Mr. Penwell."

"Yes! Ms. Franklin! Mr. Penwell is looking forward to meeting you." Her shoes clicked on the marble floor as she came around the desk. "Let's go to the conference room. I'm sure he'll want to show you your new office himself." Then she paused, turned around, and whispered to Ella, as if confiding a secret, "You're going to love working here!"

Ella just smiled.

She accepted coffee and sat at the long, dark oak conference table. She noted the framed professional-looking photographs on the wall—buildings, parks, and plazas the firm had designed, no doubt. She admired the hardwood flooring, the inset ceiling, the videoconferencing technology. Then her mind wandered.

Barry wasn't a bad person. He was good-looking, athletic, smart in his way. They got along fine when the biggest challenge was a test or a book report, and the solution to everything was to make out in his pickup. But married, trying to do life together? That was different.

Ella knew quickly she'd made a mistake.

At first, she'd tried to light a fire under him, but he simply wasn't flammable. Pushing him just made her miserable. He was unfazed. She was a powerful force, but he was an immovable object. Finally, she gave up. Chalk one up for inertia.

Ella built her own life, a superwoman: two kids, two jobs, a college degree with honors. She battled her way through law school, got Andrew to soccer practice and Natalie to dance lessons, and took care of her good-old-boy husband. It took a toll, but it deepened her reserves.

Barry's plan seemed to be to work as little as possible. He hung out with his high school buddies, played pickup basketball, and watched sports constantly. On Saturday nights, they would come over, drink beer, and play video games into the wee hours. Ella had to be the grownup, poking her head into the room to remind them the kids were asleep. It was like having a house full of teenage boys, only she was married to one of them.

The conference room door opened, and a distinguished gray-haired man in a tailored suit walked in and extended his hand. A warm smile creased his face.

"Hi," he said. "I'm Roger Penwell. You must be Ellie Franklin."

"Ella," she said, rising, smiling, and extending her hand. "It's good to meet you, Mr. Penwell."

"Please, forgive me, *Ella,*" he said. "And call me Roger. Have a seat."

He gestured toward a chair and sat down across from her.

"We are really excited to add you to our team," he said, his gaze open and friendly.

"I'm excited about the opportunity," she said. "It's going to be a little bit of a learning curve at first, but—"

"Nah," he interrupted. "Once you see what we've got for you, I have an idea you'll feel right at home. Lawyering is lawyering. Contracts and responding to litigation are pretty much the same everywhere. We're just thrilled to find someone of your background and caliber who wants to do this instead of hanging up a shingle and becoming a millionaire."

Ella laughed. For a man who was undoubtedly a millionaire many times over, he had that classic down-to-earth charm. She'd seen the same quality in successful lawyers: brilliant legal strategists, ruthless litigators, who came across in court like slow-talking, easygoing country boys. They usually went by two first names, like Jim Bob or Billy Ray.

After more conversation and the promise of lunch with a few key people, he rose and offered to walk Ella to her office.

"This used to be a partner's office," he informed her. "He decided to go out on his own, so it's just been sitting here empty, waiting for you." He pushed open the solid, dark-stained wood door, which already bore a plaque with her name and the title "Chief Counsel."

*A partner, huh?* Ella thought. *That explains the size.*

"Wow," she said aloud. "Mr. Penwell—Roger, this is too much."

"Nah," he said again. "Besides, it's about the only thing we have available."

"You could subdivide!" she said. They both laughed.

After he left, she hiked around behind the desk and sat, feeling lost. This office was bigger than her apartment. Looking over applications for the assistant she would soon hire, her mind drifted back to what had brought her here.

Barry had hired on with a well-servicing company and been issued a brand-new pickup. He spent his days driving to and through oilfields, checking on a dozen or so "stripper" wells—old wells that only produced four or five barrels a day and required little maintenance. They didn't care when he checked them, and they paid him far more than the effort merited. He joked that he "got paid to hang out with strippers all day."

He never raised a hand to Ella, but never lifted a hand to help, either. Once the kids were in school, her happy place became the law library. She read Supreme Court decisions and savored their clarity and logic. It surprised her how intensely she came to love the law's neatness and precision, its ultimate rightness. Through a contact in the district attorney's office, there was a job offer before she even took the bar exam. Before long, her courtroom performances became a must-see for colleagues. She had a soft, brutal honesty, an ability to look people in the eyes and ask the toughest questions without seeming unkind. People would open up to her even as she gently placed a noose around their necks.

No one had ever seen anything quite like Ella in court.

Those moments seemed spontaneous and effortless, but they were the result of hours of preparation. She read reports, talked to detectives and witnesses, went to crime scenes to reenact what had happened. She did so much homework that when she had a witness on the stand, it was as if she'd been there when the crime was committed, taking notes.

She was already being mentioned as the next DA when Barry's company told him they wanted to transfer him to Roswell, New Mexico. For once, his logic was unassailable. He needed *this* job, he told her. She could easily sign on as a prosecutor in Roswell, go to work for a local law firm, or open her own practice. She could do her thing anywhere.

The last thing Ella wanted to do was snuff out the only glimmer of ambition she'd ever seen in her husband, so she quit her job, and the family went west. She thought about going to work in the Chaves County DA's office, but decided instead to switch gears. A friend's father was senior partner in the biggest firm in town. She called and they encouraged her to send a resumé. She was hired after one interview to work in the oil and gas sector.

Andrew and Natalie adapted easily to their new surroundings. Andrew thought it was cool living so near where an alien spaceship had crashed; he was on constant alert for creatures from other planets. Some of the locals, and a lot of the tourists, merited suspicion. Natalie discovered she was the fastest runner at her school and was quickly becoming a star athlete.

Ella represented a widow whose husband had died in an oilfield accident and sued on behalf of a brother and sister who had been cheated out of royalty payments. She also defended oil and gas companies against an endless parade of frivolous, almost comical, lawsuits. Her trial experience set her apart, and she had the ability to grasp, then explain, the most technical issues without being patronizing. Juries liked her. She was quickly the firm's rising star.

Barry went in a slightly different direction.

"Ready for lunch?" The gelled head of a young man poked through her office door.

"Uh, sure!" she replied, rising and extending her hand. "I'm Ella."

"Brett," he said, taking her hand. "Head of engineering. Good to meet you, Ellen. Lunch is in the conference room. It's Joe T's—and I think we have you to thank!"

She must have given him a blank look, because he clarified, "Joe T. Garcia's? Stockyards? Fajitas? World famous?"

"I'm new," she half-apologized.

He shook his head. "You'll see. We'll have to go there sometime." With a look like he was doing the new kid a favor, he grinned and was gone.

"It's *Ella*," she muttered. "And I'm old enough to be your mother." Biologically, it wasn't quite true, but it made her feel better.

She met a dozen new colleagues on the way to the conference room. Lunch was followed by a tour of the offices led by the young Mr. Penwell. She and Henry exchanged conspiratorial grins when the tour breezed through his cubicle, down with the "worker bees." By mid-afternoon her head was spinning with new names, a new vocabulary, new ideas, and a new culture.

*These people* build *stuff*, she thought. *All I've ever created is the kind of paperwork that keeps people up at night.*

Ella decided to make herself some notes. As soon as she logged in, she saw an in-house email from Henry.

> *Hey! I saw you're in the system already, so I decided to be your alpha tester (or is it beta? I never get that right). Let me know what day you're free for lunch. Since you probably haven't gotten your first enormous paycheck yet, I'll buy ($10 limit!).*

She replied quickly with her schedule and her phone number, smiling as she typed.

**Thurston: 1950**

Arnold truly was an accident. Evelyn was only 15 when her drunken father's drunken gambling buddy staggered into her bed after a poker game. Evelyn never even saw his face. Jolene, her father's latest girlfriend, found her the next morning, curled up wide awake where he'd left her, one eye blackened, lip swollen, nightgown ripped. She sat on the side of Evelyn's bed with a sad smile and stroked her hair without saying a word. Then she walked out of the room, out of the house, and Evelyn never saw her again.

When she finally eased out of bed, she threw up, took a bath, then inspected her wounds in front of the mirror before getting dressed. Her father was gone; she did not know where. She didn't see him for several days, which was neither unusual nor unwelcome. She went back to school and did her best to act as if everything was normal. Her injuries didn't raise any eyebrows; her father inflicted worse on a fairly regular basis.

The bruises had faded by the time she realized she was pregnant. Having never known her mother, she had no clue how reproduction worked and had been trying very hard to forget the whole awful thing. She'd felt sick a few times but thought she'd just caught some disease from her attacker. It never occurred to her to report it to law enforcement. Finally, Evelyn told her symptoms to the school nurse, who handed her a pamphlet with downcast eyes. She went to the school library and furtively gathered what information she could find—very little, given the time and place. She kept her condition a secret, wore loose-fitting clothes, and agonized over what to tell her father, and when.

She caught him one evening, sitting in his chair, staring at nothing, a glass in his hand.

"Hey, uh, Daddy?" she started tentatively.

"Leave me alone," he muttered. "Can't you see I'm busy?"

"But Daddy, I'm . . . I'm pregnant."

He stared, open-mouthed, then lunged and took a swing at her with his open hand. She stepped back in time to dodge it and he fell back into the chair, spilling his drink.

"I knew you'd turn out bad," he yelled. "Just like your mother! Slut!"

She didn't even try to explain. She didn't care what he thought. But she told him about a place she'd seen in one of the pamphlets in the school nurse's office: a "home" in Fort Worth where they took in girls who were in trouble. She wanted to go live there, put the baby up for adoption, let it have a good home.

"Hell no!" he bellowed. "Not my grandson!" As if he had some claim.

Instead, he imprisoned her in the house. Not knowing how to drive, she was trapped in the run-down shack, miles from the highway, halfway up the side of a flat-topped hill everyone called the Mesa, her life suspended. One day, the county truant officer came up the road to inquire about her extended absence from school. She listened through the door.

"Well," her father coughed—a wheezing, over-dramatized cough. "I guess I could try to (cough) bring her but I (cough) don't get out much since I got the (cough) tuberculosis."

"Oh, in that case, I . . ." the man said, feeling behind him for the door.

"She's got it, too, they think (cough, wheeze) and the doctor said we ought to quart (cough) quarter (cough) I mean . . ."

"Quarantine?"

"Yeah! That's the word!" And he launched into a fit of coughing and wheezing worthy of Lawrence Olivier. Given her father's alcohol-emaciated frame, the story was fully believable. The truant officer couldn't get out of the house fast enough. Her father's coughs gave way to cackling laughter as the car raced away.

She stayed in her room and became a voracious reader, thanks to the Bible and a few other books she found lying around the house: *The Little Prince, Animal Farm,* and *Cannery Row*. Her favorite was *Diary of a Young Girl* by Anne Frank—a teenager like her, trapped in a basement for two years under the threat of being sent to a Nazi death camp.

Her father brought her whatever food he'd fixed for himself, often cold leftovers with bites missing. He still drank heavily, and on weekend nights, he had groups of men over for poker and booze. Peeking through the cracked door, she looked for her assailant. She wasn't sure if she would recognize him, or what she'd do if she did.

She wished him dead. She wished them all dead.

When her father passed out or disappeared, she would go outside and walk among the yucca and mesquite and breathe the fresh, clean air. At night, she would look up at the stars, so many and so close she felt she was among them. Sometimes she'd try to pray, but she didn't know much about God and was convinced he had no time for her. She thought about walking down to the highway and hitching a ride into town, but it was a long way. She was in a bad spot, but she knew from experience that things could get worse.

* * *

On a freezing wet February night, Evelyn's water broke and she went into labor. It took a lot of screaming to wake her father from a drunken stupor to take her to the hospital, 20 miles away. When she finally rousted him, he panicked, shoved her into the back seat of his Lincoln and roared toward the highway. Evelyn remembered thinking this must be what seasickness felt like. Either the accelerator or the brake, or both, were all the way to the floor at all times.

They hadn't been on the highway five minutes when he lost control on the ice and crashed, head-on, into the pillar of an overpass. Evelyn was slammed into the floorboard, stuffed face-down into a coffin of upholstery, twisted steel, and broken glass, the hot driveshaft hump directly on her bulging belly. She was terrified the car would catch on fire, but she could not move. Before long she began to almost relish the idea of a fire as the damp cold began to work its way into her body. Her quiet agony was interrupted only by contractions that got stronger and more urgent until each one felt, not like birth, but death.

She heard no stirring from the front seat, no breathing. She was sure her father was dead. She was surrounded by the sickening smell of blood, alcohol, and gasoline. The engine cooled and stopped clicking, fluids stopped dripping and night sounds took over: the wind, the plink of sleet on the metal and the ground around them, and her breathing, fogging the air in front of her face. With increasing frequency she broke the silence, screaming with each contraction, rage as much as pain. The cry welled up from deep inside her and felt like it would rip her throat out. Then it would subside, and there was only the sleet and her ragged breathing.

After an eternity, she heard a car, close. The crackling of a police radio and a flashing strobe light that popped through the wreckage told her it must be a policeman. A door opened and slammed shut, and she heard footsteps around the car. The bright beam of a flashlight shone through gashes in the metal, and a man's low whistle confirmed he had seen what was left of her father.

Then quickly, the gravel crunched away, and the car door slammed shut. It had not occurred to her that he might not see her. She heard him radio for help, but he stayed inside the car and her next volley of screams went unheard.

After another eternity, more vehicles, more strobe lights piercing her coffin. The cold air crackled with the sound of police radios and hushed voices, even laughter. She tried to speak, to call for help, but she was too exhausted to make herself heard. Suddenly, she felt a jolt. The car was being hooked to a wrecker. They were going to tow it in.

Just then, another contraction hit, and Evelyn's unearthly hoarse scream filled the night. By the time it subsided she heard shouts, and a scramble for tools. The wrecker driver lowered the car back to earth and they closed in, banging, calling to her. She called back, her voice weary and weak—but now they were listening. They had to pry a back door open, but finally, carefully, many hands pulled her out. Moments later, she gave birth in the ambulance.

Evelyn heard later that it took them another hour to get her father's body out of the mangled car. He was pronounced dead at the scene. Somehow, Evelyn survived.

The boy was chubby, pink, miraculously unscathed. Evelyn was cut up and bruised, but no bones were broken. They put the baby in a bassinet in her hospital room until she was well enough to go home. The nurses brought warm bottles, changed diapers, offered example and instruction, but after two weeks she was dismissed. A social worker drove them back to the rickety house on the mesa, where old leftovers were crawling with roaches and mice skittered boldly along the baseboards. The woman helped her clean the place up, gave her some basic childcare supplies, and promised to come back and check on her once a week.

Evelyn watched her drive away. As soon as the car was out of sight, she began throwing things out, starting with her father's liquor bottles, shattering them into the burn barrel one by one. At some point she realized she and the baby were both screaming. She picked him up and nursed him, then placed him gently into his crib and returned to her purge. She threw away everything that smelled of her father, looked like him, or reminded her of him: clothes, toiletries, even the pictures on the walls. She couldn't bear the thought of living with it. She lit the barrel, then continued to throw items into the flames until all that was left of her father's life was ashes.

She kept three things: his Bible, a bank bag she found under his mattress containing $1,875—probably winnings he'd set aside to ante into poker marathons—and a small handgun she found in a cloth bag under the bed, along with a box of bullets.

She might need it, she thought, if any of his drinking buddies came back around.

* * *

The social worker kept her promise. Once a week she brought groceries, helped Evelyn clean, and played with the baby. Together they applied for what meager welfare existed, and those checks started coming every month to the mailbox down at the end of the road. Evelyn convinced the social worker to cash them for her. It all went into the bank bag.

As spring warmed up, Evelyn explored the place during the baby's naps. The house's paint had all weathered off years ago, and there was no insulation in the walls. It had a roof, though, along with a tiny kitchen and two bedrooms, a living room, and a bathroom. Some distance away stood a sheet-metal barn Evelyn's father had kept locked. Once, when she was about eight years old, she'd explored in that direction and when he caught her, he gave her a cruel beating. But now this was her place, so one warm spring day, she grabbed the overloaded key ring she'd found in the dresser drawer and rolled Arnie's stroller in that direction, determined to see what was inside. After several tries, the dry lock opened.

Streaming sunlight revealed a bare lightbulb hanging from a wire. She pulled the string and it clicked on. In separate bays behind two sliding doors, covered with dust, sat an old pickup and an antique tractor. The tractor looked valuable, but the truck seemed more practical. She searched the glove box and found the original service manual, and after glancing through it, she decided to try and get it started.

Evelyn unlatched the sliding door and dragged it open, then worked the entire morning. She got shocked several times and had to stop and nurse little Arnold when he cried, but just before noon the engine finally sputtered to life. Quickly she threw the baby into the passenger seat and propped him in place with towels. With some effort, she coaxed it into reverse, backed out and headed toward the house, but she got up too much speed, and when she jammed the dusty brakes, the car lurched and dumped him screaming into the floorboard.

Leaving the engine running, she slipped it into neutral, set the parking brake and got out. She picked him up and comforted him, then moved the towels to the floorboard and repositioned him in a makeshift bed he couldn't fall out of. Experience had taught her you couldn't fall if you were already as far down as you could get.

Finally, they were set, and the old pickup jerked out onto the road, gears grinding, down to the highway. She stayed on the shoulder, learning the clutch on the fly. After a nauseating two-mile journey, she pulled into Dewley's Humble, Thurston's only service station.

The owner was sitting in the office, feet propped on an unlit gas heater. She coasted to a stop at the pumps and the truck jumped one more time, then died with a loud backfire and a cloud of exhaust. The man stood up, walked through the propped-open glass door and followed his substantial belly around to the driver's side window, a red rag sticking out of his back pocket and a toothpick in his teeth. He looked puzzled to find a teenaged girl and a baby inside.

"Ain't this Mason Chitwood's old pickup?" he asked.

"Yeah," she croaked.

Since the wreck, Evelyn's voice had retained a sandpaper-like quality due to the hours she'd spent screaming into the frozen night. She had come to accept it as her new normal. She didn't talk much anyway.

"He was my daddy," she said. "I guess it's my pickup now. If he owed you any money, you're outta luck."

"Hmph," the man snorted. "I heard he died. Wrecked his big ol' Lincoln."

"Yes," she said. "Crashed out on the highway, the night this boy was born. I was in the back seat. We was going to the hospital. I was hurt pretty bad . . ."

His look softened, as if he were seeing her for the first time.

"Well, uh, I'm sorry about that," he said awkwardly. "So, what can I do for you? Gas? Oil change? Maybe a tuneup? I'm Dewley, by the way. Dewley Edwards."

He stuck his hand in through the open window for a shake. She flinched, hard, and he withdrew it. "I'm Evelyn," she said, annoyed.

She wanted to just ask him to fix whatever needed fixing and charge her a fair amount. But life hadn't taught her to trust anyone, particularly middle-aged men with big bellies.

"I guess it needs one of them tune-ups," she ventured, having seen that advertised on a hand-lettered sign. "It's been in the barn awhile. I don't have much money."

He looked her up and down and glanced at the baby.

"Girl, you ain't no bigger'n a minute," he said. "What are you, fifteen?"

"I'm seventeen," she lied. "And I'm big enough to take care of myself, and him." She nodded toward little Arnie, down in the floorboard. "Look, if you don't want to mess with it, I'll go on down the road—"

"No, no . . . let me take a look," he said. "But honest, even if you was John D. Rockefeller, you wouldn't want to put too much money into this old wreck."

She just looked at him, eyebrows raised in question.

"I can probably get it runnin' okay without a whole lot," he said. "We'll see."

She sat on an aluminum-framed vinyl chair in the stark station lobby, a place that smelled of grease and dust and gasoline, bouncing little Arnie on her knee. He was a good-natured baby, a refreshing innocence in her life.

She watched as Dewley tried to restart the truck, then called an employee to help him push it into the bay, where they put it up on the rack. The air wrench chattered as they pulled the tires off. They used a grease gun to lubricate the crankcase and bearings. Now and then she looked away as Dewley continued to glance in her direction. Finally, she got up and walked over to the door.

"Hey!" she hollered over the compressor noise. "You know I can't afford a bunch of work, right?"

Dewley straightened up, wiping his hands on a rag.

"Don't worry about it," he yelled, but it was obvious she couldn't hear him. He walked to the doorway where she stood. Just as he started to speak, the compressor stopped.

"DON'T WORRY ABOUT IT!" he yelled, then lowered his voice, looking around sheepishly as his guys chuckled. "Look," he told her, "I gotta get this thing safe to drive. I can't send you out of here with a baby in something that's going to break down and get y'all killed."

He turned to look back at the truck. "Honestly, I don't know how you got it here. It's a good thing it was downhill." He laughed. Evelyn didn't. He continued.

"It needs a battery, and we're changing the oil—well, puttin' oil in it—and greasin' everything. It was dry as Egypt. I've got some used tires that are a whole lot better'n what you had, and they didn't cost me nothin'. When I get it down, I'm gonna change out those plugs and check the carburetor and put on a new air filter. Other than that, a tank of gas, and you'll be good to go."

He looked her in the eyes.

"You pay me whatever you can, whenever," he said. "I ain't worried about it."

It suddenly hit her that this was a good man. She smiled, and on impulse she stood on her tiptoes, baby balanced on her hip, and planted a prim kiss on his rough cheek. He blushed and looked around.

"Now you're tryin' to get me in trouble with my ol' lady!" he said with a chuckle. "You sit back down there. We'll be done in about a half-hour."

When he gave her back the keys, she fanned out a handful of $5, $10, and $20 bills. He reached in and picked out a $5.

"You use the rest to buy that baby some milk," he said. "When he gets big enough, he can come bust tires for me for a week or so, and we'll call it even."

The truck started right up and drove much better. From that day on, Evelyn never bought gas or got it serviced anywhere else. And if she needed something moved or hauled, she knew she could call Dewley.

**Lamesa, Texas: 1983**

The old, gray-barked elm was the tallest tree in Henry's yard. His arms didn't go halfway around the trunk, but he could jump and grab the lowest branch, flail his sneakered feet, catch the trunk, and walk up until he could hook a leg over and pull himself up. Then he'd flip around and rest on his belly, arms and legs swinging, cheek pressed against the rough bark, loving a tree the way only a little boy can love a tree. After a brief dangle, he would carefully pull himself up to the next split, then the next and the next, wedging his sneakers in the crotches between the branches, finding handholds in the deep valleys of bark until he reached the height that took his breath away, where he felt like God must feel.

He was there, surrounded and tickled by whispering leaves, when his mother came out the back door looking for him. He saw her. He could see everything as he clung to a branch not much bigger than his leg, swaying with the wind that never rested. In his imagination, he was hanging onto the mainmast of a tall sailing ship in the middle of an ocean. She called his name, but he didn't answer. He was at sea. He, the tree, and the wind were living things, all one. Even his boy's mind knew that if he let go, he was done. The risk made the moment exhilarating.

Again, he heard his mother's voice.

She walked to the front yard and called again. She seemed unlikely to give up, so Henry finally, reluctantly, answered.

"Mom! I'm in the tree!"

"Where?" she called out, walking over to the trunk and peering up through the leaves. "I can't see you! Henry?"

"I'm pretty high up," he answered, thrilled to be so well-hidden. "Do you need me?"

"No, I just wanted to know where you were. How high are you?"

"I'm fine, Mom," he said. "Probably a twenty-hundred feet."

"You be careful!" she said.

"I am! I'm okay!"

Finally, she muttered a reluctant "Okay" and walked away.

Quickly he was back at sea, sailing above his neighborhood.

He could see his roof below him, the backyard and the fence—all so vast to him on the ground, now shrunken by perspective. He saw the steep vaulted roof over the church down the street, punctuated by a spire that rose to look him eye-to-eye. Farther away was the flat roof of his school and street after street of houses, lined up in architectural precision, to the end of town. In the fields beyond, rows and rows of cotton that ran to the edge of forever, also precise and even, trucks and cars crawling along distant highways, their speed distorted by distance, like airplanes crawling across the sky.

Just then, he spotted someone walking down the street. It was a girl, about his age, wearing shorts and a tee-shirt, her skin brown, her short hair dark.

"Hey!" he yelled. He loved teasing people from the safety of his hiding place. She stopped and looked around, saying nothing.

"Who is that?" she yelled back. He froze, confident she would not look up. People never did.

She looked up, her dark eyes squinting as she scanned for the source of that taunting voice. She took a step toward the tree, then walked to a spot where the leaves no longer hid him. "I see you!" she said matter-of-factly. "Who are you?"

It was over. He'd been discovered. He looked down.

"What do you want?" he said.

"What do *you* want?" she answered. "You're the who yelled."

"I don't know . . ." he muttered. "I just—"

"Cool tree," she interrupted. "Can I come up?"

He paused. He didn't want to share this world, especially not with a girl. But it looked like he would have to. He doubted she was as good a climber as he was.

"Oh . . . kay," he stammered. "You just grab that—"

As he spoke, she leaped and caught the lower branch and pulled herself up the same way he did, only faster. She quickly scrambled higher, working her way from branch to branch, just like he had, and in a few seconds, they were face-to-face. She wasn't even panting. There was a big grin on her face, her white teeth shining except for the space where a front tooth was missing. She looked at him for a long time.

"I'm Ella," she finally said.

"Okay," he said.

"Who are you?" she asked.

"I'm Henry."

They stayed in the tree, climbing around, changing places, talking a little, but mostly just looking outward, until Henry's mother called him to come in for supper.

It became an almost daily thing that summer for Ella to come and join him in the tree. Sometimes she brought peanut-butter-and-jelly sandwiches, wrapped in a bandanna, and they would sit high above the world, observing. One day, someone came walking along below them.

"Hey!" Henry yelled, almost instinctively.

It was a kid named Ray from down the street, one of the older boys who bullied kids on the school bus. Henry got goosebumps as he stopped and looked around. *If he comes up this tree, I'm probably dead,* Henry thought.

He gave up and started on his way when Henry heard his own voice yelling again.

"Hey!"

He looked at Ella. Her eyes were wide with danger and delight.

Ray stopped again. But like everyone who wasn't Ella, he didn't look up. He began instead to look intently at the house next door to Henry's. He sneaked down the side of the house, into the backyard, and began looking around. Henry and Ella were silent, paralyzed. Ray never raised his eyes, but as he walked back out, he stopped at a window and peered in. Suddenly, he broke and ran.

Just as he sprinted past the front door, it flew open, and a chase began. Henry's next-door neighbor was tying the sash around her billowing bathrobe as she ran and caught him about halfway down the block. She tackled him like a linebacker and sat on top of him, yelling and pummeling his face as he covered up and cried. She finally released him and stomped home, straightening her robe with dignity.

Ray ran away, crying. Henry and Ella laughed until they had to stop and breathe.

**Fort Worth: 2015**

No, Ella was *not* his "childhood sweetheart," Henry told his coworkers. He'd seen the knowing smiles, that little head-cocked-to-one-side, shoulders-shrugging "awww" Texas women give when they think something is just so *cute*. He had a reputation around the office as a loner—a "character"—but after Ella came along, they began to see him differently. Word got out that Henry and Ella had grown up in the same small town, known each other since they were kids, and graduated high school together. It looked like a romantic comedy playing out before their eyes.

That was not the way Henry saw it.

What was happening, he believed, was just real, grown-up friendship. Sure, he'd "loved" Ella from afar, forever. But this was different. This was two adults truly getting to know each other, taking their time, but with a little head start. He felt no need to make it anything more. They had lunch together two or three times a week, depending on whether she had meetings or not. It was like sitting in that tree again, eating her mother's sandwiches, looking out in the same direction. Some days they would walk to a cafe, but if the weather was nice, they'd take their lunches to one of the little tables in Sundance Square, which stretched out in front of their building. They'd sit and eat under the big live oak trees, resisting the urge to climb.

They had a lot of catching up to do. They talked about jobs, their families, Fort Worth, living downtown. Ella knew Henry's family and he knew hers. Her dad had passed away, but her mom was still alive and lively. She had been Henry's second grade teacher. They'd kept up with different people and could fill gaps in each other's knowledge. Henry knew Neil had become an engineer. Ella knew Karen had gone to Rice, then worked for an oil company in Houston. Henry knew Eddie had gotten hooked on meth and been executed for murdering a cop in New Mexico. Ella knew Darlene had gotten cancer and was gone.

One weekend, Ella's daughter Natalie came from college to hang out with her mom. Ella called Henry to meet them in Sundance Square.

The first time he laid eyes on Natalie, he almost had to look away.

"Oh, man!" he told Ella. "She looks *exactly* like you did in high school."

Ella grinned, as if she had known it would freak him out. "No, she's quite a bit cuter, I think," she said. He looked back at Natalie and stuck out his hand.

"I'm Henry."

"Natalie," she said with a grin, casting a sideways look at Ella. "Mom, he's not a complete dork!"

Ella laughed, blushed a little, then looked at Henry.

"I did *not* say that!" she said. "This kid . . ."

"Good to meet you, Natalie," he said, then whispered, "We'll talk later."

They walked through the square as children played in the fountain, past the cattle drive mural, and over to Razoo's for lunch. Henry was sure Natalie was bored five minutes in as he and Ella talked about their friends, the class of '96, all the things they'd done together and where they'd ended up. Finally, he looked at Natalie.

"So, first year in college," he said. "What are you studying?"

"As little as possible," she said, pushing her mother's buttons with obvious glee. "No, I'm just taking general stuff right now, but I'm going into nursing. They have a really good program, and you graduate an RN with a bachelor's degree."

"Boyfriend?"

"Singular, or plural?" she countered. After a pause, she said, "No, not yet. I've, uh, been conditioned my whole life . . ." She cut her eyes over to Ella and continued, ". . . to put that kind of stuff on hold."

"Good answer," Ella said.

Henry nodded. "Probably a good plan."

After lunch, he excused himself so they could have some time.

He hadn't met Andrew yet, but meeting Natalie made Henry feel closer to Ella. It was another tie. They didn't talk about Barry. She was bound to her ex-husband by two decades of marriage and two kids, and was diplomatic when his name came up. Henry wondered what Barry had done to lose this woman. He was sure it wasn't Ella's fault. Barry was popular in school, but he was always a bully and had few real friends. Henry was never one of them—in fact, he had been a frequent target of Barry's cruel humor.

One day, Henry and Ella were having lunch in the company's break room when she mentioned a movie she would like to see.

"I haven't seen that, either," Henry said casually, through a bite of egg-salad sandwich.

"Well, do you want to?" she said. "See it? I don't even know where the theaters are."

"Uh, sure," he said. "Wait, did you just ask me out? On a date?"

She leaned over, as if to whisper some endearment, and he leaned in expectantly. But instead of whispering, she punched him lightly in the sternum. The element of surprise made him almost spit out a half-chewed pickle. The other three people in the room glanced their way.

"Heimlich," Ella said, putting her hand to her throat. "He was choking. I'm a hero."

Then she leaned in again, with a sly grin, and whispered, "No! I did not ask you on a date. I would never ask you or anyone like you out on a date."

She took another bite of her sandwich.

"Well, for the record," he said, leaning in from his side of the table, "there's not anyone else like me, thank God."

"Yes. Thank God. I just need someone to show me where the theater is."

"They have this thing called Google Earth now . . ."

"And walk me through the big, dangerous city."

"There are lots of cops. Some on bicycles. Some on horses. It's one of the safest cities in America. And you're tougher than I am anyway . . ."

"And fetch my popcorn." She leaned toward him again, smiling.

His eyes narrowed, wondering if she was going to punch him again. Finally, he nodded.

"Okay, it's not one of those food-service theaters, so I guess I'll just have to go with you."

They decided to meet for dinner that Friday at a deli near her apartment, then walk to the downtown theater. It was a horror movie that, refreshingly, did not involve zombies.

**Thurston: 1953**

Small-town Texas in the early 1950s was no place for an unwed mother. Evelyn found few pockets of kindness amid the disapproving stares, but she made her way.

Postwar Thurston was a fairly lively place. She became a familiar sight, a curiosity, driving that old pickup into town to get groceries at Sonny's, visit the tiny branch library, or just sit on one of the benches along Main Street, although those spots were usually reserved for World War I veterans with tobacco juice dribbling down the front of their bib overalls. She would sit and read while Arnie toddled around, fascinated with bugs, rocks, and cigarette butts, or slept in the stroller the Methodist ladies Sunday school class had given her.

She would have liked to go back to school, but that was out of the question. There was no such thing as daycare, and she had to support herself and the baby. To supplement her tiny welfare checks, she started cleaning up items from the vast collection of junk her father had accumulated and selling them at area flea markets. Everything she made went into the bank bag, and she took as little out as possible. She learned how to wash diapers and hang them up to dry over the tub, how to fix toilets, paint, and replace fuses. Dewley taught her how to change a flat tire and helped her sell the old tractor. At his suggestion, she planted a garden and started to enjoy cooking. She got better at driving a clutch—also with coaching from Dewley—and learned from experience how little money it took to keep her and little Arnie alive.

He babbled incessantly and smiled for no reason. In time, the hand-to-mouth desperation she'd known all her life began to fade. For a couple of years, this was her life.

One warm January morning, she was outside hanging clothes to dry when a car drove up the road and a man in a suit got out.

"Are you Evelyn Chitwood?" he asked, holding a sheaf of papers in his hand.

She fingered the revolver inside her thin housedress, but this young, well-groomed man didn't look like any of her father's friends.

"Yeah," she answered. "Who wants to know?"

"My name is Arthur Williams," he said. "I'm the county attorney for Logan County, and I'm here on official business."

"I ain't broke no laws," she said. "I didn't—"

"No, ma'am," he interrupted. "You're not in any kind of trouble. I just took office in January, and I'm trying to work down the backlog of cases the previous . . . well, never mind. The county is just now settling your father's estate. You seem to be his only surviving relative."

She laughed, bitter and brittle.

"Estate? Don't that sound fancy! I'm pretty sure he drank every dollar he ever got his hands on."

The man shook his head.

"No, as it turns out, he didn't. He had a few possessions, and they're yours now. This . . ." He waved the papers. "This is the deed to the property where we're standing. One hundred and twenty acres, free and clear."

She looked around in disgust, saying nothing, but relieved that at least this suited man hadn't come to run her off it. Then he picked a paper out of the sheaf and waved it dramatically, as if he'd practiced for the moment.

"And this, young lady, is the deed to the Cotton & Cattle building, down in Thurston. As best we can tell, he was the legal owner."

"The hell he was!" she barked in disbelief, her sudden anger surprising both of them. "Can't you see this house, see how he lived?" She waved her arm at the shack behind her. "He didn't have nothin'!"

The man frowned, as if this wasn't quite going the way he had imagined. But he forced a smile and continued.

"Well, actually, he did. Obviously, he just didn't let you know about it." Then he delivered the punchline. "Funny thing is, he won that building in a poker game."

"Poker game?" Evelyn said. "How—?"

"The title was signed over to him six months before he died. The previous owner is a banker with a pretty good reputation, but he has a drinking problem. And when he drinks, he has a gambling problem. I had to lean on him pretty hard, but he finally told me about the game, the night he bet the building. It's a wonder no one got shot. He admitted Mason Chitwood, your father, won it fair and square. Mr. Chitwood was sober enough to make the banker write him a bill of sale, and he got it signed and witnessed that night. I've got it. It's legit."

Evelyn nodded and pretended she understood every word. The man continued.

"I was looking through the records and saw the taxes hadn't been paid in three years. I filed a suit to collect them, but when I went after the banker, he said he didn't own it anymore. The contract was in a safe deposit box in your father's name, at the bank. I had to get a court order to open it, him being dead and all.

"There was no will," he added. "Nobody filed anything. It took a while, but eventually, Miss Chitwood, it led me to you. You are the only heir. That makes you the rightful owner."

She ignored the baby crying inside the thin-walled house. The roaring in her ears was much louder.

"So, what's this mean?" she finally asked. "I'm . . . rich or something?"

"Well, the building does have a tenant—Abbott's Department Store occupies the whole ground floor and uses the second floor for storage. The third floor is vacant. But there's a nice rent check coming in, every month," he said. "It gets drawn at the bank and goes straight into an account at the same bank. That account is yours now. And without your father around to spend it, a fair amount of money has piled up over the last two-plus years."

"What's a fair amount?" Evelyn asked suspiciously.

"I didn't see the exact balance, but it's . . . substantial," he said. "Five figures."

Evelyn's expression made it clear she did not understand.

"That's more than $10,000," he clarified. "In this case, quite a bit more."

She stared intensely at him, her teeth clenched, involuntary tears filling her eyes. His voice seemed to come from a great distance.

"Anyway, if I could just come inside and get you to sign a few documents, the building and the bank account, the safe deposit box, and of course this property, will all be yours. I don't know if that makes you rich, but I'm betting it's more than you thought you had."

Evelyn invited him in, still reeling, picked up the baby and sat him on her lap. She cleared off a spot on the table so the man could spread out the papers. He seemed to be honest, but she still asked him for identification. He chuckled and showed her his driver's license and a business card that stated he was indeed the county attorney for Logan County. She signed where he told her to sign, and when they were through, he handed her a thick envelope with copies of everything, then folded the rest of the papers and tucked them inside his coat.

"I'll file all this at the county courthouse," he said. "And if you like, I'll drop this form off with the bank. Do you have any questions?"

Her eyes narrowed. "Yeah. How'd you come to do all this for me?"

"Well, it's my job," he said. "To be honest, I'm relieved just to get this all cleared up, get the taxes paid—you will have to pay a few hundred dollars in taxes—and for the building and this property to have clear titles."

He paused and looked around. "It's fun to be the good guy now and then."

She followed him outside, holding back her tears until he was out of sight, his car throwing up a smokescreen of dust as he rolled down the hill. Then she set Arnold down and began to sob, slouching against the rough siding, sliding down until she sat on the ground, knees up, face in her hands. He toddled over to comfort her, and she grabbed him, holding him tightly as her tears flowed.

From where she sat, she could see the C&C building in the blue distance. It was a landmark, solid and substantial, a skyscraper among the rolling hills. She could not yet grasp the idea that it belonged to her.

Even though she'd burned her father's things, his memory hung like cigarette smoke, heavy in the air. Now she had the means to escape it. After a lifetime of having nothing, she had something. Along with it came the task of reconciling her contempt for her father with the revelation that he'd endowed her so generously.

The resources came in the nick of time; her stash of cash was shrinking. Although Evelyn had the survival instincts of a coyote, she had no diploma, no skills, and not even the prospect of a job, especially in Thurston. A few people had been kind to her, mostly because of the baby, but pity has a brief shelf-life. She was the dropout daughter of the town drunk, pregnant at fifteen—no one cared how. Her life was what it would always be.

Now, everything had changed. She had land, a building, a bank account, all courtesy of that horrible man who, if he'd lived, would have never shared a penny with her. She breathed deeply, and the air of freedom in her lungs made it feel like she'd only been half-breathing all her life. In that moment, Evelyn changed. The anger that had been seething inside her as long as she could remember transformed into determination. Ambition. Her ferocity did not dissipate, but it pointed her in a new direction, quieter and more deliberate. A verse she'd hit on in her Bible reading popped into her mind: *I know the plans I have for you to give you hope and a future.*

For the first time, she dared to think it might apply to her.

Suddenly, all she wanted to do was clean. She finished washing all their clothes in the big sink, along with sheets, towels, and blankets, hanging it all out to dry in the warm breeze. She took the mattress off her bed, wrestled it outside and beat it with a broomstick until she was panting like a sprinter. She pulled the pickup into the yard, dropped the tailgate, swept out the bed and began filling it with her possessions: Arnold's crib, her bed, the dining table and chairs, a few books in an old bookshelf, a couple of suitcases. It wasn't much; it all fit easily in the short bed of the old truck. By the time the sun was high overhead, everything she wanted to take with her was loaded up.

Finally, she sat Arnold in the passenger seat and surrounded him with rolled-up towels. He was big enough now to sit up and watch the road, chattering in a language only he understood. She started the engine, depressed the clutch, and pulled to the edge of the dirt road.

She paused for a moment, wiggled the gearshift knob into neutral and set the parking brake, leaving the engine running. She sternly told Arnie to stay put, giving him a toy to keep him occupied. Then Evelyn took a deep breath, got out and walked back down the gravel drive, through the dusty yard that still had more shards of glass than blades of grass. She circled the old house one last time, her hand brushing paint chips off the walls, her fingers flecking at the aged and shrunken caulk around the windows. So many memories, none of them worth keeping.

She walked up the makeshift concrete-block steps and stood in the open doorway.

She took a matchbook out of the pocket of her dress, leaned in through the screen door, and looked around. She struck a match and held it under the thin cotton curtain. It caught fire right away. She stood there a moment, then tossed the whole matchbook inside. The old shack lit up quickly. By the time she turned to walk away, flame was flowing up the walls and cascading like water across the ceiling. She felt the heat on her back. She drove the two miles down into town with a big smile on her face. No firetrucks passed her on the way up.

When she got to town, Evelyn went straight to the C&C building, parked out front, got her boy out, and put him into the stroller. She looked up, shading her eyes, catching details on the three-story building: intricate brickwork at the roof level, round stone columns and a triangle at the peak with the year "1905" set into the brick.

She thought about the work that had gone into all that detail, brick and stone and mortar, high above the street, just for show. A round turret started at the door, supported by columns, and ran all the way to the roof where it was capped by a dome. The two front windows were topped with wide brick arches. Just above one window was the big Abbott's sign, neon-lit at night but still highly visible even in the daylight. Looking at the building—her building—gave her a feeling she could not describe.

She put the envelope from the county attorney on top of the stroller and covered it with a blanket, then rolled through the front door of Abbott's Department Store.

She had never been inside. Big-band jazz was playing in the background. The whole place smelled of clean clothes, leather, and perfume, stirred by lazy fans that descended on black steel pipes from the high embossed-tin ceiling. A dapper, middle-aged man approached as she stood gawking at the rich, colorful miracle of retail, spreading in every direction.

"Can I help you with something, young lady?" he asked politely, although he seemed eager to escort her out.

She turned and looked him up and down. He was bald, with a bowtie, a thin mustache, and a tight, forced smile.

"Yeah," she croaked. "Show me around. I own the damn place."

* * *

Evelyn was determined to move in that very day. She didn't have anywhere else to go. All her worldly possessions were in the bed of that pickup, parked at the curb.

Charles, who turned out to be the store's manager, tried to talk her out of it.

"Miss, I don't think you understand," he said. "This is not a residential building."

"I wanna look at that top floor," she said, ignoring his objection. "I don't think I can drag this baby carriage up the stairs. Is there another way up?"

"Well, there is a freight elevator in the northwest corner, but we only use it to bring boxes down from the second floor," he said. "I wouldn't—"

"Northwest? That's this way, isn't it?" She took off, pushing the stroller down the aisle, past the racks of dresses, past the purses, toward the shoes. He ran to get in front of her.

"Miss! I'm going to have to insist that you not use that elevator! It's not for the public and, uh, it's not safe . . . uh, for a little one!"

She stopped and looked him up and down with her intense dark eyes. She'd never seen a man so pink. A tape measure streamed from his left hand and straight pins were stuck neatly into a flower on his lapel. She looked directly in his eyes. Channeling her father's gambling skills, she quickly decided he was bluffing.

"Alright, then," she said. "Let's just try it out. You run on up to the top floor and I'll send a box up to you. We'll see if it works."

He balked, as if searching for a reason to call that a stupid idea. Finally, he walked over and muttered something to an older lady in the ready-to-wear section. Evelyn kept going.

"You comin' or am I goin' up there myself?" she called back, impatient. He looked around, as if seeking a way to escape. Finding none, he gave in. Evelyn stepped through a metal door into the stairwell, where the elevator was located, and pulled open the cross-hinged lattice door as he rushed to catch up. She found an empty box, pushed it into the compartment with her foot, then turned and smiled at him.

"Go on up," she said, waving her hand toward the metal staircase. "I'll send it to you. We'll see if it gets there alright."

He sputtered an objection but began to trudge slowly upward. She was a force.

"We've called the sheriff, you know," he said when he was a safe distance away.

As soon as he got out of sight around the corner, she scooted the crate aside and rolled the stroller, with the sleeping boy, into the elevator car. She stepped out, pulled the door shut, pushed the button, then spun and ran up the stairs. The old elevator creaked and groaned, but it started moving. As she rounded the second-floor landing, she could see the cables spooling and unspooling and hear the whir of the electric motor. Little Arnold slept on. Evelyn went on up, and her head was at floor level just in time to see it arrive.

Charles gasped when he saw the stroller. What? You put the *child* in there?" he cried, obviously wanting to yell at her but afraid to awaken little Arnold.

By that time, she was standing right behind him.

"Well, don't just stand there huffin' and puffin'—roll him out!" she said, pivoting briskly toward the big double door. "I guess he made it, didn't he?"

Charles gave the stroller a weak shove in her direction, then scampered back down the stairs, mumbling something about a crazy woman and deputies being on their way. She paid no attention.

She tried the knob, and it was not locked. Pushing it, she entered a dark, wood-paneled hallway that led into a large open space, sunlit through dirty windows on the north and south sides. More light filtered down through rows of skylights in the high ceiling. On both ends were suites of offices that had served farmers and busy cotton and cattle buyers during the building's heyday, before and after the First World War. The open space in the middle was obviously where buyers and sellers had gathered to conduct business in groups of chairs around coffee tables, most of which remained, islands in the dusty vastness. On the back wall was a long chalkboard, rows of tables permanently marked by the prices of cotton, peanuts, soybeans, beef, pigs, chickens, and other agricultural commodities written in chalk, erased and rewritten, up-to-the-minute, now decades out of date.

She ran her hands over the marble wainscoting, topped by dark-stained wood that matched the tall baseboards. The richness of the building was like nothing she'd ever seen, wood trim around every door, ledges outside the windows, gargoyles at the corners staring down at the poor unfortunates outside.

Shuffling across the solid wood floor, she reached down and picked up a piece of yellowed paper that read "Bill of Sale." In neat, crisp printing, it recorded forty pigs shipped by a farmer named McCafferty from Cisco to the Fort Worth Stockyards, where a grisly fate awaited them at the hands of Armour & Company. It was dated 1937.

Arnold slept peacefully while she rolled him along, exploring the space. Coming from that shack on the hillside, where the walls shook when a norther blew in, this place felt like a different planet. It was built to last a century or more, with bones of stone and steel. The pressed-tin ceiling over the coffee-table-and-chair groupings was stained where men of commerce had sat for years puffing clouds of cigar smoke into the air. She crossed, parked the stroller, and stepped through a door into the office suite on the far side. By itself, it was bigger than her old house: a reception area, a hallway, and three or four offices, a bathroom and a break room with a kitchenette. She found her way out and circled the floor, exploring the suite at the other end, split by the hallway she'd just come through but similarly equipped.

"There must be a hundred chairs in here," she whispered to herself.

Suddenly Evelyn felt like a woman of substance. Those were her chairs. These were her walls, her floors, her roof. Brick and stone, roof and rain gutters and plumbing, ducts and wiring, lights and windows had all been crafted into this place decades ago. How strange to receive all this permanence as a parting gift from a father who had given her nothing but bruises and violence and meanness.

She drew some furniture together: a few chairs, a coffee table, even a couple of small couches. They all slid easily on the dust-slick floor to form a little grouping. By the time Arnold's hunger awoke him, she'd nested a place for them off to the side in the middle area. She'd picked out a spot for their bedrooms in that far office suite, but there would be time later to decide what would go where. It was a lot of space for a small woman and a toddler. She gently lifted him out of his stroller, took a bottle from the bag that hung on the handle, and fed him while sitting on the old couch, rocking slightly, singing a barely audible lullaby.

Afterward, suddenly mindful of her own needs, she put him down so he could explore his new surroundings. At the back of an office suite she found, to her surprise, a fully equipped bathroom, beautifully tiled and appointed, though neglected and dirty. She was grateful there was no fluid in the brown, disgusting toilet. There was also a tub, dry as dust, and it didn't appear the sink had held moisture since the Great Depression. When she turned the taps on, the only sound was dry, creaking air. She was surprised they turned at all.

She was on her hands and knees, looking under the sink for a water cutoff, when she heard a throat clear behind her. She turned and stood up. A tall, cowboy looking man took off his Stetson and regarded her.

"Who are you?" she asked.

"I'm the sheriff," he said, in the deepest voice she'd ever heard. "Bud Lamkin. Charles, the store manager? He called me to come find out who you are."

She just glared.

"Ma'am, I see you've got a little one here. I ain't here to arrest you or treat you like a criminal, unless you are," he continued. "We can help find you a place to stay, if you need one. But you can't just . . . squat in a commercial building."

"It's my building," she said. She reached under the blankets on top of the stroller and felt for the envelope. She could see him tense up, his hand going to the grip of the pistol holstered at his side, until her hand emerged holding only papers.

"Your building," he repeated. "You're telling me you own this building?"

"Yep!" she said, handing the papers to him. "Your county attorney come out and drew it all up, and I signed it. Don't y'all talk to each other? This building is mine. That store down there? I'm their landlord. Land . . . lady."

He leafed through the papers, noting seals and signatures, nodding his head as she talked.

"Thing is, my house burnt down . . ."

"Yes, I heard about that, Miss Chitwood," he said, without looking up. "Place out there on the side of the mesa. Total loss. Might've started a grass fire if there'd been any grass."

When he looked up, his eyes burned a hole in her.

"We aren't sure how it started," he said. "Maybe it was arson."

Evelyn didn't blink.

"I don't know nobody named Arson," she said. "But I need a place to live—me and my boy here. I figure since I own this building, I can live here if I want to."

He handed the papers back to her and sighed.

"I don't suppose I could talk you out of it?" he asked.

"Nope," came the quick reply.

He sighed again, then went back down the stairs to his car, got on the radio, and told a deputy to bring a couple of trustees over from the county jail to carry her possessions up in the freight elevator. It was a 20-minute wait, but soon after they arrived, the pickup was empty. While they were working, the sheriff called in a favor from a plumber friend and told him the tub, sinks, and toilets on the third floor of the C&C building needed to be operational by nightfall. It was an emergency.

The plumber complained a lot, but he got it done. By the time the sun disappeared from the skylights, Evelyn and little Arnold had a new home, with running water, on the third floor of the C&C building.

**Fort Worth: 2015**

It was a cool fall evening, and Sundance Square and Main Street glistened, lights in the trees, streets crowded with families, tourists, couples on dates. Henry and Ella went to a multi-screen theater near the Bass Performance Hall, detouring to walk beneath the outstretched gold trumpets held by the carved marble angels on the facade. She paid for dinner, since he had already bought the movie tickets online. A kid at the door scanned the tickets on Henry's phone and waved them in. They skipped the escalator to run up the long stairway and found seats during the previews. When the movie got scary, she laced her arm through his, casually, like she'd done it a hundred times. Her touch still electrified Henry, but if she felt the current, she didn't let on.

Henry was a throwback, the same person at thirty-eight that he'd been at eight, closer to his inner child than any normal person should be. This accounted for the quirky, offbeat, vaguely childlike personality some women found appealing, or at least intriguing. But it also made him difficult to get to know. It was the reason he and Rhonda never had a chance—and the reason he and Ella got along so effortlessly, even after all those years. She was uniquely qualified to break through. She got him. As a result, they could move on to other things.

She told him, up-front, that she was not interested in changing him, polishing him, refining him, directing or redirecting him—or "dating" him.

"Been there, done that, got two great kids and a t-shirt," she said laughing. "Actually, it's kinda nice to hang out with a guy I don't need to work on."

He smiled proudly before she quickly added, "Not that you don't need work! Oh, man, you're a project, for sure. I'm just not applying for the job."

She did, however, begin working on Henry to join her in a newfound, and to him, strange hobby: going to storage unit auctions.

"C'mon, Henry! You'll like it! I promise," she said as they ate lunch one day near the fountains in Sundance Square. At first, as he did with any new idea, Henry resisted.

Ella had gotten interested in storage unit auctions when she and Barry split. She moved into a smaller house, and some of her stuff had to go into storage. The reality TV show *Storage Wars* was popular about that time, and after seeing a flyer for an auction, she decided to go see what it was like. She was quickly hooked. When she moved to Fort Worth, she found there was an auction somewhere almost every weekend, always within easy driving distance.

"It's exciting, Henry! It's got a little mystery to it. I really think you'll like it. There's an air about it . . . I don't know . . . that you might discover—"

"Someone's old junk?" he interrupted.

"Or someone's treasure!"

"Or someone's forty-year-old shoes? Maybe that's the 'air' you're talking about . . ."

She covered her mouth with her napkin, trying not to laugh pasta salad through her nose.

"Hey, forty-year-old shoes are more interesting than baseball!" she said.

"At least a baseball game has the *potential* to get interesting at some point," he said. "This has no—"

"This has all kinds of possibilities," she said, cutting him off. "You really don't know what you're going to find in one of these units."

"Have you ever bought one? Or even bid?" he asked.

"No," she said.

"And why not?"

After a pause, she said, "I . . . just haven't gotten up the nerve."

He threw back his head and laughed. "Ella! You've got to be kidding! You've got more nerve than anyone I know. You make the Hulk look like a chihuahua!"

"But Henry-Baby, I need a partner!" she said, covering his hand with hers. "This kind of thing isn't fun unless somebody does it with you."

"Kinda like organ donation?" he suggested.

"I heard somebody found an unpublished manuscript by some famous writer in one of these units," she said, ignoring him. "Somewhere around here. Maybe Dallas."

He stopped laughing.

"Yeah, I read about that. Pearl Buck, Nobel prize winner. But Ella, that was a once-in-a-lifetime deal," he said. "You can buy a million storage units and not find anything remotely—"

"And you can go sit in the stands at a million baseball games and not see a no-hitter, or a walk-off grand slam, or—"

"Okay," he said, stopping her. "Statistically, that's not true, but I give up. Calf-rope. My objection is withdrawn, your honor. It does sound like it might, possibly, be . . . sort of fun, in a weird way. With you. Somewhat."

"So you'll do it?"

"I'll do it."

She laughed. Even though she was gloating a little, her laugh was a song that played in his head the rest of the day.

**Thurston: 1953**

One morning, not long after they moved in, Evelyn got up early and made the short drive back up the mesa to tend her garden. She returned around 8:30 and was walking along the sidewalk, little Arnie toddling along in her wake, when she met a woman coming from the opposite direction, with a little girl holding her hand. The lady was tall, trim, and sophisticated looking. The child was beautiful, wispy blonde curls tossed in the gentle breeze, her face as perfect as a Norman Rockwell painting in the *Saturday Evening Post*. As soon as the woman saw Arnie, she knelt down to his level.

"Well, hi there!" she said. "I'm Mary. What's your name?"

Arnie looked at her, mouth open, then looked back up at his mother.

"I'm Dottie," the little girl chimed in a sing-song voice, beaming a perfect smile.

Arnie just stared, open-mouthed, from one face to the other. Evelyn watched the scene play out, hoping Arnie wouldn't pick his nose in front of these high-class ladies.

The woman extended her hand and Arnie continued to stare. Evelyn leaned down to speak to the woman.

"That's Arnie," she rasped, nodding her head toward the boy. "He's three. He ain't been around people much."

Mary stood up to address Evelyn.

"Well, he's a cutie. I'm Mary," she said, putting out her hand. Evelyn took it tentatively. "This is my daughter," Mary said, gesturing toward the little girl, who was still smiling expectantly at Arnie. "Her name's Dorothy, but we call her Dottie. She's almost three."

"You comin' to the store?" Evelyn asked. "Abbott's don't open 'til 9."

"No," Mary said. "I work there. I do the alterations. Sewing."

"Oh!" Evelyn said, brightening a little. "My name's Evelyn. I'm the landlady. Me and Arnie live upstairs."

"Oh, you're the one—uh . . . Charles was . . ." Mary started, then she laughed, a flippant, dismissive laugh indicating that was a thought she was not going to finish. The two women stood for an awkward moment, then looked back to their children, whose staring contest had dissolved into smiles and conversation—Dottie talking like a little grownup and Arnie interrupting now and then with a burst of earnest but unintelligible babbling.

"We'll have to get these two together sometime, let 'em play," Evelyn said.

"That would be great," Mary said. "Some days—like today—I bring her down to the shop with me. I have a little playpen in a back closet. Maybe he could—"

"You have what?" Evelyn interrupted. "She don't have to play in no closet! She can come upstairs and play with Arnie. We got lots of room, and he's got toys and books and stuff. I could watch 'em while you get your work done."

Mary hesitated. It didn't occur to Evelyn that she might be reluctant to put her daughter into the care of a single teenage mom who'd inherited the building from her drunken father.

"That sounds . . . great," Mary said. "Next time I bring her down I'll—"

"What about tomorrow?" Evelyn asked quickly.

"Well, I guess I could . . ." Mary stammered. "My husband usually—"

"Bring her tomorrow," Evelyn said as she stepped away, holding Arnie's hand. "He could use a kid to play with. I'll make sure they don't kill each other. Just come up to the third floor and give me a good loud knock."

"Oh . . . kay," Mary said nervously as Evelyn walked away.

The next day, just before 9 a.m., there was a light knock at the third-floor entry. Evelyn opened the door, wearing a dress she had found at an estate sale with an apron over it. She looked like a 1930s farm housewife, missing only the pitchfork. She was barefoot, and she'd tried unsuccessfully to tame her thick, curly brown hair.

"Hi," she said, half-smiling, then quickly turned away and led them down the hallway. Her social skills weren't much better than Arnie's.

With the prospect of company coming, every surface had been dusted and mopped. Evelyn had made herself and Arnie bedrooms in the far corner office, and she was in the process of taking down a wall, to open up the break room to the vast area in the middle of the floor. Her old dining table and chairs were in that space, and she had gathered up furniture to create a corral where the toddlers could play but not easily escape.

"Wow, this is really . . . interesting," Mary observed, looking around.

For the first time, Evelyn smiled at Mary. "It's a work in progress, for sure. It'll take a while to turn it into a real apartment," she said. "But there's a lot of room, huh? We'll fix it up as we go. It's already way nicer than where we used to live."

She invited Mary to have a seat. There was a bag of cookies, and she was brewing coffee on an old hot plate she'd found in a closet.

The kids seemed to get along. Even though Dottie looked like a porcelain doll and Arnie crashed around like a tiny football player, they played well together. He was a natural follower, and Dottie was born to lead. They were both obviously happy to have another child to play with.

At nap time, Evelyn sat on the couch between them and read a book—she had discovered a new children's author with an unusual style and the strange pen name Dr. Seuss. She did all the voices, her croaking a perfect fit for the nonsensical lyrics. Afterward, she bedded them down on little couches on opposite sides of the room with a pillow, a blanket, a book, and a stuffed animal. Then she went and read at the kitchen table, where she could watch them until they fell asleep. They were still sleeping when Mary came softly up the stairs.

When she saw them, she tiptoed over and sat beside Evelyn.

"You know, this is really going to be nice," she said, looking around.

Evelyn beamed.

The two women quickly settled into a routine. Mary would drop Dottie off before heading down to the store. When she took a break, she would come back up and they would sit and visit. Evelyn craved company and instinctively trusted Mary, picking her brain about style and decorating, how to raise a child, cooking, toys, how to discipline.

Mary could not have imagined how blank Evelyn's slate was. Evelyn saw her as the quintessential modern mother: efficient, confident, a good cook, and housekeeper who was also trim and fashionably dressed. Although Mary worked a fairly menial job, she carried herself with an almost aristocratic air.

One day, she came up the stairs with a bag from Abbott's. Smiling, she held it out to Evelyn. "This is for you," she said.

"Aw, you don't have to buy me stuff," Evelyn said as she took it.

"It's not anything I bought," Mary said. "These are just clothes my son outgrew. He's 10 now, and we're not likely to have another one, so I don't need them anymore. He grew so fast, he was out of them before he could tear them up."

Over time, Mary became as important to Evelyn as the nurses or the social worker had been, a window on a world as foreign to her as the moon. She simply knew things Evelyn did not: the things little girls learned from their mothers.

Mary enjoyed the expansiveness of Evelyn's apartment—she

called it the "penthouse"—after spending her days trapped in a small cubby out of the public's view. Aside from her trips upstairs, she only stepped out to measure ladies as they tried on clothes, pinning hems and marking darts. Charles measured the men, then tossed the clothes on her table without a word. Mary cheerfully did them all, always by the next day, getting never a word of thanks.

Her friendship with Evelyn did not endear her to the boss, but she didn't care.

At lunchtime, she and Evelyn shared soup or sandwiches and fed the kids. Sometimes Mary would bring something she'd cooked. After a few months, Evelyn bought an electric range, so she would often cook for them all, occasionally trying out a recipe Mary had shared.

One Friday, Mary invited Evelyn and Arnie to attend her church that Sunday, and they did. Evelyn found herself captivated by the music, the parishioners' fine clothes and courtly manners, and awed by the pastor's eloquent command of the scriptures. She remembered the charity of the Methodist ladies when she was so poor, and secretly yearned to be one of them—one of the respectable people. Evelyn wanted to do good and be good, just like Mary.

Evelyn refused to accept pay for watching Dottie—in truth, the little girl had helped Arnie, teaching him social skills his mother did not have. In lieu of payment, Mary convinced Evelyn to accept clothes: a dress that had been brought in for alterations and never picked up, or something Abbott's had taken off one of the mannequins because it had gone out of style. Evelyn learned to accept these gifts graciously, and her wardrobe and taste began to improve. Mary's gracious manners and proper English became Evelyn's model, and often their conversations veered toward books Evelyn was reading, as if they were a two-woman book club. In time, the penthouse apartment, like Evelyn herself, began to reflect Mary's good taste.

As surely as the men who pulled her out of the wreck the night Arnie was born, Mary's friendship saved Evelyn—more slowly, but more thoroughly.

**Fort Worth: 2015**

In Roswell, away from his buddies for the first time, Barry began to change, focusing on the job, growing up a little. He came home in the evening talking about tertiary recovery, fracking, and injection wells. One of his jobs was installing electronic monitoring and controls for remote oil wells, which would eventually eliminate the kind of job he'd had in Texas. Someday, he predicted, half-joking, they would move "everything but the holes" to Houston.

Ella sensed he was growing frustrated with his job, bumping up against the ceiling. His lack of education kept him from moving up, as jobs he felt qualified for went to "kids" with degrees in engineering, geology, or other related fields. Ella offered to support the family while he went back to school, but he said he would rather find another job than have to go to college to keep this one. Barry had begun to look like equipment from a bygone era: used and useless, stacked up to rust in a deserted pipe yard.

Finally, his pessimism came true: the price of oil fell and he was laid off. He concealed it from Ella as long as he could, but it was a small town, and she had lots of friends. When she called him on it, he was surly and defensive. He drew unemployment compensation for a while, but instead of looking for another job, he became a regular at the strip clubs out on the highway. Ella found out about that, too.

It was only a matter of time before he began to make decisions that didn't involve his brain at all. Ella was surprised at how little emotion she felt when she confronted him. It felt like she was coolly eviscerating a felon on the witness stand. Years of neglect had eroded the thin foundation that supported their marriage; his unfaithfulness quickly shattered it. Ella drew up the divorce petition herself, then quit her job and moved back to Lubbock with the kids. She joined an oil- and gas-related firm, and her widowed mother moved in to help her care for Andrew and Natalie, who were now teenagers. She didn't try to bludgeon Barry over visiting rights or child support; she'd always made more money. She wanted her children to have a relationship with their father, but she was done with him.

When his unemployment checks ran out, so did his popularity at the clubs. He sobered up, moved back to Lubbock, got a job and settled into a new and very different life. Most of his friends were gone. When Andrew graduated high school and went to Texas Tech to study engineering, he moved in with his father as much out of pity as need. A year later, when Natalie enrolled at the University of North Texas, Ella decided to move that direction. It felt good to have a fresh start in an exciting new place.

Finding Henry? That was her signing bonus.

**Thurston: 1950s–1960s**

Evelyn Chitwood became a fixture in downtown Thurston. Word got out that she owned the C&C building and was living on the third floor. Rumors flew. She was somehow related to Howard Hughes, or he had bought the building for her because he was the father of her child. She was in the mafia. Or hiding from the mafia. Abbott's was about to be evicted so she could put in a bar, a brewery, a brothel—all financed, of course, by Howard Hughes.

She had no job that anyone could discern; she spent her days upstairs, watching her boy and the sewing lady's little girl. No one could figure out that friendship: Mary Sinclair was a fine, upstanding Christian lady. Did she not know this girl's story?

Evelyn regularly drove her pickup back up the mesa to her old place—she called it "the farm"—to tend her ever-growing garden, which flourished around the burned-out ruin of the house and provided most of her groceries. Dewley had been a great inspiration and coach, and of course Evelyn read everything she could find on Texas gardening. Although she had money, she continued to live as if she didn't, scrounging for odd pieces of furniture, scrap metal, farm implements, chicken coops, feed troughs, or other "country junk" she could sell at flea markets. She seldom missed an estate auction or a garage sale, selling or buying, and furnished her third-floor suite with her finds: a table she found on the curb, a lamp set out with someone's trash. If something was too big for her to handle, she'd call Dewley.

Her formal education had been cut short, but Evelyn continued learning on her own. She had always loved to read. Once she settled in Thurston, she read almost every book in the little branch library. When Dottie and Arnie started school, Evelyn started going once a week to the main library in Loganville. She liked the western stories of Zane Grey, the whodunnits of Sir Arthur Conan Doyle and Agatha Christie, and the stark realism of Ernest Hemingway, John Steinbeck, and Willa Cather. She also devoured textbooks of almost every kind, particularly history. As the owner of a building, she delved into architecture and construction, and as a businesswoman, she read everything she could find on accounting, math, and business. There was no subject she found uninteresting.

Even Mary, who had attended junior college before she and George were married, came to respect the breadth and depth of Evelyn's self-education.

To the surprise of almost everyone, Evelyn was a good landlady, too—better than the old banker had been. At first, Charles would challenge her with a plumbing or air conditioning problem, smugly certain she would fail. But she would go to work on it right away, often getting it done for nearly nothing or through some kind of barter arrangement. One day, he came to work and found the sheriff's jail trustees cleaning up the sidewalks, fixing cracks in the curb, making sure the steps were secure. A few weeks later, they came back and painted the trim on the building's first floor. All Evelyn had to do was supply the paint, which she got at cost from the lumber yard. She discovered she'd get a tax break if her building was designated as a historic landmark, so she did the research and went through the Texas Historical Commission's red tape. The county historical society held a ceremony to mount a plaque on the building, with a narrative commemorating its role as a market for cattle and cotton—two things the town and much of Texas had been built on.

Evelyn beamed through the whole ceremony. Charles cried a

little.

She raised the rent slightly at the end of every year, but since she was taking care of them, the store's owners didn't seem to mind. No one guessed Evelyn was simply matching the consumer price index, staying ahead of inflation—just as her textbook had recommended.

By the time Arnie started fifth grade, Evelyn was the richest woman in Thurston. Admittedly, there wasn't much competition, but based on where she'd started, it was still a noteworthy achievement. Even in the 1950s, owning a big old building in a dying town like Thurston was not a ticket to riches. Evelyn was simply a lot smarter than people expected her to be, and lived much farther below her means than most people would have imagined possible.

When the welfare department found out she owned a building, they quit sending her checks, and the social worker, the only friend she had before Mary, stopped coming by. Evelyn missed her, but she understood. She began keeping books for Dewley's station as a trade-off for gas, and he kept her old truck running. He said her penny-pinching was the only thing that kept him in business, especially after the big truck stop opened down on the highway.

She read an article about how landowners could make money by leasing grazing and hunting rights, so she ran an ad in the Loganville newspaper and quickly leased her place up on the mesa. Her new tenant put up fences and cattle guards, and she got some steady income. A couple of years later, a utility company paid her for the right-of-way to put power transmission lines across it, and not long after that, a pipeline company came through with a big gas line. She leased the highest point, up on the mesa, for a 350-foot radio tower—the tallest one in the county. Another nice check, every month.

The first time she'd seen her bank balance, those "five figures" seemed to her a vast fortune. In less than ten years, five figures had turned into six.

Her relationship with Dewley had raised some eyebrows, even among the fine ladies at church. Evelyn didn't care, but she was curious. He was the first man she'd known who treated her like a real person. One day, when she returned the ledger to the station, she decided to probe a little. He was looking at the numbers when she came behind him.

"Everything look okay?" she asked.

"Yeah," he said. "Wish there was more money comin' in, but the way this town is dryin' up, I guess I oughta be happy the doors are open. You doin' okay?"

"Sure," she said. "As long as I can feed that eating machine I'm raising. Have you seen that boy?"

He turned his chair around. "Not in a while," he said. "You need to bring him around more often. Now that he's in school I miss him playin' out here. Won't be long before he can come in and bust those tires, pay off that original repair job."

"Yeah . . ." she said. After a long pause, she continued. "Hey, Dewley?"

"Mmm?" he said, not looking up.

She hesitated. "How come you're so . . . nice to me and Arnie?"

He looked down at the ledger, then softly closed it.

"Girl, where does that come from?"

"I don't know," she said. "I just . . . I wonder sometimes. You fixed my pickup practically free that first time we met, and ever since then, you just sort of look out for us. Why?"

The big man squirmed a little, then sat silent. Finally, he took a deep breath.

"Evelyn," he started, "me and Fran, you know . . . we never had no kids. I don't know if it was me or her, but it just never worked. That day you drove that rollin' wreck in here, that was my birthday. I was forty that day. You told me you was seventeen."

She looked at him, her dark eyes intense.

"I got married when I was twenty-two," he continued. "If we'd had a baby right away, that kid woulda been pretty much your age. I guess what I'm sayin' is, I figured maybe the good Lord gave me a birthday present that day—a daughter I never did get to have on my own. I decided that, best I could, I was gonna take care of y'all. When I talked to Fran about it, she was all in."

"You . . . you just decided?"

"No, I know," he said with a chuckle. "It's weird. And you was doin' fine on your own. Hell, you're way smarter than me, and with that buildin' and all, and as much as you read, once you got a leg up, you was on your way.

"But," he continued, "you are kinda little, and I figured every now and then you might need somethin' loaded or hauled somewhere. I just wanted to be there for you—for you to know you had a guy who could do the heavy stuff."

"You *decided*," she said, still pondering his previous sentence. "You *decided* to just . . . treat me like a daughter. A daughter? A daughter."

She repeated the word as if that would help her absorb it. Tears filled her eyes and spilled down her cheeks. "So . . . you're just doin' what a father would do . . ."

"Dear God, girl," Dewley said. "You ain't never seen a real father, have you?"

He held out his arms. She hesitated at first, then leaned into his embrace, sobbing and breathing the smell of grease and oil that was such a part of his presence. Finally, he patted her shoulder, and she raised up.

"It ain't a big deal," he said. "I just wanna be there for y'all. A backstop. Somebody to lift the heavy stuff. A good friend—that's a dad. Somebody who's on your side."

"You are, Dewley. You are. And I thank you for it."

"This don't change nothin', I hope?" he asked.

"Nope," she said, sniffling as she walked to the door. "You still need to sell more oil and see if you can't find a cheaper jobber for your gas. A nickel a gallon would be night and day—"

"Okay, okay!" he said, raising his hands in surrender. "I'll work on it. Just . . . you know, let's keep this little talk just between us, okay?"

"Sure." She smiled and walked out the door.

Driving home, she cried, then had to laugh. Her first thought was to wish to God that Dewley had been her dad—especially on that drive to the hospital the night Arnie was born. But just as quickly, it hit her: if her real father hadn't been a drunk, and hadn't died plowing into that concrete pillar, her life would have never changed. She might not have escaped him. She certainly wouldn't have inherited that building—he would have lost it as quickly as he won it. She probably wouldn't have even met Dewley.

It was the ultimate irony: without that awful father, and that awful night, she would have nothing.

While she was pregnant, she'd read the Bible a lot. She continued to read, listen to the pastor, and talk about his lessons with Mary. As she drove, she thought about what Jesus went through. He spent, what, six hours on that cross? Evelyn was in that car almost that long, in labor, crushed and freezing and screaming.

She would never compare herself to Jesus—but it did compare, in a way. His horrible six hours on the cross, that's what set everybody free, wasn't it? Those hours in that wrecked car set Evelyn free. It wasn't a cross, but it was worse than what most people ever go through. And it was surely the devil who put her there.

Her tears were flowing as she pulled up to park in front of her building. She nodded, answering the question that hadn't been asked. Yes. It was worth it. In one night, she'd gone from abused child, to orphan, to mother—from being a victim, a prisoner in her father's house, a slave to his alcohol addiction, to being free, in charge of her own life.

Pain fades. Freedom stays. It was the closest thing she had to a philosophy.

And Dewley was the closest thing she'd had to a father.

* * *

When Evelyn first moved into the C&C building, there were complaints about the eccentric woman living downtown. But as the years went by, there were fewer people around to disapprove. Little by little, the businesses that had provided a living for the people of Thurston shut down, and the people left.

The cotton gin was first. There was a big, modern gin near Loganville, and the dwindling number of farmers who still grew cotton took their crop there. Sonny's Grocery closed when Sonny died, and his wife moved back up north to be near their kids. The cafe closed a few years later, a casualty of competition from the shiny new truck stop with its twenty-four–hour cafe. The businesses along Main Street gradually boarded up as their owners' children moved away.

Whenever a building emptied out, Evelyn quietly bought it for next to nothing. She liked owning real estate; no one could take it from her.

After the branch library closed, Evelyn took home boxes of books for pennies. When the bank sold, the new owner shut down the Thurston branch. She bought that building on credit, with generous terms, because no one else wanted it, and besides, she was one of their biggest customers. Even the Methodist church, in a historic stone building on the other side of the library, lost its full-time pastor and had to settle for a visiting preacher who only came once a month. They'd returned to the days of the circuit-riding preachers.

With no police department, the sheriff handled law enforcement. Water came from a rural utility district, electricity from the co-op that had first brought power to the area in the early 1940s. Wastewater was going into septic tanks already; the town had never put in a sewer system. The county commissioner kept Main Street paved, and volunteer firefighters tried, with mixed success, to keep things from burning down. Other than the truck stop out on the highway, no one had built anything in Thurston since the 1940s. The town's only neighborhood, a couple of streets of houses on the west edge, slowly and quietly transitioned to growing more tumbleweeds than kids.

Abbott's Department Store held out as long as it could, but by the mid-1960s, the family that owned it accepted the fact that none of their kids wanted to stay and run it at an almost certain loss. Charles was well past retirement age, and the only people who still came to town were ranchers who didn't buy much. The year Arnie and Dottie started high school, the store announced a going-out-of-business sale that lasted three months. On the last day, Evelyn went downstairs just to look around, and they invited her to take her pick of whatever was left. Charles stood and watched, tape measure in hand and tears in his eyes, as she carted off every lady's hat and every pair of shoes she could find.

The next year, Dewley shut down the Humble station. With Evelyn's guidance, he sold the property to the corporation that owned the truck stop, and he and Fran began raising flowers and cantaloupe. They only lived a few miles out in the country, so he continued to be Evelyn's go-to guy.

Mary asked Evelyn if she could still rent her little corner of the building, which had its own street entry, and keep doing alterations and repairs for her long-time customers. Evelyn quickly agreed. Mary offered her $100 a month, but Evelyn would only accept $50. As time went by, Evelyn suspected there were some months Mary didn't make $50. She never raised the rent, and unbeknownst to Mary, she even placed a standing ad in the *Loganville Ledger* for Mary's Alterations to try and send a little more business her way.

Long after Arnie and Dottie enrolled in high school, Evelyn continued to fix sandwiches and stop in at Mary's shop, where they would spread their lunch on the sewing table and visit, as old friends do. It was the highlight of Evelyn's day. She was always aware that only through Mary's example and advice was someone like her able to sit down as an equal with such a cultured lady.

Mary would have been stunned to know how deeply and fiercely Evelyn loved her.

The gradual clearing-out of Thurston was lamented by a few old-timers, but it didn't bother Evelyn. Arnie and Dottie's class was still a fairly big group, and school activities gave Evelyn something to do. Dewley and Mary were all the friends she needed.

As renters slipped away, Evelyn found other ways to coax income from her empty buildings. She rented the still-furnished Abbott's space for a five-day flea market once a month, advertising it in the *Ledger* and helping turn it into an area-wide event. She even had a banner made and roped to the building, so it was visible from the highway. Once a year, she rented out another building she'd bought, just down the block, to the Thurston High School student council for a month-long Halloween spook house. She also bought up land along the highway—a move that paid off during a drilling boom when an oil-field supplier needed yard space to park their trucks and equipment.

Her interest in real estate prompted her to get her broker's license. But rather than open an agency and be subject to the whims of the market, she opened a title office in the old bank building. She hired a church friend to run it but handled the closings herself, pocketing a nice check every time there was a sale. It was steady income, but it was also a way to stay on top of the market—to know what was for sale and for how much. She heard about deals in progress and deals being contemplated, and used that knowledge to buy or sell land around them before anyone else knew what was going on. She always used her own money; the only loan she ever took out was to buy the bank building, and she paid it off years early.

There was another reason she didn't miss Abbott's rent. When Arnie was in junior high, during one of those drilling booms, a landman for one of the big oil companies came to see her at the title office. He pulled out some papers, then unrolled a map of her property up on the mesa. He said his company's geologists believed there was oil up there, and he was prepared to offer her $10,000 on the spot for the drilling rights. For years, she'd wondered if there was oil under her property, given that most of the ranches around her were dotted with pumpjacks and tank batteries. But for some reason, she'd never had an offer. Finally, she'd hired a geologist, and his report had told her the same things this guy was saying.

But she let him make his pitch, lying in wait to pounce. She studied his map as if she'd never seen anything like it, taking a perverse joy in playing the naive little woman who knew nothing about business. Finally, with a benevolent flourish, he pushed a document across the table for her to sign. She pushed it away without a glance.

"I'm not interested," she said, smiling.

"What!? Are you sure?" he asked. "Mrs. Chitwood, this is found money! Don't you want to talk to your husband about this?"

"It's *Miss* Chitwood, but you can call me Evelyn. I don't need to talk to anybody. How about I make *you* an offer?" she said.

"Uh, okay," he stammered. Clearly, he had a practiced response to "yes" or "no," but nothing for this. Evelyn's dark eyes were dancing.

"I know there's oil there," she said. "I had a geologist thump it three years ago. I've just been waiting for somebody to come along and show an interest in drilling on it. I don't live on it. You can put pumpjacks all over it as far as I'm concerned—it won't bother anybody but cows and coyotes. But I'm not interested in ten thousand, ten percent, or whatever else you want to throw at me. I'm not looking to be a 'royalty owner'—I'm looking to be a partner."

The man's mouth fell open.

He made a few phone calls, and by the end of the evening he and Evelyn had agreed to terms in which she bankrolled the drilling as a 50-50 partner with his company. That gave her not a one-time payout, but half of the production profits for the lifetime of the lease.

Over the next year, they drilled five oil wells within a quarter mile of Evelyn's old house, each of them a prolific producer. Chitwood #1, #2, #3, #4, and #5 made a nice little field, and every stroke of those pumpjacks poured more money into Evelyn's growing bank account. Within a few years, six figures had turned to seven.

Now and then a suitor would come along and try to elbow his way into her life. At times she enjoyed the company of a certain widowed rancher at various events, but she never let him get to know her well. He was a gentleman, and that was all she required. A few evenings a year was all he got. He eventually found someone else.

Thurston dried up, but it didn't blow away, and Evelyn thrived in spite of it all. By the time Arnie was ready to graduate from high school, she owned almost everything she could see from the top floor of the historic C&C building.

**Lubbock: 1995–1999**

English was Henry's best subject in high school, so that was his college major. He played a few intramural sports and suffered through the required math and science, but he spent most of his college years in the library, chasing down obscure references in little-known poems by forgotten poets, writing paper after paper, looking for dots that hadn't already been connected.

The majority of his fellow English majors became teachers. Henry supposed he could probably do that, too, but he never took a step toward making it reality. In the back of his mind was a vague notion of himself, someday, as a pipe-smoking professor discussing books with his grad students while waiting for the review of his latest novel in the *New York Times*. He had no idea what it might take to get him there, or what would put milk on his cereal in the meantime. He did write a couple of letters to the college newspaper, and one day he got a call.

"Is this . . . uh . . . Henry? Henry Palmer?" the voice on the phone said.

"Yes," he replied. "Who's this?"

"This is Joe Woods, editor of the *Campus Daily*. We've noticed you've written a few letters, pretty good ones, and we were looking for somebody to do a little reporting. You interested?"

Henry was flattered. It was something he'd considered but didn't think possible.

"Uh, sure," he said. "We could talk about it. I'm not taking any journalism—"

"We know. That's not a problem. You're an English major, right?"

"Yeah . . ."

"It's all good. Come see me and we'll talk. Gosling Hall. Just ask for Joe."

The line clicked.

Later that day, when Henry got a break, he found the newspaper's office, jammed into the ground floor of the oldest building on campus. The walls were plastered with clippings, pithy sayings, posters, scandalously doctored photos—a density of hipness, cynicism, and aggressive intellect he had not encountered in the monastic citadels of literature. He found Joe's office at the center of this hurricane and stepped in.

The small, dark-bearded young man at the desk was barely visible beneath a ball cap and behind piles of marked-up paper, posters, and stacks of newspapers. There was an array of computer screens, phones, cameras, tripods, and other paraphernalia of the profession. Joe had a call on speaker, so he held up his finger when Henry stepped in. A campus police radio chattered noisily in the corner. He was also typing.

"You Henry?" he said, without looking up.

"Uh, yeah. Yes sir."

"Hah! Write that down! Somebody called me sir!" Joe yelled, to no one in particular. "Have a seat."

While they talked, Joe never did fewer than three things at once. The end result was that Henry was "hired." There was no pay, but he ended up doing a fair amount of writing: offbeat columns, stories on issues like academic freedom, censorship by the administration, parking—things college students get frothed over. He even wrote a few editorials and was admired for his ability to find just the right words. He became a mascot in the newsroom, the token "ordinary guy" who came from a small town, wrote well, and had no plans to overthrow any government.

All he got was self-satisfaction, and a decent portfolio of clippings.

Academically, he continued to study literature. His growing expertise meant that someday he would know more about poetry and fiction than most people. He figured he would get a job somewhere, doing something, and the fact that he had a degree would help.

After graduation, the pace of his education accelerated rapidly.

Henry quickly discovered a degree in English did not impress construction folk; in fact, most found it hilarious. Architectural firms were worse. Unless you had a degree in engineering, drafting, or some other specialized field, you didn't get so much as a look.

Henry thought about going to the state employment agency, as he'd done for a summer construction job, but he knew if he went that route, there would be no chance of advancement or long-term employment. Instead, he turned to journalism. He took his file of clippings from the campus paper to the local daily, got an application, and filled it out, then laid them on the desk. The guy at the desk glanced at it and looked at Henry, sizing him up.

"We require a degree in either journalism or English," he said, in the least expressive voice Henry had ever heard.

"Yeah, I have that," Henry replied. "It's right there," he added, pointing at the form.

"Congratulations!" came the response as his eyes pored over the application. "We also require two years' experience at a real daily newspaper, which you don't have."

He pushed the form back toward Henry.

"How am I supposed to get experience if you won't hire me?"

"Well," he said, leaning forward as if to confide a secret, "somebody else is going to have to hire you. This," he waved an arm around him, "is not an entry-level job. We hire experienced reporters, not kids. Go to a smaller paper, get some experience, then come back."

He pushed the questionnaire away again.

"You can keep it," Henry said. "File it. Call me if you get an opening."

"Dude! We won't call you!" the screener said angrily. "Ever!"

Henry took his application and walked away. On the way back to his apartment, he thought of Rhonda.

They had gone on one date, sophomore year, set up by a friend of hers. She was cute, an elementary education major. They had a couple of classes together. But during the date, Henry discovered a quirk that was intensely annoying: everything he said, she would scrunch up her face and, in the most annoying Shirley Temple voice possible, say, "Poooooor boopsie!"

Not all of his anecdotes were bad-luck stories, but they all drew the same response. C on a science test? A paper cut? A losing night of poker in Wilson's dorm room? The scrunch, then, "Poooooor boopsie!"

It was a long, weird evening.

But there was one other thing he remembered about Rhonda. Her father owned the newspaper in a small town in East Texas—Glendale or Glenwood, something like that. Maybe he could "network" that into a job. He was willing to do almost anything to keep from having to go home to the tire shop and get back on a broom. He dug out his college phone book and found Rhonda's number. She answered right away.

"Hey Rhonda! This is Henry. Henry Palmer?"

"Oh," she said. "Henry. Henry?"

"Yeah, you remember—we went out that . . . one time."

After a long pause, he prompted, "Rhonda?"

"I'm here. Of course I remember you," she said tersely. "You're the only guy my age I've ever known named Henry. What can I do for you?"

He swallowed, shook his head and continued.

"Well, I was, uh, kind of looking for a job, and I remembered you said your dad was involved in a newspaper . . ."

"Yes, he's the publisher of the *Glendale Gazette*."

"Yeah," he stammered. "Well, I was wondering if I could, uh, talk to him about a job."

"You want my dad's number? You called me because you want my father's phone number?"

Henry was sweating into the phone. "Uh, yeah." He apologized. "I'm, uh, actually having a little trouble finding work."

"Poooooor boopsie!" she said, and hung up.

She called back a few minutes later.

"Listen," she said. "That was probably a little rude."

"I had it coming," Henry said. "I'm sorry about . . . every—"

"Anyway," she interrupted his apology. "I called my dad, and they actually are looking for a reporter. He wants you to call him. Are you ready?"

She gave him the number and told him to ask for Gus.

"I think he's looking for someone to write obituaries," she said.

"You know, the little stories about people when they die?"

"Yeah, I know," he said, relieved. "Hey, I really appreciate it. More than you realize. I was like, 'Help me, Rhonda!' and you did. Hah!"

Dead silence.

"You know, the old Beach Boys song?" Henry stammered, then sang, "Help me, Rhonda, help, help me Rhonda . . ."

"I'm familiar," she said icily, followed by more silence. But she didn't hang up.

"So, what are you going to do?" he asked, sweating again.

"I'm moving back to Glendale myself," she said. "Got a job teaching first grade at my old elementary school."

"Hey, maybe if I get this job, we could get together," he said, almost involuntarily.

"Yeah," she said, deadpan. "That would be great."

The next day, Henry called the number and talked to Gus, who seemed like a stand-up guy. Rhonda must have mentioned him, because after a few questions about his work on the college newspaper and how he felt about President Clinton, he was hired.

"I'll start you at eight-fifty," Gus said. "Don't want my daughter to think I'm a tightwad."

*Eight hundred and fifty dollars a week sounds great,* Henry thought.

"And," Gus continued, "I'll guarantee you at least 30 hours."

"Oh." Henry choked a little. "Eight-fifty an *hour?*"

"Sure!" Gus said. "I usually start reporters with no experience at six-fifty, so you ought to feel pretty good about that, huh?"

"Uh, yeah! Yes, sir. Thanks, sir," he said. "When do I start?"

"Monday," he said. "You should probably come on over this weekend and find a place to live. I'll give Rhonda a couple of leads and she can help you out, since you two are friends."

"Uh, right," Henry said. "I . . . look forward to meeting you, sir."

"It's all set then. See you Monday." Henry was about to hang up when Gus added, "Hey, uh, mind if we call you Hank?"

"Uh . . . sure, I guess," Henry stammered, making another face.

"Whatever, sir."

"Sounds better than Henry, don't you think? Hank. Hank Palmer. Probably look better in a byline, too. Sportier. I went by my given name, Eustace, until I started seeing it in print."

**Glendale: 1999**

Henry moved to Glendale and began his newspaper career as an obituary writer named Hank Palmer for the twice-weekly *Gazette*. He was surprised at how much he enjoyed it. The *Gazette* covered the entire county, but there were at most a half-dozen deaths a week. The job wasn't nearly enough to occupy a writer for thirty hours.

Henry couldn't do anything about the death rate without becoming news himself, so he enlarged his job description. He picked up assignments from the sports editor, wrote a few features and covered the police beat when other reporters were out of town. He got to know people down at the police station and city hall, and got a taste of all kinds of writing: wrecks, fires, they even let him take one gruesome murder. His clipping file grew.

That fall, he started seeing Rhonda.

The first time was awkward, but it beat sitting at home watching TV. A week or so later, they got together again, and eventually they started hanging out whenever he got a free evening; neither of them had anything else to do. All they had in Glenwood was each other.

To his surprise, and undoubtedly hers, they hit it off. Rhonda was pretty, smart and funny, and rarely said "poor boopsie" anymore. They saw every movie that came out, played miniature golf, even went to a nearby city now and then for dinner and just to get away. After a few months, she started introducing him as her boyfriend. Her dad promoted him to associate editor and seemed to be sizing him up for the job of son-in-law.

Not knowing what else to do, Henry asked her to marry him.

It was just like one of those movies: guy moves to small town, meets girl, they fall in love, get married, and live happily ever after.

All they skipped was the "falling in love" part.

As the engagement stretched on, it became obvious to Henry that they were only seeing each other because there was no one else in Glendale to see. Whatever spark they might have had, the prospect of being married snuffed it out completely. For most couples, love overrides the differences that inevitably arise, allows them to make the needed adjustments. But Henry simply didn't love Rhonda, and he was increasingly convinced she didn't love him, either.

Every little thing created more distance between them. She was a cat person; he was a dog guy. She was a morning person. His job was quickly turning him into a night person. She liked country music; he was a rock guy. She liked historical romances; he read thrillers, the more cerebral the better. Getting on the same page would have taken a lot of work even for people who were passionately, desperately in love. They just weren't.

One evening after dinner, they were invited over to visit with several other young couples, most of whom had grown up there, married high school sweethearts, and quickly started families. Rhonda flitted from group to group, chatting with everyone, connecting with them all. Henry had no interest in connecting. He felt like a total outsider and wanted to leave.

"Just give them a chance," she hissed, maintaining a smile that said she and her fiancé were just having a little chat.

"A chance to what?" he whispered back. "Recruit me to sell cleaning products? I can think of a thousand places I'd rather be."

When she was ready to go, she found him on the porch, having an animated conversation with the family dog. She harangued him all the way back to her parents' house, and for several more minutes after they pulled up in front. It didn't help that just as she'd come out the door, he had called the dog "poor boopsie" in his best Shirley Temple voice.

The following Monday, Gus walked into his office, looking deeply uncomfortable, and dropped a ring on his desk, along with a check for two weeks' pay.

“Be out by this afternoon,” he muttered. “Good luck.”

“Thanks,” Henry said, but Gus was already gone.

Henry hung around Glendale for a couple of weeks, riding out his lease. He was about to leave town when Gus called.

“Hey, uh, Hank—uh, Henry, how ya doin’?” he said.

“I’m okay,” Henry answered. “Listen, no hard feelings or anything, boss. It just didn’t work out. Better to find out now than after three kids, I guess.”

“Yeah,” Gus said. “I understand. Stuff happens. It takes two to tango. Water under the bridge.”

Henry gave a quick, nervous laugh, although he wasn’t sure what all that meant.

“But listen,” Gus continued. “I’m a partner in a couple other newspapers, and we have an opening for a sports guy in Covington. You found anything yet?”

Henry assured him he hadn’t and said he would go talk to the editor the next day. Covington was about an hour away. The interview went well, and it was obvious Gus had recommended him. He took the job, and within a few months he was the associate editor.

With no one to disappoint, Henry found he liked the job even better. He threw himself into it, got involved in every event, every cause, every controversy. His columns made people feel like they knew him—it was the perfect way for a guy who was not very outgoing to put his personality on display. He played on a city league softball team and drank beer with the guys afterward. He hung out with the police dispatcher and even fended off a few potential girlfriends.

He heard Rhonda’s high school boyfriend had returned to town as a coach, and they were going out. That was fine. He was happy for her, and for himself, too. He found life much simpler when he faced it alone.

**Thurston: 1957–1963**

Until they started school, Arnie and Dottie played together every day, but most of the time they remained in their own worlds. Arnie's was filled with cars crashing, toys fighting, leaping off cliffs—all of it accompanied by those universal spit-flying, clearing-your-throaty boy noises. Dottie's world was orderly and refined. Every doll and stuffed animal had a distinct personality and a complex backstory. The dolls attended school (which Dottie taught), held social events, and engaged in deep conversations, commenting on Arnie, Evelyn, Dottie, and her family.

Their favorite topic of conversation? Dottie's big brother, Ted.

Now and then, if Mary had to work late, her husband would send Ted upstairs to get Dottie. He greeted Evelyn respectfully and seemed genuinely glad to see his little sister, but in spite of his efforts to make conversation, all he ever got from Arnie was an open-mouthed stare.

When they started school, Dottie was in the top group, with the best students. Arnie was near the bottom. After school, the bus would drop them off at the C&C building, and they would walk in together. Dottie went straight into a hug at her mother's little sewing office, while Arnie headed upstairs. Often his mother was off taking care of business, so he would come back down and hang out in Abbott's. If he had a penny, he'd buy a gumball from the glass-globed machine just inside the front door; if he didn't, he'd go see how many pins he could dig out of the dressing room carpet before the ladies ran him out. He also liked to spin around and around on the sturdy stools that were bolted to the floor in the fabric department. That, too, always ended when Charles shooed him away.

One sunny fall day when they were in the fifth grade, Arnie walked in with Dottie, watched her hug her mother and tried to listen to what sounded like an adult conversation. He couldn't figure out the topic, so he turned to trudge up the stairs. When he reached the top floor, he called out for his mother, but the silence told him she was gone, again. He found a cold piece of fried chicken in the refrigerator and poured himself some chocolate milk.

As he chewed, he could hear the sounds of commerce in the store below, cars going down the street, trucks on the highway, birds calling as they darted past the high windows. Suddenly he felt very alone. He finished his milk, left the empty glass and chicken bone on the table, and headed back downstairs to explore.

To avoid Charles's prying eyes, he tiptoed down to the second floor. The windowless door was never locked; he turned the knob and stepped into a strange world, dimly lit from windows that fronted the bright street below. The windows were dirty and mostly blocked by stacks of boxes that went nearly to the ceiling. He looked around. Old display counters and dress racks were lined up neatly on either side of an aisle that ran through the middle of the vast space, with smaller aisles branching off in both directions, offering access to the boxes. On both sides were boxes that seemed to have been hastily opened and rifled through, spilling dresses, shirts and pants, hats, shoes, belts and wallets, handkerchiefs, socks, and other inventory.

It was a little spooky, he thought, but his heartbeat attested that it was more exciting than sitting alone upstairs.

He walked slowly down the center aisle amid piles of festive decorations: fake greenery, ropes of tinsel, boxes of bows and ribbons, and plastic Christmas trees. A neat forest of aluminum trees stood in military precision to one side, shimmering in the afternoon sunlight despite the dust settled on their curled faux fronds. When he turned, he let go an involuntary yelp. Occupying an entire corner of the room was a jumble of mannequins—not standing neatly, like the Christmas trees, but tangled together like guests at a party where a bomb had gone off. Almost all were missing body parts, including heads, and all were naked. He stood paralyzed, puzzled, terrified, unable to take his eyes off the spectacle. He was sure he shouldn't be looking.

When he finally turned to retreat, he knocked over a stack of boxes. They fell into the mass of mannequins, and a wigless, unsmiling head bounced out and came rolling toward him. He ran back out into the stairwell, shut the door behind him, and took a deep breath.

Charles was there almost immediately to frown him away.

Over time, Arnie began to explore the whole town, hopping fences, darting across streets, and cutting through yards. He liked alleys the best. One day he found a bunch of long fluorescent light tubes leaned precariously against a building, having been replaced. He reached to touch one but accidently knocked it over. It shattered in a small explosion of glass and gas.

"Cool!" he exclaimed.

He carefully picked up another one and tossed it several feet; it landed with the same result. Grabbing another tube, he took a few steps and let it fly like the javelin throwers in the Olympics, watching it arc through the air until it landed with a spectacular explosion. The last one was still in the air when a man stepped out the back door of the building.

"Hey! What are you doing?" the man yelled, just as the glass javelin crashed to earth.

Arnie ran. He could hear the man yelling behind him about broken glass. The phrase "I'm going to call your mother!" echoed as he rounded a corner.

He kept his word, and as a result, Arnie spent a good hour the next day with a dust bin and a broom, trying to get the tiny shards of broken glass off the rough pavement under the disapproving eye of the hardware store owner.

With the streets more hostile, Arnie decided to further explore the C&C building. Even though he'd grown up there, he'd never seen the basement, which he'd always been told was off-limits. He crept quietly down the stairs to the second floor, then the main floor, hugging the wall to avoid being seen. When he reached the door, he put his hand on the knob, turned it, pushed it open, and stepped through. Only when it clicked behind him did Arnie realize there were no lights down here, no dirty windows, no dangling bulbs, not even shards of light leaking through the floorboards from the store above.

Just before the door shut, he had glimpsed a vast space with a low ceiling, beams above and dirt below. Suddenly, it was the darkest place he'd ever been.

Arnie stood motionless, holding onto the doorknob, afraid if he stepped away he would lose his bearings and be trapped in the dark forever. There was nothing for his eyes to adjust to: there was no light, anywhere. His hand in front of his face was invisible. Suddenly he found it hard to breathe. He eased back over to the door, but he could feel the weight of the darkness crushing him, smothering him.

Finally, he turned the knob and, almost in a panic, stepped back out into the stairwell. He was leaning against the door, working to breathe normally when Charles's voice broke the spell.

"Hey! What are you doing down here?"

"I . . . I don't know," he whined. "I was just—"

"You weren't in the basement, were you? You're not supposed to go in there," the older man lectured. "Don't you know there's no light in there? You could hurt yourself, boy. There's probably snakes down there, and *lots* of spiders—the poisonous kind! Nobody goes down there. Now get back upstairs to your mama and stay out of things that are none of your business."

Arnie dashed past Charles and ran up to the top floor apartment, slamming the door behind him. His brow furrowed; the more he thought, the angrier he got at Charles.

"That ol' man can't boss me around," he muttered. "My momma owns this building!"

But he never went back to the basement.

**Thurston: 1965**

Arnie and Dottie had just started high school when the empty Thurston's Thrifty Hardware store, just down the alley from the C&C building, burned down. It was a major blaze that drew fire departments from 30 miles away and threatened for a few anxious hours to reduce the entire block to charcoal. Arnie, now six-foot-two and weighing at least 250 pounds, stood on the street with his mother, part of a small crowd watching the flames. Evelyn couldn't help noticing the way Arnie's eyes danced. Now and then, something would blow up inside the building, or a beam would collapse, and he would yell like a fan at a football game. When other onlookers, including the firefighters, took notice, Evelyn made him go sit on the curb across the street.

She was agitated, too. She wanted to ask the firefighters to spray some water on her building, but never did. They were busy and didn't seem worried, although the wind was blowing billowing clouds of smoke and embers directly toward the C&C building. She walked around it, peering anxiously at the roof to make sure nothing had ignited. Fortunately, the smoke wasn't rising that high. At least the pacing helped use up some of her nervous energy.

Arnie wanted to stay until every ember was out, but once the flames settled down, Evelyn decided it was time for them to go. Her son was acting very strange, his eyes darting from the flames to the firefighters. Seeing the local chief and some other area firefighters getting a drink of water at the tailgate of someone's pickup, she walked over.

"'Bout got it out?" she asked, trying to control her voice.

Ed Harkness, the Logan County Volunteer Fire Department chief, looked up, his face blackened, his eyes red and weary. "Hi, Evelyn," he said. "Yeah. I don't think there's much left to burn. Your building's going to be okay. Probably took in a little smoke, is all."

She looked back at the rubble as hoses sprayed it down to keep it from reigniting. "Any idea how it started?" All four veteran fire chiefs looked at each other. Finally, Ed spoke.

"We haven't been able to get in there, Evelyn," he said. "But it's pretty obvious." He looked at the other chiefs and they all nodded.

"What's obvious?" Evelyn asked, a big catch in her throat.

"It started in that back corner," another chief said. "We could tell the door had been kicked open. And there was footprints."

Another one spoke up. "The investigator won't come out from Fort Worth unless we call him, but I can tell you, it's gonna be arson. It was either deliberately set, or some kids got in there playin' with fire and it got away from 'em.

"Maybe it was a short," she started.

"The power was cut at the pole two years ago," Harkness said. "It wasn't electrical."

Evelyn's heart was pounding. She looked at Arnie, still jumpy. When she looked back at the firefighters, she could tell they had all seen where her eyes went.

"Your boy's pretty agitated," Harkness said. "Be okay if I talk to him?"

"Sure," Evelyn said. Her head was spinning.

He walked toward Arnie, but when Evelyn started to follow, he motioned her to stop. One of the other men said, "Why don't you stay over here with us, ma'am? Would you like some water? You've been out here a long time—probably ate a little smoke yourself, huh?"

She walked back to him and took the cup he held out. Her hand was shaking so hard most of it spilled. When she turned around, she could see Arnie looking at the ground, kicking rocks and shaking his head, while the fire chief talked. It was not a long conversation. Arnie sat down on the ground and put his head in his hands. Harkness walked back to the group.

His eyes met Evelyn's.

"I don't think we're gonna need to call Fort Worth," he said. "It's just an old, vacant building. Nobody got hurt." After a moment he added, "My biggest worry is all these departments that came so far and used so much manpower. It'd be nice if we could take care of everybody, do something for their trouble . . ."

"We sure can, Ed," Evelyn said quickly. "There's no way any of you guys oughta be out a penny for this. We all appreciate your work. I'll make some calls Monday."

The group watched in silence as she walked over to Arnie, slapped him on the head, and walked on without looking back. He followed, head down.

* * *

The upper floor of the C&C building had indeed taken in some smoke, through vents under the eaves and loose old windows. By the time Evelyn and Arnie made it to the top of the stairs, the smell was strong. They went downstairs and slept on a couple of old beds in Abbott's furniture department.

The next morning, she kicked Arnie awake. They trudged back upstairs and opened every window to the clean morning air. Evelyn could see the caulking around every pane of glass was dry and curled-up, just like the caulk she'd seen years earlier on her old house. The fresh air helped, but she knew everything they had would reek of smoke. She gathered bedding, towels, and clothes and sent Arnie down to the big commercial washing machine Abbott's had installed on the second floor, with instructions to wash it all. He knew better than to complain.

After a few hours, Evelyn headed for the laundry room to check up on Arnie, and he stuck his head out the door.

"Hey, Mom, what about lunch?" he yelled. "Maybe we could—"

"You can go up and make yourself a sandwich," she said, cutting him off. "I ain't hungry."

He started to speak again, but she silenced him with a withering look. Evelyn went on about her tour, silently vowing to start putting all this junk in the flea market.

On the first floor, the space vacated the previous year by Abbott's still smelled of rich leather and perfume, the subtle bouquet of ladies' dresses lingering among the counters, display tables, drawers, and dress racks. She descended to the dark, untouched basement, feeling the wall until she found a switch that turned on one bare lightbulb hanging in the middle of the space. Over in a corner sat an old boiler that hadn't worked since shortly after the war. In the center, workers had left a stack of bricks and a couple of bags of mortar from the original construction.

The brick piers were solid, supporting huge steel beams that held up the floor. Evelyn should have been relieved, but that night, when she collapsed into her own bed, terror seized her—fear that fire would devour her building. She lay in the darkness, heart pounding, mind racing.

Her son was an arsonist! She knew what the word meant now. Was it her fault? She thought back to when he was a baby, and she had torched the old shack up on the mesa. Had he taken that in, at some level? Had that somehow led to this?

Finally, she put aside the gnawing fear and slept. But in a vivid dream, she was homeless again, pushing a stroller down a street where every building was on fire. The sidewalks were lined with people, yelling, cursing, blaming her. She felt their eyes and wondered where she and her baby would sleep that night. She woke up in a sweat again and again, the nightmare an endless loop playing in her head.

Between the lack of sleep, the smoke, and the vinegar, she was dizzy for days.

The building was uninsured: if it burned, the loss would be devastating despite Evelyn's resources. With the town virtually abandoned, any fire department capable of fighting a blaze in a multistory building was hours away. Evelyn knew no insurance company would touch it.

She acquired a new mission: fireproof the building and fireproof her life.

On Monday, she went to the bank in Loganville and directed sizable donations to every volunteer fire department that had responded. The next day, she quietly bought a house on the edge of town that had been for sale for years and hired a crew from the lumberyard to fix it up so she would have a place to go in case the nightmare came true. She even had it furnished.

She called the owner of the hardware store, now a blackened ruin. He had no idea what he was going to do. Her timing was perfect: he agreed to let it go for what he owed in back taxes. She rushed the title transfer through and made a trip to Loganville, where she paid the taxes in cash, that afternoon. The next day, she hired a front-end loader and a dump truck to scrape the foundation clean and haul the rubble to the landfill. By sundown, the slab was bare.

That evening, she began reading up on how to fireproof a building.

At her request, the city building inspector come down from Loganville on Friday to look at her roof and windows. He confirmed the glass should be replaced with fire-resistant panes and better caulk. The building's clay tile roof was fireproof, but he noted there were a few tiles missing. The biggest safeguard against fire, he said, would be to put in a sprinkler system. They were expensive, but some cities were already starting to require them on new construction.

That Saturday, the crew came to start on the windows, which could be done from the inside. Cardboard boxes of double-paned glass; ten-gallon buckets of window glazing caulk, tools, and gloves; and a couple of big trash bins came up the freight elevator.

"What's all this, Mama?" Arnie asked as she sat at her desk, going over files.

"What's all what?" she rasped, not looking up.

"All this stuff, that's what!" he yelled, waving an arm in the direction of the boxes.

She closed the book and looked up at him. "Boy, don't you ever raise your voice to me, you understand?"

"Yes, ma'am," he said meekly.

"All these windows . . ." she made a sweeping gesture with her hand, "they're all coming out. Every last piece of glass is coming out of those frames, and it's all going to get replaced with this new-fangled, double-pane, fire-resistant glass, caulked in real tight."

"What am I gonna do?" he asked.

"You're the cleanup crew," she replied. "You sweep, and you pick up every bit of that old glass and caulk and haul it down to the dumpster. These guys work fast. You've gotta keep up."

"But Mama—"

"No buts, Arnold! That's it! If I hear one word of complaining or whining, there'll be hell to pay. You understand?"

"Yes, ma'am," he muttered.

She pointed Arnie to the push-broom and the big dustpan and headed for the door.

"Where are you goin'?" he asked.

"I've got some errands to run," she said. "This place better be clean as a whistle when I get back, y'hear? Remember: these guys are pros. This ain't their first rodeo."

"This is a rodeo?"

"Never mind," she sighed. "Just get this cleaned up before I get back."

By the time the sun was down, the windows had been removed, the glass panes replaced, and one side glazed. They would have to dry overnight, then be flipped over and glazed on the other side before they could be reinstalled. When the job was done, Evelyn could feel how much tighter they were just standing in front of them.

But there was still work to do. The sprinkler crew was coming the next week.

**Fort Worth: 2015**

With the movie date, Henry and Ella had crossed another line. They were in each other's lives now, so it was not a big step when, the following Saturday morning, she swung by his house—a rented two-bedroom in an old neighborhood near downtown—to pick him up. He met her at the curb. She drove to a U-Store-It in an industrial area south of the city, parked beside the highway, and they walked through the gate.

By 10 a.m. they had joined a small crowd that looked like characters from a TV show: chain-smoking old ladies in sweats and visors, middle-aged guys with big bellies, most wearing gimme hats and t-shirts with questionable slogans. Women of indeterminate age and hair color. A middle-aged married couple who looked like someone you'd meet at church and an oily, hair-gelled man with gold chains and a thin mustache—someone you'd meet in a casino.

It was humid; heavy clouds hung low as the group moved down narrow rows between metal buildings. The aisles were just wide enough for a pickup. Henry got a little claustrophobic walking elbow-to-elbow with the colorful entourage, following the lady auctioneer from one padlocked roll-up door to another. The facility's owner, an earnest-looking young man, followed too, holding bolt-cutters and a clipboard.

Whenever they reached a unit to be auctioned, both he and the auctioneer checked and double-checked their lists and nodded to each other. Then he quickly read a required public notice officially announcing that the contents of this unit, owned by so-and-so, were being sold at public auction for unpaid rent, as allowed by law. The renter had been sent a registered letter at their last known address, the unit had been advertised for two weeks in a newspaper of general circulation, and there had been no response. Now, the facility could sell it to recoup lost rent, but that was all they could get. Anything over that went into a trust fund for a required number of years, and if it was not claimed, it went to the state.

With the formalities out of the way, the lock was cut, the door was flung upward, and the crowd was allowed to look inside. At that moment, even if the owner of the unit was present, he or she could not stop the auction.

Potential buyers could look in but not touch. They couldn't even reach into the unit. If they did, they were disqualified from bidding. Bidders were given a minute to look, then the auction started at a bid determined by the auctioneer based on how it looked to her, and how much rent was owed. The unit's contents were sold in one lot, all or nothing.

Henry's reporter muscles were twitching, not at the slim possibility of finding something priceless in one of these abandoned rental units, but at the stories behind them. Why was this unit abandoned? A prison sentence? A fatal car wreck? A divorce? A sudden move to a distant place, perhaps as part of a witness protection program? He wanted to poke and probe and ask questions, but there was only one way to have a shot at that: you had to be the highest bidder.

For the first few auctions, Henry and Ella just traipsed with the crowd, stood, and watched the bidding. They all seemed to know what they were doing. It almost felt as if they'd decided in advance who would get a unit, like the whole thing was more family reunion than competitive auction. Several of them seemed to know Ella. Henry thought it was hilarious that his cool, corporate-lawyer friend was a card-carrying member of this menagerie.

"Hey Ella, you bring your boyfriend?" an older lady said with a cackle.

"He's just here to carry the piano I'm gonna buy!" Ella quipped, sparking laughter.

"I hope he's got some friends!" one man shouted.

Another said, "You might have to settle for a ukulele!"

More laughter. But when the bidding started, everyone got quiet and serious. Ella did too, and he followed her lead. Each of them had their own signal: a head nod, a subtle wave of the hand, a spoken word or phrase. It reminded Henry of some Pentecostal churches he'd visited—interactive, with its own language and customs. Like church, the auction was a culture, and he was the outsider. Everybody knew what was coming but him.

He began to sense when someone really wanted a unit. Their facial expression and body language would change. Urgency would creep into their voice. Usually, the others would back off and let them have it, rather than bidding the price up. That was how they stayed friends, he guessed. He did wonder, though, why some units attracted big bids while others drew almost no interest. They all looked the same to him. What was it that made someone want a specific unit? He made a mental note to ask Ella when he got a chance.

One, for instance, had four televisions visible inside but sold for only $150. Another, with clothes in bags hanging from the rafters and stacks of neat storage boxes, brought almost $1,000. Items like ceramic owls, scooters, a garden hose reel, bicycles, pianos, and toys drew no interest; furniture generated excitement. As they walked down to the end of a row and turned, Henry caught up to Ella.

"What's the difference?" he asked, running to get in front of her and walking backward to face her. "Why do some go so much higher? That one back there had a bunch of TVs and nobody seemed to want it."

She was happy to educate him.

"Well, first off, if a TV worked, it wouldn't be in there," she said. "Nobody wants to throw a TV away, but the ones in storage units are usually dead. There's going to be a TV and a mattress in almost every unit, just because they're hard things to toss out. But who wants to sleep on some worn-out mystery mattress that's been in storage? I get itchy just thinking about it.

"Most of this stuff is junk," she continued. "People either don't want to throw it out or don't know how. They just want it out of their sight. They'd rather pay to store it than take time to go through it and toss it."

Henry nodded, catching on.

"And eventually," he said, "they're not even willing to pay. They walk away and it's someone else's problem."

"Right! Or someone else's treasure!" she said, looking at him like a proud teacher as the owner clipped another lock. "You're catching on. It's fun, isn't it?"

"Fun. Other people's junk." He shrugged his shoulders and gave a noncommittal nod. But he had to admit, he was intrigued.

With the sky low and stormy, the auctioneer picked up the pace. One unit had a saddle, a hutch, and a big metal desk. It sold in less than a minute.

"That saddle would look good on my donkey," a middle-aged man quipped. Then he looked over at Ella. "Hey, Ella! Make you a deal! You can buy it for your hoss there!"

She just smiled.

"I'll take it for my goat!" someone yelled, as the crowd walked on.

The sweet-looking older lady trailed the pack while her husband went to the front. She told Henry they had an antique store in a small town up north and were stockpiling merchandise, most of which they knew wasn't going to sell.

"It fills the shelves." She smiled. "And you never know. You might get lucky."

Finally, the group rounded a corner and gathered in front of what would be the last unit of the day. The disclaimer was read, the lock clipped, and the door rolled up. Ella went on high alert. Henry sensed she was going to try for this one.

The deep, narrow space was about three-quarters full, and it looked like the items had been there a long time. There were lots of very old-looking cardboard boxes, a few plastic storage containers, and a steel file cabinet. A table-mounted sewing machine was strapped to a pallet. An ancient TV was visible along with several army-issue duffle bags, a collapsed playpen, an old suitcase, and a couple of antique-looking dining chairs.

It was a deep unit, so there was a lot behind all that, hiding.

"I'll start the bidding at $200 on this nice-looking unit," the auctioneer began. "What am I bid? Can I get $200? Can I get $210? Two-ten, can I get $225?"

It went on, with three or four people bidding. When it got to $350, Ella rose to her tiptoes and waved at the auctioneer.

"Three seventy-five!" she said in a calm, businesslike voice. Henry wasn't the only one shocked. The auctioneer turned toward Ella, made eye contact, and pointed at her.

"Three-seventy-five!" she cried, then looked around. "Can I get $400?"

She did, from a big, rough-looking older man who had been on the fringes, quietly observing, not part of the group. After the price went up a couple more notches, the rest became observers. Ella and the man continued to go back and forth in $25 increments. When Ella bid $625, the stranger looked uncomfortable—almost angry—and paused for a long time before going to $650. He never glanced at Ella.

She squeezed Henry's arm, her dark eyes hot as coals, then

turned to the auctioneer and nodded.

"Six seventy-five!" the auctioneer yelled. "Do I hear seven? Can I get seven?"

For the first time, the man looked at Ella, his eyes angry, almost pleading. He looked down and started breathing hard. Henry steeled himself, thinking the guy was going to blow up.

Then, abruptly, he turned and walked away, muttering to himself.

"SOLD!" the auctioneer said, clapping her hands and pointing back at Ella. The owner tore the last ticket off of the form on his clipboard and gave it to her. She had three days to get the stuff out or she'd owe rent for the next month.

A couple of people walked up and shook hands with Ella as the crowd quietly scattered. Henry looked for the guy who had bid against her, but he was gone. They stood there in silence in front of the unit that was now hers.

"What just happened?" Henry asked her, finally. "Why'd you do that? Six hundred and seventy-five dollars? Are you nuts?"

She looked exhausted.

"I don't know," she said, surveying the horde of junk she now owned. "I can't explain it. I just got a strong feeling we were supposed to have this one."

* * *

They stepped in reverently, like British explorer Howard Carter entering King Tut's tomb, walking among the debris of someone's life. Henry ran his hand over the dusty roll-top desk, then reached to open a cardboard box.

"Don't!" Ella said. "Let's just go get a lock, lock it up, and get out of here. We can come back tomorrow and get it."

"You don't want to just grab something?" Henry asked.

"Like what?" she asked, sounding annoyed.

"I don't know—maybe there's a book, a file, some papers, or whatever in one of these boxes that will tell us something, help us identify the owner. Aren't you curious?"

She took a deep breath, like an athlete still recovering from a race.

"Okay, yeah," she said, relenting. "One thing. I'm just . . . a little spooked. All of a sudden, I feel really weird about this."

The boxes were sealed with packing tape that was coming loose, but all were labeled: dishes, baby clothes, china, towels. Henry's eyes went to the suitcase, a big old Samsonite, with sides made of alligator skin. He picked it up, placed it on top of a box, and tried the old locks. They were not rusted, just dry and unwilling to let go. He forced one open, then the other, and lifted the lid. It was filled with clothes, but they were tucked around several books, including an old high school yearbook in mint condition. He grabbed it, lowered the suitcase lid and snapped the locks, then stepped back out, pulling the door down behind him. Ella was standing there.

"What'd you get?" she asked. He held it out and she cocked her head to read it. "That's it? Thurston High School, 1969? This is what looks interesting to you?"

"Hey, reference books like this are great sources of information," he said. He glanced down at the cover and laughed.

"The Thanatopsis!" he read. "Thanatopsis? Why would a high school name its yearbook the 'Thanatopsis'?"

"Are you talking to me, or just muttering to yourself?"

"I'm muttering," Henry said. "Everything's not about you, sweetie."

She took a half-hearted swing at him, but he ducked. He decided to explain anyway.

"Thanatopsis is a Greek word," he told her, leaning into his nerdiness. "It literally means 'looking at death.' Isn't that a weird thing to name a high school yearbook?"

"Are you sure it's a yearbook?" Ella asked. "Maybe it's a memorial or something. Sixty-nine? Vietnam was hot and heavy then. Maybe the school lost some kids."

Henry flipped through it. It had the usual pages of portraits for each class, sections on activities like sports, band, ag, choir, and ads in the back.

"No, it's a yearbook," he said. "This is their annual. The 'Thanatopsis.'"

He looked inside the front cover and there was a name, written in neat cursive.

"'Dorothy Eileen Sinclair, Class of 1969,'" he read. "See? Aren't you already intrigued? Maybe we can find her and return this—and ask her why they named it the 'Thanatopsis.'"

As he was flipping pages, a few cards with names in calligraphic script fell out. He quickly reached down and picked them up, reading them as he put them back.

"Melvin Douglas Davis. Adeline Audelia Pounds. Arnold Ray Chitwood," he intoned, like he was reading them off at graduation as each one passed. Then he closed the book. "Every name has a story, Ella. Maybe they all signed it."

He ran to catch up with her, hoping to infect her with his enthusiasm.

"You're so weird," she said, shaking her head.

"Hey, I'm a journalist," he said, getting defensive again.

"Didn't you tell me a journalist is just a fancy name for an unemployed reporter?"

"Well," he said, brandishing the book at her. "There are some stories in here."

"Yeah? I hope they're good ones, because they cost us $675," she said.

He stopped. "Us?"

She turned to look at him. "Yes. We're splitting it, right?"

"Splitting it? I didn't tell you to bid, and I sure didn't tell you to bid $675. And I don't remember agreeing to split anything. I don't remember getting asked."

"Oh, c'mon, Henry. Please?" she begged. "It's a good deal. I know we'll come out ahead when we sell the stuff."

He looked skeptical.

"Okay, how about you do $300 and I'll do $375?" she asked. "Whatever we get for what's inside, we'll split it 50-50."

"Okay," he muttered. He couldn't say no to those big, brown eyes. "Once we both recoup our original investment."

"Wait, you—"

"And you buy the new lock," she added, with a smile.

"And you buy lunch," he countered quickly.

"Dutch," she said. "I drove."

"Dadgum lawyers!"

**Thurston: 1965**

Arnie was going to help with the next phase, too: hanging iron water pipes above the pressed-tin ceiling, then extending sprinkler heads down through the tin. Each sprinkler was equipped with a trigger—a glass bulb that held the water line shut but would shatter at a specific heat (usually 155 degrees) letting water flow through the pipe. The flowing water would spin the sprinkler head, and the resulting shower would extinguish, or at least slow, the fire.

Most multistory buildings had been required to install them since the 1940s, but the C&C building predated that by decades. In many smaller cities, building owners had fiercely resisted installing fire sprinklers, calling it an expensive bureaucratic burden. But in several towns, entire blocks of historic buildings had burned down because of outdated construction that omitted firewalls. In almost every case, sprinklers would have helped.

Thurston was no longer an incorporated city, so no agency could require Evelyn to install them. It was expensive, but a bargain, she thought, to escape those nightmares.

The plumbing and pipefitting involved was beyond Arnie's skill level, but Evelyn had asked the foreman to find something he could do. When he saw the boy's size, he assured her he could put him to work.

The next Saturday, she rousted Arnie out of bed early, and they headed to the first-floor stairwell, where the crew was already fitting the fire riser to carry water up to the third floor. Arnie helped the guys maneuver the heavy twenty-foot sections of black-iron pipe up the stairs.

He was eager to show off his strength, so the veteran ironworkers put him at the bottom, letting him bear most of the weight while they guided it up the stairwell and finally through the doorway. Once they got a section inside, Arnie rested briefly while two grown men carried each joint and set it on the floor. By breakfast time, he was sweating like he'd been through football practice.

When they invited him into the space above the ceiling, he recovered quickly.

The workers had carefully removed a piece of the pressed-tin ceiling to allow them to get the long joints of pipe into the attic, but they accessed the space by way of a staircase hidden in a closet off the hallway. Once Arnie had climbed the stairs, the only place to step was a narrow catwalk, three two-by-fours wide. Later, they would bring up bright work lights, but for now, aside from the light flooding in through the ceiling opening, only a few shafts of sunlight sliced through random gaps and hung in the empty darkness.

Arnie stood and looked around as his eyes adjusted. After a few moments, he could see the ancient wood trusses, rough-cut timbers that held up the building's roof, the lath strips the tiles were nailed to, perforated by thousands of nails. Below the catwalk, a grid of nailing strips held up the ceiling. Stepping there would be a disaster for anything that weighed more than a rat.

Arnie was transfixed by the otherworldly space just above where he slept and ate.

He proved to be such a handy tool-carrier and errand-runner that they decided to let him help hang pipe. An extra body was always handy when you started lifting the long, heavy sections into place. Besides, the crew had started a pool on how long it would be before the large, awkward teenage boy made a false step and fell through the ceiling.

They didn't *want* him to, but if it was going to happen, they sure didn't want to miss it.

One evening, the plumbers had gone home when Arnie poked back up into the attic space to pick up some tools. Suddenly Evelyn heard him scream. There was a loud crash, and she braced herself, certain he was about to fall through. Instead, he came crashing down the stairs and landed in a heap on the hallway floor, wild-eyed. She rushed to him.

"What happened?" she demanded. "Are you okay?"

"Mama—there's—it's not . . ." he stammered, more scared than hurt.

"What is it?" she repeated. "Calm down, boy! You're okay. What is it?"

"There's somethin'—some*one*—up there, Mama," he said, fighting for air.

"What do you mean?" she said. "What's up there? Who's up there?"

She thought maybe one of the pipefitters had hidden, just to mess with him.

He pointed at the opening and tried to talk, then burst into tears. Evelyn stood up, then stepped carefully up the stairs and poked her head through the opening. Arnie yelled again. "No, Mama! Don't go up there!"

She looked at him calmly, half-smiling at the sight of this big, strong boy whimpering in a heap on the floor. "Okay. So, tell me. What's up there?"

He just shook his head. She sighed, grabbed a flashlight, clicked it on, and started back up. As soon as her head was fully inside the attic space, she shined the beam all around her, half-expecting to look into the glowing eyes of a raccoon or a rat. At first, she saw nothing but wood beams and the dark skylight channels.

Then she saw what Arnie had seen. In one remote corner there was an old metal opening, sealed off for years, that went through to the roof. She later learned it was a chimney, connected to the old coal-burning stove in the basement. It had been capped after the building was plumbed with gas. Apparently, a section had come loose and fallen to the side.

It was quickly obvious that someone had knocked it loose. He was still there.

She whistled softly as the flashlight's beam revealed a human skeleton, fully dressed, upside-down, with one foot still in the upper part of the chimney. She stretched up until she could see the grinning head, with a few bits of leathery flesh still clinging to it. It was against the top of the solid brick wall at an angle that clearly illustrated the cause of death. Apparently, the deceased dove into the chimney head-first, expecting a joyride, and instead landed directly on top of the unyielding brick, breaking his neck.

Death had been instantaneous. A bag was still clutched in the bony fingers. He had probably intended to burglarize Abbott's back in its heyday.

Evelyn could hear Arnie muttering. She clicked her flashlight off and came down a few rungs to look at him. "You okay?" she asked.

He was sitting up, rubbing his shoulder. "Yeah. What is it?"

"It's a dead man, son," she said, patting his head. "What's left of him. Whatever happened, it happened a long time before we moved in. It's creepy, but you and me don't have nothin' to be afraid of."

He picked himself up, trying to salvage a little dignity. "I ain't afraid," he said.

She couldn't stifle a grin as he walked away. The next morning, she called the sheriff, and he came out with a couple of deputies. They had a good laugh when they saw the skeleton. The Loganville newspaper reporter, having heard it on the police radio, came and took photos from every conceivable angle before they finally brought a stretcher up, lifted the fragile corpse down, and zipped it into a body bag. A few pieces fell off, and they tossed them into the bag before closing it.

Evelyn was glad Arnie was at school, although he'd begged her to let him stick around and watch the retrieval. She imagined he was the center of attention with this story, which no doubt omitted his fall and all that whimpering on the floor.

The new sheriff seemed genuinely grateful.

"I think you just solved a cold case for us, Miss Chitwood," he said. He was younger and far less of a cowboy than Sheriff Lamkin, the veteran lawman who'd confronted her the day she moved in.

"I'll have to dig through a few files, but I think this is a guy who went missing around 1937," he said. "Glen Barkey. Small-time thief. Wasn't much count, so nobody ever got too worried about finding him—figured he'd just run off to ply his trade somewhere else. But he's been right here, minding his own business, all these years. Kinda sad nobody missed him."

"It's a wonder we didn't smell him," Evelyn said with disgust.

"Well, the attic space is pretty well ventilated, and with the summer heat, I think he was already a mummy by the time y'all moved in, what, around '51? '52?"

"Hmmph," she snorted. "I guess he got what was comin' to 'im."

The sheriff nodded in agreement. "Is your boy alright? That's a pretty good fall."

"Oh, he's fine," she said. "I'm just glad he didn't break nothin'—himself or anything else. He's a big kid." They laughed.

"Be glad he didn't end up like that guy," the sheriff said. "Some of these old buildings, there's places nobody's ever gonna find you. Not even the rats."

He and the other deputy were still laughing as they accompanied the corpse down the freight elevator. Evelyn didn't think it was funny.

* * *

Arnie's mother was right: at lunchtime, he drew a small crowd in the cafeteria with his story about finding a skeleton above the ceiling of his apartment. When he saw some of the girls were smiling, he included his hasty tumble down the attic stairs and the smiles became laughs. He did leave out the part where he lay in the floor crying while his tiny mother went up and identified the apparition. But the kids were fascinated with his detailed description of the corpse—taken word-for-word from his mother's account.

Arnie was just a couple of months into his freshman year, but he was beginning to feel at home. The classes were harder, and at first, he had struggled with changing rooms all the time. Some of the older kids picked on him, but most just ignored him. After a while he began to notice that even though he was a freshman, he was bigger than most of the upperclassmen. In fact, he was one of the biggest guys in school.

One day a senior named Jack who had been giving him a particularly hard time came up behind him in the hallway.

"Hey Chitwood!" Jack sneered. "Guess what I got today?"

Arnie turned, just in time to see him turn his new senior ring around so the stone was on the inside. In the next instant, he swung his palm at Arnie's head, trying to pop him with the ring. But before he could make contact, Arnie reached up and caught his forearm. He gripped it so hard the much smaller senior could not escape.

"Ow! Let me go, you moron!" he yelled. A crowd quickly gathered. Arnie didn't know what to say, so he just stood there and held Jack's arm while he squirmed, unleashing a barrage of profanity. Finally, Arnie tossed the arm away like a used hotdog wrapper, causing the smaller boy to stumble backward and nearly fall down. He continued to curse, his eyes bugged out with anger, although he maintained a safe distance.

"Don't you ever turn your back on me, you punk!" he hissed. "I'm gonna get you for this. You are going to regret messing with me."

The crowd looked at Arnie expectantly.

"Well," Arnie said, slowly, "seems like you was the one messin' with me. Maybe you regret that already, huh?"

Jack turned and stomped away down the hall, muttering. He never approached Arnie again, and the large ninth grader began to take on a bit of a reputation as a tough guy.

The hard work he was doing at home was indeed transforming him. The baby fat melted off, his arms began to show some definition, and his belly shrank. A few days after the incident with Jack, Arnie was walking down the hall between classes and passed the football coach, who was standing in the doorway of his math classroom. Arnie felt a solid punch in his right arm.

"Hey!" he said, whirling around, thinking Jack might have come back. But all he saw was the coach leaning against the door frame, chewing on the stub of a cigar with a grin on his face.

"Hey, Chitwood, when you gonna come out for football and hit somebody instead of just getting hit all the time?"

"Uh . . . I don't, uh, sir . . . I ain't thought about it," he stammered.

The coach's smile faded, and he leaned into Arnie's face.

"Well, I'm sayin' maybe you oughta think about it," he said in his most patronizing tone. "We can teach kids how to block and tackle and use their arms to move guys around. Only thing we can't teach 'em is how to be big— but it looks like you're learnin' that part on your own."

"Uh, okay," Arnie mumbled. "I'll see what my mama says."

The coach gave him a practiced look of disgust.

"Okay," he said. "You ask your mama. Tell her you want to play football, and the coach thinks it might be your sport. If she says no, you can always go out for the cheerleading squad."

With his mother's full support, Arnie changed his schedule the next morning.

**Thurston: 1968**

Dottie was utterly disinterested in her English class. That was unusual, given that English was her favorite subject. She'd already been anointed valedictorian of the class of '69, having made every A possible since the first grade, but on this Tuesday, she just couldn't focus on Mr. Posey's lecture about John Steinbeck's robust prose.

It had been three weeks since they'd heard from Ted.

Her brother, serving in a combat engineering battalion in Viet Nam, had written his family every week since he went overseas. About a month ago, the letters stopped. As the weeks went by, a hush settled over the home like a stifling blanket. Conversation was already scarce, but the lack of news about Ted built a tension unlike anything Dottie had ever felt. Dinnertime became as quiet as a graveyard. What few words were exchanged were carefully crafted to skirt the fear on all their minds: Ted was gone. Dottie could feel it. That unconfirmed and certain reality was a cloud, about to break into a storm any second.

It was the centuries-old dilemma of military families: desperate for news, but terrified at what that news would be.

Dottie's father drew more deeply into himself, while her mother carried on as if nothing was wrong. Dottie was screaming inside—a pulsing cry of pain with no sound and no ceiling. The longer it went on, the deeper her panic became. She felt certain she would never see her brother again, never hear his voice, join his laughter, or smell his shirt when she stood on her tiptoes and reached up to hug him. He was gone. Her soul knew it.

The war was ramping up. Every day there were body counts on the evening news, Walter Cronkite telling America how many of theirs we got, how many of ours they got. We were "winning," but it was eighteen American boys yesterday, twenty-four today, each one an empty place at a dinner table somewhere. On top of that was the live footage: reporters following troops through the jungle, the pop of gunfire in the distance, flag-covered coffins coming off of transport planes. Behind it all played the music of the era—defiant music, the soundtrack to a war at home that was as dangerous and violent as the one in Viet Nam. It wasn't just protests against the war, but growing racial tension in city after burning city. Taken together, it gave Dorothy and many others the feeling that the America she knew was going away, or, like Ted, was already gone.

The turmoil was a long way from Thurston. But now that the war had almost certainly taken Ted, it was personal. Dottie couldn't go get him, couldn't save him, couldn't make her life, her country, or even her family feel like it used to feel.

Ted and Dottie were seven years apart, but they were close. In many ways, Ted had filled in for her cold, distant father. He was the classic big brother—protecting her, advising her, taking her places he shouldn't have, bringing her back unharmed and better-educated. He could open doors that were closed even to parents, and especially to quiet, bookish little sisters.

Dottie was book-smart. Ted was brilliant in practical ways. He learned by seeing things, touching them, experiencing them. He played a vital role in her education. He rounded her out, challenged her and helped her rise to challenges. He showed her how to drive a stick-shift, how to change a flat tire, how to dance the twist and get the best of a bully. Ted was the reason Dottie constantly surprised people who didn't expect a lot of spunk from a girl who looked like her most vigorous physical activity was turning a page. She was every bit as literary and romantic as she appeared, but thanks to Ted, she was also a tough Texas country girl.

She didn't care much for Ernest Hemingway, but Ted was her hero.

Their father, George, was older than their mom, a product of the Great Depression and a veteran of World War II, stoic and distant. He never hugged, never said "I love you," never showed emotion. When they took Ted to the bus station to leave for basic training, he offered his son a firm handshake, then quickly turned away, muttering about warming up the car. His silence deepened after Ted left for Vietnam. He spent his days at work, out on the road as a lineman for the electric cooperative, and when he got home, he was in his shop or on the tractor until after dark. When Dottie spoke to him, all she usually got was a grunt from behind the newspaper.

Dottie's mom had always done her best to make up for that distance, tenderly caring for her son and daughter, cooking and cleaning and getting them off to school every day. Dottie's earliest memories centered around her mother reading to her, helping instill a love for books. Dottie had spent many happy hours in her mother's shop at Abbott's or upstairs playing in the third-floor apartment of the building's quirky owner, Evelyn Chitwood, who babysat Dottie and her son, Arnie, on days when Mary was working. The store had closed in '65, after the last of the Abbott brothers decided to move away, but Mary continued to sew there. It didn't pay much, but it covered the rent for the space and provided money for her to buy extra things for her kids.

Dottie came back to the present just in time to hear Mr. Posey's question.

"So how is Steinbeck's realism different from, say, Hemingway's?" he asked. It was the kind of question that motivated the entire class to turn and look at Dottie, because hers was usually the only hand that went up. This time, she kept her hands on the desk.

Finally, Mel Davis raised his hand and tentatively offered, "More words?"

Mr. Posey was deeply into Steinbeck. To Dottie, his lecture on twentieth-century realism sounded like a buzzing insect, droning on in the distance. She much preferred Wordsworth, Byron, Keats, Shelley—the romantics, who painted pictures with words that took the reader to a different time and place. She loved literature where there was magic, not just a reality even harsher than Thurston's. For the last several days, she'd been reading Wordsworth's "Lines Composed a Few Miles Above Tintern Abbey," memorizing it despite its length. She could hear in her mind the poet's voice—the big brother—talking to his "dear, dear sister" about the natural wonders of that beautiful place. It made her think of Ted.

After Mel's answer, a soft giggle ran through the classroom as Mr. Posey tried to hide his look of resigned frustration. Just then the office aide came into the room and spoke quietly with Mr. Posey.

"Oh," he said. "Oh, my. Well, uh . . . Dottie?"

She looked up.

"You need to go to the office with Teresa, please," he said softly. "Right now."

There was an audible buzz as she stood. Her friend Abby grabbed her hand and whispered, "Dottie! What do you think they want?"

Dottie smiled and looked back at her. "It'll be fine," she said.

But she knew what it was about, even before she saw her mother sitting at Mr. Chesterton's desk, or the sunken look on both their faces. And she knew, just as surely, that nothing would ever be fine again.

* * *

The Sinclair family had lived in Thurston for years, and news of Ted's death traveled like a brush fire through the little town.

Evelyn only had one real friend. She was among the first people at Mary's door that day. Mary's husband opened it without a word, then stood there looking at Evelyn as if she were responsible for Ted's death. She would soon realize he looked at everyone that way. Evelyn felt uncomfortable in his lifeless glare, but after an awkward standoff, she put the casserole dish she was holding into his hands, told him she was so, so sorry for his loss, then stepped past him. Mary was seated on a couch, talking on the phone. Evelyn waited patiently as Mary listened, speaking at intervals. As soon as she hung up, Evelyn reached to hug her.

Mary stood and smiled, accepting the embrace, but it was a formal, obligatory hug, not the sheltering hug of a friend. As people continued to arrive, Mary made the rounds, seeing that everyone had something to eat, being the gracious hostess. Evelyn could see it was a pose. There was no spark in her eyes, like something inside her had died.

Evelyn busied herself around the house, helping greet visitors, taking dishes, managing the growing buffet. It hit her that only through her friendship with Mary had she been exposed to the funeral customs of small-town Texas. Nothing in her upbringing resembled this ritual.

Evelyn's previous encounters with death had been shocking and violent.

When she was about ten, her father had gotten into a fight during one of his poker nights at their house up on the mesa. As it escalated, it moved outside. A small crowd gathered to watch what they expected would be a fistfight, until the man who had accused her father of cheating reached into his pocket, retrieving and flipping open a switchblade. Evelyn's father calmly urged the man to put it down, come back inside, have another drink, and discuss the matter. It was his best salesmanship—cajoling and persuading, playing to the crowd as much as the man with the knife.

But instead of putting it down, he lunged at Evelyn's father. He dodged but suffered a light slash across one arm, causing blood to stain his ripped shirtsleeve. As he pulled back, he reached into his pocket and produced a small revolver. When the man regrouped for another attack, he was looking down the barrel of a gun. Evelyn's father told him to drop the knife, get in his car, and leave. Instead, he proclaimed loudly that Evelyn's father was a cheat, and he wanted his money back. After another brief standoff, with a sneer he lunged again. The pistol popped loudly and there was a flash at the barrel. Evelyn's father stepped aside like a bullfighter who had just plunged his sword home, and the man's thrust ended on the ground as he fell and lay motionless, a bullet hole in his forehead and a spreading pool of blood pulsing out beneath him.

The rest of that night, Evelyn hung on the fringes, wide-eyed, as police lights flashed and deputies browsed the scene, taking statements from witnesses. A group stood around, talking and laughing, and she heard the sheriff use the phrase "misdemeanor murder." All that time, the man's body lay there, the sneer frozen on his lifeless face. No one bothered to put a sheet over him; no one tried to shield a little girl from the gruesome sight. His dead eyes, the unnatural twist of his body, the smell—gunpowder, sweat, and blood—burned into her memory. Her father, who likewise had no thought for her or what she was seeing, was treated like a hero, his wound attended by the ambulance driver, who happened to also be the undertaker. He wasn't taken in for questioning, and no charges were filed. They didn't even take his gun.

The night of Arnie's birth had been even more violent and horrific: the smell of blood and alcohol and radiator fluid, the eerie quietness as she lay trapped in the wreckage. Death again, not knocking at the door but kicking it to splinters. Finding the burglar's body above the ceiling was another macabre encounter that fit perfectly within her experience: death was quick and gory, no sugarcoating, no one patting anyone on the arm and saying, "There, there."

Just a person alive, then suddenly, not.

Evelyn knew Ted's death, in war, thousands of miles from home, had been brutal. It was far removed from this ritual, which was designed to quickly and completely create a different reality, to gloss over and distance people's minds from death. The casket would be delivered to the church, sealed. The US military had gotten quite smooth and professional at returning fallen soldiers to their loved ones. At the Sinclair home, there was only a framed photo of Ted in his uniform, smiling and handsome, and a few artifacts from his life: a baseball glove and bat, his high school letter jacket, some shoes. They could remember him that way.

With the casket closed, at least they would be spared the barbaric ritual of filing past, Evelyn thought. She didn't know what to think of the visitors, the never-ending stream of food, as if eating would somehow assuage their grief.

After school let out, a few of Dottie's classmates filtered in: her best friend Abby and some other seniors, the band, and the yearbook staff. At her mother's urging, Dottie came in and greeted them, but she looked like she wanted to be anywhere else. Unlike her cheery mother, she made no attempt to hide her grief, sobbing as she hugged Abby. A couple of the boys offered her side-hugs, and a girl Evelyn hadn't seen before grabbed her for an intense embrace.

"It's okay," Dottie said finally, just wanting it to end. The girl let go and they all stood awkwardly, wiping their eyes. Arnie came in with several of his friends to join the circle. He went straight to Dottie and wrapped her in a bear hug. Finally, she pushed him away, and they all stood and looked at each other.

After "I'm so sorry," no one had a clue what to say next.

Evelyn slipped in beside her son. He continued to look at Dottie, but Evelyn noticed the younger girl kept glancing at Arnie. She tugged at the sleeve of his letter jacket.

"Who's the girl over there by Abby?" she whispered.

"Who?" he asked, still looking at Dottie.

"The one with the dark hair, who keeps looking at you. I don't think I've seen her."

"Oh," he said. "That's Sherry Statzenburger. She's a freshman. She's kinda weird."

Evelyn knew what it felt like to be the weird girl with the hand-me-down clothes. It was obvious she was watching Dottie's every move, trying to fit in. She couldn't have picked a better role model, Evelyn thought.

Arnie and his pals decided they'd paid their respects and headed for the food. Evelyn followed and poked her head through the kitchen door.

"Hey boys, slow down on that, okay?" she cautioned them. The boys, all members of the football team, were laughing and talking among themselves as they loaded their plates.

Arnie looked up. "Okay, Ma," he said with his mouth full. Evelyn's disapproving look quickly quieted them all. She stepped in and pulled the door closed behind her. Her fierce demeanor brought them to a standstill.

"This is a grieving home, not an all-you-can-eat buffet," she hissed. "You boys take one plate and go out in the yard, but don't be laughin' and cuttin' up in here. This is a place of sadness, and this food is for the family, not y'all."

Arnie had worn Ted's hand-me-downs as a little boy, but he and his friends were too young to remember him. As they slunk out the back door, Evelyn muttered, "None of y'all know nothing about dying!"

**Fort Worth: 2015**

Henry was clutching the yearbook when he and Ella stepped into the office to buy a lock so they could relock number 705 and come back for their stuff the next day. It was $5.95. Henry paid in cash, but he did have a question for the young woman behind the desk.

"Do y'all ever get the story?" he asked. "You know, the reason people don't come get their stuff? Aren't you curious?"

She gave a quick laugh. "Sometimes we do. Usually, it's nothing dramatic. About half the time, people just move away and forget they had things in storage. By the time we notify them, they've done without it so long, they figure they don't need it, so they just let it go."

"I guess I was looking for the dramatic ones," Henry said with a chuckle. "You know, bitter divorces, murders, mysterious disappearances, kidnappings by pirates . . ."

"Yeah, those are few and far between," she said, with a laugh. "The guy we bought this place from did tell us one story, though . . ."

She began flipping through a dog-eared record book. "I'm trying to remember the name . . . It was before we got here, but I remember looking it up, just because of the story. In fact," she said before pausing. "What was the number of your unit?"

"705," Henry confirmed quickly. Her face got serious.

"Are you sure?" she asked. "Wow. I think that was the unit. The man that rented it came and put his stuff in, and then . . . I'm not—oh . . ." She stopped midsentence.

"What?" Ella asked, suddenly interested.

She laughed, but it was forced.

"Oh, nothing. It's just . . ." she mumbled, pushing the book aside.

"What?" Ella pressed. "It's just what?" She was cross-examining.

"I just remember this story," she said, shifting from one foot to the other. "It was sad. He said an older gentleman rented that unit, put his stuff in, bought a lock, and paid a year's rent in advance. He said he was renting it for a friend and gave them her mailing address."

"So," Ella said. "Then what happened?"

"They heard the old man got in a wreck on the way home and . . ." her voice trailed off.

"And what?" Henry asked. "He died? Someone rented this unit and then died?" He looked at Ella, then back at the woman.

"So, when did all this happen?" he asked. "Was it recent, or . . . ?"

"Oh, no, it was years and years ago, back in the '80s," she said. "We've had that unit forever, and the rent's been paid like clockwork—right up until this last time it was up for renewal, back in February."

"Wonder why they stopped?" Henry asked.

"Uh . . ." she thumbed through the ledger. "I don't know. We sold the place, and the home office took over the billing. They said they sent letter after letter to that address and got no response. Finally, we had to list it."

"What about the man who bid against Ella today?" Henry asked. "Have you seen him?"

"No," the woman said. "No one had, which is unusual. It's kind of a club, in case you didn't notice."

"Did he have to register, give you his name, anything like that?" Ella asked.

"No," the woman said, closing the book and looking down at it. "We don't get anyone's information unless they buy a unit. But he's definitely not one of our regulars."

She looked at Henry and Ella again.

"Why do I feel like you already knew this story?" she asked. "Did you know the old man?"

"No," Ella said. "We don't know anything. We just got a wild hair and bought it."

The woman turned to help another customer. Ella picked up the lock, took Henry's arm, and pulled him aside.

"Let's lock this thing up and get out of here," she said. "You're not a reporter anymore, remember?"

"But Ella, there's something *off* about that story," he whispered, turning his back to the table. "I need to see that book. I want to know who was paying the rent, and why they stopped. I want to know who that old man was. I want to know more about that wreck. I want to know who the guy was who bid against you."

"Henry, stop it!" she said, pulling him farther away from the counter. "You aren't working today. And anyway, they don't have good addresses or phone numbers on these people. If they did, they'd just go collect the rent. That's why they auction it off—they can't find them."

"So you aren't just a little bit curious that a guy rented this unit, put all that stuff in there, and then went off and *died?*"

"No," she shot back. "People die, Henry. Often at inconvenient times. I'm actually a little creeped out by it all. Let's get out of here!"

"Okay," he said, surrendering. When he turned back to the desk, the woman was still helping the other customer. The book was on the table, open. One of Henry's reporter skills was upside-down reading. While Ella was picking up his receipt, he quickly scanned the page and found the number 705. There was a name beside it: Chitwood.

Where had he seen that name?

She saw what he was doing, reached over, and gently slammed the book shut. "Those records are private, sir," she huffed. "Is there anything else?"

"No thanks," Henry mumbled. He turned and Ella was waiting in the doorway.

"See anything?" she asked as they walked back to the unit.

"Just a name," he said. "Chitwood. Maybe that was the one who started paying after the guy died. Seems like I saw that name somewhere else, just recently."

She began to chuckle softly as they walked.

"So, is this going to be some biiiig mystery?" she asked.

"Maybe. Probably not. But I did see that name somewhere recently."

"Yeah," she said. "Maybe this one belonged to Lee Harvey Chitwood, the guy who shot Kennedy. Or the godfather, Don Vito Chitwood. I'll bet Jimmy Hoffa's in one of those bags!"

"Stop it," he said.

"Maybe several of those bags . . ." she said ominously.

"C'mon, Ella. You said you got some kind of feeling, like we were *supposed* to get that unit. What if your gut was right? What if it's, I don't know, haunted or something?"

He knew he was being dramatic, but she wasn't going to play. Instead, she laughed.

"Yeah! Maybe we're its next victims!" she said. "There's probably a psycho clown hiding in there with a big knife, waiting all these years for us to come in! The Slasher of 705."

"Stop it," Henry said. "I just want to know who that guy is who bid against you."

After a moment he added, "Why'd you have to bring a clown into this?"

They continued talking as they walked back to the unit. Henry rolled the door down, banged it shut, and locked it. He was glad it was midday instead of night.

"G'night, Krusty!" Ella said as the door closed. "See you tomorrow!"

"Ahhh! Knock it off!" he said.

They decided on fast food for lunch because they both suddenly felt poor. He picked up the yearbook to take it inside.

"No," Ella said. "Don't bring that thing in. Just leave it."

"We can look at it together," he countered. "It'll be interesting."

"Henry, I don't want to," she said. "Seriously. It'll be depressing, and you'll get ketchup on it."

"Okay," he said and tossed it back into the car. "You've seen me eat."

The lunch conversation centered around when and how to get the stuff, and where to put it. Her compact car and third-floor apartment took her out of the running. His car, a beat-up old Beetle, was not an option, and the tiny garage at his house was already full of his landlord's junk. He had two bedrooms, but he really didn't want it in his house.

"There's no telling what kind of bugs are going to crawl out of there," he said. "Maybe snakes. Maybe mice."

"Maybe clowns," she said wickedly.

Then he remembered his friend.

"Oh!" he said. "I have a buddy, a guy named Nick that I used to work with at the *Star-Telegram*. He was a photographer, a really good one. Now he shoots for *National Geographic*. He's in Sri Lanka or

Singapore or somewhere like that, on an assignment, and he said I could use his pickup if I needed it."

"That's nice," Ella said. "But still, where do we put the stuff?"

"I can call him and ask, but I'm sure he wouldn't mind us using his garage to sort through it. It's a big house, and it's almost like he doesn't live there because he's gone so much. We could work on it there, lock it up whenever we leave, and keep coming back until we're done. He left me his keys." After a pause, he added, "He's in Seoul. I remember now."

"So call him," Ella said.

"I'll have to check the time difference," Henry said, pulling out his phone. After a few clicks, he said, "Yeah, it's the middle of the night there. I don't want to wake him up."

"Well, call me when you find out," she said. "We need to get that stuff tomorrow, and we have to take it somewhere, or else we'll have to start paying rent. It's cost us enough already."

She seemed distracted as she dropped him off.

Henry let himself in, tossed the book on his kitchen counter, clicked on the TV, and settled into his comfy chair. It was a golf tournament. He called Nick and left a voicemail, then just as he dozed off he heard the rain start pattering down on the roof—ideal nap conditions. The phone woke him up at 4:30. It was Ella.

"So?"

"So what?" he said sleepily.

"What's in the yearbook? Whose is it? Did you find anything exciting?"

"Ella," he yawned, "I didn't even look at it yet."

"Are you . . . are you napping? What are you, eighty?"

"Maybe," he said, stretching as he dropped the footrest. "All that walking around and wondering about stuff wore me out. What do you do in your free time?"

"Henry, I have so much to do, I'll never catch up. So?"

"Just a minute." He got up and walked over to where he'd laid the book.

"Hang on, I'll tell you what's in there," he said as he sat back down and opened it. "Hmmm . . . hmmm!"

"What?" She sounded exasperated. "What is it?"

"Oh, Ella, you're not going to believe this," he said dramatically. "The photographer just happened to catch every one of these girls by surprise, looking over their shoulders at him while wearing the same feather boa. Incredible!"

Hearing nothing but sardonic silence, he continued.

"And Dorothy Sinclair? She was homecoming queen AND valedictorian AND most likely to succeed . . . and everyone who signed her yearbook told her to keep smiling, and—get this," his voice lowered ominously, "predicted she would go far."

Finally, Ella spoke. "Dorothy Sinclair? So it's her yearbook?"

"Yes," he said, chastened. He flipped back to the front page, where she'd written her name in neat cursive, and below it, "Class of '69."

"And," he continued, flipping the stiff, glossy pages. "Pretty much everybody in school signed it. Including . . . wait, this really is something. A kid named Arnold Chitwood. Chitwood! That's it! The connection!"

"Hooray!" Ella said unenthusiastically. "Anything else?"

"He called her Dottie and told her she was groovy. Sounds like he had a crush on . . . Ew! That's embarrassing."

"What about the 'interesting' part? Any of that in there?"

"I told you, I'll let you know," he said. "I haven't even gone into reporter mode yet. Dorothy was the yearbook editor—maybe she's behind the weird name, Thanatopsis."

"Well, let me know if you learn anything or hear anything from Nick," she said. "I'm getting antsy."

"You'll be my first call," he said. They had barely hung up when his phone buzzed. It was Nick, who said he was glad Henry caught him early because he was about to go shoot wildlife photos in the demilitarized zone between North and South Korea, and he would be out of contact. He would be gone at least another month, probably more. He was glad for Henry to use the garage and check his fridge—

but, he suggested, hazmat gear might be in order.

Henry called Ella back to let her know the pickup and garage were all theirs. They made a date to go get the stuff the next afternoon. She sounded distant.

"You okay?" he asked. "You seem kinda down. I didn't mean to give you a hard time over this—I was just cutting up. I'm really okay with the $300."

"No, I'm fine, Henry, and I appreciate it, I really do," she sighed. "I'm just . . . I don't know. This whole thing, going through somebody's old stuff. It makes me sad. Tired-sad. Maybe we should get hold of that couple that has the antique store and sell it all to them. Let them pick it up, even if we take a loss. I just don't know if I have the energy to go through all this junk and, you know, vet it—try to decide if any of it is worth anything. Just thinking about it . . ."

"I think I know what this is," he said quietly, after a pause.

Another long silence. "Okay. What is it?"

"You just moved, right? So you just finished going through your own stuff—and it wasn't fun, was it? I mean, it wasn't a particularly happy move, right?"

"No," she said. "You're right. It wasn't."

"Well, that's it. I've been there. You just went through this big life-changing upheaval and had to sort through all your own stuff—sort through your life, really. It's depressing. So it's understandable—sorting through someone else's life doesn't sound like fun right now."

After another long silence, she said, "Dang it, Henry, you're pretty good. I hadn't thought about it that way, but I think you might have nailed it. It's just a weird feeling."

"The hunt—going to the auctions and wondering and speculating—that part's fun, right?" he asked.

"Right! Actually buying the stuff . . . this is a whole different deal," she said.

"You were the dog chasing the car!"

"Did you just call me a dog?"

"Of course not," Henry laughed. "I'm just saying the chase is what's fun. The dog doesn't really want to catch the car."

"Yeah," she said. "What you're really doing when you buy one of these things is putting yourself into someone's life, usually at what might've been a rough time. I'm not sure I need to go borrow that kind of stress from someone else right now."

"And this is the first one of these you've ever bought, right?"

"Right."

"So, neither one of us really knows how this is going to go," he said. "We can explore this new territory together, okay?"

"You don't want to just sell it all to the antique people?"

"No! Number one, I think we can get our money back, and more. And number two, I think we'll find some interesting stories," he said. "This Dorothy Sinclair sounds fascinating. Maybe I can give her back her yearbook. She'd be, what, in her late sixties now? She would probably appreciate it."

Ella sighed. "Okay. But let's just keep it light. Remember, this is strictly for entertainment. And honestly, most of it's probably going in the trash anyway."

"Absolutely," Henry said. "We may need a drop-off dumpster."

Henry said he would get Nick's truck and pick her up the next day around 2:00.

**Thurston: 1968**

Dottie's family made it through the funeral, the official visits of sympathy, the twenty-one–gun salute, the folded flag. Mary did not weep—at least not within view of anyone, including Dottie. She thanked everyone, comforting those whose sorrow was visible. Dottie stayed at her mother's side, wordless and angry and alone. Her heart broke for her stoic father, who, she thought, must be tormented by the things he wished he had said to his son but simply could not say. She could only speculate; he didn't say them to her, either. He offered no comfort, took none. Instead, he sank deeper into gray, silent sorrow. By the time they walked away from the mound of flowers in the little Thurston cemetery, Dottie felt her family had ceased to exist.

In its place were a widower, a widow, and an orphan, three strangers sharing a house.

George Sinclair was well-suited to his solitary job, riding alone, scanning mile after mile of electric lines. When they had construction to do, they worked in crews, but most of the time, he patrolled by himself. It was only about six weeks after Ted's death that he got an outage call on a weekend and decided, against the co-op's rules, to go fix it himself. He was on a pole when the transformer exploded, dousing him with scalding hot oil and knocking him to the ground. It was never determined if he'd died from burns, electrocution, or the fall.

Dottie and Mary mourned, but they both knew he had been gone a long time before the accident. His death was merely a ratification.

Another funeral at the Sinclair house, so soon, was a lot to ask, but the Sunday school ladies were there, ready to swing back into action. Mary cut them off summarily. There would be no food, no living room full of people talking in hushed tones after stopping by for snacks. Fine Christian women, standing on the front porch with casserole dishes in hand, were thanked and turned away, encouraged to take the food to someone who needed it. Mary and Dottie did not.

What they needed was to comfort each other. Instead, they crept to separate corners of the house and nursed their sorrows alone.

No family members came. George Sinclair was buried with full military honors, next to the fresh grave of his son. Most of those in attendance were Mary's church friends and George's coworkers. Evelyn and Arnie came, but Arnie could not get close to Dottie. Sherry sat next to him. At Mary's request, they skipped the twenty-one–gun salute and just gave her another flag at the end of a quiet, quick ceremony. As soon as she took it, she stood up, motioned to Dottie, and they walked to the black limousine. There was no passing-by, no squeezing of hands, no more words of sympathy. Just a fleeing from death.

Mary had quit going down to the sewing shop after Ted died, but now she resumed her work; in fact, she immersed herself in it.

At home, she cooked and cleaned and did laundry, even boxed up George's clothes and took them to the Salvation Army. She repainted Ted's old room but hung onto his things. Dottie offered to help, but Mary said she'd rather work on it alone while Dottie was at school. When Dottie tried to talk, Mary dismissed her airily, as if all was well. What could possibly be wrong? Dottie felt her mother had retreated to a place where no one else could go, so she did the same. She took on every school activity she could find, staying late working on the yearbook, directing the school play, or rehearsing for solo and ensemble contest with the band.

She was the most active, popular, and sociable senior. But what should have been the best time of Dottie's life, a triumphant senior year leading to graduation and a bright future, was just a grim wait until she could leave—leave home, leave Thurston, leave her vacant mother behind, and never come back.

Dottie began to think of her home as "a whitewashed tomb," Jesus's phrase for the hypocritical Pharisees: pretty on the outside, full of death on the inside. One evening, as the TV droned, Dottie glanced up from a book and caught her mother looking at her, eyes wide and frozen, as if they were strangers, seated together on an airplane spiraling down, about to crash.

At school, Dottie found comfort in the library, gravitating toward poetry. Her romantic poet heroes didn't suppress their feelings about death; they explored them. They didn't flee death, they reveled in it, ripping open their souls to capture it in words.

Keats's "Ode on Intimations of Immortality" and Gray's "Elegy in a Country Churchyard" spoke to her powerfully. Wordsworth's "Lines Composed a Few Miles Above Tintern Abbey" played in her head constantly. Tears filled her eyes as she recited it under her breath and walked, hand-in-hand in her mind with her brother, to a cool, leafy place, looking down from the heights over green hills, hearing the waterfalls and rejoicing in timeless beauty far from tiny Thurston.

For all appearances, she was a normal high school student: popular and surrounded by friends. But inside, like her mother, she was completely alone.

A few classmates told her Ted was a hero. Abby came up and gave her a wordless hug as soon as she returned to school, but they were already drifting apart. Sherry followed her around as if she were her bodyguard. Now and then, someone would approach Dottie like it was an assignment, avoiding eye contact, and say, "Sorry about your dad." Most just looked at her with sad hesitation, afraid to speak. One day, after band, a couple of freshman girls she barely knew walked up, and one of them said her brother and the other soldiers were baby-killers. She looked at them, smiled politely, then heard her voice, like someone speaking from a distance.

"You go straight to hell," she said.

The two girls looked shocked and quickly walked away. Sherry followed them.

The next day, Dottie noticed Sherry wasn't at school, and word got around that she'd gotten into a fight with two girls and been suspended. One of the girls had had to go to the hospital. Dottie was not surprised. Everyone knew Sherry had a rough side.

Losing her brother, then her father, had bought Dottie a little distance from most of her classmates, and she embraced it. After word got around about the freshman girls, a wall went up around her. The state was still a few years away from its "Don't mess with Texas" slogan, but "Don't mess with Dottie Sinclair" was a real thing at Thurston High in 1968.

A few boys in her class were painfully infatuated with her, drawn to her mystery and sadness as well as her fragile beauty. Mel Davis wrote her poems. Dale Kelly tried to impress her with his muscles, unsuccessfully. Arnie was the worst—a big, lovesick puppy. It would have been hilarious if he wasn't so serious.

Romance was the farthest thing from Dottie's mind. In every way except chronologically, she was already grown, marking time until high school was over. She could see herself having a relationship someday, but she had no time for high school boys. When they pressed, she did her best to let them down easy, but she didn't want to lead them on.

Arnie would not give up. She refused to go out with him, though she grudgingly admired his determination and did her best to offer him friendship. He had always been a sweet, harmless kid. They'd been playmates as babies, upstairs in that odd apartment where his mother had raised him. But lately, it seemed he had come to believe their childhood experiences gave him a claim on her—an inside track.

One day, after school, she went to the library to read until they locked the doors, which she often did just to avoid going back to her sad, silent home. The yearbook staff was looking for a theme for next year's book, and Dottie wanted it to be literary, the more obscure, the better. They had decided to look for words that began with "th" so the title could be alliterative: "The Thurston Th . . . whatever." They'd brainstormed a little during lunch, but nothing seemed right. Sherry brought a photo of a hitchhiker she'd cut out of a magazine and suggested "The Thurston Thumb." Dottie did her best to stifle a laugh.

"The Thurston Thicket," "The Thurston Thumper," "The Thurston Throat," and "Thurston Thoughts" were also quickly eliminated. Eddie Baker, who was very much into insects, suggested "The Thurston Thorax." "The Thurston Threat" came from Dale, who wasn't nearly as much of a threat as he thought he was. "The Thurston Throcket" —a tribute to NASA's upcoming mission to the moon—got some consideration, to Dottie's horror, but in the end she prevailed upon them not to coin a new word. "The Thurston Thruster" was also floated but immediately vetoed for obvious reasons. She pointed out that no one in the class had a connection to NASA or was planning to be an engineer, an astronaut, or even a pilot.

Dottie thought "The Thurston Thread" had possibilities. She could envision a common thread running through the yearbook's pages, tying everything together. It made her think of her mother's sewing machine and connected to several literary references, like the weaver and the loom in *Moby Dick* or the gold thread in the letter "A" that Hester Prynne was forced to wear in *The Scarlet Letter*. She even considered coming up with a different alliterative heading for each section: conceding to use the Threats for the football team, Throats for the choir, Throwers for the baseball team, Thinkers for the honor society, etc. But she wasn't sure they could come up with enough. Would there be Thugs? Thuds? Would anyone, or anything, Throb? It could easily get out of hand.

She had pulled several encyclopedias from the shelves and was just sitting down when Arnie came up, as usual wearing his letterman jacket, and sat across from her.

"Hi, Dottie," he whispered, smiling. "Whatcha doin'?"

She smiled back, looking around to see if they were disturbing anyone. No one was around except Sherry, who was sitting in the corner, furtively avoiding eye contact.

"Just looking up a few things," she said softly. "Actually, I'm trying to come up with a theme for the yearbook. Something that begins with 'th.'"

Arnie looked puzzled. "A theme?"

"Yeah, something to kind of tie it all together," she explained.

"Doesn't . . . doesn't 'theme' begin with 'th'?" he whispered, his brow furrowed.

She couldn't help but laugh. "Yes, it does!" she said, reaching across the table to pat his leg-sized arm. "It's . . . we were looking for something a little more complicated. Something we can do more with. But you're right."

He beamed, obviously thrilled that he had made her laugh.

"Glad I could help," he said. "I was looking for comic books."

He sat there, smiling at her, until finally, she broke the silence.

"Well, I appreciate it, Arnie," she said. "We'll take that into consideration, and if we can't find anything else, we may just use it. If we do, I'll make sure you get credit."

He continued to sit. And smile.

"I'd better get back to this," she said, gesturing at the stack of reference books.

He finally picked up on the dismissal and stood up quickly,

knocking his chair over backward. A few students looked their way, and the librarian glared at them over her glasses.

"Dammit!" Arnie yelled, then looked around sheepishly and added, "Sorry!" in a loud whisper. He picked up the chair and scooted it noisily back under the table.

"I . . . I'll see you, Dottie," he said. "Hope you find . . . what you're lookin' for."

"Thanks," she said, then added, "And you, too."

* * *

Evelyn missed her friend. Although Mary had resumed working regularly at the sewing shop, Evelyn seldom saw her, and when she did, Mary treated her like a stranger: she was polite but acted as if they were mere acquaintances. Evelyn didn't press, preferring to let Mary come back to her when she was ready.

One day she decided to just pop in at the shop. Mary was busy at the sewing table, head down, running a long hem through the pounding needle. Evelyn waited until the run was over, then called, "Hi there, stranger!"

Mary looked up, and Evelyn almost gasped. She looked twenty years older.

"Oh!" Mary said. "Evelyn! You startled me."

"I didn't want to make you stitch your finger," Evelyn joked, still horrified.

"No, no, don't want to do that," Mary said, not laughing. After an awkward silence, she asked, "What can I do for you, dear?"

"I'm sorry, Mary," Evelyn began. "I just . . . I don't know, thought maybe you'd like to take a break and come up for some coffee or something. Like in the old days."

Mary's smile was distant, the pause long.

"I don't know, Evelyn," she sighed. "I don't think so. Dottie's probably home by now. I should go, I guess. We just want to be alone right now, Dottie and I."

"I understand," Evelyn said. "Is there anything I can do?"

Mary looked at her, and in her eyes, Evelyn saw her falling away.

"Thank you," she replied. "No. Thank you. No." She shook her head and looked back down at her work, dismissing Evelyn.

"Okay, maybe some other time, then?"

Mary did not look up.

A few nights later, Evelyn saw the light on in Mary's shop and decided to try again, this time with some pound cake and tea. She tiptoed down the stairs and tapped lightly at the door.

"Yes?" came the faint voice. "Who is it? Evelyn?"

Evelyn opened the door with the tray in front of her. As she had expected, Mary was too polite to refuse the gesture. She offered Evelyn a chair, and the two of them sipped tea, silently at first, and talked about the weather, their children, and the way the town was drying up. It wasn't quite like old times, but it was something.

"Now Evelyn, I don't want you to think you have to do this every evening," Mary said as Evelyn got up to leave. "I really should get home to Dottie."

"Well, I figured she was probably practicing for the band contest," Evelyn said.

Mary looked at her guiltily. "You've done your homework," she conceded. "They practice every night. If it's not band, it's yearbook, or the library. I have to stay up late just to see her when she gets in."

"It's that senior year," Evelyn said. "They get so dang busy—I think it's just God's way of preparin' us to see 'em drive away!"

"Oh!" Mary looked stricken.

"Aw, Mary—I didn't mean anything by that," Evelyn said, kicking herself. "I mean, they're all going to leave at some point. Even Arnie, and goodness knows there aren't a lot of colleges courting him like your little girl!"

"You're right, Evelyn," she sighed, leaning on the table. "I know she's going to leave—I might as well admit it."

Evelyn stepped over, set the tray down, and laid her hand on Mary's arm.

"It's what you raised her to do, Mary! She couldn't stay in Thurston any more than a wave can stay on the beach. She's got to go. She's got such a bright future! That girl can do anything—and the last thing you want to do is hold her back, right?"

"You're right," Mary said. She lifted her arms and pulled Evelyn into a hug.

The following week, Evelyn came down to see Mary almost every evening. A couple of times Mary put her to work, sorting thread and rewinding bobbins. They talked like they'd talked when their children were little.

Evelyn looked for Mary and Dottie at church, but they almost always came in late, sat at the back, and left early. But when Evelyn caught her eye, Mary always smiled.

They didn't drive to the football games together, but with Dottie in the band and Arnie on the team, they usually sat together and talked nonstop over the crowd noise. And most afternoons, Evelyn still went down to the shop with tea. When they were done, often Evelyn would just sit silently, reading while Mary sewed.

Their friendship had weathered a storm.

**Fort Worth: 2015**

Ella seemed to have cheered up by the next afternoon. It was sunny and cooler, and they stopped and got drinks before heading out to the U-Stor-It on the Burleson Highway.

After tooling around in his old VW Beetle, Henry felt like an over-the-road trucker in Nick's big F-150. He had to reach down at the gate to punch in the code they'd been given to make it slide open. Going down the narrow aisle between storage buildings, he was careful not to scratch the borrowed truck. They got to number 705 and Ella hopped out to unlock the door.

"Watch out for clowns!" Ella joked as she pulled the door up.

"If there's even a clown nose in here, I will just flat-out die," Henry said, shutting off the truck and hopping out. He joined her and they began to work their way through the unit.

The dust-covered boxes got a quick look before they went to the pickup. Many held swatches of cloth, spools of thread and other tools of the sewing trade. Others were full of clothes, shoes, even old-style ladies' hats. Then came the TV, the suitcase, and several duffle bags. The dining chairs came with an antique table that had not been visible from the outside, a pleasant surprise. It was disassembled, the legs and top separated, but clearly high-quality.

"Oh, man," Ella said, running a hand along the mahogany top. "I bet we can get $200 for this! Have we got all four chairs?"

"Nope," Henry said. "Six!"

"Excellent!" Ella said, rubbing her hands together like a cartoon villain. "Three hundred."

A folded-up playpen that looked like it was from the 1950s was not in good shape. But a roll-top desk, hidden behind the table and chairs, was.

"Jackpot!" said Ella. "This thing is gonna bring serious money at resale."

"Okay, but not until I go through the drawers and look for hidden compartments filled with diamonds or Confederate gold coins," Henry said.

"You have a rich fantasy life," she said, deadpan.

Henry was glad he had thought to bring a dolly. He tilted the file cabinet on, leaned it back, and got it to the tailgate where they were able to lift the end and slide it in on its back. There was also a guitar in an old cardboard case, with strings so old they felt like bridge cables. There was an antique lawyers' bookshelf with stacking units, each with its own glass front, filled with books that looked like they were printed in the early 1900s. Other boxes held textbooks.

The heaviest item was the sewing machine, permanently mounted to a large table and strapped to a pallet. A forklift would be needed to move it.

"We ain't lifting that puppy," Henry said.

At Ella's suggestion, he walked to the office and asked the woman they'd met the previous night if, by any chance, they might have a forklift. She seemed to have forgotten Henry's peek in her book. She said her husband would be happy to load it for them as soon as he got back. Henry told her they would take this load, then come back for the sewing machine and the rest of the items.

About thirty minutes later, they pulled into the driveway at a sprawling stucco bungalow on a tree-covered corner in one of west Fort Worth's old neighborhoods.

"Wow!" Ella exclaimed. "Photographer pays better than reporter, huh?"

"Yeah, if you're shooting for Nat Geo," Henry said. "It also helps if this was your parents' house and they moved to Arizona and your brother didn't want it. And it also helps if you've never been married, never been divorced, never had kids . . ."

"Oh, man," Ella said as she dropped the tailgate. "People who don't have kids, I don't know what they do with all their money, right?"

She immediately caught herself.

"Aw, Henry, I—" she started.

"Hey, it's okay," he said, laughing. "I haven't made any kids *or* any money. But you know," he grunted, lifting the suitcase, "as much money as we're going to clear on all this stuff, I may just get myself a place like this."

In spite of the cool weather, he sweated as he carried in box after box, stacking them against a side wall.

"I wonder if these are fardels?" he asked.

Ella gave him a quizzical look.

"You know, like, 'Who would fardels bear, to grunt and sweat under a weary life?'" he quoted from Hamlet's soliloquy.

"You're a fardel," she said. Ella didn't quote Shakespeare, but she carried as much as Henry did and did not break a sweat. Once they got everything in, he locked the garage and the house, and they drove back to get the rest.

They got back to Nick's house, parked, and stood in the shaded driveway under the live oak trees. Henry knew someone who might want the sewing machine, so they left it on the truck, then stared into the open garage, where treasures awaited.

"So, how do you want this to go, partner?" Henry asked.

Ella took a deep breath, looked over at him, and smiled.

"How about I start on the boxes?" she said. "You can grab that suitcase, pull out the drawers on the desk, hit the file cabinet, or look through the books for hundred-dollar bills."

"Cool," he said.

He found a couple of lawn chairs hanging on the wall, dusted them off, and set one up for Ella, the other for himself. There was also a folding card table, which he placed in the middle.

"Anything you find that you think is worth another look, you can put it here," he said. "The rest . . ." He dragged a big trash barrel over by the table.

"That's not near big enough," she said.

"I've got extra bags," he said, pointing to a box on a shelf. "I'll do the hauling."

"Yeah, this is quite a haul!" she said with a laugh.

Henry remembered how much he enjoyed her laugh.

He had also brought a radio, so he found an oldies station and they set to work with Christopher Cross's "Sailing." It was a perfect late-fall afternoon, with a cool breeze and a steady stream of walkers, joggers, and bicyclists heading to and from a neighborhood park. He couldn't think of anything he'd rather be doing, or anyone he'd rather be doing it with. He was just about to open the file cabinet when Ella gave a little scream and jumped back.

"Snake?" he asked, heading her way.

"No, worse!" she said, pointing into the box. Henry peeked in, expecting to see a scorpion, or a tarantula, or a mouse. Instead, it was a handgun, an old revolver.

"It won't hurt you—unless it's loaded," he said. He reached in and grabbed the handle with two fingers, making sure it was pointed downward. He'd been around guns his whole life, but he didn't like handguns. He'd reported on plenty of shootings, accidental and otherwise. On the hip of a law officer, they made him feel safer. Anywhere else, they had the opposite effect.

Lifting the hammerless revolver, he could see the exposed rims of the bullets.

"It *is* loaded," he said. He found the latch and rocked the cylinder open, spilling four bullets and one empty casing into his hand and laying them gently on the card table. He looked it over carefully to make sure that was all there was.

It was an unusual gun, a Smith & Wesson five-shot .32, probably made before World War II. It appeared to have been a long time since it was fired, but it wasn't rusty. There was a little cloth bag with it containing a few more bullets, a brush, and a folded-up oily rag that had probably been used to clean it. Ella watched with a pained expression as he examined it.

"Man, that creeps me out," she said.

"Guns don't kill people—" he began.

"Maybe not, but they make it a lot easier for *people* to kill people!" she said. He realized she'd probably prosecuted more murders than he'd reported on.

"Just look at it as something we bought in the auction," he said. "This one's a collector's item, probably worth at least a couple hundred dollars—maybe a lot more. And . . ." He laughed nervously. "I wonder what kind of stories *it* could tell?"

"I don't want to hear 'em!" she said.

It fit easily into the bag, so he put it back in, along with the bullets and the empty casing, tightened the drawstring and laid it on the card table. Ella looked at the bag, then at him.

"You just make sure no little kids come in here, okay?"

"Okay," he said, moving it to the top of the file cabinet.

"And when we leave here, you're locking that thing up."

"I'll take it with me," he said. "I know a guy who collects guns. He can probably tell me what it's worth. He might even buy it."

"Do you have a permit?" Ella asked.

"C'mon, madam district attorney," he said. "You need a permit to carry it on your person, not to own it. We bought it, fair and square."

"Hmmm," she said. "That's a gray area, and you're a pretty seedy looking character. Just our luck, you get pulled over for speeding, they do a search, find that thing, and go all Bonnie and Clyde on you." She made a little gun with her thumb and forefinger.

"Next thing you know my old Beetle's got 167 bullet holes in it and my skeleton's inside, up on a flatbed trailer, going from town to town so the schoolkids can all come out and be scared away from a life of crime."

"And on the documentary, Ken Burns is interviewing your third-grade teacher," Ella went on in mock-teacher voice. "'He was a quiet kid, just kept to himself . . . can't imagine he'd do such a thing.'"

"No," Henry said. "If they found my third-grade teacher, she'd say, 'I *knew* it! That little punk! How come they only shot him 167 times?'"

They laughed, then went back to work.

**Thurston: 1968**

Dottie buried her head in the *Encyclopedia Britannica*. She flipped over to where the "th" words began and quickly found one that caught her attention.

"Thanatopsis."

It was Greek for "a meditation or observation on death." Most famously, it was the title of a poem by William Cullen Bryant, published in 1817. Quickly she closed the volume and sat for a moment. She liked it. "The Thurston Thanatopsis," she murmured, repeating it softly a few times, then louder. "The Thurston Thanatopsis," she announced loudly, with conviction.

The librarian gave her a look that said, "Strike two."

Quickly she pulled out her pen and spiral notebook. She printed it, wrote it in cursive, all caps and various fonts. She liked the way it looked, liked the sound, literary, obscure, even slightly medical. It occurred to her that using the title of a poem about death might be a problem, but she quickly realized it was unlikely anyone at her school would know that. She'd read more poetry than all of them put together, and she'd never heard of this poem. She went to the card catalogue and there was only one reference, to an old anthology of American poetry.

She tracked it down. The three-inch-thick volume had been sitting on the shelf for decades in dusty serenity. It was the first poem in the collection. She found a chair far from the librarian's desk, sank in, tucked her feet under her, and flipped to it. The first lines did not disappoint: He sounded like Wordsworth.

As Dottie read, a blush quickly rose to her cheeks. She looked around to make sure no one was watching. Suddenly, she wasn't sure she was ready for this. She wanted to stop, but looking down at the words inked on that musty page, she felt the poet was speaking to her personally.

The words stuck like a knife in her heart. It was as if he knew her, and was holding her pain in front of her eyes, forcing her to look.

*. . . Thou shalt lie down*
*with patriarchs of the infant world—with kings,*
*The powerful of the earth—the wise, the good,*
*Fair forms, and hoary seers of ages past,*
*all in one mighty sepulchre. . . .*

"So . . . the earth is just one vast tomb," she whispered. "That's cheery."

*. . . The hills*
*Rock-ribbed and ancient as the sun,—the vales*
*Stretching in pensive quietness between;*
*The venerable woods—rivers that move*
*In majesty, and the complaining brooks*
*That make the meadows green; and, poured round all,*
*Old Ocean's gray and melancholy waste,—*

*Are but the solemn decorations all*
*Of the great tomb of man. . . .*

She closed the book, then shut her eyes and took a ragged breath. This was powerful: Nature didn't shroud the dead in grim terror; it cradled them in beauty. Clutching the book to her chest, she actually began to feel better. Bryant placed death in the inevitable flow of nature.

Literary as she was, this the deepest dive Dottie had made into a poem. Bryant's concept was bigger than country, bigger than war, bigger than an accident on a utility pole. Universal. Cosmic. Her perspective was changing.

She flipped back to the biography page and was stunned to learn that William Cullen Bryant wrote this when he was . . . SEVENTEEN? That hit her like a hammer between the eyes. How could a boy her age think and write this eloquently about death? What had he seen? The biographical sketch said he'd been accused of plagiarizing. Critics simply didn't believe a boy so young could write something so profound.

Dottie had to smile at the irony. Here, at last, was a boy she could have fallen for. She'd only missed him by 150 years.

She read through it again, then again, seeing more each time. It could have been written specifically for Dorothy Sinclair in the fall of 1968.

*. . . All that tread*
*The globe are but a handful to the tribes*
*That slumber in its bosom. . . .*

Tears welled up at the thought that both Ted and her father were now members of that tribe, finally one with the natural world, part of eternity. It was comforting to think of death not as strange and frightening, but as natural as life itself. She closed her eyes, breathed deeply, and let the tears run down her face.

She wondered what her brother felt when the gunfire stilled for him, and he stepped into a realm that knows no war, no pain, no loss. Or her father, as he flew from that pole, finally free from the heartache and loneliness he had buried so deep inside. Dottie found peace in that. Death was not a horror, but a friend who released you from the horror life had brought you.

Lost in the poem, she had forgotten her search for a "th" word. Now that she'd found it, she felt her mission even more fiercely: she must convince her classmates to name to their yearbook the *Thanatopsis.* She began weaving a story to explain where she got it. She wouldn't tell them it was a poem. She'd just say it was Greek and let them think what they wanted—a city in ruin, a war, something to do with Helen or Zeus. It was classical, she would say, and their eyes would glaze over.

She liked the way it sounded. No one would investigate further.

If Mr. Posey found out, she would do what she had to do: explain how much the poem meant to her, how it comforted her in her terrible loss. She wouldn't be lying.

As it turned out, no one objected, and if Mr. Posey caught on, he kept it to himself. The kids all thought it was a groovy-sounding word. And besides, it was Dottie's idea, and Dottie always had great ideas.

**Fort Worth: 2015**

Instead of starting on the file cabinet, Henry went back to the suitcase where he'd found the yearbook. Amid a jumble of t-shirts, shorts, socks, and feminine underwear, he found three more yearbooks—the entire collection. Given a graduation age of eighteen in 1969, Henry figured Dorothy would have been sixty-four or sixty-five by now.

He promised himself he'd try to find her and return the yearbooks. It would be a challenge, not knowing if she had a married name, if she had moved away, or even if she was still alive. But if he found her, it might make a cool freelance story. He tempered his enthusiasm with a reminder to be pessimistic: just assume Dorothy

Sinclair isn't around anymore. That would explain why her possessions were no longer in her possession.

He took the yearbooks out and laid them aside.

But something about this suitcase intrigued him.

"Hey," he said to Ella. "What do you think about this?" He motioned her over.

"Think about what?" she asked.

"This suitcase is all packed like someone is going somewhere. But here it is, forty-five years later, and it's never been unpacked."

"They probably just used it to store these clothes and the yearbooks," she said.

"Yeah, but when you pack clothes to store them, aren't they usually folded and neat?" he asked. "You're saving them. They're special. We've got boxes and boxes of nice clothes. But this isn't Grandma's needlepoint or baby's first clothes. It's socks and underwear, jammed in here. It's toothpaste, lipstick, deodorant."

Ella scratched her head. "So, you're a detective now?"

He ignored her sarcasm. "That's not the kind of stuff you put in storage," he insisted. "This was packed by someone who was going somewhere and never got there."

Ella looked at him, half-disgusted, half-admiring.

"I hesitate to say this twice in twenty-four hours, Henry-baby, but you may have something there," she said. "I can see grabbing clothes to cushion the books. But toothpaste?"

"See? I told you!" Henry almost shouted. "There's a story here. A mystery!"

They looked at each other for a heavy minute, then Ella dug into the suitcase.

"Let's see what else is in here," she said. In a side pouch she found a small, leather-bound book. She turned back to Henry, clutching what looked like a diary.

"Hey Clark Kent, look what you missed," she said.

She held it out to him. The title said simply, "Journal: 1969, Dorothy Sinclair."

"Whoa," he said, taking it from her hand reverently. "That's Dottie! The yearbook editor, the valedictorian. This is about to get really interesting."

"Well, my, my," Ella said with a sarcastic smile. "Let's see . . . you've got her yearbooks, you've thumbed through her panties, and now you're going to read her journal. You're starting to look like a stalker, my friend."

"You're the one whose hobby is buying other people's stuff," he said. "You knew I was a reporter when you brought me in on this. What am I going to do, not read it?"

Ella turned and resumed going through the bags on her side of the garage. But Henry wasn't done.

"Wait a minute," he said. "Are you jealous?"

She turned around, giving him her most withering courtroom stare. "Jealous of what, exactly, Mr. Palmer?"

"Uh, I don't know," he said, suddenly a bumbling witness. "Jealous that I'm trying to get to know this person we keep getting glimpses of?"

"A seventeen-year-old girl who is now a sixty-something-year-old lady?"

"Exactly! She's a . . . what do you call it? A 'person of interest'?"

"Hmph," she said, turning back to a bag full of women's shoes. "Your interest."

She quickly changed the subject to shoes. Each pair was in its own cloth bag with a drawstring. Despite being outdated, they all looked brand-new.

"Man!" she said. "If these belonged to your little friend Dorothy, she had some tiny feet." She held one of the shoes next to her foot; it was a good two inches shorter.

"And you've got yourself some water skis," he said, quickly ducking as a shoe came flying at his head.

They went back to their work. Items were stacking up on the table, but the trash bag was still empty. Ella found another bag, this one filled with ladies' hats.

"I should donate all this stuff to a high school drama class or a community theater group," she said. "If someone's doing plays from this period, these would be a gold mine. Look at this hat! I think they called them 'fascinators.'"

She perched a little black one on her head, the veil coming down over her face, and leaned in close to Henry.

"Whoa!" he stammered. "You look like the sexy widow at a funeral, acting sad even though she killed her husband just to get his money so she could run off with her lover."

Ella raised an eyebrow. "Well, maybe I did . . ." she intoned mysteriously.

"I'm watching you," he said. "And I'm hiding that gun . . ."

"See?" She smiled. Their faces were inches apart. "It worked. Pretty soon, you'll be as fascinated with me as you are with little Dorothy."

"I don't know," Henry said. "She's, uh . . . literary."

"But I'm real, and I'm right here, and . . ."

Their eyes held for a long time. In his mind, he lifted the veil, and they kissed.

"And I'm fascinated," he whispered, then cleared his throat. "Do you have a journal?"

"That's none of your business!" she said, turning away.

"Okay, so you don't need to worry if I delve deeply into Dorothy," he said. "She's research. You're real."

As they continued to pore over the contents of the storage unit, Henry finally arrived at the filing cabinet. He opened a rusty drawer and began flipping through files, all of which seemed to hold old legal documents: copies of land transactions, deeds, contracts, and bills of sale.

"This looks more in your wheelhouse," he told Ella.

"What is it?" she asked.

"Looks like titles, sales, stuff like that," he said. "Maybe this person was a lawyer."

He held out the file to her.

"Most of this stuff is from the 1950s and '60s," she said, flipping through it. "Yeah, it looks like all this is from a title office."

"So, a lawyer?"

"These days, most of the time," she said. "But back then, a lot of title offices were just run by people who owned land, knew about transactions, and how to research. Real estate people. Surveyors. It's not a requirement that a lawyer be involved."

"Hmmm . . ." Henry pretended to nod off. She gently tapped his head.

"Pay attention, young man!" she said. "There will be a test!"

"You're a test," he said. "So, any of this worth anything?"

She leafed through the rest of the file and looked at the other drawers. "Probably not," she said finally. "Looks like it's just copies, although it might have historical value."

She kept reading, and a moment later said, "Y'know?" then stopped short.

"What?" he asked. "Did you see something?"

"This title office . . ." She leaned down to read the fine print, "Logan County Title—it's probably still there. These kinds of businesses rarely close down; they just pass from generation to generation, owner to owner. If they're there, they might like to have this stuff back."

She laid the file on the table, and they both went back to work.

As he leafed through, a document caught his attention. It had fancy scrollwork around the edges and it was signed in different-colored ink. The notary stamp was pressed deeply into the heavy paper.

"Hey, Ella, look at this!" he said. She laid down a scarf and walked over to him. He held it up, not saying a word.

"That's not a copy," she said. "That's the original title to a piece of property."

"Property? Does that mean we own it now? Where?"

"No," she said. "It doesn't work that way. You're supposed to hang onto the title, but what matters is that it's recorded in the county courthouse. If you're trying to establish ownership, it helps if it's *your* name on the title. In this case, it's . . ." she held it up closer to the light, "Evelyn Chitwood."

"There's that name again! What kind of property is it?" Henry asked. "Is it a ranch? A house? A factory?"

"Hmmm," she said, reading. "Looks like it's a 'three-story masonry building in the 100 block of Dallas Avenue in Thurston, Texas.' It's big—17,000-and-something square feet, with a full basement, if it's still standing."

"When did she buy it? Does it show that?"

"The date is May 12, 1953," Ella said.

She handed the deed back to him. He returned it to the file, and she went back to sorting through a box of antique shawls, scarves, and gloves.

"I tell you what, though," she said, looking up at him. "It makes me want to take a little road trip over to Thurston, maybe try to find this title office and see this building."

"Road trip!" Henry exulted. "Man, I hope we own that building."

"We don't," Ella said. "My guess is they got a duplicate title."

"Thurston is a famous ghost town. I used to go through there all the time before the interstate looped around it. In fact . . ." he smacked himself on the forehead. "I'm pretty sure I've seen this building."

"It's still there?" she asked.

"Yeah," he said. "I think it's visible from the highway."

"It's probably a 17,000 square-foot pigeon roost by now," Ella said.

"Then we can mine the pigeon guano and sell it for fertilizer!"

"Yuck!" Ella said. "If that ends up being the best use of this property, I will give you my half of the title. You can mine guano by yourself."

"You don' guan to?" he punned.

"Don't start that crap!" she played along.

He began swaying and singing, "Do you guano dance, under the moonlight . . ."

"If I had a bat, I'd hit you," Ella sighed.

"If it was bat guano, we would *really* be rich," he said.

Ella returned to counting spools of thread. After another hour, they were both ready to call it a day. She grabbed the file with the deed, and Henry picked up the journal.

"We've both got some homework to do," Ella said. "You use your English-major skills on that, and I'll use my lawyer skills on that deed. I'm sure I can find out who owns this building."

"A reporter could find that out," he muttered.

"I know, sweetie," she said. "But I need a job, too."

He took her home. They promised to get together soon and compare notes.

That evening, he picked up the journal. He flipped a few pages and saw that it was handwritten in small, precise cursive, and easily seventy or eighty pages. Pasted onto the back of the front cover was a sheet that folded out. On it was typed a poem: "Thanatopsis" by William Cullen Bryant.

"Thanatopsis," Henry muttered to himself. "I guess I'm gonna have to read this thing."

**Thurston: 1968**

After Dottie asked him to be her escort at homecoming, Arnie's whole demeanor changed. Evelyn was accustomed to a little swagger during the football season, but this was different. He was walking on air. After the halftime ceremony, he spent the rest of the game bouncing up and down on the sideline, playing very little since the team was so far ahead. When the game was over, he high-fived everyone he saw. He endured the postgame traditions—a speech from the coach, the school song—then scanned the field for Dottie. He spotted her just as she stepped through the chain-link gate, headed for the parking lot.

"Dottie!" he yelled as he ran, his cleats crunching in the gravel. "Dottie!"

She stopped and turned around. She was carrying the homecoming queen's crown in one hand and a dozen red roses in the other.

"Oh. Hi, Arnie," she said. "Good game. I'm glad we won."

"Yeah, well," he stammered, looking at his shoes. "Thanks. Everybody tries to schedule Bosworth for homecoming. They suck."

"Oh," she said with a half-hearted laugh. "That makes sense. Sad for them, though. At least you weren't too tired to walk around with me a little at halftime. Thanks for that." She turned to go, walking toward her mother's car, where Mary sat waiting, the engine running.

"Uh, Dottie?" he said, taking a step in her direction. "I was, uh, wondering if you . . . if you're going to the senior banquet next Saturday."

She had feared he would see the invitation to be her escort as something more.

"No, Arnie. I'm not," she said firmly. "I'm . . . I just don't feel like it."

His face fell and he exhaled a sigh, again closely examining his shoes. "Oh," he said. "I was hoping you'd go with me. I—"

"Arnie," she interrupted. "I think you're a good guy. I like you as a friend, but I'm really busy right now. And honestly, I don't give a hoot about the senior banquet. It's just a bunch of joking around, wills and all that, and I think me being there would make everyone sad."

He looked her in the eyes for the first time.

"You don't make me sad," he said. "I . . . I don't care about the stupid banquet, either." He took another step toward her, a big puppy again. "But . . . maybe we could get a burger sometime. If you'd . . . if you'd just go out with me, it would make me really, really happy."

She glanced at the car where her mother was waiting, then looked back at him and took a deep breath.

"Wait right here," she said firmly. She walked to the car and motioned for her mother to roll down the window. They spoke briefly, then she walked back to Arnie.

"Do you want to go get a hamburger?" she asked.

"Now?" he said. "I'm all, you know . . . I just played a football game. I'd have to go home and get cleaned up and all."

"Have you eaten?" she asked.

"No! I never eat before a game," he said. "I'd hurl. All the running and stuff."

"So, you're hungry? You could stand to eat something now?"

"Well, yeah," he said. "I could eat a burger." He laughed. "I could eat five."

"You know where I live?"

"Sure!" he said.

"Pick me up in twenty minutes," she said. "We can go to the truck stop."

She turned and walked to the car, got in with her mother, and they drove away.

Eighteen minutes later he was at her door, his hair still wet from the shower. He was sweating, but he wore his letter jacket anyway. She opened the door almost before he knocked, then turned and told her mother goodbye.

"I'll be home in an hour, Mom," she said. "Love you."

He and Dottie didn't talk until the pickup was in motion.

"The truck stop's pretty greasy, but it's the only place open at this time of night," she said. "I'm not really hungry. I'm just feeling a little weird, you know."

She had decided to go out with him, just this once, and get it over with. There was a homecoming dance, so none of the kids from Thurston High School would be at the truck stop.

When they arrived, she hopped out and headed for the door while he half-ran to catch up. He tried to put his arm around her, but she picked up her pace and was at the door before he could make a move. She didn't wait for him to be the gentleman but pulled it open and walked right in. He caught it and followed, undaunted.

The place had atmosphere: dark and cheap, with wood-paneled walls, windows covered by louvered blinds, and low lights over every table. Cigarette smoke billowed and hung like a cloud below the ceiling. The bells of pinball and the click of pool balls punctuated music in the background: Ernest Tubb singing "A Guy Named Joe." Eyes followed them as they seated themselves, Arnie's size and Dottie's beauty drawing equal amounts of attention.

She slid into a booth, and he started to slide in beside her. Wordless, she refused to scoot over and pointed to the opposite side. He frowned but complied. The menus were on the table in a chrome holder that also corralled salt, pepper, ketchup, and Tabasco sauce. Each table was equipped with a remote-control jukebox that allowed diners to feed it one song for a dime, or three for a quarter–then flip through pages of songs and pick their own tunes without getting up.

"Hey, how 'bout you pick one and I'll pick one?" He grinned, digging two dimes out of his pocket and slapping them down on the woodgrain Formica. She began flipping through titles.

"Don't tell me what you pick," she said with a pleasant smile, "and I won't tell you what I pick."

"You go first," he said, covering his eyes.

Dottie quickly settled on "Do You Know the Way to San José?" by Dionne Warwick. She put a dime in, made her selection, then rolled the menu several pages so Arnie wouldn't guess what she'd picked. She covered her eyes while he picked. Before he could finish, a worn-looking waitress came by and set sweating water glasses on the table, then looked from one to the other, her order pad in her hand.

"Do we know what we want, kids?" she asked tiredly.

"Just fries for me," Dottie said.

Arnie punched in his song selection, then rolled the dial as the waitress and Dottie both looked at him expectantly. Finally, he said, "Double cheeseburger, no onions, extra pickles, and a double order of fries."

"Drinks?" the waitress questioned.

"Dr Pepper," Dottie said.

"Chocolate shake," Arnie said. The waitress turned to leave, and he added, "Large! *And* a Dr Pepper!" She waved that she had it without turning around.

"My mom never lets me come in here," he said. "This is the place that kinda put Dewley out of business. But I like it here. The football team used to come down and hang out, play pool, and eat and listen to the music."

Dottie was a little surprised to see Sherry Statzenburger bussing the table across from them. She was going to say hi, but Sherry kept her head down, tossed all the dirty dishes into a plastic tub and was trying to hurry away when Arnie saw her.

"Hey Sherry, whatcha doin'?" he yelled.

She turned around, balancing the tub on her hip.

"Oh, hi Arnie. Hi Dottie. Just workin'," she said.

"Hi Sherry," Dottie replied. "I didn't know you worked here."

"Yeah." She gave a little hopeless laugh and shrugged her shoulders. "It don't pay much, but my daddy says if I wanna eat, I gotta work. Pull my weight, y'know."

Dottie couldn't think of a reply, but Arnie did.

"We'll try not to make too big of a mess!" he said, with a loud laugh. Sherry ducked her head and turned away. Dottie shot him a dirty look he clearly didn't understand.

A few travelers milled through the cafe and the adjacent gift shop, probably on the way home from a football game. Weary long-haul truckers trooped up and down a fluorescent-lit hallway that led to the back, carrying overnight kits, showering and shaving before they returned to the road.

"It's an interesting place, isn't it?" she said, looking around. "I feel sorry for these guys, though, just driving all the time. That seems incredibly hard and boring."

"I think it's exciting," Arnie said. "Getting to see new places all the time, always going somewhere . . ."

"I guess so," she said, drumming her fingers on the table.

In just a few minutes, the waitress brought the food, and Arnie tore into his cheeseburger like someone was about to take it away from him. Dottie nibbled at her fries and finally offered them to Arnie, who gladly inhaled them along with his, pausing only to suck down more of the chocolate shake. When he was done, he gulped the Dr Pepper too.

A shouting match broke out between two truckers at a nearby

pool table. It was loud, but it was over quickly, a little shoving and cussing before bystanders separated them. Just then, Dottie's song started, and she sang along.

"Is that the one you picked?" Arnie asked.

"Yep," she said, then smiled at him and continued singing softly.

"Oh, man," he said. "I don't know if these truckers are Dionne Warwick fans."

Dottie laughed. "Who cares? Are we trying to impress them?"

"We can go," Arnie said, looking nervously for the waitress.

"Don't you want me and your trucker friends to hear your song?" Dottie asked.

"No, that's okay," Arnie said, fidgeting. "Hey, Dottie, I gotta go to the bathroom. Will you be okay here?"

"Sure," she said, playing drums on the table and grinning at him as he walked away.

She was pretty sure the next song that came up was Arnie's. Electric guitar chords pounded, and Jim Morrison's provocative growl started, "Hello, I love you."

Dottie didn't sing. The Doors were not her favorite. Suddenly she was ready to go, too. She got up, walked through the smoky cafe and waited for Arnie outside. Through the glass, she saw him emerge from the restroom. He saw Sherry again and they talked for a moment. When he stepped outside, he seemed relieved to see her.

"Dottie! I thought I'd lost you!" he exclaimed. "I didn't know you were—"

"Let's just go, okay?"

"Okay . . ." he said.

They got in the pickup and sat in silence while Arnie fumbled with the keys. Dottie thought he was acting strange. Maybe eating so much, right after a game, had made him sick.

"How old is this truck?" she asked.

"I think it's a '41," he said. "Pretty old, but Dewley still takes care of it. It runs good."

They bounced out of the potholed parking lot and onto the farm-to-market road. As soon as they got on the pavement, Arnie gunned the engine and headed for the road that went under the highway. Her house was on the other side.

"So," Dottie yelled, a little nervous as he sped down the deserted road. "Is your mom going to get you a car for graduation?"

Arnie blushed, glanced in her direction, and drove even faster.

"I don't know," he said. "She says she might get herself something new and let me have this one. I don't want it, though."

"Why not?" she said. "I think it's kinda cool."

He laughed somewhat cynically. "I didn't think you thought anything of mine was cool."

"Oh, Arnie . . ." she said.

"What about you?" he asked, getting off the gas, mashing the clutch, slipping it out of gear, and letting it coast as they approached a four-way stop. "Are you gonna take your mom's car to Austin, or get a new one?"

Dottie got quiet.

"What?" he asked. "What's the matter?"

"Nothing. I just don't want to talk about cars anymore, okay?"

He looked puzzled. After a moment, she relented.

"We just got my brother's car back," she said. "My mom wants me to have it. I don't think I can do that."

Arnie let off the clutch, took his foot off the brake, and eased into the intersection as he reached over to comfort her. She was sitting as far away from him as possible, hugging the door, but his arms were long. He patted her leg, and she pushed his hand away.

Just then, he looked up and cut the wheel hard to the left, slamming on the brakes as an eighteen-wheeler blew through the stop sign at highway speed, crossing right in front of them. Arnie reached to restrain Dottie, but ended up just pushing her into the door. Pressed against the glass, she was looking directly at the truck's headlights as it roared past them in a cloud of dust, air horn blaring. She screamed, but they had stopped just in time.

As soon as it passed, Arnie straightened the wheel, gunned the engine, popped the clutch, and skidded across the intersection into the parking lot of a long-abandoned cotton gin. He took it out of gear and shut off the engine. The windows fogged immediately.

"Dottie, are you okay? I'm sorry!" he gasped.

Finally, she spoke, her voice trembling just a little.

"I'm fine," she said. "Just take me home, okay? Now."

He restarted the engine and turned on the defroster. They drove the rest of the way to her house in silence. He pulled up in front and stopped.

"I'm sorry," he said again. "I didn't see that guy—he was going way too fast. I think he ran a stop sign."

"He was, and he did," she said with measured anger, her voice low. "But if you hadn't been trying to grab my leg, you'd have seen him."

He ignored the accusation, turned toward her and reached out again, as if he expected a goodnight kiss. She quickly tugged the door handle and slid out, her sneakered feet bouncing in the street. She turned around and stood in the open door, her eyes burning a hole in him.

"Goodnight, Arnie!" she said as she slammed the door. She had a lot more to say, but the words would have been wasted.

He watched as she disappeared into her house. He sat awhile longer, staring at the door, seeing a light come on inside as the porch light went off. As he sat there, trying to process what had just happened, his expression slid from disbelief to grief to anger. His teeth clenched and his breathing became audible. He slid his hand over to the spot where she'd been sitting, resting it lightly on the upholstery, then smashed his fist into the spot in fury, over and over.

Finally he put the truck in gear and headed home.

* * *

Evelyn didn't know where her son had been. He had rushed in after the game, showered and changed, then rushed out again. He just said he was going out and wouldn't be too late. She was happy for him. Arnie had never been very social. Before he started playing football, Evelyn knew the other kids made fun of him. Now, at least he was good at something.

But if his exit was hasty, his return was just strange.

He came crashing up the stairs, muttering, threw his keys and jacket on the table, and stomped directly to his bedroom. Evelyn wanted to try and talk to him, find out where he'd been and what had happened. She walked quietly across the open space and tapped on the door.

"Go away!" he yelled, his voice betraying tears.

"Arnold," she said. "I don't know where you've been, but I'm here if you need to talk."

"I don't wanna talk!" He sniffed, but she heard him get up and cross over to the door. She stood there, quiet, and the knob clicked. He opened it a crack, then turned and went back and threw himself on his bed.

"Then you can just listen," she said, standing in the doorway but not following him in. "I know this is a big time in your life. You've got big ideas and big dreams, but everything's not always gonna go your way."

He laughed bitterly, his face still buried in the rolled-up blankets. "How about NOTHIN' goin' my way? EVER! How about that?"

Part of her wanted to lash out, call him spoiled rotten, and tell him it was time to grow up. But she didn't. He was almost eighteen. He needed space, and to tell the truth, Evelyn was a little scared of him. Since he'd gotten so big, and particularly since he became a football star, she had begun to pick her battles carefully.

She never saw his father, but she had a feeling he took after that man in some ways. It bothered her that, aside from Dewley, he had never known a father. Maybe she'd been wrong not to marry—Lord knows, she'd had chances. Arnie had had a much better childhood than she did, but she worried about what he'd missed. She worried what would happen when he got out of school and started having to do grown-up things.

Getting his heart broken was one of those things. He was not in Dottie's league, and his mom knew it—but she also knew that was not going to be an easy lesson for him to learn.

"You gonna be alright?" she asked.

"Yeah," he said, sniffling. "Is there any of that pizza left?"

"Yeah," she said. "Help yourself. But clean up after yourself, too, y'hear?"

"Yes, ma'am."

**Fort Worth: 2015**

Henry hadn't read a poem since college. Poetry wasn't his thing. He preferred Steinbeck, Hemingway, J. D. Salinger, or Saul Bellow—writers who captured a time and place with a minimum of description. But in the last few years, Henry had mostly quit reading fiction.

Nevertheless, he picked up the little diary, took a deep breath, and dived in.

The poem was old and felt even older. Ancient. To Henry, it sounded exactly like all the other poetry of that era, the stuff he'd been forced to read and "explicate" in order to get a degree in English. He'd known he was just blowing smoke. This felt different. This time, he was a reporter, trying to get inside the mind of a seventeen-year-old girl who had graduated from a little high school in a tiny town nearly fifty years earlier.

The town was a ghost. The girl? To be determined.

The poem's premise, that death somehow made us one with the universe and put us in fellowship with all those who had gone before us, was a little big for Henry. Like most people, he preferred not to think of death. When he was forced to, he thought of it as something distant and scary, something that happened to other people. But this poem, pasted into the front of her journal, made him even more curious about Dottie Sinclair.

He wondered how a girl like Dottie would have lost track of her journal. Was that suitcase hers? Where was she going? Did she ever arrive? How did this journal make its way into someone's abandoned junk? He wondered, too, about the connection between Dottie and the Chitwoods. All their stuff seemed to be mixed up together. He made a mental note to ask Ella what she thought about that. But as soon as he started Dottie's journal, he was fascinated.

*I want this to be about my life. But when I talk about classes and yearbooks and boyfriends (Don't have one!) it all seems so trivial. I guess I could write about homecoming but honestly, isn't this a democracy? Why do we need kings and queens and royalty and courts? Are we reverting to our British roots? And why did I have to be escorted onto the field by a boy? A queen can't walk without a boy to hold her upright?*

*Picking Arnie Chitwood to escort me was a huge mistake. He's a big football player now, but we've known each other since we were little kids. Our moms are friends. I like him okay, but not the way he likes me. I felt super small holding onto his arm, and he was sweaty. What really bothered me was the way he looked at me, real slow, up and down, smiling, like I was something he wanted to eat. Arnie is* <u>*not*</u> *cool.*

*I went out with him, afterward, to get a hamburger, hoping it would calm him down. We nearly had a wreck, because he was trying to put his hand on my leg and almost ran a stop sign. Just what I needed, another brush with death! It was undoubtedly our first, last, and only date. He's starting to give me the creeps, and I'm starting to wonder if I'll make it out of high school alive.*

*How about a new subject?*

*I could write about yearbook. It's kind of fun, getting to be the editor this year, but I really wish I had done it as a junior and then just sat this one out. So much of the book is about me, and I hate hate HATE having to put all that stuff in there. I know people will think I'm just stuck on myself, and I'm not. There has always been a page on the homecoming queen. There's always been a page on Most Likely to Succeed, the Valedictorian, etc. I can't not do those pages, even though doing them looks like self-aggrandizement, like I'm just me-me-me all the time. Oh, well . . .*

*Funny thing about the yearbook this year—my title, Thanatopsis, got past everyone! I'm dying (hah!) to tell someone what it means and why I chose it.*

*All the kids on the yearbook staff, even Abby, treat me differently now. I used to feel like we were friends. Now it's more like they're fans, trying to get in good with me for some reason, trying to be like me. There's this one sophomore girl, Sherry, who copies everything I do. It's obvious to everybody. I should be flattered, right? But it's a little creepy.*

*I guess Death is maybe my only friend now. I know that sounds morbid, but what else am I supposed to think? First my brother, then my dad. In a sense, my whole family. I know I need to talk about this with someone, but I don't know who that would be. So, I write. The words do not come easily, even on a page.*

*My father was just . . . distant, as long as I can remember. I think he loved me—he just didn't know how to express it. He pushed me away my whole life. I think when he was growing up, that was how they dealt with little girls: turn her over to her mother, make sure she learns the things girls are supposed to learn. When I think about my father, I don't even remember a scent—you know how when you hug somebody, you bury your nose in their shoulder and take a big breath, and that's how you remember them? I have no scent memory of my father. That may be the saddest thing of all.*

*I'm pretty sure he spent more time with Ted than he did with me, teaching him man-things—how to shoot, how to drive a tractor, all that stuff. But I always sensed tension between them. I don't think anything Ted did was ever good enough for him.*

*I loved everything Ted did. Even though he was seven years older than me, we did a lot of things together. He was the classic big brother, the experienced one, the guide. He never hesitated to take my hand and lead me where I would have been afraid to go by myself. We played, we laughed, and we had adventures. I can't imagine what my opinion of men would be if I hadn't had Ted in my life.*

*I want to write down every memory I have of him, every detail. More than anything, I want people to know how good he was, and how smart he was—better than me, smart in a completely different way. His intelligence didn't come from a book—it came from life. He knew a lot about things that mattered.*

*When Ted graduated, with the class of 1962, he went to Texas A&M to study engineering. He wanted to be an architect. He was in college almost three years before he got drafted. Because of where he had gone to college and what he was studying, he was assigned to an Engineer Combat Battalion. I understand that's one of the hardest jobs in the army, the first to enter the battlefield and the last to leave it. In one letter, Ted said, "We build stuff for our guys, and we tear up their stuff." His outfit's job was to clear trees and flatten out runways so airplanes and helicopters could land. But first, they had to build the roads they needed just to get their equipment in. It was nothing but jungle and sand. Ted said it was hotter than Texas, and during the rainy season, it often rained more in a day than it rained in Thurston in a whole year.*

*To read his letters, you'd have thought he was having the time of his life. He was just that way—always positive, everything a big adventure. He was learning drafting, surveying, using maps, and topography. He got to drive bulldozers and road graders. I think they all just did whatever needed doing, with whatever equipment they had. They even had to build a mine, to collect some kind of material off the top of a mountain and mix it with the sand to try and harden it, so everything they drove wouldn't just sink in. He said if their mission had been filling sandbags, they'd have all gotten medals.*

*They were getting the place ready for the boys to come in and fight the Viet Cong, so now and then the Viet Cong would attack to try and stop the work. I guess that's what happened when Ted got hurt. We didn't know anything for three weeks, but when they finally told us, they said he'd gotten hit by a sniper while he was running some equipment on a road in a place called the Am The Valley. They didn't find him right away, and when they did, it was too late.*

*But the last part of Ted's life was only a fraction of his story. I remember going to his Little League baseball games, his school programs at Christmas and Thanksgiving (how he hated them!) before I was even in school. He taught me to read, he read to me and helped me learn the letters and words so that when I went to first grade, I was ahead of everybody else. I would take books home from the school library and read to him, and he would always listen even though he was so much older. He was in junior high, playing tuba in the band and liking girls, but he still took time for me. It was his nature. I think it helped that we were so far apart in age, because we never competed or anything.*

*When Ted was in high school, he used to take me to the school dances. He acted like he was proud of me, and all the big kids thought I was cute, but then he'd ditch me for the first pretty girl that glanced in his direction. I'd sit on the side and stay out of the way until it was time to go. That was okay. I still got to spend time with my big brother and venture out into a much larger world than a ten-year-old girl would have otherwise known. I loved the music, the lights and colors and fast-moving cars. Hanging out with Ted showed me how big the world is, and how fast it moves.*

*He did a lot of living in just twenty-three years. I'm glad, because I would hate to think he missed something. A lot of those boys in the army probably live as if they are likely to die any minute. Maybe that's the way all of us should live. Death can happen as easily here as in Viet Nam. Ted had done a lot more living than I have. I'm ready to start catching up.*

*When I sat down to write this, it felt like it would be a novel. But it's barely a short story. My memories of Ted are wonderful, I just don't have many. I remember him making us grilled cheese sandwiches when we'd camp in the yard in his Boy Scout tent. He invited me even though I was a girl. We'd climb trees together, out in the yard, and he worried about me falling. I can imagine Ted coming home from the war, finishing college, marrying one of those pretty girls and having a big family. He'd have been such a great dad! And I would have been their funny aunt who read to them and spoiled them by buying them things.*

*I'm pretty sure my dad would have related better to Ted as an adult. They could have talked about grown-up things, farming, politics, whatever. And if he'd had some grandchildren, Daddy might have even smiled, done some tickling, and let them crawl up in his lap now and then. My mom would have been a wonderful grandmother, not the sad, gray lady she is now, lost in her sorrow.*

*That's the thing about war, I guess, especially this one. It doesn't seem like anyone is winning. Those people over in Viet Nam, I know we've torn up their country and killed a lot of their people, and I'm sorry about that. But our country has lost a lot, too—not buildings or farms or forests, but sons. Hope.*

*It wasn't just Ted who lost a future. Our family lost a future.*

* * *

Henry was lost in Dottie's journal. It didn't read like something a seventeen-year-old girl would write. He made his living writing, and he would have been proud to produce something so insightful and eloquent. It was late, but he didn't want to put it down. It made him feel he knew her.

The next morning, when he got up and headed to work, she stayed on his mind. As he had done a few times as a reporter, he began to be obsessed. He went through the motions all morning, answering emails, setting up appointments, looking things up for people in the office archives. Ella had a meeting and couldn't make lunch, so he ate at his desk and searched for Dorothy. If anyone had walked in on him, he had another page ready to switch to so they would think he was simply reading the day's headlines.

Where was she? He felt sure she would have been successful, whatever she did. He could see her as an author, a professor, playing some role in publishing, or even television or film, as pretty as she was. But internet searches yielded nothing. He searched Facebook, LinkedIn, every engine he could think of. There were lots of Dorothy Sinclairs. Of those in her age bracket, several were in jail, their mug shots a sad witness to lives gone wrong. One Dorothy Sinclair had testified repeatedly before Congress, but that wasn't her, either.

He decided she must have moved, married, or changed her name. It was hard to keep a profile that low, but if anyone was bright enough to pull it off, it was her.

He called the circulation desk to see if he could get access to the *Star-Telegram* archives. The person he needed to talk to was at lunch, so he left a voicemail. He wondered if the Fort Worth paper had covered goings-on in Thurston.

"Somewhere Over the Rainbow" started playing in his head. Maybe this Dorothy went over the rainbow, lost those ruby slippers, and couldn't come home. He couldn't wait to get home and continue reading. He walked in, tossed the mail aside, and picked up where he'd left off.

*A lot of girls want to marry a man like their father. I most certainly do not. I loved my father and I'm terribly sad he's gone, especially so soon after we lost Ted. I grieve mostly for my mother, but honestly, I don't think she got much companionship from him. Maybe behind closed doors he was a completely different person, but I don't think so. It breaks my heart to say this, but I think the silent, angry man I saw every day was who he really was. He was a puzzle with very few clues. I was just a kid who didn't bring much experience to the job of solving him. Maybe my mother understood him. If she did, she never bothered to enlighten us. I felt like a footnote in the story of his life.*

*If there's a model for the kind of man I'd like to marry, it would be Ted. I realize if he'd come back alive, he would just be plain old Ted, not the saint I've built from dreams. He'd be bored and boring, tired, preoccupied, not the fountain of wisdom and rightness I remember. I understand that. Still, a girl could do worse.*

*My all-time favorite memory with Ted was when I was in fourth grade and he was a junior in high school. He had just read this wonderful new book,* Goodbye to a River *by a Texas author named John Graves, about a canoe trip down the Brazos, while it was still wild. The river comes pretty close to where we live, so Ted decided to recreate the trip as far as he could. I read the book after Ted finished, and I understood.*

*Ted wanted to do a big multiday excursion with his buddies, but none of them could make it. He decided to go anyway, by himself, but Mom wouldn't hear of it. She threatened to get Dad involved, and Ted knew that would be the end of his trip. So, he agreed to take me, and Mom gave in. She thought I should get outside more, and she knew Ted would be more careful if I came along. She would drive us down to the bridge where we'd put in, then pick us up several miles downstream. It was a one-day trip—a letdown for Ted—but a huge adventure for me.*

*When John Graves canoed the Brazos, the water was pretty low, with lots of sandbars, and he had to carry his canoe for some fairly long stretches. Ted's concern was that I wouldn't be able to help him. I promised him if he'd put all the gear in the back end, I could carry the front end. I remember showing him how I could lift my half of the boat. He gave me a paddle, cautioned me not to drop it, and helped me in. Mom had stuffed an ice chest with sandwiches and Shasta Cola so we wouldn't starve. She waved from the bank, Ted kicked us off, and suddenly we were paddling, the river carrying us along. I can still feel the thrill of the wind in my hair, the banks sliding past, trees reaching out over the water. Ted pointed out fish below, birds all around.*

*We had only been on the water a few minutes when it started rising. At first, we just noticed we weren't having to carry the canoe. A few minutes later, we didn't need to paddle, either. The current was strong, and the water was getting deeper. Ted was overjoyed, but I was a little scared. He told me it was okay, they had probably opened the spillway, or there'd been rain upstream. We were lucky to be out on the river at this moment, he said. He made sure I had my life vest on, told me to sit low and steady and just let him do the steering. We started singing as we sailed along.*

*Then the rain came. You could see it ahead, drops of water that looked like they were boiling up from the river rather than falling from the sky. The line swept toward us and then we were in it, pelted by cold needles. At first Ted thought we could just keep going, but we didn't have ponchos and it was raining hard. Finally, I heard him yell, "Paddle hard left! Go right!" and we headed for the sandy bank. He beached the canoe, pulling it well up above the water while I was still in it. I jumped out and as soon as Ted got us up high enough, he took our stuff out, picked the canoe up, turned it upside down, and propped one end on the cooler. We sat under it, facing each other, and laughed for no reason while the rain pounded down all around us. Ted switched his backpack for the cooler so we could eat while the rain beat down on our aluminum shelter. When the rain calmed down, he told me more about his favorite sections of the book.*

*After about a half-hour, it stopped just as suddenly as it had started, and the sun came out, bright and steamy. We stood up to move on. Ted picked me up in a big wet hug and sat me in the boat. I can't describe how happy I was. When we got back on the river, all Ted had to do was steer, making sure we stayed in the middle. He pointed out a few landmarks and we got a taste of why rivers were so important to the early settlers. You could get places on water, fast, with no roads. It was one thing to read that; it was something else to experience it. Ted talked about the different tribes that controlled much of the territory we were going through, too. Once he yelled he'd seen Kiowa up on a ridge above the river. I screamed and ducked. He laughed so hard he nearly ran us aground. I was mad, but eventually I saw the humor.*

*I also saw, in action, almost everything I loved about Ted that day. He relished a challenge; the tougher, the better. He was stronger than I realized and had skills I didn't know about. He took care of me, not just physically, but keeping my spirits up, making sure I wasn't scared (except when he was the one who scared me). I saw him calm and in control, and it quieted my fears.*

*Our time on the river went by quickly. The pull-out point came after we rounded a bend, and Ted steered us to where Mom was waiting, waving like she was afraid we would miss her. We found a little area of still water and Ted jumped out to pull the canoe in. He got thoroughly wet, but he was so jubilant he didn't seem to mind. He beached the canoe, fetched me out like I was a little doll, and set me on dry land, then went back in, waist-deep, to where the backpack and cooler were sitting. He let go of the canoe and waded over to the shore with them. Just then a big surge came down the river, lifting the canoe and pulling it away from the bank. Ted dove and swam after it, caught it, but couldn't get in. Soon the current was carrying him and the canoe back out into the center of the powerful river. I know I screamed, terrified he was going to float away.*

*He told me later he had been tempted to just float on down, but when he looked back, the expression on my face persuaded him to fight his way out. I was so relieved when he came back, swimming powerfully, pushing the canoe in front of him, until finally he could touch bottom and walk up out of the water.*

*I thought about that moment last year, when I realized he was not coming back from Viet Nam. I could close my eyes and see him, out on a swift, powerful river. He couldn't make it back to us, so he just smiled, waved, and let the current take him away. When I think about it now, it feels like he was preparing me to lose him. Back then, we could have just gone on downriver and picked him up at the next spot. On a river, that's how it works. With life and death, I just have to trust the same thing will happen. He's not gone, just gone on. We're on the same river, and we'll see each other again, around some bend.*

*I remember looking at my mother, while Ted was working so hard to get back to us. She didn't seem worried at all. Maybe she didn't want to scare me, or she was just sure he'd make it. I think it's her nature to put a cheerful face on everything, no matter how bad it is. I can't just smile and act like everything is alright. I know sometimes it isn't, and it won't be, and there's nothing any of us can do about it. But I think you can embrace the joy of life more deeply if you can also embrace the sadness.*

*One of the many things Ted taught me, that day, without even trying, was to just enjoy the ride. Go with the current and trust you'll come out okay. Canoeing that river with his little sister wasn't his first choice, but it was one of the highlights of my life. I wouldn't trade that time with him for anything in this world.*

*I would give anything to have more.*

**Thurston: 1969**

Graduation was the biggest social event of the year in Thurston. Most people couldn't wait for it to arrive. Dottie couldn't wait for it to be over. She had turned in her final papers, finished her tests, and gotten the official word that her grade-point average ranked her at the top of the class of 1969 at Thurston High School. No one else was even close. She had been accepted to the liberal arts honors program at the University of Texas at Austin. Her brief valedictory address was written and had been practiced repeatedly.

She was not looking forward to the ceremony.

All her life, she had imagined her mom, dad, and brother would be there to see her walk in at the head of her class. Her brother would grin and applaud, maybe with his wife and a kid or two in the bleachers beside him. Her mom would glow with pride, and even her dad might manage a smile. But her brother and dad were gone, her mom hollowed out by grief. The only thing Dottie looked forward to now was getting out of high school and moving on with her life.

After school, she was reviewing her speech in the English classroom, which doubled as the newspaper and yearbook office, when freshman Tim Potts walked in, carrying a heavy box. The yearbooks had arrived.

"Hey Dottie, look here!" he said, his voice cracking. "It's the yearbooks! Do you wanna sign mine? I could sign yours . . ."

"Thanks, Tim," she replied, feeling old in the face of his adolescent enthusiasm. "I've got some work to do first—you know, look up the orders, make sure the books are right, see who's paid and who hasn't. We'll pass them out tomorrow."

He and a couple of other freshman boys set boxes of yearbooks down on a table. Dottie hadn't noticed Sherry over in the corner, but when the boys came in she wandered over.

"Need any help?" she asked, smiling at the boys. They didn't even look at her, staring at Dottie like they'd never seen a girl before. She dismissed them quickly, grabbing a pair of scissors to cut a box open and handing another pair to Dottie. They unboxed and stacked the books. When they were finished, Sherry took one and retreated to the corner.

Dottie grabbed a copy, too. It was slick and shiny and had that new-book smell. A smile spread across her face when she saw "The Thanatopsis" embossed in the dark leather. She opened it and flipped a few pages, checking a couple of items she'd had second thoughts about, particularly a photo of her and Mel Davis as valedictorian and salutatorian.

She sighed. The previous Friday, Mel had told Dottie he would always love her and presented her with a sonnet sequence he'd been working on all year. It was all about her hair, her eyes, her voice, her everything. She thanked him. That was obviously not the reaction he'd hoped for. She told him he would undoubtedly get over her at some point. And, she added, at least he got some good poems out of the deal.

She prayed she'd be forgiven for the lie. They were awful.

Arnie Chitwood wasn't writing any poems, good or otherwise, but he was considerably more worrisome than Mel. For one thing, he was the size of three Mels, with the intellect of a doorknob and the persistence of a pit bull. Their homecoming-night date, meant to placate him, had only made things worse.

Dottie was leafing through the yearbook when he stepped into the doorway.

"Hi Dottie," he said. "Whatcha got?"

She looked up. "Oh, hi Arnie," she said coolly. "It's the new yearbook." She turned away and started checking the list, who had paid and who still needed to. But she didn't want to be mean; Arnie was pitiful, and she had a soft heart. She picked up a book and flipped to the football page.

"Look," she said. "Here you are!"

He took a couple of steps and loomed over her, looking down at a football photo. He was throwing a block to free up a running back for a modest gain. Other than the team photo and his class portrait, it was his only appearance in the book. He grinned when she pointed it out.

"I look pretty good, huh?" he asked.

"It's a good picture," she conceded.

Arnie had been courted for a college football scholarship, with a few major universities showing interest simply because of his size. But after coaches visited and saw his transcript, they concluded he was not college material. He had decided to go to an area junior college to try to improve his grades, but those who knew him had little hope he could do even that.

Dottie went about her work as he watched.

"So," he said after a long silence, "tomorrow night is the big night. You comin' to my party? I'm pretty sure everybody's going to be there."

"No, Arnie, I'm not," she said. "I don't like parties. It's just me and my mom now. I'm just going to go home and hang out with her."

His eyebrows plunged and his face crunched into a scowl. Suddenly, he banged his fist on the table, making all the yearbooks, and Dottie, jump.

"Dammit, Dottie!" he said. "My whole *life* it's been just me and my mom! This is graduation night! You only get one of those! Forget your mom! You need to have some fun."

"Arnie!" she said, shocked by his sudden outburst. "I don't remember asking you for advice on how to live my life. Besides, I haven't heard anyone else mention anything about a party up on the mesa."

"So, what are you saying?" he asked defensively. "You don't think there's gonna be a party? You think no one's coming? You think it's going to be . . . lame? Hey, it's going to be a great party—the best party ever!"

"You need to leave," she said, walking over to the classroom window. He followed, blocking her in behind a row of desks. She turned to face him and saw she was trapped. "I said go, Arnie. Leave me alone. I've got a lot to do."

"You think you'll get a better offer?" His voice turned mean as he closed in on her. "It's our last night in high school, Dottie. We need to be together."

Her hands curled up into fists at her side, but she knew she could hit him with everything she had and not faze him. It was obvious he knew it, too. He reached out and touched her hair where it tucked behind her ear. She slapped his hand away.

"No!" she said. "It's not 'our' last night anywhere. Our last night already happened. Homecoming. Remember? That's it! We're done."

"Oh, Dottie," he said, creepy calm despite her agitation. "I've known you longer than anybody. Let's face it. I'm the biggest, strongest guy in school and you're the smartest, prettiest girl. We're meant to be together."

*Smart*, she thought, her heart pounding. Yes, smart. That was it. She turned to the window, pretending to see someone outside, tapped on the glass and waved.

"Hey, Donna!" she yelled.

When Arnie turned to look, she hopped onto a desk, kicked her legs up, and slid deftly across, out of the trap.

Arnie turned. "I didn't see Don—"

"Shut up, Arnie!" she said, turning back to face him. "Now you listen to me. I'm not your girl, and I'm never going to be your girl. Got it? There's no way in hell we will ever be together. Your mother babysat me. We played together. That doesn't mean anything, and neither does homecoming. You don't know me. You have no idea who I am or what I want. 'We' are not meant for anything. I don't know what you're meant for, but I mean to get out of here and once I do, I'm gone. Not you, or anyone else, is going to pin me down or hold me back. Understand?"

Dottie shocked herself. She had never talked to anyone like that. But she had to get through to Arnie, somehow.

"And," she added, leaning in and pointing a finger at his face, "if you ever put your hand on me again, I swear you'll go to jail!"

Arnie stood there as she spoke, his mouth open. Then, his reaction chilled her.

"Jail?" He forced a laugh. "I don't think so. My mother's friends with the sheriff. Hell, they didn't even do anything to me when I burned that building down. I can do whatever I want. My mom owns this town."

Her response was to turn and walk briskly out of the classroom. He stood there a moment, expressionless, then left as well, working to regain his swagger.

Sherry, sitting quietly at the far end of the room, had heard every word.

**Fort Worth: 2015**

Through the newspaper archives, Henry learned that Thurston Independent School District had consolidated with the nearby town of Budlong in 1972. Thurston-Budlong CISD lasted for a few years, but enrollment continued to dwindle as cities kept pulling families away from rural life.

In '76, they consolidated with Loganville and closed the old Thurston campus, the last nail in the coffin of the old town. The population steadily dwindled: less than one hundred by 1980, less than fifty by 1990, and finally, only a dozen by the 2000 census. A Dallas TV reporter had done a prize-winning series on Texas ghost towns in the early 2000s, and Thurston was at the top of the list. Henry found the series on YouTube and decided to take a look.

After a slick intro and some traveling music, he found himself looking at the old C&C building, the three-story landmark of the little town. He hit pause, went to the file, and found the deed he and Ella had discovered. Sure enough, that was it. He reached for his phone to call Ella. She answered on the first ring.

"Did you find something?"

"Hello to you, too," Henry said.

"You know me," she said with a laugh. "I like to cut to the chase.

What did you find?"

"Well, I'm sitting here holding a deed to the building this reporter is standing in front of, in a video that aired in 2003," he said. "How about that?"

"What's it say?" Ella pressed.

"I haven't watched it yet," he said. "As soon as I saw it, I called you."

"I was about to call you!" she said. "I found something, too."

"Do you want to come over?" he asked.

There was a fairly long pause. "Henry, it's after 10 o'clock."

"Okay, if you don't want to come, don't come," he said. "Do you want me to wait and watch this with you when you can?"

Ella paused again, then sighed.

"I'll be there in ten minutes," she said. "Warning, though. I do not look good."

She arrived in five. She'd thrown on a sweatshirt, some khaki shorts, and flip-flops, and pulled her hair back into a ponytail. She didn't wear a lot of makeup anyway; seeing her without it convinced Henry she didn't need any.

He met her at the door, and she hugged him as he looked around furtively. "Quick, get inside! People will start talking about my late-night visitor!"

"You have nosy neighbors?" she asked.

"Is there any other kind?"

He shut the door and they walked into his living room, where his big TV was located in a floor-to-ceiling bookshelf made of crates, two-by-twelves, and cinder blocks.

"I love what you've done with the place," she said.

"Really?"

"No!" she scoffed, laughing. "What are you, still in college? No one would ever dream you work for an architect."

He absorbed the blow and offered her coffee. She wandered around the room while he started the coffee, then returned and opened his laptop.

"Have a seat," he said. She found a big pillow and curled up on the hideous but comfortable sectional. "I can't believe you've never been here."

"You've never been to my place, either," she reminded him.

"Don't remember being invited," he muttered.

"What's that?" she asked.

"Nothing," he said. She grinned. He knew she'd heard him.

She was probably just as uncomfortable as he was, Henry thought, although she looked pretty cozy. But it was different, seeing her here. It was personal. It brought home that they were more than coworkers, even more than old friends. He looked at her as she thumbed through a magazine. What in the world was this beautiful woman doing here? Who was he? It was another in a series of strange feelings Henry had been dealing with ever since that day at the elevator—another feeling he thought he'd like a chance to get used to.

He tapped a key and the image on his screen popped up on the TV. He hit play, and the reporter was talking.

"Once upon a time, there was a store called Abbott's, on the ground floor of the old C&C building—the Cotton & Cattle Building—in busy downtown Thurston," the reporter said. A black-and-white video began to play, with jaunty bluegrass music behind it. It was shot during the store's heyday in the 1950s. The grainy film showed a bustling department store, people walking up and down the busy street outside. Then the video switched to color, and to the present day. Vacant houses lined the streets, and all the storefronts along the main drag were empty. Finally, there was a close-up of the historical marker on the building before the camera moved inside, panning empty space where only a few built-in fixtures remained. Then it went back outside, and there stood a tiny lady—the owner of the building—who still lived on the top floor. She was in her late sixties, a lively woman who, as it turned out, owned the entire town.

Her name was Evelyn Chitwood.

"Whoa!" Ella yelled. "Stop it!"

Henry sat up, hit pause, and grabbed the deed. Evelyn Chitwood's name was right there. He handed the document to Ella, and they looked at each other.

"That's our girl!" Ella said, sitting up on her knees. "And guess what? She's still there—that's my news! I called the county clerk yesterday, and she knows her. Everybody knows her. Apparently, she still lives up on the third floor."

"Let's see the rest of the interview," Henry said.

The camera zoomed in on Evelyn Chitwood's face, which looked surprisingly young.

"I got this building in 1954," she said, in a voice that sounded like a three-pack-a-day smoker. "I was only nineteen. My daddy had won it in a poker game. When they finally found me and told me it was mine, I was living in an old shotgun shack up on the mesa. I packed up and came down here to live in the penthouse." She laughed, then continued.

"I raised my boy up here. It was a nice place, a nice little town for a boy to grow up in. After he grew up, I just stayed here," she said. "This is my home."

The reporter's voiceover came back, talking about the school closing and the town drying up, "but Miss Evelyn isn't going anywhere."

A few more images, past and present, flashed across the screen, then the clip ended with a shot of the C&C building as the sun set behind it. The reporter's voice came back.

"Evelyn Chitwood doesn't like people calling Thurston a ghost town," he said. "In fact, when we told her that was the theme of our series, she objected strongly."

"There's no ghosts here," she said, in a closeup. Then she laughed. "Well, maybe a few." She paused, looked into the camera, eyes wide, and said with a cackle, "Maybe it's me! Boo!"

Henry sat there, staring at the screen as the credits started rolling. He looked at Ella, leaning forward on the edge of the couch, then jumped up and ran to get the coffee.

"So, what did you think?" he called from the kitchen.

"Man, Henry, I want to meet this lady," Ella said, taking a cup. "I want to give her back that deed, if she wants it, and some of this other stuff. I'll bet those are her shoes, and probably her hats, too. She's tiny, and intriguing, but . . . the ghost stuff is a little creepy."

"She seems pretty spry," Henry said. "I'll bet she has some stories to tell. She could probably fill in a lot of gaps for us. That was shot, when? 2002 or 2003?"

"Yeah, I think so," Ella said. "So she would have been around sixty-seven. She would be about, what, eighty now? It looked like she was in good health, one of those independent, tough old Texas women."

They sat in silence for a moment. It felt good having her in his house.

"I like those tough Texas women," he said with a grin.

She smiled back at him. "You left out 'old.'"

"Yeah," he said. "On purpose."

"It's a good thing," she said, smiling again. After a pause, she added, "You know, there's just one thing I can't figure out."

"What's that?"

"Doesn't it seem like there's two families' stuff in our unit? What's the connection between this lady and your girl, Dottie Sinclair? How did their stuff get mixed together?"

**Thurston: 1969**

Graduation evening for the class of '69—the biggest in Thurston's history—turned out dry, although storms were forecast for later. Everyone hoped they would hold off, because if it rained, the school was in trouble. Neither the auditorium nor the gym could accommodate all the family members, friends, and well-wishers. The principal's personal nightmare was Grandma driving in from Arizona, then not getting a seat because they had to move the ceremony indoors, causing her to miss the biggest (possibly only) accomplishment of her precious grandchild's life.

Tonight, in the football stadium, there was a gentle breeze, clear skies overhead, and seating for everyone.

The junior cheerleaders, dressed in white like vestal virgins, were passing out programs. The student section was filled and buzzing, boys in their letter jackets and girls in dresses they'd wear to church on Sunday. The band members, half of them seniors in graduation robes, were tuning up when Evelyn walked up the ramp to the bottom of the bleachers, turned, and scanned the crowd for Mary. She squinted against the evening sun as she continued to climb, running her eyes down each row until she heard a voice at her side.

"Looking for anybody in particular?"

It was Mary. She smiled, then threw her arms around Evelyn for a quick hug.

"Yeah! You!" Evelyn greeted her warmly. "Wanna sit together one last time and watch these kids of ours?"

"I would love that," Mary said, "as long as I can squeeze your hand if I need to, to keep from bawling like a baby." She took Evelyn's hand.

"We'll just pool our tissues and cry as much as we want," Evelyn said.

They walked down the row until they found a space where they could slide in side-by-side. Evelyn spotted Dewley and waved. After a few more greetings, they sat down.

"You must be so proud of Dottie," Evelyn said. "Valedictorian and all. She's a really outstanding kid, that girl of yours."

Mary turned around and looked Evelyn in the eyes.

"Yes," she said. "She's all I've got left." A sob caught in her throat, although her smile remained fixed. "And she can't wait to get out of here. She's going to summer school. Says she wants to get a head start on the fall. She's leaving Monday morning. She doesn't want to spend even one more day here with me."

Evelyn laid a hand on Mary's shoulder, and they sat in silence for a moment.

"It's not you, Mary," she said. "That's natural. A lot of these kids feel like that. It's a little town, a little school. They all want to go see the lights."

"It's more than that, Evelyn," Mary said. "She—"

"I know," Evelyn said, cutting her off, her hand on Mary's shoulder patting and comforting. "She just . . . she wants to get away from all the . . ." She shook her head. "From everything. You know."

"Yes," Mary agreed. "I know. I'd feel the same way, in her place. I just don't know what I'm going to do."

There was another pause, less awkward.

"We'll just have to start getting together again," Evelyn said. "We don't have to just sit and watch kids, you know. We can do whatever we want."

Mary looked at her and smiled, then patted her on the leg. "Yes. We sure can."

Just then the music started. The band was seated in folding chairs arranged in a semicircle at the thirty-yard line. At the fifty yard line, in chairs on a raised platform, sat the school board, superintendent, and principal. In front of them stood a microphone behind a podium. On the track, facing the platform, were thirty chairs in two rows, where the graduating seniors would sit. The band director raised his baton and the band launched into "Pomp and Circumstance." A beat later, the principal rose and motioned for everyone to stand as the cap-and-gowned graduates walked slowly out from behind the concession stand, led by another white-clad girl.

Dottie wasn't in the lineup. She was first-chair clarinet, playing with the band one last time. Arnie walked in third, behind Bennie Aguilar and Janie Baker, based on alphabetical order. His grades placed him squarely at the bottom of the class. But when she saw him, Evelyn squealed quietly.

"Aw," she said, surprised by the flood of emotion. "That's my baby boy! I never thought I'd see this day."

Mary took her hand again. When they were all standing in front of their chairs, the band stopped playing and the seniors quietly put down their instruments and filed in an orderly line to the open chairs. Dottie and Mel Davis, who played trumpet, went up the steps to fill two empty chairs on the platform, facing the graduates and the crowd. When everyone was in place, they sat down as a group, and the audience sat down as well.

A few of the parents and siblings yelled things like, "Way to go, Billy boy!" and there was almost always a cowbell or two, but those outbursts were frowned upon. Mr. Chesterton welcomed the audience, congratulated everyone for making it this far, and reminded their families that "this is not a rodeo" and they should confine their celebration to clapping and polite cheers, out of consideration for others. He made the same plea every year, to no effect.

After the national anthem and an invocation, Mel made a brief talk as salutatorian, thanking parents, teachers, and everyone who had gotten the class of '69 to this crossroads in their young lives. He was almost finished, urging everyone to stretch out their wings and fly like birds, when a sudden puff of wind tried to relieve him of his mortarboard hat. Instinctively he reached to catch it, knocking the microphone over as his pages flew away like birds. The microphone crashed to the platform with a sharp, loud bang and the principal jumped to stand it up again. He got it back upright quickly. It took Mel a bit longer to recover. His voice cracked as he shouted his last line, "Wildcats forever!" while his pages fluttered toward the end zone. By the time he sat down, he was soaked in sweat and looked like he might pass out.

Mr. Chesterton came back to the podium, thanked Mel, and called on Dottie for her valedictory address. The stadium went quiet as she approached the microphone, blonde hair blowing back from her fine-featured face like a model's in a photo shoot.

"She looks like a movie star!" Evelyn whispered to Mary, who smiled calmly although her whole body was rigid with tension. Dottie looked down at her notes, then up, past the audience and into the crowd, finding her mother. Mary smiled and waved covertly as her eyes glistened with tears.

"Mr. Chesterton, faculty, board members, friends, and family," Dottie began. "It's hard to believe this night has finally come, and our time at Thurston High School is nearly over. When you are waiting for something, it seems the days crawl by, doesn't it? But time's pace never changes: it is inevitable. And this day we saw so far in the future, so long ago—this day is finally upon us.

"I'm glad for that. I believe most of my classmates are, too. We've done our best to be the sons and daughters, the students, and the citizens you wanted us to be. Sometimes we succeeded and sometimes we failed, but we've persevered, and now it's time for us to go. We're ready, and you should be ready, too. This is what you raised us for. This is why you taught us, fed us, encouraged us, and equipped us. The future calls, and wherever it takes us, we're ready to get going.

"I wish, like Bilbo Baggins at the start of the *Lord of the Rings*, that I had a magic ring I could just slip onto my finger and become invisible. I would say my goodbyes, wish you all well, and assure you that very soon, you would see me no more. Then I would reach into my pocket, slide my finger through the ring, and it would be done—I would be off on my great adventure.

"But I have no ring, no cloak of invisibility. So, I'll say goodbye to all of you anyway, right to your smiling faces, and wish you the very best. I hope you'll wish the same for me and my classmates. Wherever the future takes us, may it be bright and full of hope, and may we face it with confidence and joy. Goodnight."

The crowd rose immediately to its feet. Most of them knew the losses she'd suffered. Many cheered out loud, and quite a few wiped tears onto their sleeves. Evelyn sniffled as she looked over at Mary, her smile frozen, her cheeks streaked with tears.

"That's just about the best speech I've ever heard," Evelyn whispered. Mary squeezed her hand—she'd been holding it all along—and nodded, never taking her eyes off the stage where her daughter stood, still waving and smiling as the applause slowly died.

The rest of the ceremony went by quickly: the announcement of names, the handshakes, and the handing out of rolled-up pieces of paper that stated a diploma would be arriving in the mail within the next five business days. Finally, the graduates moved the tassels on their hats and filed out as they had come in, with "Pomp and Circumstance" played weakly by the band without seniors. After a benediction and a shaky rendition of the school song, the ceremony was over. Hats flew into the air, and Mary and Evelyn let go of each other and focused on finding and hugging their children before the wide world swept them away.

Arnie, large and lonely, was easy to locate.

"Aw, son, I'm so proud of you!" Evelyn said, wrapping her arms as far as they would go around him. He accepted her hug matter-of-fact-ly, scanning the crowd for friends and finding few who wanted to greet him.

"Thanks, Ma," he said. "I think I'm going to be out pretty late tonight."

Evelyn looked up at him. "Just make sure you don't do any drinking," she said. "Do you hear me?"

"I dunno, Ma," he said. "I mean, it's graduation night . . ."

"Arnold," she said, pulling him by the ear down to her level. "You don't need alcohol to have a good time. Stay sober! Have fun you can still remember the next day. Y'hear?"

"Yes, ma'am," he said, in a singsong voice.

"I mean it!" Evelyn yelled.

He stepped back, frowning. "Ma, I get it! Stop embarrassing me!"

Mary had spotted Dottie and joined the crowd around her—parents, visitors, teachers, all wanting to shake her hand. Mary waited like everyone else. Ironically Dottie, although "most popular" in the yearbook, didn't have any more friends than Arnie. They were at opposite ends of the spectrum: he brought little to a friendship; she brought far too much. No one knew what to say to her. No one understood her. She had decided that was okay—it would make it easier to leave.

She smiled and accepted the compliments. When Mary finally got to her, they hugged and held onto each other in a brief embrace, avoiding looking into each other's eyes.

Arnie walked up. "Hey, Dottie! Hey, Mrs. Sinclair!" he said. "Wow, just think! Here we are!" He looked at Dottie. "Great speech!"

He reached out to hug Dottie, and reluctantly she leaned in and disappeared in his overlong embrace.

"That was a terrific speech, Dottie," Evelyn said. "Just wonderful. Made me proud to know you." There was a long pause, and finally Evelyn tossed out a question.

"Anybody got plans?"

Dottie started into a well-rehearsed speech about summer school at the University of Texas. Evelyn interrupted her. "Oh, honey, I know all that," she said with a laugh. "I meant tonight!"

Dottie glanced at Arnie, who didn't say a word.

"Oh," she replied, acting embarrassed. "I don't know. I've heard about a few parties. But I think I'll just go home and hang out with my mom. We don't have too many more evenings to do that, do we?"

"No, baby," Mary said. "But it's okay. You do whatever you want; you don't have to come home and sit around with me on your graduation night. Just let me know where you are."

Evelyn envied their level of trust. She relied on Arnold's lack of creativity to keep him out of most troubles. He was a good-hearted boy, she often said. It was his head that worried her.

"I can give you a ride, Dottie," he said.

"That's okay," she said firmly. "I'm going home."

"I'll take you wherever you want to go. You choose.". I'll be your driver. You know, like, the one who doesn't drink. The destinated . . . detonated . . ."

"The designated driver," Mary said.

"But I'm not drinking, so that's not necessary, right?" Dottie said. Arnie looked completely puzzled. "I'll drive us home, Mom," she said.

Decisively, Dottie took Mary's arm, and they waved goodbye to Arnie and Evelyn.

Evelyn looked at her son and saw not just embarrassment, not even anger, but a seething undercurrent of rage. She stepped back, chilled.

"Arnold? You okay?" she asked him. "Arnie?"

He turned away without looking at her and stalked off. She had told him the pickup was his for the evening, since she could easily walk home from the football field. She was worried, but there was nothing she could do about it.

He hadn't learned anything in school, she thought. Maybe he would learn something on graduation night.

**Fort Worth: 2015**

Henry walked Ella to her car, and she drove the five minutes back to her apartment. They had decided that having found Evelyn, they would ramp up the search for Dottie.

The next day, Henry took a half day and went to the *Star-Telegram* office to look through archives. The database was searchable, but if you got a hit, you still had to go get a microfiche and put it in a reader. He found Dottie's brother easily, in the fall of 1967. Edward Randall "Ted" Sinclair. Henry saw a photo of his name on the Vietnam Memorial Wall in Washington, D.C., and read his obituary. He was survived by his parents, George and Mary Sinclair of Thurston, Texas, and younger sister, Dorothy, also of Thurston, as well as grandparents and a few aunts and uncles, mostly in Ohio.

No surprises. He decided to go forward from that point and just search for pairings of the word "Sinclair" and "Thurston."

Less than two months later, he found her father's obituary. This was back in the day when everyone who died got an obit, and if a death was unusual, or the person was prominent in their community, it might be fairly detailed.

George Sinclair had died in an accident while working on a power line. The story said it was made more tragic by the fact that he'd recently buried a son who had died in Vietnam. George's death left behind a grieving widow, Mary, and one daughter, Dorothy.

That was all. Even in the 1960s, events in Thurston didn't get a lot of ink in Fort Worth. Henry decided whenever he and Ella made their road trip to Thurston, he would like to hit the archives of the *Loganville Ledger*, the weekly newspaper in the county seat a few miles south. Ella wanted to go to Loganville, too, to check some records at the county courthouse.

He hoped there might be more detail in the local paper, about both George's death and Ted's. He kept following the thread, but there was nothing else in the *Star-Telegram*.

That afternoon, when he returned to the office, he called Ella, but the receptionist told him she was in consultation with the Penwells and some of the other big shots about a lawsuit. She asked if she could take a message, but Henry said he would just email her.

When he got back down to his cubicle, an email from Ella was waiting for him.

> *Hey, don't know if you found anything, but I've got this big lawsuit going and I have to go to Albuquerque for a couple of days. Apparently, some substandard brick fell off one of our buildings and injured some people. I want you to keep me posted, but if you find something really big, I'd much rather see it and talk to you about it in person. Isn't this fun? See!*
>
> *I'll be back Thursday evening and they owe me a comp day on Friday. Do you think that might be a good day for our road trip?*

He replied immediately to let her know that he had a few vacation days coming, and he would put in for one on Friday.

> *I have a lot to tell you. The mystery is getting more mysterious every day. And I agree that I would much prefer to show-and-tell you this in person. You just focus on getting the company out of hot water in Albuquerque. We can talk it out on the drive to Thurston.*

In that instant, an afterthought in his mind flashed involuntarily through the synapses of his brain directly to his fingers, which had been trained from years of newspaper writing to type things as quickly as he thought them. He hit send just before he became aware that he had typed:

*I'll miss you.*

He sat there for a moment, then took a deep breath. It was yet another unfamiliar feeling.

It was true. He did miss Ella. Down deep in his gut, he wanted to see her so badly he ached. He felt cheated, envious of Albuquerque and whoever the lucky sap was who got to sit across from her, hear her voice, watch her work, and deal with her—even if it was the guy whose tail she was kicking in legal combat. He missed her every moment he wasn't with her.

So, it was out there. Worse-case scenario, she would shoot him down, laugh at him, or not even notice it. He scooted his chair back and got up. He was two steps on his way to the break room when his computer beeped with an incoming email. He lunged back over to the screen to see what it said. It was from Ella.

*Miss you too. See you Thursday night. I'll call when I get in.*

He quickly clicked off the screen, but a smile lingered on his face.

That evening, he went home and cleaned house in a manner worthy of his obsessive personality. He took rugs outside and shook them, beat couch cushions with his old racquetball racquet, swept and vacuumed, scrubbed the kitchen and the bathroom—he even cleaned out the refrigerator, tossing out food he could identify only by the takeout containers it was breeding in. Pushing furniture aside to vacuum, he decided to rearrange, moving things around until he found a new look. It didn't look much different, but it smelled noticeably better.

He hoped Ella would like it.

**Thurston: 1969**

Sherry stood in front of the mirror. She wasn't as beautiful as Dottie—nobody was. But she was pretty in her own way. She was about the same size as Dottie, and there were a lot of things she could do to make Arnold notice her. She'd been making do with very little her whole life. Tonight, she was going to pull out the whole arsenal.

She had saved up, bought some peroxide, and dyed her hair blonde. It was curled and tied back in a loose ponytail. She had casually asked Dottie at school what kids wore under the graduation gown—the typical question of a naive sophomore. She was delighted to learn that even though she didn't have a lot of clothes, she could easily match Dottie's wardrobe of cutoff jeans, Mexican blouse, white sneakers, and no socks. It was the summer uniform of girls at that time. She put herself together, looked at the effect, and was not disappointed.

She'd been in love with Arnie ever since she came to Thurston. He was big, strong, and rich. He had the confidence, the swagger, of someone who'd been in one place his whole life, knew everyone, and was known by everyone.

Sherry had spent her life shuffling from one place to another. She was raised near Waco, but not in a happy home. When she was ten, her mom went to prison for trying to kill her dad. She'd only wounded him, and the woman he was in bed with got away without a scratch. But a twelve-gauge shotgun can do a lot of damage, especially to a marriage. Her dad was a faithless, no-good drunk, but after the shooting, he was a victim. As a result of the trial, her mom was taken away and Sherry became a "ward of the court." That meant one foster home after another, until one day, her daddy showed up. He was clean and sober—she almost didn't recognize him. He told the judge he wanted her, said all the right things. In reality, all he wanted was someone to wait on him, hand and foot.

They wound up in a trailer park in Morenci, Arizona, where he drove a truck in the open-pit copper mine. She liked her school and made friends, but that was no home for a little girl.

One day, he went to work and just never came home. Sherry was on her own for nearly a week until a neighbor noticed the dad's pickup was never there anymore—at any hour—and the girl was walking to school every morning by herself. The neighbor called the law, and they took her into juvenile custody, as if she'd committed a crime.

A few days later they found an aunt—her mother's sister. She drove all the way from Wichita Falls to pick Sherry up. She was about thirty and looked just like a younger version of Sherry's mom. After she had gathered her niece and her few possessions, she complained all the way back to Wichita Falls about what a great inconvenience it was to have to take care of a kid.

She talked as if Sherry wasn't even there. After a couple of weeks of minimal care, she decided to put her back into a foster home.

An agency in Abilene agreed to take her. She spent her junior high years at the children's home, going to a nearby school and settling into a routine. Then one day, the director called her in and told her they had found her a foster home, with an older couple in Cisco. They were about the age Sherry's grandparents would have been. He was a preacher whose congregation wouldn't let him retire. His kindness was his best sermon, and his wife, although she was in poor health, was his greatest asset. Sherry quickly fell in love with them and the quiet stability they offered.

She hadn't been in their home three months when he had a stroke. After a terrible week in the hospital, he died. His wife could not take care of the girl by herself, so the agency was called.

It was routine in such situations to do a search for relatives. To everyone's surprise, they found her dad again, this time in Thurston, working an oilfield job. He showed up in Abilene and once again said all the right words: he had a good job, he missed his daughter, and he was deeply sorry for abandoning her in Arizona. Thurston was a nice little town where she could start and finish high school, and there was no trouble to get into.

The good people at the home were eager to reunite a family. But as Sherry and her father got in the truck, he made it clear she was on her own. He did not have time for a kid—he just didn't want her living in some children's home. He would let her live in the house on one condition: she had to take care of her own needs. Even though he made good money, she would have to earn her own. He would buy some groceries, but if she wanted to eat, she would have to fix it. She could sleep there until she turned eighteen, and then she was gone.

After all she'd been through, that arrangement didn't seem so bad. If he would just leave her alone, she could make her own way. He worked almost all the time, often staying at a well site almost a hundred miles away for days or weeks at a time. In Thurston, unlike Arizona, no neighbors were watching. Her father treated her as if she didn't exist, and she knew that any day, he might disappear as he had before. She was certain if she disappeared, he would not notice.

More than anything, she wanted to run away with Arnie and never see Thurston again. And she had no intention of waiting until she was eighteen.

* * *

Dottie wasn't thrilled about spending graduation night with her mother, but she had few options. Mary, on the other hand, was almost insistent.

"Honey, you know you can go out tonight if you want to," she said as they drove home.

"I know, Mom. I just don't want to," Dottie said, her hands at three and nine o'clock on the steering wheel. She had shed her graduation robe and was wearing cut-off jeans and a loose-fitting bright red Mexican peasant blouse with lots of embroidery. With the window down and her loosely tied hair blowing, she was a vision.

"I just hate for you to spend your graduation night sitting home with boring old me," Mary said.

"Mom! I'm fine with it!"

"If Arnold wants to take you somewhere, to some party or something, you ought to go. This is the only graduation night you'll ever—"

"Dammit, Mom!" she said, surprising herself. "I'm not going out with Arnie Chitwood. If you knew anything about him, you wouldn't encourage me to."

Mary shrank at Dottie's outburst. Then, uncharacteristically, she lashed back.

"Oh, stop it, Dorothy!" she said. "You can't go through life thinking you're so much better than everybody just because you're smarter. Come down off your high horse! His mother came from the worst possible upbringing, but she's been a good friend to me all these years and worked so hard to make something of herself. She used to babysit you, you know?"

Dottie was dumfounded. It was as if her mother was reading from Arnie's script.

"Mom, you—"

"No, you listen to me, young lady," Mary said. "I know Arnold isn't as smart as you, but it's obvious he likes you. If you're ever going to have a boyfriend, you're going to have to bring your standards back to earth a little bit. Not that many people—"

"Mom! Stop it!" Dottie was aghast. "Do you even know me? You could not be more wrong! I don't not want to go out with Arnie because I think I'm too smart, or too good, or too anything! He's . . . he's got this idea that because we played together when we were kids, he's got some kind of claim on me. He's creepy, Mom."

Tears welled up in her eyes.

"I can't believe you don't see it," she said. "I can't believe my own mother would encourage me to go out with somebody like that."

Dottie's words seemed to bounce all around Mary without registering.

"Oh, Dorothy," she said. "He's a nice boy. He's just slow. And he's so big, everything he does is magnified. He's like that man Lennie, in that book . . ."

"*Of Mice and Men*?" Dottie asked, incredulous. "That man?"

"Yes, him!" Mary said, as if by referencing a book she'd found common ground with her daughter. "He's lovable, just a big, slow guy."

Dottie wanted to scream, but she took a breath and answered in a slow, measured tone. "Mom, do you know how that book ends?"

"I . . . uh . . . no, I guess not," Mary stammered. "I probably read it a long time ago. I do remember seeing the movie once, parts of it. He's big and he's slow, and . . ."

"And he *kills* a woman!" Dottie said, her voice rising. "He's big and slow and stupid, and he breaks this woman's neck because she's pretty and he doesn't want to let go of her hair. Is that what you want for me, Mother?"

"Dottie! No! Of course not! I'm just saying . . ."

They pulled up in front of their house, and Dottie stomped on the brake, threw the car into park, and quickly got out, slamming the door. She was truly furious. She could hear her mother protesting as she walked back down the driveway and out to the road. She was almost to the gate when her mother called to her.

"Dottie! Come back! We can talk this out!"

She stopped. The thought of going back, sitting in that sad house and having another long, one-sided conversation with her sad mother was more than she could bear. A pair of headlights was approaching. She looked back toward the house one more time, then shook her head, turned, and walked through the gate.

The lights had stopped. Lightning flashed in clouds that were growing closer. Dottie took a deep breath, looked back toward her house, then turned and walked toward the headlights.

**Fort Worth: 2015**

Henry picked Ella up early Friday morning at her place. He wanted to kiss her, but they weren't quite there yet. He did get a hug, though, and she smelled wonderful. She told him about her work in Albuquerque, where she had secured a settlement that saved the company hundreds of thousands, if not millions, of dollars. Through her preparation and diligence, she had gotten them off the hook for the brick incident.

"How'd you do that?" he asked. "Did you bribe somebody, or have somebody whacked?"

"No!" She beamed. "That would have been simpler. I just did my homework, homeboy."

"So what did you find?" he pressed. He was truly interested in how her mind worked, how she made things look so easy when everyone else found them complex and difficult and daunting. "Was there a smoking gun?"

"Yes!" she said, pounding his chest. "That's exactly what it was! A smoking gun!"

"So let's have it," he begged. "This isn't all sealed in some settlement file, is it? I'm still a reporter, you know. I dig for information. It's in my genes."

"Keep your jeans on, big boy," she said, laughing as she strung him along. "The smoking gun was, we didn't pick that brick."

"We didn't? What do you mean? Doesn't the architect usually do that?"

"Yep," she said. "But not this time."

"Then who picked it?"

"The client!" she said triumphantly. "In fact, our engineers recommended against it. They'd seen it used in some other applications, and it just wasn't good quality. It should never have been used—especially on a multistory building.

"But it turns out—and this is the smoking gun—there was a family connection between the client and the company that makes the brick. I found phone calls, a clear paper trail, and connected the dots. When I showed it to them, they had to admit it. We nailed 'em."

Henry nodded, impressed. "So the client was more interested in throwing business to this company than he was in the quality of the building?"

"That's right," she said. "And the thing that gets me is, they knew all that, but they were still trying to hang us for it and let us write that big settlement check. We couldn't let that stand. It was their call, their responsibility."

He loved seeing her excited about what she did. But he still had to poke a little. "So, you kinda hit a home run there, huh?" he asked.

"Yeah," she bragged. "I kinda did. I made myself, and the company, look good."

"So . . . I guess we won't be doing any more work for this client," Henry said. "When you nail their hide to the wall like that, they don't exactly come rushing back to hire you the next time they need a building."

Ella glared at him. "Thanks," she said. "Way to throw a cloud into my silver lining."

"Hey, I'm messing with you!" he said. "Seriously. I'm proud of you. Really. I'm sure we don't need their business anyway."

"No!" she said, animated again. "No, we don't! We don't need clients we have to be codefendants with, because of their stupid choices that keep us from doing our job." It was a glimpse of what it might feel like to face Ella in a courtroom. "We don't need clients who pressure us into bad decisions, then try to make us take the fall."

After a moment, she added, "Honestly, we probably did have maybe 20 percent liability. But after I showed them what I found, they owned it."

After another brief silence, she spoke again.

"And you know what, Henry? I'm still the new kid on this block. I'm really jazzed about this one. I needed a win, to feel like I was earning my keep. It would be nice if you could just cheer for me and let it go at that."

"I was kidding!" he pleaded. "Ella, I'm your biggest fan! Seriously, if you didn't already have a big office, I bet they'd give you one. Maybe they'll give you a raise!"

"I'm fine," she said. "Office-wise and pay-wise. I just want to be worth it. And I want my . . . I want you to support me."

"Of course!" he said. Then he paused, suddenly intrigued. "Wait, your what?"

"You," she said.

"But I'm your what?" he pressed. Now she was on the witness stand.

"My very own personal Henry—that's what you are," she said, tousling his hair as he drove up the entry ramp onto Interstate 30, going west. She reached out and took his hand, gave it a squeeze, and held on. He was certain she had been about to say "boyfriend."

He couldn't stop grinning as they drove in silence for a few minutes while she checked her phone. Then suddenly, she yelped.

"Henry! I forgot to ask! What did you find? Did you find Dottie?"

He heaved a big sigh as eighteen-wheelers blotted out the horizon.

"No," he said. "That's what bothers me."

"What do you mean?"

"She was the valedictorian, smart, beautiful, articulate—and she just dropped off the face of the earth after graduation," he said. "She was accepted into an advanced program at UT-Austin, but I can't find her there. All I know is, she left Thurston and never came back."

"Well, that's not unusual, is it?"

"Maybe not," he admitted. "But I feel like she'd pop up somewhere. This kid had a bright future. And I can't find anything, anywhere, after graduation night."

**Thurston: 1969**

Arnie was not having a good night. First, there was boring graduation with boring speeches—although it had been funny seeing Mel's papers flutter across the field. Dottie's speech was okay, although she referenced a book he'd never heard of and talked about a magic ring.

His mom had embarrassed him in front of everybody. Then Dottie flat-out turned him down, also in front of everybody. When his mom started walking home, he decided to just let her go.

After a while, everybody drifted away and he found himself alone at the football field where he'd been a star just a few months ago. He felt like a nobody, mad at his mom, mad at Dottie, mad at the world. He trudged out to the pickup, not knowing where to go.

There was, of course, no party on the mesa. He had just been trying to get Dottie alone. He kicked his feet in the gravel in the parking lot, climbed up into the old truck, and slammed the door. He cranked up some music and just sat there for a minute.

Finally, he stomped the clutch, threw it in reverse, tossing gravel, then slipped it into drive and headed out of the parking lot. He wasn't sure where he was going, but he knew it wasn't home. He saw a girl standing beside the gate. As he got closer, he could see it was Sherry.

"Well," he muttered to himself. "Maybe this is the consolation prize."

He slowed down, turned the radio down, and grinned a big, cheesy grin through the open window as she approached.

"Where you headed, young lady?" he asked.

"Just walking home, I guess," she said, smiling through the open passenger window. "Nothin' goin' on that I can see."

"I could give you a ride," he said.

"A ride where?"

"Pretty much anywhere you want to go, doll," he said. "The night's just getting started."

She smiled. "Sounds good to me!" she said as she climbed in, looking like she'd just won the lottery. She scooted straight over to the middle and Arnie put his massive arm on the seat-back behind her. It was the girlfriend position—a place he'd always reserved for Dottie. He thought of his and Dottie's "date" with her hugging the door, as far away from him as she could get. This was more like it. He cranked the radio back up.

"Hey Arnie! Did you get your senior ring?" Sherry asked.

"Sure!" he said, waving his hand in front of her.

"Wow, can I see it?"

"Yeah," he said. "Hell, you wanna be my girl? You can have it!"

Her eyes lit up as she took it from him.

"What do I do with it?" she said. "I can't wear it—it'd fall right off."

He grinned down at her.

"Them shorts look pretty tight," he said, leering. "I don't think it'd fall outta there."

She smiled primly and tucked it into a front pocket. "I'll get a necklace and put it on there as soon as I get home," she said, glowing that she was now Arnie's girl.

"Hey, since you're my girlfriend now, you wanna have some fun?" he asked. "Let's hit the liquor store, go up to the mesa and watch the storm roll in."

She looked at him nervously.

"Uh, okay," she said haltingly. "It's just, I ain't old enough to drink, Arnie."

He laughed. "Neither am I!" he said. "But they don't even ask to see my ID here! I think it's 'cause I'm kinda big."

"Okay, but . . . I've never had beer or anything like that. I'm just not sure—"

"That's okay, doll!" he said, trying to ease her mind. "You don't mind if I get a beer, do you?"

"I don't guess so," she said, relaxing a little. "Maybe one won't hurt."

"That's my girlfriend!" he whooped. "This is graduation night! We're going to get us a six-pack and go up to the mesa, and we're going to drink it together! Maybe we'll watch the sun come up."

Sherry was suddenly uneasy at the thought of spending the night with him. But this was what she had been dreaming of: in the pickup with Arnie, his date on graduation night, and now his girlfriend. His arm dropped from the back of the seat onto her shoulders as he drove. It was heavy, but she endured it without a word.

He drove fast, getting out on the highway and heading for the liquor store just over the county line. The music blared, and he started singing along.

As he drove, Arnie's hand slid off her shoulders and rested on her leg. He sang, badly. The nagging voice in her head would not be quiet. His hand slid up her leg and reflexively, she grabbed it.

He put his hand back on the wheel but stopped singing. When he turned into the store's parking lot he skidded to a stop in the gravel and turned to her. There was a look on his face she'd only seen once before—the day the yearbooks were delivered, after Dottie eluded him in the window of that classroom.

"Listen, babe," he said. "You got in with me. Nobody put a gun to your head. This is my graduation night, y'understand? I'm getting some beer, and I'm gonna party tonight, with you or somebody else. When I come out of that store, if you ain't in the mood to be with me tonight, I don't wanna see you sittin' here in this truck. You got that?"

She didn't answer. He stepped out, slamming the door so hard the pickup shook. She watched him walk into the store and knew she didn't have much time. Being with Arnie was all she'd wanted since she came to Thurston. If he loved her, maybe this was where she was supposed to be. But this didn't feel like love. Through the store window, she could see him standing at the counter, his back to her, a six-pack in his hand.

When Arnie came out of the store and climbed into the cab, she was gone.

"Well, there's my answer," he said, and pounded his fist into the dashboard. He set the six-pack on the seat where she'd been, took a deep breath, and decided it was good riddance. She wasn't the one he wanted in that seat anyway. He started the engine, grabbed a can of beer, opened it, then reached up and slid open the glass window behind the seat so he could toss the empty cans into the pickup bed the way all the cowboys did.

He wasn't sure of his next move, but the truck seemed to know where it wanted to go. The sunlight was gone by the time he turned down the road in front of Dottie's house. There was a light breeze, and the smell of rain hinted that a storm was coming.

Arnie squinted, slowing the truck to a complete stop. He could see someone—a girl—walking down the middle of the road, a silhouette in the dusk. As he got closer, he could see it was Dottie. Finally, she drew up beside him.

"You lost, young lady?" he said with a smirk.

"You followed me home?"

"Uh . . ." he stammered, the smirk gone. "I was just out driving around, that's all. I saw you walking and just wanted to . . . make sure you got home okay."

"Yeah, right," she said, her hand on the door handle. "I live right back there. I can go home anytime I want. I just had a huge fight with my mother—about you!"

"Well," he said, "here I am. What's it gonna be?"

She took a deep breath. She didn't want to be with Arnie, but her only alternative was to go home and be with her mom. She pulled the handle. As she climbed in she saw the six-pack, and his face broke into that big scary grin. She hugged the passenger door, and in case her body language wasn't clear, she spoke.

"Arnie, you need to understand nothing is going to happen between us tonight, or ever. I'll go to your party, but I'm not staying late," she said. "I'll walk around and say hi to people, but when I get ready to go, you've got to take me home. Got it?"

"Got it!" he said. The grin just got bigger.

"I'm serious!" she said. "I'm not your date, and I'm not staying out half the night. If you don't want to take me home, I'll get somebody else to."

"Whatever you want, doll." He had a smirk on his face she'd never seen before.

"And don't call me doll," she said.

Arnie drove under the overpass and out toward the mesa. Lightning flashed as the storm drew closer. Dottie finally broke the silence.

"So, the party's up on the top of the mesa?" she asked.

"Yeah," he said. "It's near where my mom lived when I was born, before she, you know, got the building and we moved in there."

"So your mother owns the mesa, too?"

"I guess," he said. "I don't know. She owns a lot of stuff. She don't tell me a lot about her business."

"You ought to ask her," Dottie said. "It's all going to be yours someday."

Arnie didn't say anything for a long time. Finally, he said, "I don't think so."

"What do you mean?" she asked. "Of course it will. You're her only relative. You're the one who gets everything when she, you know, dies. Someday."

As familiar as Dottie was with death, it seemed like Arnie had never entertained the idea that his mother would die. Dottie could tell from the emotions flashing across his face that she'd touched a nerve. She reminded herself that for Arnie, she had to keep it simple.

"It's no big deal, Arnie," she said. "I'm sure your mom is going to be around for a long, long time. She was really young when you were born, so—"

"Okay, let's just *shut up* about my mom, okay?" he yelled. "I don't want to spend my graduation night talkin' about my mom. I don't want nothin' from her, and you know what? It'd be fine with me if she died tonight! I'm tired of her tellin' me what to do all the time, like I ain't a man! I don't want her truck, or her building, her land, nothin'!

"I'm a man!" he said emphatically. "I don't need her."

He pounded on the steering wheel as he drove, his fists clenched. Dottie was taken aback.

Just then they went through the gate, bounced across a cattle guard, and started up the road to the mesa. She heard thunder growing closer. Other than the flashes of lightning, there was no light at the gate, no cars on the road, no other activity she could see. And no sign of a party.

"I'm . . . sorry, Arnie," she said. "I didn't mean to—"

"Seriously, just shut up now, Dottie," he said, looking straight ahead. "I'm tired of all this talkin' crap. It makes my head hurt."

She kept silent as they wound up the road, past the oil tanks and the pumpjacks, past the old barn and toward the top of the flat hill. There was no one else around.

"I just . . . where are the people, Arnie?" she asked softly.

He didn't say anything. His hands were glued to the wheel and his eyes were fixed on the winding caliche road. Raindrops began to patter on the windshield.

"Arnie!" she said, louder. "Where's the party? I don't see anybody."

In a quiet voice, eyes forward and hands on the wheel, he replied, "We're the party, Dottie. Me and you. This is a pry . . . it's a private party."

She reached for the door handle, but his hand came across and grabbed her wrist. With his big right arm, he held onto her while his left hand held the wheel. He sped up, even though the road was winding and rough. Bigger raindrops pelted the windshield and the roof of the cab.

"Arnie!" she yelled. "Let go of my arm. Take me home! I'm not doing this!"

"Not doin' what?" he said, glaring at her. "Not goin' out with me? Not bein' seen with me? Not partyin' with me? You know what? I think you are!"

She began pummeling his arm with her free hand as he drove, causing him to swerve all over the potholed road. A moment later the truck topped the mesa, and he cut the wheel hard and slammed on the brakes. Dottie's head hit the side window and she sat, stunned, still trying to tug her hand away from his viselike grip.

"Arnie, ow!" she moaned. "You're hurting my arm."

It didn't appear he had any intention of letting go.

He killed the engine, stomped the parking brake, and turned to her. Rain was pouring, little drops splashing in through the open back sliding window. His intent was obvious. Dottie shook her head, cleared her mind, and remembered: he had the size and strength, but she had the brains. She'd always been able to get him to do what she wanted, just by pushing the right buttons. She would have to be quick.

"Arnie, let go!" she said.

"I thought I told you to shut up," he growled, tightening his bruising grip.

"You did," she said. "But I know you didn't mean it. And I know you don't want to hurt me. Ow! Arnie, I know . . . you love me."

Lightning flashed and a gust of wind shook the truck, but the menacing behemoth in the seat beside her was still looking forward, downward. She saw his face soften. It was working.

"Let's talk, Arnie. It's raining. It's graduation night, and we're spending it together—talking. Then you can take me home."

He held onto her wrist.

"Arnie!" she said. "You're hurting my wrist! Let me go, okay? I'm not going to run. It's really starting to come down out there. Let's just talk for a minute. C'mon . . ."

He relaxed his grip. Finally, he began to speak.

"Dottie, I do . . . I love you. I've always loved you. There's never going to be nobody else for me . . ."

In that instant, she twisted her arm free and pulled the door handle. Another gust of wind shook the truck as Dottie opened the door, kicked against the floorboard, and launched herself out. Her eyes fixed on him, she stepped off into . . . nothing.

Arnie had stopped on the very edge of the mesa. On his side the flat, level terrain stretched out. But on the passenger side, the tires were almost off the road. Below her was a steep drop of at least five hundred feet—essentially a cliff, with only a few outcropping ledges. Grasping for the door handle, she turned back to look at him, etching her face into his memory forever, a look of terror and disbelief and sadness.

He lunged across the seat to grab her, but it was too late. Her hand released and a gust of wind shook the truck. He heard a scream as she disappeared.

"Dottie! Dottie!" he yelled, diving after her and almost falling himself. Instead, he held onto the door and peered down into the darkness. Lightning flashes illuminated her fall in macabre snapshots as she bounced like a rag doll down the steep slope, tumbling all the way to the bottom. When she finally came to a stop, the strobe flashes of lightning revealed her form deathly still at the bottom of the canyon.

His scream was lost in the night as the rain continued raging.

**Fort Worth: 2015**

Henry had the woman of his dreams right beside him, but he couldn't stop thinking about Dottie. He was truly obsessed. He had read her journal, looked through her yearbooks. He even knew the backstory behind "Thanatopsis." He knew about her dad, her mom, her brother, and her concerns about Arnie.

He glanced over at Ella, who was watching the road.

"I wish we knew where Dottie is," he said. "I was really looking forward to meeting her, returning all that stuff, learning how her life had gone. I just know she did something noteworthy—she had so much going for her. She had it all . . ."

"Okay, Henry," Ella said. "I might actually be a little jealous."

"Hey, if I'd known her in 1969 I'm sure I would have been head-over-heels," he said, laughing. "But I would have been one more face in a big crowd—just like the one around you."

They drove on in silence for a while.

"I can't help thinking something happened, Ella. People like her don't just disappear. She would have been on the honor roll, joined a sorority, graduated—she would have made the hometown paper a dozen times while she was in college."

"But Thurston didn't have a newspaper," Ella pointed out.

"Loganville did."

"But she's not a Loganville girl—she's a Thurston girl. The college probably didn't send her stuff to the *Loganville Ledger*. And when girls get married, their names change, and it gets harder to track them."

"Y'know, you're right," Henry said. "UT is so big, and they were always one of the worst about sending news releases. We got stuff from the small colleges all the time—they wanted the ink—but UT couldn't have cared less. Most of their dorms had more people than Logan County."

"We can't request her transcript, but I think we can find out if she was enrolled," Ella mused. "You didn't find anything in the *Star-Telegram*?"

"Nope," he said. "I found her brother's and dad's obituaries, but nothing on her."

Ella was silent for a while. Finally, she spoke softly.

"So what's in her journal, Henry? Something scary?"

He pointed to his briefcase. She grabbed it, shuffled through the papers and pulled out the small book.

"I bookmarked the parts where she mentions Arnie," Henry said. "That last entry especially."

Ella found the marker and began reading.

"Read it out loud," Henry urged. "Start right there." He pointed to a paragraph.

"You just keep your eyes on the highway, buddy," Ella scolded, pulling the book away from him. She started reading.

*Arnie cornered me in a classroom yesterday. He said we were meant to be together because we played together as kids. I can't think of anything less appealing. He even said he loved me. I was able to slide across a desk and get away, and I chewed him out good. He's scary big, but he's just kind of a simpleton.*

*He keeps talking about this party he wants me to come to, on Saturday night after graduation, up on the mesa where he and his mom used to live. It sounds creepy. There's probably going to be all kinds of stuff going on. As weird as it sounds, I'd rather spend the time with my mom. I don't know if he's really even having a party. I haven't heard anyone else mention it.*

*His mom and my mom are such good friends, and I think when I'm gone, my mom will need a friend. I don't want to burn that bridge for her, but going to a party with Arnie is a high price to pay. I want my mom to live again, but Arnie has really started to creep me out. I'm going to stay away from him.*

Ella hummed contemplatively. "That looks bad," she said. "It isn't evidence of foul play, though, unless we find a body or someone files a missing person report. She may have just left and never come back. She said in the journal that was what she wanted to do."

"Yeah," Henry said. "There are a lot of questions, though, right? Was there a party? If so, wouldn't there have been witnesses? Surely if she went out with him, someone must have seen them together."

Ella sat in silence for a long time. Henry could tell her mind was spinning.

"That was nearly fifty years ago, Henry," she said. "There's no statute of limitations on murder, but there's nothing here to make Arnie anything more than a person of interest. And this little town has dried up. Finding a witness would be a huge challenge."

"You think we should keep going with this?" Henry asked, seriously. He could see her wheels were turning.

"We're about to cross a line, Ella," he continued. "This is beyond going to storage unit auctions and having fun. We're about to get involved in the lives of real people who may have good reason not to want anyone snooping around."

"This is still just conjecture," she said. "I agree it's not just fun anymore, but we can't walk away now—we've come too far. Let's see what we can find out. We found Evelyn. We may need to find Arnie, and we sure need to find Dottie.

"Right now, all we know is a girl fifty years ago was nervous about a boy coming on too strong, then she seems to have disappeared," Ella continued, as if summing up her case for the jury. "That doesn't mean somebody got murdered."

"Well, finding out more is why we're here," he said.

"Right," she agreed. "I want to hit that courthouse. There have to be some records on these people."

"The newspaper may have something too," Henry said. "I want a look at their morgue."

"A newspaper keeps a morgue?" she asked, aghast.

He laughed. "Not bodies in drawers. The morgue is the newspaper's archives—bound volumes of back issues. But maybe I can find out where the bodies are buried."

"Yeah," Ella said, relieved. "Maybe there's an old-timer who remembers this story."

They drove on, deep in thought, until they saw the exit sign for Thurston. It was only about a mile off the highway; they could already see the top of the C&C building. Henry looked over at Ella. Their eyes met; she nodded and without a word, he took the exit. Both of them had driven past Thurston dozens of times, but now it was the pivot point of a story they were just starting to uncover.

"A ghost town looks different when you know the ghosts, huh?" he said.

Ella gave a little shiver, then glanced again at Dottie's journal. They were at a stop sign when she shut the book and looked at him, her dark eyes intense.

"Henry, let's not tell anybody about this, okay?" She stuffed the journal back into his bag.

"Okay," he answered. "Why?"

"If this is an unsolved murder, it was buried a long time ago," she said. "We don't want to breeze into town, two city people, two outsiders, looking to dig it all up. We don't know who to trust. That old lady," she tilted her head toward the C&C building, "she's been here since before dirt. She probably has a lot of friends, and we have no idea who they are."

"Yeah, but we've got to go see her, right?" he asked.

"Eventually," Ella said. "It may depend on what we learn on this trip. She may have the answers, but she may not be happy to hear the questions."

As Ella was speaking, they drove into the shadow of the big, ghostly building; it loomed above them like a silent ship. The Abbott's sign was still there, and as they drove by, they could see the historical marker. Henry wheeled into a parking spot and they both jumped out to read it. Ella finished first and walked up to peer into one of the windows. There was no light and no movement, but she could make out the fixtures of a long-dead department store.

There was no sign of life on any of the streets. Thurston was truly a ghost town.

They both did a little more window-peering before they got back in the car. Without a word, Henry backed out, turned around in the big empty street, and headed back to the highway.

Neither of them saw the woman watching through a slit in the curtains over a darkened window on the top floor.

* * *

It was only eight miles to Loganville, a town of about twenty-five hundred where the courthouse, the school, and what little commerce the county had was centered. It was a desperately charming little town trying to capitalize on its history with a quaint old square and a restored theater. A closed-down Walmart had been converted into a community college, and the square featured a cafe where Henry was certain the waitress would call him "honey."

He parked next to the courthouse, right across from the *Ledger* office. It looked open, but on a Friday, there was probably just one person there. His best-case scenario was to walk in and find the old editor sitting at a roll-top desk, the guy who'd been there more than fifty years and remembered the Sinclair case in vivid detail. But most likely, that person was dead, had moved away long ago, or was beyond remembering anything.

Henry was still staring at the newspaper office when Ella opened her door, then reached back, smiled, and gave him a pat on the leg before she got out.

"See you later," she said. "I'm going to do some courthouse digging. Remember to play it close to the vest! And don't get lost, Henry-baby."

"You either!" he said just before the door closed. He watched her walk up the courthouse steps. "Don't *you* ever get lost," he said under his breath.

**Thurston: 1969**

Arnie buried his head in the seat Dottie had just vacated, moaning "No! No! No!" as if he could erase what had just happened. When he finally looked up, the only sound was the driving rain and almost constant thunder. In the pauses, he could hear the lazy *pop-popping* of the motors on the pumpjacks.

Sitting up, he decided he had to go get her. Maybe it wasn't as bad as it looked. Maybe she would be okay. He slid out the driver's side door and stumbled around behind the truck, quickly soaked by the driving rain. He stopped at the edge and looked down. The drop-off was so close he couldn't walk to the passenger-side door. It was a wonder the truck hadn't slid off. Unable to walk down the route she'd fallen without falling himself, he set off back down the road, looking for a place to cut over. Finally, about halfway down, he found one and headed off-road as the rain made walking ever more treacherous.

He staggered across and down, making his own switchback route through exposed boulders, loose rocks, and scrubby yucca and briar. He slipped and slid, getting scratched bloody, working his way down to where he thought she was. The rain in the darkness was blinding. Once or twice, he almost lost his balance and was tempted to let himself just tumble on down. But he had to find Dottie.

He spotted her near the bottom, her blouse illuminated by a flash of lightning through the rain. She was not moving. He approached fearfully and, for only the second time in his life, saw death. But this was no ancient skeleton—this was the beautiful girl who only moments ago had been beside him, the girl he'd loved as long as he could remember. He fell to his knees.

She lay face-down, her head pointing down the hill, her body twisted at unnatural angles. He could see her neck was broken. He gently turned her over and gasped. Her delicate face was battered and bloody, unrecognizable, her blonde hair tangled and matted with mud and blood. He turned away and vomited. Turning back, he reached to pick her up, and it felt as if her body was held together only by her clothing. She was completely and irrevocably broken.

He carried her in front of him, her weight almost nothing in his big arms. He trudged back to the road and then up toward his truck, walking for what seemed like an eternity as the rain pelted his face. He half-cried, half-groaned all the way up, panting. When he reached the pickup, he stood there, not knowing what to do. Finally, with the rain whipping down in sheets, he knelt and laid her gently on the ground, then stood and dropped the tailgate.

He looked around, and in a flash of lightning spotted a blue tarp caught on a clump of yucca. He went over and got it, then came back and gently scooted her broken body onto it, gasping for breath, nearly drowning in rain and regret. He wrapped her tightly, scooped the bundle into his arms, and placed her on the tailgate. He gently slid her in, tucking the edges of the tarp beneath her. He stood back and raised the tailgate slowly until the latch clicked.

Then he fell to his knees in the wet caliche, leaning on the back bumper as if he were kneeling at an altar, sobbing as the rain poured.

* * *

Evelyn was still angry when she got home. She let herself in and skipped the elevator, walking all the way back upstairs in an effort to settle her nerves. Several times on the way up she had to stop and lean against the wall. When she finally reached the top, it hit her that she was about to be alone. She felt the sadness of a lifetime, a river of sadness flowing from the past into the future.

She was sitting at the table, having a cup of tea, when she heard Arnie trudging up the stairs, his steps slow and heavy. The squishing sound told her his shoes were wet. She was prepared to unleash her anger on him, but when he opened the door he stood there, dripping wet, covered in white caliche mud, blood, and scratches. He appeared ready to collapse. Evelyn's mothering instinct quickly took over.

"Arnold! Baby! What happened?" she said, rushing to him. He held up his hand to ward off her affection. "Did you have a wreck? Good Lord, boy! You look like you got in a fight with a tree full of mountain lions."

"Mama," he began, but his voice broke immediately, and he bowed his head.

"What it is?" she said, reaching to stroke his hair. He pushed her hand away.

"Mama, I'm in troub—we got trouble," he said. "It's . . ." His face, streaked with mud, crumpled. "Mama, it's Dottie. She fell. Up at the mesa. She fell a long way. She's—"

"What? Where is she? Is she hurt? Bring her in! We got to take care of her!" She tried to get past him, but he blocked her.

"She's dead, Mama."

Evelyn's mind would not accept the words.

"Let's just get her inside," she said, nervous energy surging. She tried again to push her way past him. "Let's get her some help. Let's call the doctor. We can—"

"We can't do *nothing*, Mama!" Arnie half-yelled, filling the doorway. "She's gone! She fell over the side and . . . she rolled all the way down." He started crying again. "I picked her up, Mama. She's broken. She's all broken."

Evelyn looked at the hulking, wet figure before her, then turned slowly and walked back to the table. Instead of sitting, she went to her knees. She knelt there for a long moment, seething between anger and sorrow as Arnie stood dripping. Finally, she rose and turned back to her son.

"Where is she?" she said firmly, although her voice trembled.

"She's in the back of the pickup," he said. "I wrapped her up in a tarp. She's . . ." His face crumpled again. "She's out there in the rain, Mama."

Evelyn's tears welled up and her voice broke. "Where'd you park?"

"Just out in front," he said, sniffling.

Her mind was racing. "You know where the delivery door is, down around back?"

"Yeah," he said. "What are—"

"Shut up," she cut him off. "Drive around there and back up to the door. I'll go down and open it, and you can bring her into the basement."

He looked up at her, puzzled.

"The basement? What are we—"

"Do what I say, boy!" she said, almost sobbing. "Did her mama see you?"

"No," he said. "I was just drivin' by and she was walkin' down the road."

"Nobody saw y'all?"

"No, Mama. We was just goin' up to the mesa to, y'know, talk. Graduation night, you feel like talkin' and stuff, and then she . . ." He started crying again.

Evelyn's mind started playing out every scenario, every question. If Dottie was truly dead, Mary had now lost everyone. If word of this got out, Arnie's life was over, too. He said she fell . . . but there were no witnesses, and he'd moved her. It would be hard to explain to the sheriff what he and Dottie were doing up there in the rain. Being her son would not help him this time.

"Go!" she barked. He turned and headed down the stairs. She stopped at a desk by the door, grabbed a flashlight and a ring of keys, hesitated, then picked up her emergency roll of $20 bills. Suddenly she was overcome by emotion and leaned over, sobbing out loud, her tears tapping on the desk. By the time she could stand, Arnie was out the door. She headed downstairs to the dark basement, using only the flashlight as she crossed the dirt floor to the roll-up door that hadn't been opened for years. She tucked the flashlight under her arm and fumbled the key into the padlock, hands shaking. When she yanked up the door, Arnie had backed the pickup so close it nearly brushed the bumper as it slid up.

Arnie came around and dropped the tailgate, and they looked together at the small bundle wrapped in the blue plastic tarp. He picked it up gently and turned around, crying again as he stood in the pouring rain.

Evelyn fought back tears, but quickly slipped back into emergency mode.

"Bring her on in here," she said. "Quick!" As soon as Arnie stepped in, she reached out and slammed the tailgate shut, stepped in and pulled the door back down. Arnie stood there with the broken girl in his arms. Evelyn pointed her flashlight down the ramp.

"Go on!" she ordered. "There ain't any lights. We've got to be quick."

Arnie started down, then nearly fell as he lurched halfway around.

"What are we gonna do, Mama?"

"We're . . ." She choked on the words. "We are gonna give this poor girl a proper resting place."

**Loganville: 2015**

The bell on the front door dinged when Henry walked into the *Ledger* office. He saw no one and heard no activity anywhere in the small building. Standing at the counter, he looked around. Several framed front pages were displayed on one wall and on the other were a few award plaques, none of them hanging straight. A small bronze newsboy figurine sat on the counter along with several signs about rates, deadlines, and returned checks. There was a bell, upon which he finally banged, twice.

A woman's voice called out from somewhere in the back.

"Be with you in a minute! I'm trying to get this dang toilet to stop running!"

"No problem," Henry called out. "Do what you need to do. I'm fine."

On the other side of the counter, in shelves that ran the length of one wall, he could see what he was looking for: the morgue. These bound volumes, usually one for each year, were the newspaper's archives, the official record of the community's history. It was a sacred trust, getting those papers trimmed and glued and bound in a big book so future generations—people like Henry—could come browse through them.

One of Henry's childhood friends had been the son of the newspaper's editor, and they had spent many happy hours exploring the old building, climbing on top of the big rolls of paper, hiding in the darkroom, finding caches of outdated equipment in forgotten closets. One day, they found the morgue. They started pulling out the big books and looking up their own birth dates, finding familiar names, then looking up historic dates like November 22, 1963, and December 7, 1941. They got a laugh out of stories about crops and weather, petty crimes and Kiwanis club programs, until the old man caught them and told them to leave the books alone.

Now most newspapers were preserving their issues digitally, in searchable databases. It was no surprise that the *Ledger* wasn't there yet, but Henry suddenly realized he liked those big old books: the way they felt, their smell. It took him back.

Just then an older lady emerged from the back, wiping her hands on a paper towel.

"I'm so sorry," she said, smiling. "Some emergencies just won't wait, so I guess customers have to! What can I do for you?"

Henry returned her smile. "No problem. I'm just chasing a little history from this area, and I wondered if I could get a look at your archives."

"Sure!" she said. "I see you've already spotted 'em. There's a table there. Just help yourself. But please handle them gently and don't put your fingers on 'em any more than you have to. If you need a copy, we'll try to balance it on the copier, but that's a little iffy . . ."

"Oh, I can just shoot a picture with my phone," Henry said. "And don't worry, I'm an old newspaper guy myself, so I'm used to dealing with these."

She lifted a section of the front counter and invited him back.

"If you don't mind me asking, what are you looking for?" she said. "I've been around here most of my life. Maybe I could help you."

"Oh . . ." Henry replied with an awkward laugh. "It's just a little hobby. I'm kind of a history buff, and this is kind of a fishing expedition. Thurston is interesting, huh?"

"Yes!" she said. "The 'ghost town.' Sounds like fun. Well, if you need any help, I'll be right over there," she said, pointing to a desk. "And if you know anything about fixing toilets, you're hired!"

He laughed. She sounded like exactly the kind of old-timer he was looking for, but he wanted to see what the books had to offer before he started picking her brain. He eyed the shelves. Years and months were printed on the spines, and the size of the volumes changed as the paper got smaller over the years.

The 1969 volume was thick. *Nice year,* he thought as he pulled it out and laid it on the table. He felt a little rush of excitement as he began to leaf through the neatly trimmed pages, front to back, working his way to May. Finally, he found a front-page story in May announcing the graduation schedules for Loganville, Thurston, and Budlong. A week later, there were feature stories about the valedictorians and salutatorians of each class.

*These guys did a good job covering the county,* he thought. Sure enough, when he turned a page, there was Dorothy, sitting at a desk beside salutatorian Mel Davis, smiling.

Henry had seen all the yearbook photos of Dottie, but seeing her in the newspaper had a different impact—proof of life. Even in the yellowed newsprint, he could see the intelligence in her face. But he also saw a sadness. The well-written story focused on her school activities and touched briefly on the tragedies she'd experienced. He learned a few things, fleshing out a character he already felt he knew well.

The next week, the special graduation section ran, with each school getting a few pages for photos and thumbnail biographies of the graduates. There were small ads congratulating them, wishing them well. He remembered the same thing in his hometown paper, and the *Glendale Gazette* and the *Covington Chronicle*. He flipped forward to the next issue, and there were photos of the ceremonies: seniors in billowing gowns, smiling, hugging, tossing their mortarboard hats in the air. In one, Dottie was making her valedictory speech at the Thurston football stadium, the evening light hitting her face, the wind blowing her hair back.

There were no stories about missing students.

From that point, he started reading through every page so he wouldn't miss what might be a small story. The next issue mentioned a big thunderstorm on graduation night. Power had been knocked out all over that part of Texas, and there'd been some flooding and hail damage. After that, headlines focused on summer reading programs at the library, the city swimming pool opening, and Little League all-stars. In mid-July, he found a column of boilerplate about who had enlisted in the military and spotted this item:

> *Arnold Chitwood, recent graduate of Thurston High School, has been accepted into the United States Marine Corps and reported to Camp Lejeune, North Carolina, on June 6. He is the son of Evelyn Chitwood of Thurston.*

Into September and all the way to the end of the year, there was nothing. No mysterious disappearance, no unsolved murder, no manhunt. Several times he looked up and caught the newspaper lady watching him. She seemed intensely curious as to what he was looking for.

**Thurston: 1969**

Evelyn's mind worked quickly. She directed Arnie to place Dottie's limp body on a ledge, high up under the edge of the building where the columns that supported it created a small niche. The area was closed in from the outside, above and below, and by columns on each end, spaced about eight feet apart. It would take only three or four courses of brick to seal the gap.

Arnie followed her directions in a daze. Dewley had taught him how to lay brick. He didn't have the right tools, but this didn't have to be pretty—just solid. He opened a sack of mortar, dumped about half of it into an old bucket, then got water by holding it out the door.

"What am I s'posed to mix it with, Mama?" he whined.

"Your hand!" Evelyn spat. "That's the only tool you need."

She began handing him bricks, until the broken figure in the blue tarp was hidden from view. A couple of courses later, Arnie pushed in the last of the mortar with his bleeding fingers, tightly sealing the tomb.

Evelyn reached into the pocket of her dress and gave him the bundle of bills. He'd sleep in the truck tonight—if he could sleep—and first thing in the morning he would go to the induction center and join the army. She was sure they would take him, a big, strapping eighteen-year-old who was probably about to be drafted anyway. Once they did, he was their problem.

"Listen, boy," she said as she squared up to hug him. "You don't tell anybody about this, you understand? Not a word, ever! Everything's going to be alright."

Then she squeezed him tight, patted him on the shoulder, and sent him off.

* * *

Evelyn banged the door down as Arnie drove away, then sat on the steps and let her tears flow at last, sobbing and gasping into the dark, empty space until she was cried out. Finally, sniffling and wiping her eyes, she stood, checked the basement one last time, and trudged back upstairs. More than once, she had to stop and lean against the wall to cry some more.

The idea of telling Mary, forcing her to deal with another loss, was more than she could bear. The only way to avoid that was for Mary to believe her daughter was still alive. Evelyn sat at her table, alone, fighting back tears and looking for a way to make that happen.

Even in 1969, downtown Thurston was deserted after dark. No one lived there but Evelyn and Arnie. Arnie told his mother he was sure Mary had not seen his truck. As Evelyn sat and pondered it all, pieces of the puzzle began to click into place.

The stage was perfectly set for Dottie to have run away: she'd graduated, made her speech, and said goodbye. She'd had a big fight with her mother, and they had parted in anger. For all Mary knew, she actually had run away.

Evelyn just had to convince Mary that Dottie was still running.

The storm moved on, and by the time the Sunday morning light filtered through the windows of Evelyn's upper floor, she had a plan.

She knew that no matter what had happened, Mary would not miss church. She bathed and dressed, got in her car, and went to church herself. Mary's car was parked in its usual spot. Evelyn went in and mingled a little in the foyer, accepting an announcement sheet from the elderly deacon at the door. When services began, she slipped into a back pew near the side exit so she wouldn't have to see him again. As soon as the first prayer started and everyone's head was bowed, she quietly edged out and headed for the parking lot.

Evelyn knew Mary did not lock her doors. She parked a good distance away and picked her way down to the creek that ran through everyone's backyard. The water was still flowing swiftly from last night's rain, but she stayed to the side and walked through the mud to Mary's back porch. She slipped her muddy shoes off, let herself in, and headed straight for Dottie's room, stepping softly with stockinged feet.

On the top shelf of the closet, she saw a suitcase.

Stretching on her tiptoes, Evelyn got it down and laid it open on the bed, then began taking outfits off their hangers and stuffing them in. She went through all the dresser drawers, grabbing socks, bras, and panties, then t-shirts, shorts, and blouses, glad it was a big suitcase. Suddenly it hit her: shoes. She looked in the closet, found several pairs, and stuffed them in.

Something else clicked, and she grabbed the shoes that looked the most worn, hurried to the back door, and put them on. She stepped off into a puddle, walked around enough to get them thoroughly muddy, then walked back in, leaving footprints down the hallway and all over Dottie's room. She went down the hall to the bathroom too, grabbed Dottie's toothbrush and other essential items, and laid them on top of the clothes.

She was about to close the suitcase when she took one last look around the room. What else would Dottie grab if she were leaving in a hurry and not planning to return? Her eye went to the neatly ordered desk. The shelf above it was stacked with novels, books of poetry, and yearbooks. Dottie would have taken books. She got them all and laid them on top of the clothes. She was just about to close the suitcase when she spotted a small, leather-bound journal, hand-lettered on the front. She grabbed it and stuffed it into a pocket inside the suitcase, then closed it and lugged it back down the hallway.

Evelyn stepped out onto the back porch, picked up her shoes in one hand, and trudged away in Dottie's muddy shoes, carrying the heavy bag through the mud, through the creek bed, and back to her car. She put the suitcase in the trunk and took a rag she kept there, using it to wipe every speck of mud off her legs and feet. She slipped back into her own shoes and tossed Dottie's muddy sneakers into the trunk.

She was back in her pew before the sermon was over. She could see Mary, several rows up, head bowed as she listened.

"Let not your heart be troubled," the pastor said, quoting John 14. "In my Father's house are many mansions; if it were not so, I would have told you. I go to prepare a place for you. And if I go and prepare a place for you, I will come again, and receive you unto myself; that where I am, there ye may be also."

"Let not your heart be troubled," Evelyn prayed silently, her dark eyes focused on the back of Mary's head. After the closing prayer, she made it a point to find her friend, smile, and shake her hand before she headed home, choking back tears.

* * *

Mary was dismayed, but not surprised, when she got home and saw the muddy footprints in Dottie's ransacked bedroom. It made perfect sense that her daughter had run away after their big fight. Mary blamed herself. She had been so lost in her own sorrow the past year that Dottie had been virtually on her own. With graduation and a quick start to summer school, she hadn't thought about how much pressure her daughter had been under.

Part of her wondered if Dottie had planned this in advance, but she quickly dismissed the thought. Her daughter was smart, not devious. Their argument was spontaneous. And as she thought back to the quarrel, Mary wondered if maybe she was wrong about Arnie. She only knew him through his mother; Dottie had been around him in school for twelve years.

Mary was sure she'd heard a car door slam after Dottie walked out of sight. It was probably someone who happened to be going by, who knew Dottie and didn't want her walking in the rain. Obviously, someone had brought her by the house this morning to get her things. She could ask Evelyn, but after the way Dottie talked about Arnie, it was unlikely he knew anything. Dottie had probably gotten a ride from a neighbor, or one of the other boys who worshipped her.

Mary was worried, but she knew Dottie would be okay; she had a good head on her shoulders and wouldn't do anything to jeopardize her bright future. She was about to leave home anyway, and she'd made it clear she did not want to drive Ted's car. Mary expected to hear from her in a few days, after emotions cooled down. She told herself Dottie was fine.

Reporting Dottie's disappearance to the sheriff never crossed her mind.

**Loganville: 2015**

Ella was sitting in the car when Henry crossed the street and opened the driver's side door. "What did you find out?" he asked as she pored over her notes.

"You go first," she said.

"Okay," he said, sliding into the seat and pulling the door shut.

"Not much. The paper covered the graduation, and Dottie spoke. She looked very nice."

"A 1960s hottie?" Ella asked sarcastically.

"More like a 1950s movie star. Old-fashioned. Wholesome. Think Donna Reed. But of course, not my type." Henry grinned. "May I go on?"

"Sure," Ella muttered. "That's a big relief."

"What?" Henry asked.

"Knowing 'wholesome' isn't your type," she said, deadpan.

Henry couldn't think of a comeback that wouldn't get him in trouble, so he continued.

"There are no more stories on Dottie. Nothing to indicate that anything unusual happened on graduation night. There was a big storm, but it held off until after the ceremony."

"Might've rained out Arnie's little party," Ella said. "Or turned it into a one-on-one affair."

"I can't see her going anywhere with him, after what she wrote," Henry said.

Ella sat for a moment.

"Not willingly," she said.

"Oh, and he joined the Marines," Henry added. "Went to Vietnam. There's nothing more about him after that, either." He paused. "So, what about you, Miss Lawyer?"

"I found a couple of interesting tidbits," she said, waving the documents she had been reading. "I asked for birth and death certificates for everybody named Chitwood and Sinclair, and guess what? Evelyn's father's death certificate and Arnie's birth certificate were filed on the same date."

"Whoa! That's weird!" Henry said.

"It said the old man died from 'blunt force trauma and extensive internal injuries from an automobile accident,'" Ella said. "Our boy Arnie was apparently born in an ambulance. Looks like Evelyn's dad was driving her to the hospital and had a wreck on the way. They got Evelyn out of the car just in time to deliver the baby."

"Wow," Henry said. "That's some entry into the world. What else?

"Wellllll," she said, stringing it out for dramatic effect.

"Well what?" Henry half-yelled. "You're making me crazy!"

Ella grinned. "Well, our girl Evelyn doesn't own that old building anymore."

"She sold it?" Henry asked. "To who?"

"No, she didn't sell it—she let the county take it for back taxes."

"Get out! And she's still living there?"

"Yep," Ella said. "Apparently after the town died, she decided paying any taxes was too much. So she just let it go delinquent, and after a couple of years the county seized it. They put it up for sale on the courthouse steps—literally—and there were no bidders."

"Kinda like a storage auction," Henry said with an ironic laugh. "Only they raise the door and everybody just says, 'Nah,' and turns away."

"Exactly!" Ella said. "So the county owns it, technically. But apparently, the old lady plans to just keep on living there until it sells or they carry her out feet-first."

Henry pondered.

"I guess she takes care of it for them," he said. "Maybe she even pays a little rent. It's probably better than if it was just sitting there empty, right?"

"I'm sure," Ella said. "It's a weird deal, but who wants to evict an eighty-year-old woman from a building she owned for sixty years, that nobody wants, in a ghost town?"

Henry laughed. "Even if she is the richest woman in the county!"

"No place but Texas," Ella said.

It was lunchtime, so they decided to go sample some of Loganville's local cuisine. The waitress at the Pie Hole Cafe looked about the age of Henry's mother and called him "honey." The special of the day was meatloaf with turnip greens, lima beans, and mashed potatoes.

Henry opted for the chicken fried steak. Ella ordered a hamburger.

"Whoa!" Ella said after a sip of sweet tea. "I think I'll skip dessert for the next month."

Henry's dinner salad arrived quickly, and he offered to share it with her. She took a forkful of shredded lettuce soaked in ranch dressing.

"Yeah, salads probably aren't the house specialty," she said, chewing bravely. Once the main courses arrived, Ella returned to the subject of their visit.

"I want to look deeper into our boy Arnie," she said between French fries. "See if he made it home from the war, where he lived, what he did, if he got into any trouble with the law. I'll hit the district attorney's office. There's got to be something there."

"Can you do that after lunch?" Henry asked.

"Yes. And what will you be doing?"

"Maybe I can help you," he offered. "I don't think I'm ready to go back to the newspaper lady just yet. She's really curious, I can tell. I probably won't get by without an explanation."

Ella held up her hand, putting Henry on pause while she pondered.

"No, I think maybe you should go back to her," Ella said. "Why don't you just ask her about Evelyn? Don't tell her we know anything, just that we saw her name on the historic marker and were wondering if she's still around. Focus on her. If she and Evelyn are best buds, you'll find out. We'll keep the Dottie and Arnie questions to ourselves."

"Y'know, that's not a bad strategy," Henry said. "If I didn't know better, I'd think you question people for a living."

"Hey, it's a skill." She smiled modestly.

"I think the newspaper lady knows a lot and is dying to help me. I'll just have to pick her brain without tipping our hand."

"Do you need me to come question her?" Ella asked.

"No, counselor, I think I can handle it. If she turns out to be a hostile witness, I'll call in the big gun."

"Well, I'm here for you," she said with a grin. "It would be nice to talk to someone who knows Evelyn—or at least knows something about her—before we try to go and talk to her. Be careful, though."

They finished, paid the check, and went back to the car with renewed zeal. They parked in the same spot and headed back to the same places. Ella disappeared into the courthouse just as Henry tried the door on the *Ledger* office. It was locked. The sign in the window said they closed at noon. He sighed and was about to turn away when the door clicked and swung open.

"Oh, hey there!" she said. "Didn't expect to see you back this quick!"

"Well, if you're closed, I don't want to keep you," he said. "I just had a couple more things to look up . . . and maybe some questions you could help me with."

"No problem!" she said with delight. She held up her fingers about a half-inch apart. "I've been around here since the moon was only this big and there weren't any stars at all! If you need to know something about somebody, I can probably point you in the right direction."

She beckoned him in, clicked the lock shut behind him, and waved him to a chair. She took the seat next to him and beamed expectantly.

"Now, I'm Vivian, but you have to call me Viv. What can I help you with?"

* * *

Ella's visit to the county clerk's office that morning had created a small stir; they didn't get a lot of visitors. Even though she was dressed casually, Ella came across as professional just by knowing what she wanted and calling things by the right names. The clerks were happy to comply with her requests.

The atmosphere at the district clerk's office was different.

"What was that name again?" the clerk asked. "Do you have a case number?"

"Arnold Chitwood," Ella said. "I don't have a middle initial, or a specific case number, I'm just looking for the entire criminal file, or files, on this individual. Indictments, convictions, incarceration records, anything you've got."

The clerk glanced toward the back. "Let me go get my boss," she said apologetically.

Ella nodded, a little exasperated. A moment later the clerk came back, trailed by a middle-aged man, suit coat off, tie loosened.

"Hi," he said, fake smiling. "Now, what was it you were needing, sweetie?"

"Sweetie" shifted Ella into a witheringly formal demeanor.

"I'm requesting any and all criminal files on an Arnold Chitwood. These are public records, unless they've been sealed by a court order. The name is Ella Franklin. I'm an attorney, State Bar of Texas number 1-8-8-3—"

The official's smile faded instantly as he interrupted her recital.

"We'll need a written request, and it'll take us a few days to respond to—"

"I don't think so, Mr. . . ." she glanced at the plaque on the wall beside his office door. "Merrill. It doesn't really take days to walk over, pull open a drawer, and pick out a file, does it? I assume you have them alphabetized?"

"Yes, of course, but—" he stammered.

"And it certainly won't take me three days to contact the attorney general's office and file an open records request for this file and probably a few . . ." she looked around the office, " . . . thousand others."

"You don't have to be so—"

"Pushy? No, I don't." Ella fake-smiled, leaning on the counter. "This doesn't have to be a confrontation, Mr. Merrill. We're not adversaries. It's public information. The public owns it, and I'm a member of the public. You're the custodian of it. If you can have this nice young lady just lay these files on this counter, I'll go right over there and sit down quietly, see what I need to see, and you can go back to whatever you were doing. I'm sure you're very busy."

He stood there, arms crossed, and took a deep breath.

"Why do you want the files?" he asked.

Ella's smile evaporated and she leaned closer to him.

"Mr. Merrill, you're a district clerk for the state of Texas," she said softly. "Surely you know I don't have to explain or justify an open records request. It's been thoroughly litigated."

The word "litigated" was still hanging in the air as he spun and headed back to his office.

"Cindy, get her whatever she wants," he muttered to the clerk. "I'll be on a call."

Stifling a grin, the girl walked over to a cabinet, pulled open the top drawer, and took out several files. She walked over and laid them on the counter.

"These are just the felony cases," she said in a conspiratorial whisper. "If you want the misdemeanors, they're down the hall at the county attorney's office."

Ella smiled and thanked her, picked up the folders, and was about to head for the chair in the corner when she turned back.

"Is he that way on all the requests, or just this one?" she asked.

"That's just the way he is," she said. "But this guy . . ." she nodded toward the files Ella was holding, "his mother owns half the county. That's probably the call he's on right now."

Ella's smile faded.

"Seriously?"

"That would be my guess," the clerk said as her colleagues nodded.

"Hmmm," Ella said, resolving to skim the files quickly and get out of there. Based on the size of the stack, she had some work to do.

* * *

Across the street, Henry and Viv were already old friends.

"Let me tell you what I'm trying to do," he said. "We work for an architectural firm in Fort Worth, and we're fascinated with the old

C&C building in Thurston. I've done a little research myself, and apparently it was a real happenin' place back in the '30s and '40s and '50s. The store there—"

"Abbott's?"

"Yes, that's it," he said. "It shut down in . . ."

"1965," she said.

Henry had to laugh, but he continued playing dumb.

"Obviously you know something about it," he said.

Viv beamed, her expression telling Henry she knew all about the old building and was eager to fill him in. He knew the feeling. It was fun to be the expert.

"Well!" she leaned forward. "It's actually quite a story. It's on the historical marker, if you haven't looked yet, but I can give you the basics. It was built in 1905—even before my time!—by an old cattle rancher who wanted Thurston to be the hub of this area. He welcomed all the agricultural folks, buyers and sellers, to do their business there and save themselves a trip into Fort Worth. The train and the highway ran right through Thurston, and for years, it seemed like a great idea. A bank rented the first floor—didn't survive the Depression, though—and there was a hotel on the second floor, a pretty nice one. The third floor is where they smoked cigars, drank whiskey, argued about the price of cows and hogs and made deals."

She was obviously enjoying herself. Henry was happy to fill in some blanks.

"When Abbott's opened, the whole town really started hopping," Viv continued. "Even though it was the Depression, it was kind of a golden age for Thurston. That was where all the farmers and ranchers went when they 'went to town' and bought everything they needed.

"The old rancher died after the war, around '46 or '47, and his kids just wanted to sell the building. Eventually, the president of the bank across the street bought it. That bank never loaned anybody any money, so it was quite strong."

She talked him through the rise of Abbott's and the demise of the local cotton and cattle trade. Better highways after the war made the trip to Fort Worth less daunting, and farming changed in ways that made the cotton exchange obsolete. Cattlemen still used exchanges, but the one at the Fort Worth Stockyards was easy to get to, and there was a lot more action.

The top floor of the C&C fell silent in the late 1940s, and the hotel shut down within a year. Abbott's held on as long as they could, but after the family failed to produce an heir who wanted to keep the store open, it, too, was doomed.

"So, who owns it now?" Henry asked, playing dumb.

"Well, that's a whole 'nother story," she said with a mischevious grin

Viv told him about Mason Chitwood's drinking and gambling, his poker win against the banker, and the wreck that took his life. Evelyn's move from the mesa into town with her baby boy was the stuff of local legend. All of it fit seamlessly with what Henry already knew.

"And she's still there?"

"Yesirree," Viv said. "She's probably in her eighties now, but she's still around."

He sensed the story about Evelyn letting the building go back to the county for taxes was not public knowledge, so he did not share it.

"Does she ever come to Loganville?" he asked.

"She never misses the Rotary meeting, but that's only once a month," Viv said. "I think she still goes to her office pretty regular . . ." She paused. "Other than that, I guess it would take a funeral to get her out of that big ol' building."

Henry was about to tiptoe into more dangerous territory.

"Whose funeral?" he asked.

"Well," Viv said, "it's been years. Most of the folks she knew in Thurston are long gone. But I remember back in the late '80s, when Dewley Edwards got killed in a wreck in Fort Worth, they had his services here."

"I heard she paid for everything," she whispered conspiratorially. "She and Dewley went way back. He had owned a service station, and she did his books. They said he'd been hauling some stuff for her when he got in a wreck on the interstate. I'm sure we had a story—it was sometime back in the '80s."

Henry quickly connected the dots. This had to be the mysterious man who had rented the unit, left, then died.

"So, she never got married?" he asked. "What about her and Dewley?"

"Oh, no!" Viv said with a laugh, shaking her head. "Dewley was like a father to her. She only had one other real friend I know of—Mary Sinclair. Now that was an odd pair!"

"Why do you say that?"

"Oh, I don't know," Viv said. "Mary was just . . . so refined. Kind of an elegant lady. Evelyn had some pretty rough edges. But they were real close."

"Is Mary still around?" Henry asked, trying not to seem too interested though his heart was pounding.

"No, no," Viv said. "She passed a good while ago—before Dewley, in fact. Now Mary, she had a sad story. Her son got killed in Vietnam, then her husband died in an accident not long after. That left just her and her daughter—a really smart, pretty girl. What was her name?"

It took everything Henry had to keep from blurting it out.

"Daisy? Dana? Darla? I can't remember," Viv continued. "But she went off to college and never came back. That's the way it is in these small towns, I guess."

Henry sensed Viv was nearing the end of her ability to fill him in. Obviously, Evelyn's story was one of the colorful local legends in this part of the world, but Viv's knowledge seemed more superficial than personal. Unless Viv was a tremendous actor, she and Evelyn were not the best of friends.

"Well, I don't need to keep you from your afternoon off," he said, standing up. "You've been very helpful, and I appreciate it." He stepped toward the door, then turned around.

"So, if someone wanted to get hold of Evelyn, how would they go about that?"

Viv looked pensive for a moment, then stood and went over to a card file on her desk. She pulled open the top drawer and began talking to herself.

"I know she gets the paper," she said. "Let's see, Campbell, Carson, Chavez . . . Chitwood! Here she is."

She pulled a card and turned to him.

"You got something to write with?" she asked as he frisked his pockets. "Some reporter you are! Here. " She leaned over, grabbed a pen and a business card from her desk, and wrote down a phone number. She handed him the note. "That top one will be her office, and the bottom one, far as I know, is her personal phone. I don't think she has a cell phone yet."

"She won't mind you giving it to me?"

"Well," Viv said slyly, "she won't know where you got it unless you tell her."

"Okay," he smiled. "I'll just let her think I'm a good investigative reporter."

"Exactly," she said, nodding. "And if you need anything else from me, that's my card on the other side. I'll help you with anything you need. Just don't let Evelyn see the logo!"

He reached in his pocket, pulled out his wallet, and gave her a business card with his information on it.

"You can call me, too, if you remember anything you think I need to know," he said.

The doorbell dinged as he stepped out into the afternoon sunshine. Ella was sitting in the car, window down, arm hanging out. As he got closer, he could tell from her face that she'd discovered something interesting—but not in a good way.

**Thurston: 1969**

After Mary lost her son, then her husband, Evelyn had patiently nourished their friendship back to life. This time, she didn't know what to do, how to start. She wanted to remain friends, but friendship is built on honesty, and now a huge lie lay at the very core of their friendship.

Dishonesty was against Evelyn's nature. Quite the contrary, she was prone to blurt out the truth even when no one wanted to hear it. But now, she had no choice. Evelyn believed with all her heart that if Mary knew Dottie was dead, it would kill her. She had to believe her daughter had run away, even if she never heard from her again. It was her only hope.

Evelyn had no choice but to keep her deepest, darkest secret.

A few days after graduation, Mary called to invite her over for coffee. Evelyn quickly said yes, asked what time, then hung up. She didn't know what else to say. It was going to take everything she had to pull this off, and she wasn't sure she could do it.

She was terrified when Mary met her at the door with a smile and a hug.

"Oh, it's so good to see you," Mary said.

"Well," she said, "it's good to see you, too. Seems like a long time since graduation. That was some night, wasn't it?"

"Yes," Mary said, ushering Evelyn to the kitchen table. "Yes, it was."

The conversation lagged while Mary got the coffee pot and cups and set them on the table, then reached back to the counter for a tray with a few slices of angel food cake. Evelyn picked up a coffee cup and admired it.

"This is really pretty china," she said. "I don't think I ever saw this pattern before."

"I didn't use this set for the funer— I don't use them often," Mary said. "They're just for special occasions, like this one."

Evelyn quickly set the cup down so Mary wouldn't see her hand shaking. She looked around. "The house looks nice," she said, still awkward. "Do you have some help, or do you do all the cleaning yourself?"

Mary smiled. "I do it myself," she said. "I don't make many messes now that it's just me."

"So, uh, Dottie?" Evelyn asked tentatively. "She off to school already? I didn't see her at church Sunday."

"Yes," Mary said, sitting down. "She was in a big hurry to get out of town."

"I'll bet," Evelyn said with a nervous laugh, dying inside. "A lot of them were. Arnie went down to Fort Worth and joined the Marines. I told him to go the Army. The Marines are out on the front lines everywhere they go. But he thinks he's tough, so he wants to be a Marine and prove it to everybody."

"Have you heard from him?" Mary asked.

Evelyn's throat was scratchy. She picked up the cup, blew, and sipped without adding her customary spoonful of sugar and shot of milk. The hot liquid warmed her throat, but her head was still spinning, and her hand was shaking so badly she nearly spilled the coffee.

"Uh, no," she said. "I don't really expect to. We aren't much on conversation, me and that boy. He'll probably come home in a week or two to bring the pickup before they ship him off to boot camp. I just hope he makes it through."

"Well, he's a big strong boy," Mary said. "I'm sure the Marines will put even more muscle on him. Do you think he'll have to go to Viet Nam?"

"Almost certainly," Evelyn said.

"I pray he can stay out of harm's way."

"Yeah," Evelyn said. "That situation over there is outta hand. Nixon said he was going to ratchet that thing down, and I think we have more boys over there now than we did when Lyndon was president. You can't trust politicians any farther than you can throw 'em."

"No, you can't," Mary said. There was another long silence.

"So," Evelyn heard her voice saying, as if she was listening from another room, "have you heard from Dottie yet? Did she make it to Austin alright?"

Tears welled up instantly in Mary's eyes.

"Evelyn, we had a fight," she said, reaching out to take Evelyn's hand. "A big one, on the way home, and she got out of the car and walked away, down the street. She didn't even say goodbye."

Evelyn's eyes filled with tears, too. She looked away, hoping Mary didn't see them. She didn't know what to say.

Mary leaned her head down, hand across her forehead as her tears dropped onto the tablecloth. Evelyn reached out and touched her hair. "It's gonna be alright," she finally said.

"I hope so," Mary sniffed. "When I came home from church Sunday, she had stopped by the house and gotten a bunch of her stuff."

She looked up at Evelyn, her eyes round with disbelief.

"She ran away, Evelyn!" Mary cried. "There was mud all over the carpet, the suitcase was gone, she's gone. She even took her books. I haven't heard a word."

"Honey, you know she loves you," Evelyn said. "She loves you! You've been a great mother. And she's going to be fine. With her good looks, and as smart as she is? Nothing is going to stop her." Evelyn stroked her hair and consoled her as best she could. It took everything she had to hold in her own sobs, thinking of the broken girl wrapped in the blue tarp, buried in her basement. But she took a deep breath and pressed on.

"Did you . . . tell anybody about her runnin' off? The sheriff or somebody?"

"No!" Mary said. "She's an adult. If she doesn't want to be here anymore, that's her right, and believe it or not, I understand. I can't stop her. I just hope . . ."

The tears returned. "I just hope she has a good life. I don't blame her for wanting to get away from all this death and sadness. I wish to God I could!"

Evelyn pulled Mary's head to her shoulder as the tears flowed. That was all she could do.

"Just let it out, sweetie," she said as they cried together. "Don't keep it locked up inside."

* * *

After the class of '69—thirty strong—graduated, Thurston Independent School District went down quickly. The next year's class was half as big, and the next few were even smaller as enrollment fell off a cliff. In '72, Budlong, a nearby rural school district, asked to consolidate, and Thurston's school board said yes. They brought fewer than forty students in thirteen grades.

In 1975, Thurston-Budlong ISD petitioned to consolidate with Loganville. The Loganville school board accepted, and voters throughout the district were asked to cast ballots to see which facilities to keep open and which to abandon.

Budlong was closer to Loganville and had built a new school in the mid-1960s. Thurston's building, from the same era as the C&C, was so outdated there was no question it would be shut down.

Evelyn thought about bidding on the ten-acre campus, which included a parking lot, the football field, a detached gym, and an ag barn and livestock pens. But after thinking about it a few days, she decided to pass, figuring she already owned enough vacant real estate. Abandoned, the old building fell apart quickly: its windows shot out by vandals, its flat roof springing leaks, bricks falling off. The parking lot became more pothole than pavement. One day Evelyn drove past and noticed a whole section of the roof had collapsed, and a tree with green leaves grew in a sunlit classroom, its limbs poking through the broken windows.

Nature was reclaiming her turf, calling everyone's attention to the impermanence of man's works. As years went by, the metal awning across the front of the building turned loose and slowly sank, like an eye closing, as the old school knelt in submission.

The C&C building held up better, thanks to better bones and Evelyn's maintenance. Mary continued to come down to her tiny shop and sew. One day, during one of their visits, Evelyn told her she could stop paying the $50 monthly rent.

"I don't need it, and you aren't making $50 a month down there," she said.

"I appreciate it, Evelyn, but it's okay. I made a promise," Mary protested. "I like coming down there. It gets me out of the house."

"No, no, no! That's not what I mean!" Evelyn clarified. "I'm not telling you don't come—I'm just saying you're my friend and it's my building and you don't owe me anything. You were always so nice to me and Arnie, gave us all those clothes, did all that sewing . . ."

"And you babysat!" Mary said. "You always found a way to repay me."

"Well, you deserved something for it."

The conversation lagged. Finally, Mary spoke up.

"Evelyn, I . . . I'm probably going to close the shop soon anyway. When I do, I'll come down and clear out my stuff," she said.

Evelyn paused, then told her, "Don't you worry about that, either, dear. Nobody's beating down my door to rent that space," she said with a wistful laugh. "You work as long as you want to, Mary, and when you're done, take whatever means something to you, and just walk away."

Mary protested again, but Evelyn cut her off.

"You work whenever you want, on whatever you want to work on. When you get ready to leave, you leave. You get ready to come back, you come back. It's your spot. As far as I'm concerned, you own that space. I'll file a deed if I have to!"

Mary laughed, and they didn't speak of it again.

As time went by, Evelyn could see sadness overtaking her friend, in spite of all she could do. They continued to meet and have coffee, but without their children, topics were fairly limited. Dottie existed only as an ache in Mary's heart.

The ache in Evelyn's heart had a different source.

Arnie survived Vietnam, reenlisted, and did a second tour. But when he came back, he was a different person. The Marines made him bigger and stronger, but the war leached out whatever sweetness was left. Evelyn figured, correctly, that what had happened with Dottie played a big role. He was hard and mean; beneath it all, he was angry and desperately sad.

Evelyn helped him get set up in the trucking business, and he stayed on the road for weeks at a time. But when he was in town, he drank, and when he drank, he got dangerous. Bar fights were common, and when a felony DWI cost him his commercial driver's license, he was no longer able to work as a trucker. Evelyn told him she didn't want him living with her anymore and gave him the keys to the house she'd bought after the fire. After that, she saw him only when he needed money, or when she had to bail him out of jail.

After a few years, most of Mary's customers had died or moved away, and custom tailoring became a relic of a bygone era. When she decided to close the shop, she called Evelyn to set up a coffee date.

She was sitting at the sewing machine when Evelyn stepped tentatively through the door, holding a tray with cookies, two cups, and a coffee pot.

"You lost or somethin'?" Evelyn said.

Mary rose, took the tray, and set it on the sewing machine table, then wrapped her arms around her friend, her eyes dancing in a way Evelyn hadn't seen in years.

"Oh, Evelyn, it's so good to see you," she said. "Please, sit down. I have news!"

"You're shutting it down, aren't you?" Evelyn asked.

"Yes, but that's not it," Mary said. "It's Dottie! I heard from Dottie."

Evelyn was grateful she wasn't still holding the tray. She felt nauseated and had to sit down. More than anything, she wanted to run from the little shop, run from the cursed old building, run from Thurston and not stop until her heart burst. Instead, she sat looking at Mary, her eyes betraying every emotion.

"What?" she finally croaked out. "You heard from her?"

"Yes!" Mary gushed. "It was late, late last night. It was a long-distance call, and she didn't talk long. She didn't tell me where she was. I had so many questions—"

"She called you on the phone?" Evelyn interrupted. "After all . . . all these years?"

"She did! She didn't have time to talk. She told me she was alright, and that . . ."

Mary's voice broke and she began to weep.

". . . that she loved me and never meant to hurt me. She's had a good life, and she said I was a good mother. There was just too much sadness here. She couldn't stay!"

Evelyn sat, mute, looking from one eye to the other, her heart pounding. Maybe someone was trying to run a scam on Mary. Maybe it was an angel. She couldn't remember ever seeing her friend so happy, and she knew there was nothing she could say or do.

"It's a miracle, Mary," she said at last. "I don't know what to say. I'm happy for you."

"That's all you have to say, Evelyn," she said. "You're the only person I'm ever going to tell, but I wanted someone to know. You're the one. It's our secret!"

Evelyn's hand was shaking as she lifted her cup. She couldn't bring herself to make small talk, afraid she would somehow put a damper on the joy she saw in her friend's eyes. She sipped coffee, skipped the cookies, and let Mary do most of the talking. After a decent interval, she felt she might be able to stand.

"Well, I better get back upstairs," she said. "You alright getting out of here?"

"Oh, yes, I'm fine, Evelyn," Mary said. "This is it, my old friend. I've put in a lot of stitches in this little shop, for a long time."

"Well, you leave it just like it is," Evelyn said. It took everything she had just to speak normally. "If you decide to come back, you can, and if you don't, don't worry about it."

They hugged again and Evelyn turned, feeling one hundred years old as she trudged up the stairs. She heard the shop door open, then Mary called, "Evelyn, what about the key?"

"You keep it," Evelyn hollered. "That way you can come back whenever you like."

She heard laughter, then the door closed and the lock clicked. She heard Mary's car start up and drive away into the night. Evelyn stood on the landing, then turned and sat down wearily on the steps, her hands over her face.

A few weeks went by, and Evelyn didn't hear from Mary, so one day she called around mid-morning. There was no answer. Over the next hour, she tried three more times with the same result. Worried, she drove to Mary's house, arriving just in time to join a small crowd of neighbors who'd come out to see what the ambulance was doing. Just as Evelyn got out of her car, the paramedics wheeled Mary out, strapped to a gurney. Evelyn ran up and took her hand.

Mary saw her, smiled, and cheerfully asked how she was doing, as if she were greeting Evelyn in the church foyer. Mary's eyes were as lively as they had been the other night, but her body looked worn and thin. Evelyn just squeezed her hand, her face as grim as the faces of the men loading Mary into the mobile ICU.

Evelyn asked them if she could ride with her friend in the ambulance, but the crew chief said that would not be a good idea. She followed them to the hospital, and by the time she parked they had wheeled Mary in. Evelyn took a seat between a mother with a sniffling child and a man who had obviously dislocated his shoulder. A few hours later, she was the only person left in the waiting room. Finally, she approached the nurse's station.

"Do y'all have a room number for Mary Sinclair?" she asked timidly.

The nurses were busy, looking down and filling out paperwork, but upon hearing Mary's name, one looked up.

"Mrs. Sinclair? From Thurston?" she asked.

"Yes," Evelyn said self-consciously. "I'm her friend."

The nurse shook her head. "I'm sorry, dear. She didn't make it. She was dead on arrival."

**Loganville: 2015**

"What did you find?" Henry asked through the open car window.

Ella looked up at him, shaking her head. "This isn't good, Henry. This is not good."

He walked around to the driver's side, slid in, and waited.

"Start it up," she said with a shudder. "Let's get out of here. This whole thing is starting to give me the heebie-jeebies."

As he drove out of town, she finally began telling Arnie's story.

"Arnold Chitwood has a big file," she said. "It starts with arson, which he was allowed for some reason to get away with when he was a teenager. There's a few reports of vandalism, but since the property owner was almost always his mother, no one pressed charges."

"Sounds like a good recipe if you're baking a criminal," Henry said. Ella did not laugh.

"There's a big gap, I guess while he was in the military," she continued. "One report references disciplinary action while he was in the Marine Corps, too, but no detail. Apparently, he was put on report several times for fighting. No formal charges and no court-martial. After he came back to Logan County he was hauled out of a few bars for fighting."

"As I recall from Dottie's journal, he was a pretty big guy," Henry said.

"I'm thinking we don't want to cross him," Ella said. "Especially if he's been drinking."

She had made extensive notes and went over it all with Henry, as if he were the judge and she was prosecuting the case. Arnold Chitwood had gotten more second chances than anyone she'd ever seen. Most of his arrests, he spent just a few hours in jail before his mother came.

Once he was pulled over on suspicion of DWI and allowed to drive himself home, with a police escort. Another time, he was driven home by a state trooper, and on another occasion, he was involved in a slow-speed chase when a sheriff's deputy, lights flashing, followed him all the way to Thurston. He pulled into the C&C building's delivery drive, turned his engine off, and just sat there. After a few minutes, the officer approached to find him leaning on the steering wheel, crying. He took his keys and walked him to the door.

"This guy should have been locked up years earlier," Ella said. "He should have gotten treatment. He should have gotten out of here."

As she said it, she thought of Barry—the high school jock everybody loved until he graduated, and they moved on, and he couldn't.

"I think the cops just didn't want to mess with him," she said after a moment's pause. "He was the perfect storm: a big, mean drunk and also the son of the lady who owned the town. Eventually, he caused an accident, nearly killed somebody, and they had no choice but to file felony DWI charges. He pleaded guilty and, as you might expect, got a sweet deal."

"His own key to the jail?" Henry offered.

"Like Otis, in Mayberry?" Ella said.

"Yes!" he said, delighted she'd understood his reference.

"No!" she exclaimed. "His three-year sentence was commuted to six months, and he was allowed to serve it in the county jail. He was out of jail before his victim got out of rehab. After that slap on the wrist, he was on probation, required to undergo drug and alcohol abuse therapy and random testing, and predictably, he came out vowing to leave the stuff alone forever."

"Did he?" Henry asked, deciding to give up on his attempts at humor.

"No more activity in the file," Ella said. "But this guy may be scarier sober."

By the time they finished talking about Arnie, they were halfway home, and the sun was going down behind them. They decided to stop in Weatherford for supper, and with the subject of Arnie off the table, the rest of the evening was remarkably enjoyable. When Henry pulled up in front of Ella's apartment, they spent a long time just looking into each other's eyes. Finally, she smiled and sighed.

"Henry, I love being with you. I'd invite you in, I really would. But I'm worn out from all this. It's been a pretty productive day, but I feel like I'm carrying a big sack of secrets around with me. I think I'm still tired from Albuquerque, too."

"I understand," he said, tearing his eyes away from her and looking down. "It hasn't all been fun, but the parts I spent with you sure were."

"I'll take that," she said. He looked up, and she leaned toward him for their first real kiss. Her hand went behind his head and her lips pressed hard against his as they breathed each other's breath, tasted each other, and touched foreheads for a long, lingering moment.

"Bye," she said as she turned to open the door.

"Sweet dreams," he replied. He watched her go in, and it was a while before he felt able to drive away.

**Thurston: 1985**

Mary Sinclair's funeral was a small affair. No twenty-one–gun salute, no flag ceremony, no military honors. She'd given a husband and a son to her country, but her own last rites were barely noted. The traveling preacher who did the eulogy had not known her well. A few folks from church attended, along with some of her longtime sewing customers and grown-up kids who had known Ted or Dottie.

In the end, Evelyn was all the family Mary had. She sat in the front pew, pious and sorrowful, but inwardly she was still haunted. As the preacher droned his out-of-a-book funeral, the finality of Mary's death hit Evelyn. She'd won. The long lie had worked. Mary died believing Dottie was still alive, still out there somewhere.

That phone call, whether from a scam artist or an angel, had comforted Mary, but it was no comfort to Evelyn. Fear had become a way of life and was not easily set aside. The next day, her heart skipped a beat when she got a call from the lawyer who had been hired to close out Mary's estate. He'd seen the will. He was calling to tell Evelyn she'd been named the executor.

"Sure," she said. "I'd do anything for Mary. Just tell me what you need."

He rattled off a long list, and she quickly found a pen to take notes. She would need to get multiple copies of the death certificate so she could close out bank accounts, settle life insurance, and stop George's and Ted's Social Security and veteran's benefits. George had had a retirement plan through the co-op that she would have to deal with. And she would need to go through the house, arrange an estate sale, sell Mary's cars, then put the house on the market.

That evening, as she ate supper alone, it dawned on her. The co-op's life insurance settlement for George's on-the-job death had been substantial, and with no debt, Mary had spent very little of it. The retirement plan was generous. Mary lived simply, so there was probably going to be a sizable amount of money left in her estate.

Evelyn's deception had no expiration date. Even with Mary gone, it had to continue.

She called the attorney back the next morning. "Can you create a trust?" she asked.

"Sure," he said. "It's pretty simple. What's going on?"

"Well, Mary's got a daughter out there somewhere," she said. "All this stuff—the house, the cars, the bank accounts—all the proceeds have got to go in trust for that little girl."

"Evelyn, nobody's seen Dorothy in twenty years. Nobody's got an address, a phone number, nothing," he said. "She disappeared. She didn't even come back for the funeral. You—"

"Nevertheless," she interrupted, "this is all hers. It sure as hell isn't mine, and you ain't getting it. Everybody's got to know that, Tommy. I'm not getting a penny of it. Everything—*everything*—goes in trust. If Dottie never shows up, I guess the state'll get it."

"It's still less than a million, Evelyn," he said.

"I don't care if it's ten dollars!" she snapped. "That's the only way to do this right. You draw it up, I'll sign it, and then it's all going to sit there and earn interest until this girl comes to get it or Jesus comes again. You got that?"

"Yes, ma'am," he said.

"Good, because you're going to be the trustee." He tried to protest, but she wouldn't listen. "And I'll pay your fee—neither one of us is taking a penny out of that estate, y'hear?"

He meekly agreed. It was no use arguing when Evelyn started barking orders.

As soon as she hung up, she started making a list. Less than an hour later, a girl from the lawyer's office dropped by to give her the keys to Mary's house and cars—the one she drove, a pickup her husband had left behind, and Ted's car. The death certificates, she said, wouldn't be ready for a few days.

Over the next several days Evelyn looked through all of Mary's things, often through tears. She truly missed her friend, but she was also determined to play her role to the end, whether or not anyone was watching. Mary's reality, that Dottie was alive somewhere, had to become Evelyn's reality. Because of that, there were things she should not get rid of. China. Silverware. Books. Clothes Mary had sewn herself. Ted's things. Mementos, honors Dottie had earned that Mary had cherished. It was the stuff of Dottie's life, everything she'd left behind.

Evelyn knew the assumptions that were out there: that Dottie had callously deserted her mother. It didn't matter that the real story was different; both versions were tragic.

She placed an ad and quickly sold the pickup. Mary's car went for $1,500. A collector bought Ted's Mustang for five times that—it was a classic and in good shape. Several companies that ran estate auctions offered to just handle it all, but Evelyn thought their fees were too high. She placed the ads herself, in the *Loganville Ledger* and a few areawide shopper publications. She moved the most precious things—the roll-top desk, the dining table and chairs—down to the old Abbott's building, then priced the rest to sell and got rid of most of it in three days. George's tools brought the most. Mary's sewing machine, still at the C&C building, did not sell.

Evelyn was thankful Dewley was still spry enough to help. She never considered asking Arnie to help. Going through Dottie's house would have been too much for him.

By the time it was over, the little sewing office was jammed with boxes, some spilling out into the old vacant store. Hidden among it all was the suitcase Evelyn had packed for Dottie, full of clothes and books, unopened since that day.

Arnie didn't go to Mary's funeral. He was old enough to know he didn't handle stuff like that very well. He did, however, start thinking about how his life would be different.

With Dottie's mother out of the picture, Arnie thought he and his mom might finally be able to relax and move past the dark secret hidden in the C&C building's basement. Of course, they still wouldn't be able to tell anyone, but at least the constant fear—fear that Mary would find out, have the body brought out and prosecute him for murder—would be gone. That threat, hanging over his and his mother's heads since graduation night, was gone.

His mother had sacrificed a lot to protect him. She should be relieved, too.

He'd been attending AA meetings since he got out of jail. It was a condition of his parole, but he talked a few of his buddies into going with him, and they all got into it. The twelve-step system was simple enough that Arnie could keep up in a way he never could in school. In fact, it reminded him of going to Sunday school as a child with his mom. He'd always believed that was a waste of time, that none of those Bible stories meant anything to him. But as he sat through the AA meetings, dots started connecting for the first time and things started to make sense.

He decided to check on the law and see if he could get his CDL back so he could drive again. He didn't want to own a business anymore—that was always his mother's ambition, not his. He just wanted to drive for someone else, get back out on the road, out of Thurston, and out of that house his mom had given him. Away from this ghost town and its ghosts.

He called his mom to see if she knew a good lawyer.

"What, are you in trouble again? Boy, I—"

"No, Mama, I ain't in trouble," he interrupted. "I just need to see if there's something I can do to get that commercial license back so I can drive again. I'm tired of sittin' around, doin' nothin', and depending on you for everything."

There was a long silence on Evelyn's end.

"Ma," Arnie continued. "With Mary gone, I figure life's gonna be different for us now, right? We don't have to pretend no more. I can—"

"You can what? Go back to your old ways until you get drunk some night and spill the whole story? In a crowded bar, with an off-duty deputy sittin' in the corner?"

Now the long silence was on Arnie's end.

"Boy, you need to understand something," Evelyn continued, slowly and deliberately. "Nothing has changed. Nothing. You and me have the same secret we've always had, and it's got to stay that way. You understand?"

"Mama, I—"

"Do you understand? You may be able to get your CDL back, but there's no relaxing, no . . . freedom from this thing. There's no statute of limitations. It goes with me to my grave, and it goes with you to yours. Got it?"

"Yes ma'am."

The next day, Arnold decided to call a lawyer himself. After a half-dozen tries, he finally got through and learned quickly that felony DWI meant no more commercial driving, ever. It was a federal law, not just a Texas thing. There was no getting around it.

So he started calling Fort Worth trucking companies, looking for work as a dispatcher or in a warehouse. One was willing to interview him, but they said there would be a criminal background check and if he had any felony convictions, for anything, it was a no-go. He went through the *Star-Telegram* looking for job listings, but most of them were for computer this and data processing that. The only jobs he was qualified for were manual labor, hard, physical jobs, and even those required skills like welding or heavy equipment operating that he did not have or could not be licensed to do. After three or four days, he was utterly discouraged.

He told his buddies all about it at the next AA meeting. They decided to continue the conversation at the county line bar.

**Thurston: 1989**

Evelyn avoided the sewing office, but knowing Mary's things were down there continued to haunt her. Finally, one day she decided it was time to just get rid of it all.

She'd heard about these new storage places, where you could rent a space and cram whatever you wanted in there for as long as you liked. No inspections, no questions. You had the only key. That sounded good. She made herself go back down to the sewing room.

As she stood there and looked around, a patchwork quilt of feelings smothered her, brought on by the smell of cloth and leather, memories of her friend toiling away at that machine, their children playing upstairs, lives stretching out before them.

*Yes*, she thought. It was time for it all to go.

Evelyn did a little homework and found a place just off I-20 in south Fort Worth. She called and booked a ten-by-twelve unit, then called back and bumped it up to ten-by-sixteen. She decided to throw in several of her old file cabinets, boxes of shoes and hats she'd salvaged from Abbott's, and other personal items she hadn't looked at in years.

A rental place delivered the trailer on a Wednesday afternoon. Evelyn called Arnie and told him to come the next morning to load it, and bring a couple of guys with him. He protested, but she convinced him it was the least he could do.

Arnie and two of his buddies showed up bright and early. By the time Dewley arrived in his big Dodge pickup, the trailer was packed and ready to go, sitting in front of the C&C building. He backed in, jumped down, and wrapped Evelyn in his arms.

Arnie gave his two helpers a disgusted glance. His mother hadn't even said hello to him.

All that remained was to hook up the trailer. Dewley stepped back up onto the running board, but Evelyn had other plans.

"Let Arnie and them hook it up," she said. "Come upstairs and let me get you a cup of coffee for the road."

Dewley tossed Arnie the keys and did as he was told. Evelyn and

Dewley took the freight elevator, and when they got upstairs, she motioned for him to sit.

"How you gonna unload that thing?" she asked. "Do you need to take the boys?"

"Nah," he said, blowing on his cup of coffee. "They told me they've got plenty of help on that end—even a forklift if I need it. I don't know how your guys got it loaded that quick."

"Well, they're all big as bears," Evelyn said.

"I should probably go help 'em hook that trailer up," he said, standing up.

"I'm sure they're done already," she said. "For Pete's sake, Dewley—Arnie's a trucker. He knows how to hook up a trailer. I just wanted to visit a minute. Seems like I never see you anymore."

"Well, you know, Fran ain't doin' so great," he said. "I'm the only one who can take care of her, so that's how I spend most of my time these days."

"Aw, Dewley," she said. "I hate that for you and Fran. Y'all deserve better. Is there any . . . I don't know, medicine you need? A special nurse or a therapist? A place she could go where she could get better? There's nothing I wouldn't do for y'all. You know that, right?"

He sat for a minute, just looking at Evelyn. Then he shook his head.

"Evelyn, you've done so much already," he said. "If it wasn't for you, I'd still be pumpin' gas and bustin' tires, making twenty bucks a day. Doin' my books all those years, then helpin' me sell that place—that was the best thing anybody ever done for me." He paused.

"We've had us a good run, me and Fran," he added, his voice breaking. "She's got the Alzheimer's pretty bad. She ain't gonna be around much longer. I don't need nothin'. I would just ask you one thing, and if you can't do it, just let me know and we're still good."

"What is it, Dewley?" Evelyn asked. "Anything—you just name it."

"If something happens to me, would you promise me you'll take care of Fran?"

Evelyn sat back in her chair, tears filling her eyes.

"Yes, of course!" she said instantly. "You and Fran mean the world to me."

"Would you promise me, Evelyn?"

"Of course, Dewley! I promise. But I still hope you outlive me!"

He laughed. "Not likely, sprout! But if I know you'll take care of Fran, it'd make me rest a lot easier at night."

Evelyn stood up and walked around the table to where Dewley sat. She leaned down from behind and wrapped her arms around him, giving him a little kiss on the same cheek she had kissed the day she brought her daddy's old pickup to the garage.

"You rest easy, Dewley," she whispered in his ear. "I won't let anything happen to Fran. Drive safe and get home as quick as you can. I'll go over and look in on her today."

"Aw, Evelyn, you do that—she'd love to see you," he said. "Now I better get on the road if I want to get to Fort Worth and back by dinnertime."

Evelyn laughed, leaned down, and patted his substantial midsection.

"You haven't missed many dinners, that's for sure!"

He laughed, gently patted the side of her head, then got up and headed for the door.

"You can take the elevator down if it's easier," she said, but he had already started down the stairs. She heard the outside door slam and the diesel engine rev as he pulled out. The door shut again, and Arnie came trudging up the stairs.

"Ma!" he yelled. She was at the sink, cleaning up from breakfast.

"What?" she said. "I hope you got that thing loaded right, so it doesn't shift on him. It was a lot of stuff."

"It's fine," he said. "I just thought maybe you oughta pay them boys for helpin' load all that stuff up. They ain't rich, y'know."

"Well, they'd have everything they need if they didn't pour it all into whiskey bottles in those cheap dives where y'all hang out," she lectured.

"Used to hang out, Ma. Ain't none of us doing that anymore," he said.

He was lying, but her preaching infuriated him. Her superior silence didn't help, either.

"Ma, they come over here clean and sober this mornin'. Early. They didn't get no coffee like the old man, and all he did was drive up," he said, his voice rising. "You offer him a donut, too? Toast and eggs? You ain't fixed me nothin' in a while. I didn't get no hug, neither."

"Boy, you—"

He cut her off.

"I don't answer to 'Boy' no more, Ma!" he barked. "Eight years in the Marines, two tours in Vietnam and I'm still a boy? What's it take to be a man around here?"

She turned around and looked him squarely in the eyes, her voice calm.

"Well, all that drinking and that hitch in jail didn't help," she said. "How about you just man up and then maybe you'll get treated like a man? Pay your own way and quit living off your mother like some spoiled brat. Get yourself a nice girl, treat her honorably, and start a family. Make me a grandmother. Come to church. Stay on that program of yours, and out of the bars. Clean up. Take care of yourself."

He had turned and was walking away.

"You want me to go on?" she said, her voice rising. "I'm just getting warmed up!"

"No, that's enough," he said calmly, as he stopped with his back to her. "I know how you feel."

Then he turned around and looked in her eyes. "But you know what, Ma? You ain't got a clue how I feel. There ain't nothin' I can do that's good enough for you, Ma—ever! You pulled yourself up by them bootstraps, and I've been hangin' on your apron strings ever since. Ain't that the story? God knows I've heard it often enough—the great Evelyn Chitwood and her no-good son Arnie. But nobody knows my story. Nobody knows the real story."

Their ghastly secret hung in the air between them.

"I'm just tryin' to play my part, Ma," he said quietly. "This ain't the way I wanted it, but this is the way it's turned out." He turned and headed down the stairs.

"You find a way out, you let me know," he called back. "I'm all ears."

She didn't say a word as he walked away.

* * *

Evelyn waited until after lunch to go see Fran. She seemed well enough at first glance, but she shuffled when she walked and was no longer capable of many of the simplest tasks around the house. There were times when she was perfectly lucid and times when she didn't even recognize Dewley. They had a housekeeper who came twice a week, did most of the cleaning, and looked after her while Dewley ran errands. Today, she had been asked to stay until he got back from Fort Worth.

When Evelyn showed up, Fran knew her at once and threw her arms around her. It was one of the good days. At about 4 p.m. there was a knock at the door. The housekeeper answered, and her face went pale. She motioned for Evelyn to come. Standing at the door was a uniformed Texas Highway Patrol officer, hat in hand.

"Can I help you?" she said.

"Are you a family member of Durwood Lee Edwards?"

She knew he must have gotten the name from Dewley's driver's license.

"I'm Evelyn Chitwood," she said. "I'm a close family friend and I'm over here with his wife. They don't have any children."

"Can I speak with Mrs. Edwards, please?"

"Sir, she is . . . she's not well. She's incapacitated. If you have some news, can you please tell me, and I can break it to her?"

"Ma'am, I'm Col. Jefferson of the Texas Department of Public Safety in Weatherford," he said. "I'm sorry to inform you that there has been an accident. Mr. Edwards . . . did not survive."

Evelyn choked back a sob and spun around, bending over double as he recited the details. All she heard were snatches, words like "Interstate 20," "multi-vehicle accident," and "trailer."

Her head was still spinning when the officer said, "Sorry for your loss" and turned away. She closed the door, gathered herself and broke the news to Fran as gently as she could, keeping the details to herself. She'd had a lifetime of practice.

**Fort Worth: 2015**

Henry and Ella's relationship had switched gears. They ate lunch together when Ella wasn't out of town or in a meeting, and as spring turned to summer, they spent most weekends together. They naturally slipped into the rhythm of going to church together as well, and he loved the way she laced her arm through his during the sermon. It just seemed natural.

When Natalie or Andrew came to visit, Henry was included. He got along well with Natalie, but Andrew was leery of this new guy in his mom's life. Ella's son was a big, good-looking kid, a clone of his dad, and he'd seen a lot more of Barry than his mom over the last year. Henry met the challenge head-on. His unique personality, his sense of humor, and his obvious affection and respect for Ella gradually won Andrew over.

Henry had lived in Fort Worth for years, but with Ella and her kids, he saw the city's sights through fresh eyes. They strolled the Water Gardens, hit the downtown restaurants, and made forays through the Museum District, walking the galleries of the Modern, the Kimbell, and the Amon Carter —with Henry talking more about the architecture than the art. He got them good tickets for the Rangers, and they toured AT&T Stadium. One weekend, they all cowboyed up and went to the Stockyards to mingle with tourists, eat barbecue, and watch the longhorns trudge down Exchange Avenue.

But Henry and Ella didn't abandon their mission. Everything

pointed to a meeting with Evelyn—it was unavoidable. One day as they shared lunch under the live oaks in a nearly deserted Sundance Square, a plan began to take shape.

"Just like with the newspaper lady—" Ella began.

"Viv," Henry interrupted.

"Okay, Viv. Your buddy," Ella said. "Just like her, Evelyn does not need to know how much we know. You told Viv you were a history buff, so how about we tell her as much truth as we can? We work for an architecture firm, you're a writer and I'm a photographer and . . . we're doing a book on old buildings."

Henry thought a minute. "Ooh. I like that," he said. "In fact, it's brilliant."

He grinned and she gloated. Then he punctured the moment.

"I can pretend to be a writer," Henry said. "But . . . do you even have a camera?"

"Yes," she said. "Of course."

"I don't mean your phone," he said. "If someone's going to shoot photos for, like, a coffee-table book on architecture, they're going to have a Nikon and some crazy lenses."

She gave him an exasperated look.

"I can play that role," she said. "But we'll have to borrow a camera."

"What about Nick?" he said. "I'm sure he's got some equipment he doesn't use anymore. I'll bet we could borrow one of his old cameras and a light meter, a bag, maybe a tripod."

"So while you're chatting up the old lady, I'm lugging all this gear around, right?"

"Well . . ." he stammered.

"How about I carry a camera, and we tell her if she agrees—and signs a release—we'll come back and I'll set up some real photography, when the light's right—all that techie stuff?" Ella said. "All I'm doing is just exploring possible angles for the book."

"Yeah, that sounds better," Henry agreed. "You can probably pull that off."

"Hey, buddy, I can absolutely pull it off," she said, bristling. He raised his hands.

"Of course you can!" he said. "And it beats the heck out of telling Evelyn you're a lawyer. But we need to be careful our act doesn't get in the way of our real mission, which is to feel her out, see what she knows."

"And boy, we've got to be careful there," she said, stealing a potato chip. "If Evelyn finds out we bought her storage unit, that takes it to a whole different level."

"Yeah," he said. "Do you want your pickle?"

"I was going to eat it with your chips," she said, stealing another one.

"Fine," he said. "So, what's yours is yours, and what's mine is—"

"Mine, too." She smiled and stole another chip. "Clear?"

"Crystal." He smiled. "So, when are we going back to Thurston?"

"I have to go to Austin Friday for a legislative thing," she said, making a face.

"So you're a lobbyist now?"

"Some of our clients are seeking tax breaks, so it doesn't hurt to have a lawyer on hand, right?"

"Right," he said. "And if she happens to be drop-dead gorgeous, that doesn't hurt!"

She smiled. "I'm just there to help. If anybody drops dead, that's not on me."

They decided Henry would call Evelyn and try to set something up for the following weekend. He would sell it as a research trip. He was a writer who worked for a Fort Worth architect, and he was working a book on Texas buildings. The C&C was high on his list.

He would ask for a tour. He was bringing a colleague, who would take photographs if that was alright. They were interested in details of the construction, along with any colorful stories she might share beyond what was on the historical marker. He was looking to create a book that would be of interest to both history buffs and fans of architecture.

When he saw Ella the next day, Henry was happy to report that it was all set.

Evelyn had sounded older on the phone than he expected, but small-town friendly and open to their quest. Her language was proper, almost courtly, and she lit up when he reminded her of the Channel 8 piece from twelve years ago. At eighty, she still sounded sharp.

Contacting someone like that, out of the blue, took Henry back to his newspaper days. The writer in him wanted to just sit down with her, turn on the recorder and listen to her stories.

But he was pretty sure there were a few she would not wish to share.

**Thurston: 1989–2014**

After Dewley's death, Evelyn wanted nothing to do with that storage unit. When she got the first invoice, she sent them ten years' rent. In 1999, she sent them another ten years' worth. In 2009, she started paying year-by-year again.

But in 2014, the storage facility sold. The new owner sent out new invoices with a new logo and mailing address. Evelyn thought it was junk mail, so she tossed it. She kept tossing them until she finally got one that said, "FINAL NOTICE." She dropped it on her desk, intending to look at it when she got time.

It was a week before she got around to opening it. By then, it was too late. The auction was the next day. In a panic, she drafted Arnie to go to Fort Worth and buy it, no matter what.

Like any large object, Arnie had a lot of inertia—especially when he didn't want to do something. He left late, went to the wrong storage place, and walked around for an hour before he realized his mistake. By the time he made it to the right spot the auction was almost over. The unit he wanted was last, but he'd never done one of these. When it became a bidding war, he was quickly flustered and out of his league.

Evelyn spotted the defeated look on his face as soon as he came through the door.

"You didn't get it?" she yelled. He shook his head no. "How do you not get it? What happened?"

"There was a lady, Ma, and she kept on raising the bid," he said defensively.

"So? Outbid her! I didn't put any limits on you! How can you just let it get away?"

"I guess the same way you forgot to pay the rent!" he shot back. "I don't know what the big deal is anyway. There's nothin' important in there."

"How do you know that?" she snapped. "You don't know what's in there, and we don't know anything about whoever bought it. They might be . . . I don't know, detectives!"

"Ma," he said, trying to calm her anger. "They weren't police. They were just regular people—a girl and a guy, just out doin' auctions for fun. Everybody else was cuttin' up with 'em. I think it was the first unit she'd ever bought."

"So why'd she buy it?" Evelyn probed. "Why this one? Did they say anything? Couldn't they see you wanted it? Why did she want it so bad?"

"I don't know," he said. "I bid it up pretty high, but she just kept on outbidding me. It was the last unit of the day. I guess they just wanted it."

"Hmmph," she muttered. "Or they wanted to poke around in somebody's business."

"Ma, it's almost fifty years since Dottie . . ." he stammered. "Ain't nobody lookin' into that anymore! For cryin' out loud—you can't spend your whole life worryin' about me! Nobody remembers, understand? Nobody cares anymore!"

She turned away from him, clutching the counter and holding her cane in the other hand. She sat back down at the linoleum kitchen table. Her hand was shaking. She looked up, slowly and deliberately, and glared into his eyes.

"I understand more than you think I do," she said. "I have spent the better part of my life worrying about that basement, hoping nobody cares anymore—but sometimes people start caring. They get curious, they get nosy, and before you know it, the whole thing unravels."

"Ma, I—"

"Arnie," she sighed. "I know you tried. This is just one more accident, like with Dottie, Dewley's trailer hitch, and everything else. It really does seem like your best is never good enough. I know that's hard for you to hear. It's hard for me to say—but it's true. I just don't want this to come out, after all these years, and ruin everything."

He laughed bitterly. "Ruin what, Ma? Ruin what? Everything got ruined a long time ago for me. I ain't got nothin' left to ruin."

He pushed the door shut and went down the stairs, through the abandoned store that once teemed with shoppers, to the street that was once thronged with traffic. *There was a time, in Thurston, Texas*... he thought. He shook his head.

"Nobody cares about Thurston anymore," he muttered.

* * *

The following Saturday, Henry and Ella drove to Thurston mostly in silence. Evelyn had been gracious on the phone. Henry had assured her he was a building nerd, excited to see one of North Texas's architectural landmarks and hoping to include the C&C building in his book. Still, he and Ella were nervous. They were about to meet possibly the only person who could unravel this mystery, but they weren't sure if she'd be helpful or hostile.

Evelyn had misgivings, but the request was not completely out of the blue. She heard from historians and writers from time to time, like the TV guy years earlier. It was the timing that bothered her, coming just a few months after the auction. Could this be the couple that had bought the storage unit? Had they already traced something back to her? She wanted to find out how much they knew and what their real motivation was.

It was unlikely they would connect any dots just from Mary's sewing machine, the files from her title company, and other odds and ends she'd thrown into the unit—in fact, the mix might confuse them. But there was Dottie's suitcase, which she had never opened. She probably should have, but it had become like a sacred trust to her. She remembered grabbing Dottie's journal. Could there be something in there that might prompt questions?

For now, Evelyn just wanted to know if these nosy newcomers were the ones that bought the storage unit, and the only way to find out was to get Arnie to lay eyes on them. They might recognize him, too, so it would be better if he were hidden. That morning, she invited him over for coffee, implying a need to hurry. He burst through the door less than ten minutes later.

"What's goin' on, Ma?" he asked.

"Oh, I just wanted to see you, son," she smiled. He gave her a skeptical look.

"No, really, what's going on?" he countered. "We ain't exactly coffee-drinkin' buddies, me and you, and I don't need no small talk. You got somethin' to tell me?"

"Yeah, I do—not to tell, but to ask," Evelyn said. "You know those people who outbid you on that storage unit?"

"Aw, Ma, for cryin' out loud, let it go!" he said, standing up to leave. "You're gonna worry yourself to death over—"

"Just listen!" she cut him off. "There's some people from Fort Worth who want to come and meet me and look at this building. He says he's writing a book about old buildings. I need to know if this is the ones that bought that unit. If it is, they may be snooping around for a different reason," she added. "Anyway, they're coming here today—this morning."

Arnie sat back down. "And you want me to ID 'em?"

"You're the only one who can," she said. "But they don't need to see you."

"What if it ain't them?" he asked.

"Well, then we may not have a problem," she said. "If they are what they say they are, I'll just tell them some stories, let them take some pictures, and send them on their way."

"And if it is them?"

"I don't know," she said. "But if they put enough clues together, they might be able to make trouble for us, even now."

She poured him coffee and he sat there, sipping, while she peered out the window that looked toward the highway. When she spotted the car driving slowly into town, she shooed him into a side office and got rid of his cup.

"Now don't you make a sound," she said. "I don't want a fight to break out. Just peek out and see if it's them, okay?"

He grunted, settling in behind a closed door that was cracked just enough for him to see who came in and sat at the table.

"Don't screw this up," Evelyn hissed. "Keep quiet. You got that?"

"Yes, ma'am," he muttered.

By the time Henry and Ella had parked in front of the building, Evelyn was heading downstairs. They were on the sidewalk, stretching legs and arms and wondering which door to knock on when she stepped out the unmarked side entry to meet them.

"Y'all must be my building people!" she said, putting out her hand. "I'm Evelyn."

"Good to meet you, Evelyn," Henry said. "I'm Henry and this is Ella. I've been looking forward to visiting with you face-to-face ever since we saw the Channel 8 piece."

"Yeah, I was a TV star for minute there, wasn't I?" she said with a laugh.

"You came across very well," Ella said.

"Missed my calling!" Evelyn shot back. "I should've been one of those weather girls! Bring a little sex appeal to the job!"

They all chuckled.

"Now you folks, y'all work for some architect in Fort Worth?"

"Yes," Henry said, "but we're not on the job right now."

"This is kind of a hobby," Ella said, taking Evelyn's hand. "This building is fascinating."

"You're fascinating, too," Henry said. "You're part of the history of this place, right?"

Evelyn summoned a blush, shaking her head. "I don't know about all that," she said. "I've been here a long time—and how I came to be here is kind of a strange little story. But it's a good building, and it's been my home since, I guess, 1953. More than sixty years.

"But y'all come on in," she said, turning toward the door. She waved a hand at the historical marker on the front of the building. "Did you see the marker yet?"

"Yes," Henry said. "We came by a few weeks ago and looked at that. It's interesting, but we'd like to hear the story from you personally, since . . ."

Evelyn laughed. "Since, against all odds, I happen to still be alive?"

Henry and Ella laughed nervously.

"And still sharp as a tack," Ella said.

"Well, let's get to know each other before you decide how sharp I am," Evelyn said. "I'm getting pretty old. Things don't always come back to me the way they used to."

They stepped through the door and Evelyn motioned them up the stairs.

"I try to stay away from the elevator," she said. "These stairs are part of what keeps me active, and y'all look plenty young enough to handle a few steps."

They skipped up the steps and paused on the landing while Evelyn trudged steadily up behind them. She opened the door and waved them in.

"Here's my humble abode," she said, gesturing toward a comfortable seating group, a coffee table surrounded by chairs and couches. The expanse of the third floor was still mostly open, with Evelyn's kitchen and living area centered along one wall.

"I love the way you converted this into a living area!" Ella said. "It's like a loft—all this open space. But you've made it . . . cozy."

"Well, I had a really good friend who spent a lot of time up here with me, and she had some great suggestions. Can I get y'all some coffee?"

They looked at each other, then Ella said, "Sure! Can I help?"

"No, honey, I've got it," Evelyn said. "It's already made—all I have to do is pour. You can grab that one for you and this one for . . ." She paused, looking at Henry.

"Henry," he said.

"Yes, Henry," she laughed. "Y'all excuse my memory. I think I'm starting to get a little of that 'Old-timers' everyone talks about." She sat down, placing her coffee on the table, and looked at Henry. "I don't see a lot of young guys named Henry these days."

"Actually, the name is making a comeback," he mused. "I guess those old fifties movies with Henrys in them are still popular."

"Or all those English kings," Evelyn said. "Henry the Eighth seems to be especially popular—you know, the one that killed all of his wives?"

Henry and Ella laughed nervously. Their discomfort grew when Evelyn gestured toward a hallway where the attic stair was located.

"Y'know, we found a body up there, back when my son was just a boy," she said. "Some guy got on the roof and took a dive down the coal chute, looking to break into the old Abbott's store and steal something. He broke his neck and just sat up there and . . . he was just a skeleton by the time my son found him."

"Oohh," Ella said, squirming. An awkward silence followed.

Behind the closet door, Arnie was seething. He had already made his identification. He didn't remember Henry, but Ella was not easily forgotten. When they finished their coffee, his mother invited them to follow her downstairs for the grand tour. As soon as the door clicked behind them, he stepped out, seething.

"Mom was right," he muttered to himself. "That's them. They know something."

He paced the floor like a caged lion, waiting for them to leave. Evelyn walked them through Abbott's, the second-floor storage, all the nooks and crannies of the old building. When he heard their voices on the stairs, he quickly stepped back into the closet, closing the door.

"... how many square feet, altogether?" Henry was asking.

"A little over seventeen thousand," Evelyn replied.

"Wow," he muttered. "And the second floor used to be a hotel?"

"Yes. Seven rooms," she said. "This floor is where they did all the cotton-and-cattle trading—cut deals, smoked cigars, and drank whiskey."

"I'm just so impressed with all the interior woodwork, the arches, the turret, and all that carved stone on the exterior," Ella said. "I can't wait to take some pictures—it's a work of art."

Evelyn stood at the door.

"Y'all are welcome to come back and visit some more," she said.

Ella and Henry looked at each other and shrugged.

"Honestly," Henry said, "I think we've taken enough of your time for one morning. I would like to set up another visit, though. Can I call you?"

"Sure, honey," Evelyn said. "You just let me know. Believe it or not, my dance card isn't that full these days!" They laughed and shook hands, then Henry and Ella headed back down.

"Oh, one more thing," Henry said, turning to catch Evelyn just before she went back into her apartment. "Is there a full basement under this building?"

She turned toward him, a quizzical look on her face.

"Yes. But you don't need to see that, do you?" she asked.

"Yes, actually," Henry said. "If not now, next time. I'd really like to see the foundation system, the piers and trusses, how they built for the weight of a multistory building like this back in the early 1900s."

"Well, it's all there," she said. "But it's not exactly a wine cellar. Nobody's been down there in many, many years, and I'm sure it's musty and dirty. There's no light, either. It's probably better if y'all don't go down there."

"Sure, okay," Henry said. "Well, it's not absolutely necessary."

Evelyn's eyes told them the tour was over. She quickly turned to reenter her apartment. Then she looked back, her smile strained. "Y'all be careful" she said, and she was gone, closing the door before they even turned to head down the stairs.

Inside, Arnie was already out of his hiding place, anger in his voice.

"It's them, Ma," he hissed. "It's them! You was right. We got a problem."

* * *

Henry and Ella knew something was off. As soon as the car doors closed, they looked at each other.

"We have a problem," Ella said. "She was all smiles until you asked about the basement."

"I know," he said. "What if...?"

They both shook their heads and stared through the windshield.

"We better go," Ella said. "What about—?"

"Let's go back to Loganville," Henry finished her thought. "Talk to Viv again."

They drove in silence until they were out on the highway. Then Ella spoke.

"Henry, this is starting to feel like we're in a mystery novel," she said. "Surely... surely they didn't, I don't know, bury somebody in that basement?"

"Hey, just because it sounds like a Stephen King book doesn't mean it might not have happened," he said. Ella gathered her thoughts as they drove.

"So Dottie rejected Arnie, and what—he killed her? And he and his mother buried her in the basement?"

"It's possible," he said. "But wow, that's a long time to keep a secret."

"A long time," she echoed. "But they sure wouldn't want it to get out. Ever."

It was a short drive to Loganville. They were both still in shock when Henry pulled up in front of the newspaper office, where they could see the light on and Viv in her customary spot at the front desk. As if on cue, they took deep breaths in unison and looked at each other.

"We have to be calm," Henry said.

"My heart is still racing," Ella said. "Maybe we should go get coffee or something."

"I'd like that, but she's seen us now," Henry said. "And as weird as her hours are, she might not be here when we get back. Let's just take a few more breaths, put on those happy faces, and act like nothing's happened."

"Okay," she said. "Man, this is more dramatic than any of my trials!"

He laughed. Then he proposed an approach.

"Let's just see if she's friends with Evelyn," he said. "If she is, we can't tell her anything. If she's not, I think we need to tell her about the storage unit and the search for Dorothy."

"I guess we're about to find out if we can we trust her," Ella said nervously.

"If she's not Evelyn's best friend, she might be ours," Henry said.

They clasped hands and put their foreheads together. She gave him a quick kiss and they got out of the car. Viv met them at the door.

"Well, what do you know? My old history detective friend is back!"

"Hi, Viv," Henry said. She offered him a little side-hug, then did the same for Ella although they hadn't met. She introduced herself, Ella reciprocated, and Viv turned to Henry.

"So, what are we up to? Need to look at some more back issues?"

"No," Henry said. "This time, I think we need to just talk. We're kind of at a crossroads."

"Sure!" Viv said, delighted to be a resource. "Y'all drag up chairs and we can visit. Like I said, I've been around here a good while."

Ella spoke up first.

"How close are you to Evelyn Chitwood?" she said as they sat down. "Are y'all, like, friends, or just aware of each other?"

Viv's smile faded. "Well, we're in the Rotary Club together, but I wouldn't say we're close friends." She half-laughed. "For a while there, she wasn't a big fan of the newspaper."

"What do you mean?" Henry asked.

"Well, after she bought up everything in Thurston, she wanted to do the same thing in Loganville, but she found out it wasn't for sale. Some of the people around here didn't like her tactics. The paper was in that group, and we worked to stop her—behind the scenes, mostly, but she knew who was on her side and who wasn't. She wasn't the kind of woman you wanted to get crossways with, but back in the day, this newspaper wasn't scared of anybody."

Henry and Ella looked at each other.

"But we're okay now," Viv added. "She runs ads now and then, and of course she's a subscriber. Where are you going with all this?"

"We bought an old storage unit in Fort Worth a few months ago," Henry said. "There was some stuff in there that belonged to Evelyn, and some things that belonged to other people."

Viv's expression didn't change.

"So?" she asked. "What was in there?"

"Well," Ella said, "there was a sewing machine and a bunch of shoes and old ladies' hats, stuff like that."

"That sounds like it was from Abbott's," Viv said.

"Yes," Ella agreed. "There were also a lot of files. Deed records, stuff like that—"

"Oh, yeah. Evelyn had a title office," Viv interrupted. "She sold it a few years ago to an outfit out of Fort Worth, and she got out of it. She kept the office, though, and I'm not surprised if she kept a few of the old files, too."

"Yeah, that's what these were . . . including the deed to her building."

Viv laughed. "I am surprised she let that get away!"

"There was a guy there who tried to buy the storage unit," Henry said. "Big guy, kind of rough-looking, on the back side of middle-age.

He bid it up pretty high, but when Ella bought it, he cut out, fast. None of the people at the storage place knew who he was."

"Ooh, that sounds like her son, Arnie," Viv said. "Without Dewley around, that's who she'd get to run that errand—and it's no surprise he'd screw it up. Yeah . . . he's big, and rough."

After a long pause, Henry spoke again.

"There was also a suitcase in there," he said. "Clothes, high school yearbooks, and a journal. We think it belonged to a girl named Dorothy Sinclair."

Viv's eyes grew wide with excitement.

"Dorothy . . . Dottie! That was her name! That's the girl I was trying to tell you about before—her mom was Evelyn's best friend." She paused, then looked at Henry. "Did you read the journal? Because that might clear up a big mystery."

"I did," Henry said. "Great writer. She talks about a lot of different things, but it ends pretty abruptly, while she was still in high school."

"Hmph!" Viv said, disgusted. "No clue as to what happened to her?"

"No," Henry said. "She did mention that she was scared of Evelyn's son, though. That he had threatened her."

"Threatened her?" Viv said. "The story back then was, he was in love with her."

"And she didn't love him?" Ella probed.

Viv laughed. "Oh, hell no—pardon my French! He was as dumb as she was brilliant. Valedictorian, yearbook editor, most-likely-to-everything. High school football was obviously going to be the high point of his life, so he'd already started downhill. She had it all ahead of her."

"So," Henry said, picking his words carefully. "She just disappeared? Where did she go?"

Viv leaned forward.

"Nobody knows," she whispered. "She may have kept in touch with her mother, but nobody around here ever heard of her again. Some people thought she must have been pregnant, the way she took off so quick. But I don't think so."

"And her mother's gone?" Ella asked.

"Yep," Viv said with a nod. "She died years ago."

The three of them sat, questions hanging in the air. Finally, Henry asked, "So the newspaper never tried to find this girl?"

She laughed. "Oh, sure! We just dispatched our crack team of investigative reporters!"

"Well, I . . ." Henry stammered.

"No, it was a mystery, for sure. But nobody seemed worried, not even her mother. She just left town and never came back. That's the story of a lot of kids who grow up here. Thing was, her mother and Evelyn stayed friends. They were inseparable."

"And you . . ." Ella started.

"When Mrs. Sinclair died, Evelyn was the executor of her estate. I wasn't surprised. Mrs. Sinclair's family was gone, so Evelyn took care of everything. She even set up a trust for Dorothy, in case she ever came back."

Henry looked at Ella and they shook their heads.

"Well, you've been very helpful," he said.

"I don't see how," Viv said, "but I hope y'all find what you're looking for. If you do . . . well, you're an old newspaper guy. Write it up and give the local paper a scoop—goodness knows, we haven't had one of those in a while! You still have my card?" she asked.

"Yes," Henry said as they got up to leave. "And you have mine, too, right?"

"Yes, somewhere" Viv laughed, gesturing to a messy desk covered in papers.

After she shut the door behind them, she stood looking through the glass for a moment as they drove away. When they were out of sight, she closed the blinds, went over to a file marked "dead subscriptions," and began looking through the cards. Finally, she pulled one out and stuck it in a pocket of her dress. Then she turned off the lights and locked the front door.

**Fort Worth**

It was a few days before Henry could find the courage to call Evelyn and set up another appointment. He told her Ella wanted to look at some specific photo locations for the book, and he would need to get more detail from her about those exact spots.

"Yes, that'll be fine," she said curtly. "I don't know how much time I can give you, but if you want to drive all the way back out here, I guess I can let you in."

"Thank you," he said. "I've learned a little more about the building's history, if you're interested."

"Sure," she said, sounding disinterested.

"The architect was the same guy that designed the Tarrant County Courthouse in Fort Worth," he said. "Did you know that?"

"No," she said. "I was just a kid when I did the research for the historical marker, and we didn't have the internet and all, like you've got today. I was happy to find out what little I did."

"Yeah, it was kind of cool," Henry said. "Louis Curtiss had left his partner, a guy named Gunn, and opened his own office in Kansas City. So, he gets this big contract with the Atcheson, Topeka & Santa Fe Railway to build terminals for them all over West Texas."

"Well, isn't that something?" Evelyn said.

"Yeah," Henry went on. "He did terminals in Lubbock, Post, Snyder, and Sweetwater, then your rancher, Robert Ellis, hired him to do the C&C building. Pretty cool, huh?"

Crickets.

"So, anyway, we'll see you Saturday," he said, finally getting her message.

"I'll be watching for you," she said, then the line clicked. He called Ella.

"Hey, I've got us set up for Saturday," he said. "I tried, but I'm not sure I convinced her we're just into architecture and not missing persons."

"When we go back in there, we'd better be ready for anything," she said.

There was a moment of silence.

"Henry, what is it?" she asked.

"I was thinking . . . maybe we should let Viv know we're coming, tell her our schedule. Like when you go backpacking in the wilderness—somebody needs to know where you are and when you plan to get back. Y'think?"

"Yes," Ella said. "I think that's a great idea. We trust Viv, right?"

"Right. I'll call her. Should I tell her what we suspect?"

"No," Ella said quickly. "Everybody is on a need-to-know basis. Just tell her we're going to see Evelyn again, and when."

**Thurston**

This time, Evelyn didn't meet Henry and Ella on the sidewalk when they pulled up in front of the building. But the door was propped open, so they looked at each other, shrugged, and headed up the stairs.

Henry had raised his hand to knock on Evelyn's door when she pulled it open and stepped out. Clearly, they were not invited in. Her greeting was terse, and she launched straight into what sounded like a well-rehearsed speech.

"Listen," she said. "I'm starting to think maybe I don't want this place in a book. It's a neat old building, but it's also my home. I'm afraid if you put it out there, I'll have people poking around here all the time, wanting to look at this or that. Maybe we should just leave it alone."

Henry looked at Ella, then back at Evelyn.

"Wow," he said, shaking his head. "But Miss Chitwood, you agreed to let us do a chapter on your building."

"I know," she said, "and I'm sorry—but I haven't signed anything. I'm sorry for your trouble, and your travel, but—"

"It's not just that," Henry interrupted. "I really think you'll love this book, and your building is going to be a terrific chapter. I've done a ton of work on this—the architect and that story. This place has a great history. I'd hate—"

"No," Evelyn said dismissively. "It would be better for y'all and for me if we just cut it off right here. Don't waste any more time on it. Find another building. Mine's not going to be in your book." She turned to go back into her apartment.

To Henry's surprise, Ella stepped forward, reached up, and stopped the door before it closed. "But really, Evelyn, it's not your building anymore, is it?" she said.

Evelyn looked up at Ella, her eyes narrowing suspiciously.

"What do you mean?" she said. "Of course it's my building!"

"No, it's not," Ella said, sounding like an accusing lawyer in trial. "I did the research. This building is the property of Logan County. They seized it for back taxes in 2010. The only reason you're still living here is because they don't want to evict an elderly woman."

Evelyn quickly shifted the focus.

"You don't sound much like a photographer, young lady," she said, stepping back out onto the landing. "Now why don't the two of you just cut the crap and tell me what you're really doing here?"

"She's not a photographer," Henry said. "She's a lawyer."

"You better have a lawyer!" Evelyn snapped, turning back to Henry. "Because whether you tell me or not, I'm going to find out what y'all are up to. You want to hold me to my promise? You just admitted you're here under false pretenses. Just because you bought a storage unit doesn't give you the right to poke around in my business, my life."

Henry and Ella looked at each other. No one had said anything about a storage unit. There was only one way Evelyn could have known that. At that moment, Arnie stepped out. His menacing face was familiar to both of them, and there was a threat in his voice.

"Maybe we ought to show 'em the basement, Mama," he said.

"Hush," she hissed. She turned back to Henry. "So, I guess you're not really a writer, either," she said, fixing him in her steely gaze.

"No. I mean, yes, I am a writer—a reporter," Henry said. "And I'll tell you exactly what we're doing here. We're trying to find out what happened to Dottie Sinclair."

Arnie stepped toward Henry with his fists clenched. Henry stood his ground. Evelyn inserted her tiny frame between them, pushing her son back.

"Y'all need to go," she said. Henry and Ella headed down the stairs.

"And stay the hell away from here," Arnie yelled after them. "You don't know nothin'!"

By the time they reached their car, Arnie was right behind them.

"I better not see neither one of you around here again," he threatened. "Ever!"

Just then, his mother stepped out, having regained her composure.

"Calm down, Arnold," she said smugly. "Maybe they do know something. Or maybe they just think they know something."

She looked at Henry and Ella. "I guess you read the girl's journal. I never read it, even though it was in my possession for many years. I guess I just respect people's privacy more than you do. Tell me, what is it you think you know?"

"We know Dottie Sinclair was worried about your son," Ella said.

"That's it?" Evelyn asked.

"And he invited her to a party, up on the mesa, on graduation night," Henry said.

"And what else?" Evelyn said, looking as if she'd won her case. "Do go on. As I said, I never read Dorothy's journal. Please, tell me, what else?"

"And there's no trace of her since then," Henry said. "She disappeared."

"You can't find her?" Evelyn said calmly. "Maybe you're not as good of an investigative reporter as you think you are. But what do I know? I'm just a businesswoman.

"Now I'm going to make you an offer: I never see you two again, and this all just stays between us. That would suit me. Come back here, and the only suit will be a lawsuit for harassing an old lady who is just trying to live out her remaining years in peace."

Henry dug in his pocket for his car keys, but Ella was in full prosecutor mode.

"What happened up on the mesa that night, Arnie?" she asked.

Evelyn laid her hand on her son's arm, calming him even as his face twisted in anger.

"What do you think?" she said. "You're the ones with the overactive imaginations. Do you honestly think if my boy did something to that girl, I could stay friends with her mom all those years? Mary was my best friend! My only friend!

"Dottie ran away," she continued. "She just disappeared. Right, Arnie?"

He didn't say a word, just turned and skulked back toward the building.

"I'd like to hear Arnie answer that question himself," Ella called out after him.

Evelyn held out her hand to stay Arnie, then turned to Ella.

"Well, write this down in your journal, Miss Lawyer," she said. "Today, you didn't get what you wanted!"

She turned to go, then turned back around and spoke slowly, her eyes going from Ella to Henry and back, her finger pointing, emphasizing every word. "Y'all better be real careful what you do next."

Henry was starting the car by the time the door closed behind them. Ella slid into the passenger seat, but as she was about to close the door, she saw a small, white card stuck under the windshield wiper, almost invisible. She got out and slid it out from under the wiper blade, then got back in and pulled her door shut as Henry quickly drove away.

"What's that?" he asked as she examined it.

"It's a *Ledger* subscription card," she said. "Viv must have put it here while we were inside. It's got an address—in a place called Chadron, Nebraska."

"Where's that?" Henry asked.

"No clue," Ella said. "Do you want the subscriber's name?"

"Sure," he said, holding his breath.

"Helen Bryant."

Henry and Ella rode in silence for a while. Ella grabbed a travel pillow she'd brought along, curled up in her seat, and leaned back to sleep.

Henry was about to burst. "So," he finally said, "who do you think Helen Bryant is?"

"No clue," she yawned. "Maybe Viv thinks it's somebody we need to talk to. Why? Who do you think she is?"

"It's Dottie!" he almost yelled. "It's Dorothy Sinclair! She took the name from the poet! William Cullen Bryant! *Thanatopsis*! Dottie's alive. She's Helen Bryant!"

Ella yawned again. "Sounds like you have some more research to do, buddy," she said. "Personally, I am worn out."

She laid her head on the pillow, closed her eyes, and was asleep almost instantly. Henry looked at her in disbelief, wondering how she did that. Later, he would learn it was a habit she'd developed when she was prosecuting criminal cases. The more intense an argument was, and the more adrenalin she pumped out, the sleepier she was when the confrontation was over. The showdown with Evelyn and Arnie had left her crashing like a five-year-old who had eaten too much cake and ice cream at a birthday party.

Ella's last waking thought was how Henry had reacted when Arnie stepped into him. He didn't back up, or even flinch. *My boyfriend's so brave* . . . she smiled to herself.

Henry looked at the speedometer and saw he was driving 95 mph. He lifted his foot slowly, until his heart was the only thing racing.

* * *

Evelyn and Arnie sat looking at each other across the table. Finally, Arnie spoke.

"Ma, we gotta do something," he said. "These people ain't gonna quit. They think I killed Dottie, and they're comin' after us."

"They may think that, boy, but they don't know that," Evelyn said. "They can dream up all kinds of possibilities, but if that girl's really a lawyer, she knows they don't have any evidence. Nobody on this earth knows what happened up there except you and Dottie. She's dead, and you say it was an accident."

"It WAS a accident, Ma!" Arnie said. "She fell!"

Evelyn patted his beefy hand. "I believe you, son," she said calmly. "I've always believed you. And I think a jury would believe you, too. God forbid you ever have to put your hand on a Bible and swear to tell the truth, but if you do, you just stick with that story.."

"What are you sayin', Ma?"

She leaned back in her chair, her mind sorting through every option. Finally, she leaned forward.

"Best case, these two just realize they're at a dead end," she said. "We stonewall 'em, and after a while they'll move on to some new treasure hunt."

"But Ma—" Arnie said.

"And if they don't, then we'll deal with them in the courts," she said, cutting him off. "I'll sue them. They are harassing me and slandering my good name!"

"But Ma—what if they figure out about the basement?"

Evelyn was silent, but her body tensed up again.

"You acted real nervous when he asked if he could look in the basement," Arnie said. "I think you might've tipped 'em off. They know something's down there now—something you don't want nobody to find."

"You threatened 'em," she lashed back. "All that tough 'Maybe we ought to show 'em the basement' talk! I might've let it out of the bag, but you made it worse!"

They both sat, looking at their hands.

"Ma, I think we gotta take 'em out," he said.

Evelyn sat silent, then finally shook her head and asked, "What?"

"Take 'em out, Ma," Arnie said. "Take care of 'em. Shut 'em up for good."

"What?" Evelyn yelled. "My eternal soul . . . Dear, God, Arnie! I am not a murderer and neither are you! Are you? All we did was cover up an accident, and I only did it because I knew the truth would kill my dearest, sweetest friend."

Arnie sat for a long moment, looking stunned. Then his gaze rose to his mother's eyes. "You what?" he said.

"Think about Mary!" Evelyn shot back. "She'd already lost her son, then her husband. Dottie was all she had left. She'd have died if she'd thought Dottie was dead, too. I had to give her some hope. I had to give her a reason to live."

"So, all those years . . ." he continued quietly. "All the lying and the secrets and the play-acting—you did all that for Mary?"

"Of course! Can you imagine . . ." Suddenly she realized how her words sounded to him.

He sat frozen, but anger was building inside him like a volcano. Suddenly he stood, knocking his chair over backward. Towering over his mother, he banged the table, hard, with both fists. Coffee splashed from the cups, and the sugar bowl flew off and shattered as it hit the wood floor, white granules strewn amid the shards of pottery.

"What about ME, Ma?" he yelled. "What about ME? What about MY hope? MY life? MY reason to live? You did all that—you made me bury that girl in the basement and keep that secret all these years—just for MARY?"

Evelyn was speechless, afraid Arnie was about to harm her.

He paced back and forth, grappling with his rage, then came back and leaned over, his face inches from hers.

"We're done, Ma," he hissed. "You and me? We're done, as of now. I'm gonna take care of these people myself, my way, and there's nothin' you can do about it, okay? There's plenty of room in that basement for two more—three, if you get in my way."

He reached for the door, then stopped and glared at her.

"You just leave me alone from now on, Ma," he added. "That oughta be easy, since you never cared nothin' about me anyway. I was a accident. You said so yourself. You're finally gettin' your wish. I'm gone!"

He slammed the door, and she heard his feet all the way down the stairs. He had parked his truck around back so Henry and Ella wouldn't see it. She heard it start. Its motor revved up and the noise echoed through the empty canyons of the ghost town she owned—a town that had somehow reappeared on the map, for all the wrong reasons.

Now, she had two problems. Arnie was by far the bigger of the two.

**Fort Worth**

Henry used his office computer to research Chadron, Nebraska—a town he'd never heard of, even though he'd had several friends from Nebraska in college. It was in the panhandle, the far western part of the state, an hour-and-a-half south of Rapid City, South Dakota, and seven hours west of Omaha. It had a population of five thousand people.

It was almost a thousand miles from Fort Worth. The closest a commercial airline could get you was Denver, and from there it was a five-hour drive. The phrase "off the beaten path" seemed to have been coined just for this place. Was this where Dottie Sinclair went to get lost?

What really intrigued Henry was that Chadron was a college town, and Chadron State College was no tiny, nondescript academic institution. Founded in 1911, it had two thousand students and several hundred faculty and staff and offered fifty-one undergraduate degrees.

Henry had pegged Dorothy for an academic career. As a big-enough college in a small town, Chadron State seemed like exactly the kind of place she might have gone.

He shifted his focus to Helen Bryant, knowing the internet would offer lots of hits for such a common name. He was right: there were more Helen Bryants than there had been Dorothy Sinclairs: bloggers, writers, influencers, chefs, moms, managers, actors, educators, felons. The only filters he had were her age, a few photos from when she was in high school, and a sense of her writing voice. As he searched,

Henry became keenly aware that he was trying to find someone brilliant—someone who had worked hard, a half-century ago, to get lost.

It was an ice-cold trail, but he had an advantage: obsessiveness. Ella had told him he could dive deeper, and stay down longer, than anyone she knew. She didn't mean it as a compliment, but he cherished the observation. Over the next several days, working during breaks and lunch, he diligently chased every reference he found.

Finally, he hit the jackpot. In 1972, a student named Helen Bryant had written a master's thesis at the University of Texas. The subject? A lengthy, little-known early American poem: "Thanatopsis," by William Cullen Bryant.

"Bingo!" he yelled, jumping up from his desk and drawing looks from nearby coworkers. "How 'bout those Rangers?" he covered—weakly, given the team's current slump.

But he couldn't have been more excited if they'd won the World Series. At last, he had solid evidence of Dottie. It looked like she was on track to be an English professor, and she may have gotten the *Loganville Ledger* delivered. It was still pretty far-fetched, but Henry felt sure he was on the right track.

He believed Helen Bryant was, in fact, Dottie Sinclair.

This prompted three observations. Number one, if she didn't die on graduation night, Arnie and Evelyn were off the hook. So why were they still so angry and nervous?

Number two, she had graduated high school in 1969, but by 1972 she had published a master's thesis. This kid had flown through the University of Texas! That alone made her harder to find, since her age and academic level were no longer tracked.

Number three, as expected, she had done a thorough job of switching identities. This was, of course, pre-computer, so it may have been easier, but she'd done it so well it was no wonder no one had ever found her. She was Helen Bryant. The Dorothy Sinclair who'd graduated at the top of Thurston High School's class of '69 hadn't died—she had simply ceased to exist.

Now, he had to connect Helen Bryant to Chadron State College. He went to the college's website and quickly found the faculty directory. There was no Helen Bryant, not even a Helen. That would have been too easy, he thought. She'd probably gone there early in her career and moved on—probably even farther away.

He scanned the directory, looking for a professor who'd been there long enough to remember her.

Everyone's office phone numbers were listed. Henry picked one who looked old enough and focused on her academic resumé, finding out she'd been at Chadron State for more than thirty years. He dialed the number, but it went straight to voicemail.

Nervous, he hung up. He wasn't sure exactly how to put into words what he was looking for without freaking someone out. Instead, he decided to call Ella.

"Hey," he said. "Have you been at Penwell long enough to get a vacation?"

"Uh, hi Henry," she said. "Pretty personal question, right up front. How are you doing?"

"I'm good," he said, forcing nonchalance. "So, vacation?"

"Well, as I recall, my contract gives me three weeks anytime in the first year, which is just about over. Why?"

"Oh, just curious," he said. "I don't have a contract, but even people at my pay grade earn a few days off after a while. I'm pretty sure I have two or three weeks coming."

"So, you're taking a vacation?" she asked.

"We are," he said. "Ever been to Nebraska?"

"Henry, you dog! You found her?"

"Not exactly," he said. "This is still part of the search. But the trail is getting warmer. Think of it as a scavenger hunt. Besides, won't it be fun to go somewhere besides Thurston?"

"Yeah, but . . . Nebraska?"

"Ella, I just know this is her. I don't know how long ago she stopped getting the *Ledger,* or when she might have left Chadron, but she was there. I guarantee you that if we go to that campus, we'll find someone who knows her."

"Well," she said finally, "I do like corn."

It took a couple of weeks for Ella to clear her calendar. In the meantime, Henry called Viv, but all she could tell him was that the subscription expired in May of 1986—less than a year after Mary Sinclair's death. She didn't know the person, but she'd always had a feeling it might be Dorothy, using the paper to keep up with her hometown. When he had called Viv to let her know about their upcoming visit to the C&C building, she had decided to drive to Thurston to check on them. When she saw their car, she slipped the card under the windshield wiper, figuring Henry would catch on.

Immediately, Henry started making flight plans. Southwest Airlines could get them to Denver, and they would have to rent a car and drive the rest of the way.

He asked Ella to handle the hotel booking, mostly to see what kind of accommodations she would get. She found a Best Western near the campus and booked adjoining rooms. That was fine with him. They'd been friends most of their lives, and he felt certain that at some point they would be much more. Her kisses told him she believed that, too.

He'd been patient his whole life. He wasn't about to rush things now.

* * *

They enjoyed the trip, even the stopover in Las Vegas. After they landed in Denver, she got the bags, and Henry got the rental car, a Kia. Within an hour, they were on their way to Chadron.

It was a scenic drive up the edge of the plains, with mountains to the west and farmland everywhere else. The drive seemed short. Their hotel was on the highway; after they checked in, the short walk to the campus sounded good after a day of flying and driving.

The young woman at the hotel desk was a student. She told them they could go straight down Tenth Street and be on campus in about a half mile. They passed a busy bowling alley on their left, open cornfields on their right. There was a cemetery, then a park, and a block later they were on campus. It was beautiful, with manicured landscaping and a mix of old and new buildings, most of which had donors' names on them.

The original administration building, where the English faculty's offices were located, was closed, but to their surprise, not locked. They entered, and after walking seemingly endless hallways, they found a small cubby of an office that belonged to the teacher Henry had tried to call, Sharon McPeak. She was not there. A sign on the door said her office hours were Monday and Thursday, 2 to 4 p.m. They had missed her.

They decided to take the weekend off and try again Monday.

On the way back, they saw groups of students studying, tossing frisbees or footballs, kicking soccer balls, or just going somewhere together. They spotted a couple seriously in love, so deeply entwined they could barely walk.

"Ah, young love!" Henry said. Ella held herself together until they were a safe distance away, then she nearly fell down laughing.

"Is that what you were like?" she said, giggling. "With your college girlfriends?"

"No!" he said defensively. "They were all over me, but I didn't . . . what about you?"

"Oh, Henry," she said wistfully. "I was already married by the time I went to college, remember?" She looked at him, took his hand, and slipped into his arms. "And already alone."

As they walked on together, into the setting sun, he admired the way the wind blew her hair back from her face. He'd never seen anything quite so beautiful.

* * *

After dinner at the hotel, they decided to give their jet-lagged, road-weary brains a break by retiring early. Henry showered, put on shorts and a t-shirt, and sat down on the bed with the TV remote in his hand. He had barely started exploring the local cable offerings when there was a tap on the door that separated their rooms. When he opened it, Ella stood there, also in shorts and an oversized t-shirt, holding two chocolate milkshakes.

"There's a malt shop in the bowling alley!" she said, offering one to him.

"You're way ahead of me," he said, taking it and immediately executing a big slurp on the straw. "I can't even find anything on TV."

"Let's look together!" She bounded into the room, flopped onto the bed, and began fluffing pillows for both of them, nesting a spot for an evening of TV watching. He watched in wonder, ready for anything.

By the time he settled into his spot, she was rifling through the TV channels, rejecting anything labeled as news, a documentary, a home improvement show, or science.

"Hey, do I get any input here?" he asked. "It is my room."

"Sure," she said, not offering him the remote. "How about we each get three strikes? You pick something you want, and if I absolutely don't want to watch it, I'll strike it."

"So, three strikes, but more like jury selection than baseball?" he said.

"Exactly! If I pick something and you're out of strikes, you have to watch it with me."

"And vice-versa, my dear," he stipulated.

"Of course, my darling. That would only be fair."

He quickly struck her first two choices, *Sleepless in Seattle* and *You've Got Mail.*

His choices, a documentary about an Everest expedition and a Science Channel special, fared no better.

"No!" she said. "I did not come all the way to Nebraska to learn about salamanders!"

"But they're adorable!" he countered. "I had a pet one when I was little. His name was Leroy, and I smashed flies and put them on the end of a stick. He would flick his tongue out and get them. But they had to be fresh. It helped if they were still wiggling."

She didn't budge. Her next choice was *Shrek* and he caved. Animated, perhaps, but a love story, and it had been a while since either of them had seen it. They giggled at Donkey's quips, sang along, and laugh-cried when Lord Farquaad tortured the Gingerbread Man. As the evening went on, they settled into each other's arms. When it was over, having never relinquished the remote, Ella clicked the TV off.

They sat in silence for a moment.

"So, Henry-baby," she said. "Where are we?"

After a pause, he answered, "If I'm not mistaken, we're in Chadron, Nebraska."

She leaned out and turned around to face him, kneeling on the bed. They spent a long moment just looking into each other's eyes.

"You know what I mean," she said. "Me and you. Where are we headed?"

He let out a long breath. "I don't know," he said. "At one level, this is just a lot of fun, and I think we both need that. But on a whole 'nother level . . . I don't even want to think what my life would be like if you hadn't come back into it."

"I'm right there with you," she said, taking his hand. "We've been obsessing on the storage unit thing, Dottie and all that, but me and you—we're more than that. We're good partners. I have a lot of fun being with you, and it's been a long time—a very long time—since anyone made me feel like that."

She paused, then added, "Honestly, I've never felt like that with anyone but you."

"Me, neither," he said. "I think . . . this is how it's supposed to be."

"Yeah," she said, melting into his arms. "When it's right."

A moment later, she whispered in his ear between kisses, "Which is new to me, too, by the way."

"Me too," he said.

They lost track of time, finding each other for the first time, over and over, until at a certain point, they both heard the same alarm bell, pulled back, and looked at each other again, for a long time. Finally, Ella spoke.

"This . . ." she said, reaching out to tenderly touch his face. "This feels right." Then she looked around the generic hotel room. "This doesn't. This isn't us."

"I know," he said. His heart was pounding, but he knew she was right.

They sat there in silence for another moment. Then she looked in his eyes again.

"Henry," she said, "I'm in. Wherever this takes us, I'm in."

"Me, too," he said. "I can't see any future that doesn't have you in it."

"But let's find Dottie first," she said. "I'm ready for that to be over—so we can go on."

"And on and on," he echoed. "You got it." He bounced off the bed and opened the door to her room. "See you for that complimentary breakfast in the morning?"

"Absolutely," she said. "I'm gonna hit that waffle maker."

"I'm thinking biscuits and gravy," he said. "Y'know, go ahead and get my cholesterol quota for the rest of the year."

They kissed goodnight and she slipped away.

* * *

Over the long weekend, Henry and Ella drove up into South Dakota, saw Wind Cave National Park, and visited Custer State Park. It wasn't far, particularly on the scale that defined this wide-open part of the country. They enjoyed the sights, and each other's company, immensely.

Monday afternoon, associate professor Dr. Sharon McPeak was right where her sign had said she would be: in her tiny office, grading essays. Henry tapped on the door and without looking up, she sang out a hearty, "Come in, and know me better, man!" quoting the Ghost of Christmas Present in Dickens's *A Christmas Carol.*

Ella's expression said she thought that was a strange way to answer a knock. Henry was delighted at the literary greeting. They stepped inside, waiting while she wrote furiously in red ink. Finally, she looked up, realized they were strangers, and immediately stood and began clearing file folders from the two chairs that faced hers so they could sit down.

"Oh!" she said. "I'm so sorry! How are you guys doing?" She looked at them again, searching their faces. "Whose parents are you? What can I do for you?"

Ella laughed as she slid into a worn leather chair.

"Don't worry," she said. "We're not anybody's parents. Well, I do have two children in college, but not here, and not with . . ." She nodded in Henry's direction.

"I don't have any children anywhere, that I know of," he said, easing into the other chair. "We just want to see if you can help us find a former colleague of yours."

"Well, sure, I . . ." The professor looked puzzled.

"We're not detectives or IRS agents or anything," Ella said. "We just . . . it's kind of a long story, but we are trying to locate this person because . . ." She looked at Henry.

"The trust," he said. "She's come into a sum of money. Quite a bit of money, actually, and we want to make sure she gets it."

"Oh!" Dr. McPeak said. "Well, that's a worthwhile errand. Most of us in academia dream about sums of money, but all we get is some, not sums. To stretch a homophone."

Henry laughed. Ella shook her head, wondering if she'd really just heard a grammar pun.

"So which of my former colleagues has come into these sums?" the professor asked.

"We believe her name was, is, Helen Bryant," Henry said.

Dr. McPeak wrinkled her brow and looked at the ceiling.

"Wow, that sounds familiar," she said. "I've been here thirty years, so I'm trying . . ."

"She may have gotten married before you met her, in which case she might have had a different last name," Ella said. "What about Helens?"

"Let's see," she said, eyes closed. "Helen? I do remember a Helen. If it's who I'm thinking of, she left quite a long time ago. But Bryant doesn't sound right."

She swiveled in her chair and began looking at the overloaded shelf to her left. A 1987 Chadron Eagle yearbook caught her eye and she pulled it out. She rifled to the faculty page, then turned it around and set it down in front of Henry and Ella.

"Helen Bryant *Porter*," she said, pointing to a photo. "She and I were friends, sort of, although she was a hard person to know. Guarded. This was her last year, I think."

Henry's eyes followed her finger to the photo, and his breath left him in one big whoosh as he recognized Dottie. He held the book so Ella could see better. "It's her!" he said. "See?"

Suddenly the professor looked concerned, as if she'd betrayed a confidence.

"Are you guys bounty hunters?" she asked. "Is this woman a fugitive?"

"No!" Henry cried. "Like I said, we—"

"Because honestly, she was a little mysterious," Sharon continued. "I wouldn't be surprised if she was in witness protection or something." Her laugh was strained. "She was just one of those iceberg people, you know?"

Henry looked up from the book. "I do!" he said. "A lot below the surface, not seen."

"Exactly!" she said. "There was always something about Helen . . ."

"Seriously, we don't know her," Ella said.

The professor looked from Henry to Ella, and back. "Helen Bryant Porter," she said. "She always used 'Bryant Porter.' You never got just 'Helen Porter' from her—you got all three names, like Helen Gurley Brown.

"Here's her CV at the time," she continued reading. "She did undergrad and masters at the University of Texas. Her field was early American literature. Yes. She came in 1980. I got here in '85, and she left in '87."

The professor continued to read, then laughed. "Yes! I remember she was obsessed with this little-known early American poet. Wrote her dissertation on him." She shook her head.

"What is it?" Henry asked.

"Oh, it might not mean anything to you, but it strikes me funny."

"What?" Ella said. "Try us."

She sat back in her chair. "Some of the kids, when they heard her name, told us it was spooky," she said. "Like she had known this guy personally. One of my students said she thought they were married in a past life. Said it gave her classes an eerie feeling."

"Who was this poet she was so fascinated with?" Henry asked.

The professor thought for a moment, then smiled. "William Cullen Bryant," she said.

"'Thanatopsis'?" Henry said.

The professor looked shocked. "Yes! You know it?"

"Almost by memory," Henry admitted, a little sheepishly.

"Then you might enjoy her dissertation: *Elegiac Echoes: Death as a Link Between Early American Poets and England's Late Romantics*."

Henry and Ella both leaned in to read her CV on the screen.

After leaving UT, she'd completed an internship at the College of Idaho. She joined the faculty at Chadron State College in 1980 and was awarded the Dean's Scepter as the College's Outstanding Professor for seven straight years. She'd left Chadron in 1987 and taken a job at the University of Victoria, British Columbia. According to the screen, she was still there.

"Oh, my," Dr. McPeak said. "I can't blame her for leaving Chadron for Victoria. That's a beautiful campus. And the connection to Great Britain would have been perfect for her to pursue that doctorate. She probably studied at Oxford."

Henry and Ella looked at each other.

"I hate to be so much trouble," Ella said, "but can you print this?"

"I'd be happy to," Sharon said. "I'm just grateful you aren't here to tell me your little darling should have gotten an A on her plagiarized essay!"

They laughed, and she handed them the paper. Thanking her profusely, they left the office holding hands. As they walked back to the hotel, Ella looked at Henry.

"You know, I'm not opposed to visiting that beautiful campus," she said. "Did you bring your passport?"

"I never leave Texas without it," he said. "You never know when they're going to secede from the Union, and you'll need it just to get back in." When they got back to their hotel, they booked the first available flight to Seattle, and headed back to Denver the next morning.

* * *

**Fort Worth**

Arnie wasn't allowed to have a firearm, but like a lot of convicted felons in Texas, that did not stop him. In fact, through gun shows and other less reputable channels, he had amassed an impressive collection: a few shotguns, a couple of high-powered rifles, and an array of handguns. He kept them hidden in a back closet in his house on the edge of Thurston in case his parole officer decided to drop by. But he also had a gunbox he'd built during his long-haul trucking days and adapted to fit under the seat of his pickup, hidden and safe. It held a loaded, easily accessible .38 special.

Nobody was going to get the jump on him.

These "researchers" who had suddenly gotten so interested in the history of the C&C building—they had a history, too, he decided. The Logan County Library wasn't exactly his home turf, but he headed there the next day to search for architecture firms in Fort Worth. It took him a while, but he narrowed it down to a dozen or so and started looking through websites. He hit nothing but dead ends until he stumbled upon Penwell, with offices in the Burk Burnett Building. He found the staff directory and, since he searched executives first, quickly came across Ella's photo. As corporate counsel, she was high on the organizational chart.

"Yeah!" he congratulated himself. "There you are! Dang, I bet you make a lot more money than your little boyfriend! Better lookin' too." A few minutes later, he was looking at Henry's photo. He sneered for a moment, then grabbed a piece of scratch paper and took down all the information that was there. He flipped back over to Ella's page and wrote hers down, too. Then he folded the note and tucked it into his back pocket.

He was going to pay this cute couple a visit.

* * *

Flying into Seattle-Tacoma International Airport, they again split up duties: Henry went to rent a car while Ella waited at the baggage carousel. He found a Honda hybrid and was eager to tell Ella he was saving both the planet and money, but when he approached the baggage area, she was beaming.

"Henry," she said, waving a flyer at him. "Guess what I found?"

"Our luggage?" he said.

"It's not here yet," she said dismissively. "But look! The Victoria Clipper! It's a ferry that leaves once a day from Seattle and goes directly to Victoria. You drive on, sail out of Puget Sound, through the Strait of Juan de Fuca—" her Spanish accent was impeccable, "—and then you drive off in Her Majesty's provincial capital! And we have a couple of hours to get there."

"Cool," he said. "I, uh, got us a hybrid."

"Cool," she agreed.

They thought about stopping for coffee at the original Starbucks, but as they drove by, they could see the line was around the block. They decided to get coffee on the ferry.

"I'm whale-watching the whole time," Henry said. "I hear Juan de Fuca is teeming with humpbacks!"

They stood at the rail as the big boat pulled out of Seattle. Looking back at the Space Needle and downtown, with Mount Rainier in the distance, water and trees all around them, it was a picture-perfect day. Henry put his arm around Ella. "Wow," he said.

"Yeah," Ella said. She pointed to the people in their seats, looking intently at their phones. "They take it for granted. But to a couple of Texas flatlanders, it's awe-inspiring, right?"

"Even here," he whispered, "the most beautiful thing I see is from Texas." She smiled.

The sun was low by the time they landed in Victoria Harbor and drove off into a Canadian city. *Another good place for a Texan to get lost*, Henry thought.

They ate fish tacos on the pier while the sun finished setting.

Ella had grabbed a map at the airport, and they began looking for hotels along the way. They found one, and Ella was delighted that her phone worked just fine. She booked a suite at the Craigmyle, and they set off. They would head for campus in the morning to locate the elusive Professor Porter.

**Fort Worth**

Arnie parked his pickup just off Sundance Square and reached down to grab the .38, then thought better of it. There were a lot of cops in downtown Fort Worth, and just possessing a gun would send him straight back to prison. This visit would just be a warning, he decided. He was big enough to be menacing without a gun.

The building's lobby was the Worthington National Bank, but he'd done his research. He knew Penwell had the top two floors. He waited for the elevator with a group of men in suits and women in skirts, wishing he'd dressed a little nicer so he didn't stand out so much.

When the doors opened, they crowded in, and Arnie took up most of the space. Just as the elevator started up, he reached to push the button for the eleventh floor and jostled two women who were deep in a personal conversation. They frowned but fell quiet when he met their eyes. By the time the car reached the eleventh floor, it contained just Arnie and two well-dressed men holding rolled-up sets of drawings.

He followed them off, but they quickly rounded a corner and disappeared. Arnie walked to a reception desk where a woman was working at a computer. He stood there until finally, she looked up.

"Can I help you?" she asked.

"Yeah, well, I dunno. Maybe. I'm looking for a guy, named Henry... Henry, uh, Palmer, I think? And Ella... Franklin. That's them. Where are they?"

The woman seemed wary. "Do you have an appointment?"

"No, I just—" he stammered.

"Ms. Franklin's office is upstairs," she said. "I'm sure you'd need an appointment to see her. And..." she touched her keyboard and glanced at her screen, "I see Mr. Palmer is out today. Can you tell me the nature of your business? Are you a builder?"

"No," he said, backing away. "I just... we're old friends, from school. I was going to see if they wanted to go get coffee or something."

Her face said she clearly did not believe him. "If you'd like to leave a message, I can give you their voicemail," she said, reaching for her phone. When he stepped back, her expression shifted to high alert. "Or I can leave a message. Can I get your name?"

"Uh, I..." Arnie looked around, wondering what he had thought he was going to accomplish. "No, ma'am, that's alright. I'll go see... Henry after he gets off work." He turned and started walking away.

"Sir!" the woman said. "Can I tell Mr. Palmer you came by? Sir? Your name?"

"No thanks!" he growled over his shoulder as he headed for the elevator. He pushed the button for the ground floor, then turned and glared at her. She was standing, phone to her ear. He was sure she was calling security. But the elevator doors opened, and he stepped in.

Alone in the elevator, he muttered to himself all the way down.

"What were you thinking? Man, you weren't thinking—that's the problem! Another screwup for the undisputed screwup champion of the world."

The security camera got an excellent view of his scowling face as he exited the elevator and stepped out into Sundance Square.

* * *

**Victoria, British Columbia**

The next morning after breakfast, Henry and Ella walked out and got their first view of Craigdarroch Castle, a national historic site that was literally right behind their hotel. It wasn't open, but they took a little time to walk around and gawk at its Victorian arches and turrets.

"Wow," Henry said. "This place reminds me of Hearst Castle. But this guy, Dunsmuir, made his fortune in coal, not newspapers."

"Impressive," Ella said without enthusiasm.

Henry was feeling philosophical. "What is it about these titans of industry, back in those days, who came out west, made tons of money, then built themselves castles?"

"Hmm," Ella mused. "Maybe . . . compensating? Like our buddy Lord Farquaad?"

They laughed all the way to the car, and Ella navigated while Henry drove. The streets looked like an English town, but Henry was grateful Canada hadn't adopted the British habit of driving on the wrong side.

They entered the campus through exquisitely tended gardens and dense forest. Henry rolled the windows down so they could smell the magnolias, rhododendrons, and camellias, dripping with morning dew under the rainforest canopy.

"Y'know," Henry said, "I don't think we're in Kansas anymore."

"Or Nebraska," Ella said. "And we're sure not in Thurston."

Within a few minutes, a sign pointed them to the Clearihue Building, which a pamphlet told them was home to the Humanities,

Technology Solutions, and the Computer Help Centre. Since most of the students rode a bus, biked, or walked to class, parking was not a problem. Reading from a guide they'd picked up at the gate, Ella noted that Clearihue was the oldest building on campus.

"Of course," Henry said. "That's where they always put the English department."

"Oh, look!" she said, holding up a picture. "The law school is super-new and modern."

"Yeah," he said. "Big rich donors."

"Well, those best-selling novelists need to pony up for their alma mater, instead of building castles," she said.

Henry was surprised that the place wasn't ivy-covered and ancient-looking, but had lots of futuristic glass-and-steel buildings set among green spaces, fountains, and tall trees. The buildings had lots of windows, and there were trails everywhere that disappeared into the woods, calling students to commune with nature.

Clearihue was a quadrangle of offices and classrooms around a green courtyard. They entered on a corner and walked down a long hallway until finally, at the bottom of a stairwell, they found a staff directory. When he saw Professor Helen Bryant Porter's name, Henry's brain started buzzing. He looked at Ella.

"Oh, my," he said. "I guess this is it." He started taking deep breaths.

"You okay?" she asked.

"I don't know," he said. "It just . . . it doesn't seem like it should be this easy?"

"Easy?" she said. "It's been a struggle, in my humble opinion! Airplanes, automobiles, a boat, a couple thousand miles . . . you do realize we're in a different country, don't you? Easy?"

They headed up the stairs and walked more hallways until at last they found an office door with her name on it. It was locked, and the lights were off. Henry looked for a sign with her office hours, but when Ella spotted someone walking down the hallway, she hailed him, remembering that Canadians were famously polite.

"Excuse me," Ella said. "Do you know where we might find Dr. Porter?"

"No worries," the young man said with a friendly smile. "She's down in the lecture theatre, I believe. I can walk you down there."

Ella said they could make it on their own, but he insisted on walking with them. "Actually, she's giving her last class today," he said. "Retiring. She's been here forever."

"Thank you so much," Ella said. As they neared the open doorway, they could hear a woman's voice. They stepped in quietly but saw to their dismay that they were at the front of the hall. To their right, about fifty people were seated at desks in rows to the back wall. Near the front, a distinguished-looking woman smiled as she spoke in a soft but authoritative voice.

"Oh!" she said. "We have more visitors! Please come in. There are a few seats left, but I'm afraid they're in the front row. You have to come early to get the back ones."

A hushed laugh rippled through the room, and Henry and Ella sank with chagrin into two open seats just inside the door. The professor looked right at them and stage-whispered loudly.

"I was nearly through anyway," she said. "I've never been a big fan of goodbyes, and that's what this is." More laughs.

Henry smiled, then gave Ella a knowing nudge. This was definitely Dottie. She was in her late sixties, but she was still the same beauty that led the Thurston High School class of '69.

"To sum up, I hope you all continue to pursue your own education as the world delivers it to you—the world present and the world past," she said. "I hope you know real learning doesn't take place only in academic settings. These poems, these images—they didn't arise in a classroom. They sprang from nature, from experience, from long walks under the sky and relationships as deep and real as a thunderstorm.

"Their lives were as busy as yours, their times just as turbulent," she continued. "They sought, as best they could, to learn from it all, to find the kernels of eternal truth, and they wrote them down for us.

The least we can do is pay attention—but those of you who've been in my classes know my mantra: 'Never do the least you can do. Do the most.'"

She closed her folder and looked with bright eyes at the faces in the room.

"I've avoided goodbyes my entire life, and I would avoid this one, too, if I could." She paused, smiled, and continued. "How I wish, like Bilbo Baggins, I had that ring in my pocket, and I could just slip it on and disappear!"

Another muted laugh filtered through the room.

"But I wouldn't want to draw the attention of Sauron, now, would I?" she winked. She smiled warmly at a group that was obviously colleagues in the front row, put a hand to her heart and the other to her lips, blew a kiss, and stepped down as the applause grew into a standing ovation. Henry and Ella stood, too, then stayed to the side as students and colleagues queued up to offer their best wishes. Finally, she turned to Henry and offered her hand.

"And who do I have the pleasure of meeting on my last day at UVic?" she said.

"I'm Henry Palmer, and this is Ella Franklin," he said, nodding toward Ella.

"You're from Texas," the professor said. "That accent is difficult to disguise. What brought you all this way?"

Henry smiled. "We were wondering if we could talk to you for a few minutes, maybe in your office."

She looked around. The room had emptied out and it was just them.

"We can stay here," she said, taking a seat in the front row and bidding them sit back down. "Now what can I do for you?"

"Dr. Porter, we've been on a long journey to find you," Ella said.

"And may I ask why?"

Without a word, Henry reached into the pocket of his coat and pulled out a small, leather-bound journal. He placed it in front of her. "I've read some of your writing."

Her half-amused expression became serious, and the color drained from her face. She took the book as if it was a sacred relic. She lifted it, closed her eyes, and pressed it to her cheek. A tear spilled out, then another. When she lowered the book and opened it, the poem she had pasted into the front cover as a teenager unfolded. "Thanatopsis."

She sighed and leaned back in the chair, and when she looked back to Henry and Ella, she was a different person. She was Dottie Sinclair.

"Where did you get this?" she asked. "How did you find me?"

Ella told her the story: the storage unit auction, their discoveries and suspicions, and their contact with Evelyn and Arnie.

"They're still there? Oh, my—it's like they're frozen in time," she said.

"We still have a lot of questions," Henry said. "All we know is that you had misgivings about Arnie. You were a little scared of him. That's where the journal ends."

She drew a ragged breath and looked toward the ceiling. Her shoulders began to shake in silent sobs, and Henry wished he knew her well enough to offer a consoling hug. All he could do was watch as she dealt with waves of memory.

"I know this is a lot to absorb, all at once," he said. "And I'm sure this was already an emotional day for you. It's just—we've been living with this story for a while, now, and we . . ."

"I'm a former prosecutor," Ella said. "We were afraid this might be an unsolved murder."

Helen leaned forward. She was a distinguished professor, accustomed to being in the driver's seat, asking all the questions and having all the answers. She looked from Henry to Ella and back again, then put her hands over her face and took several deep breaths.

"Arnie got a little scary," she said finally, moving past the shock. "But I was tougher than everyone thought. My big brother saw to that. I wasn't about to go with Arnie that night—I was going home to stay with my mother. But we had a fight in the car. A big fight. I never even went inside. I walked away, down the street. And there was Arnie, in his old pickup truck."

"You got in with him?" Ella asked. "After all that?"

"Yes!" Helen said. "I had confidence in myself. He was bigger, but I was smarter—and there was a big storm coming."

"So, what happened?" Henry asked.

Helen smiled. "I've thought about writing this as fiction, but it would be too implausible. He drove us up onto the mesa, in the pouring rain, and stopped the truck. Then, yes, he started to threaten me, grabbed my arm and wouldn't let go. It hurt. When I finally twisted free, I opened the door and jumped out . . . and I fell."

"You fell down?" Ella asked.

"I fell off the mesa," she said. "He had parked so close to the edge, there was no ground under me when I stepped out. I thought I was going to die. If I hadn't caught onto a scrubby mesquite tree, I would have. I managed to scramble back under a little overhang just a few feet below the edge."

"So what did Arnie do?" Henry asked, his mind working to reconcile Arnie and Evelyn's actions to what Dottie was saying.

"This is the implausible part," she said, her voice solemn. "At the exact moment I fell, a girl jumped out of the back of that truck. I heard her scream. Remember, it was pouring rain and pitch-dark. She sailed right over the edge, over me, and went flying down the side of the mesa. She never had a chance. It was the most horrible thing I ever saw. I could see her bouncing, tumbling in the flashes of lightning, down and down and down. There was no way anyone could have survived that fall."

"But who was it?" Ella asked.

"It had to be Sherry, a girl we knew in school. I had no idea she was in the back of Arnie's truck, but I'd seen her at graduation and noticed we were dressed alike. She'd even bleached her hair blonde, like mine. It was creepy, one more reason for me to want out of there.

"Arnie leaned out of the truck and screamed my name, over and over, only a few feet above my head. But he never saw me."

Henry and Ella sat in silence, dumfounded.

"And that was your chance," Henry said at last.

"That was my chance!" Helen said, leaning forward. "My chance to leave Thurston and all the sadness and smallness behind, forever. A chance to start completely over, to be someone new. Few people ever get that kind of chance. I had to take it."

"But your mom?" Ella said.

"My mom had Evelyn," Helen answered. "Arnie's mother. She was such a good friend. She cared for my mom, and I knew somehow, she always would."

"How did you get out of there?" Henry asked. "Did you hitchhike?"

"I had to wait until Arnie left," she continued. "He was sobbing so hard I was afraid he was going to jump, too. But he went back to the road and worked his way down the hill. God bless him, he picked up the body and carried it back up to his truck in the pouring rain."

"And he never saw you?" Ella asked.

"No," she said. "He thought the girl in his arms was me. He loaded her in his pickup and drove away. That's the last time I saw him.

"I walked down later, after the rain stopped, cleaned up at the truck stop, and found somebody who was going to Austin. Catching rides with strangers wasn't that unusual back then. Once I got there, I had a spot in the dorm."

"As Dorothy?" Ella asked.

"Yes," Helen said. "Dorothy was registered, fees paid, everything all set. But I knew I couldn't get completely lost as long as I was still Dorothy Sinclair. I started going by a different name—Helen Bryant—kept a low profile and avoided relationships. I tutored and wrote papers for people, waitressed at the Nighthawk on weekends, and saved up enough money to get all the documents I needed for a new identity."

"And you went through UT fast," Henry said.

"I took a lot of tests for credit, and a lot of hours," she said.

"And you fooled everybody!" Henry gushed, sounding like a fanboy. "How did you get away with it at a big school like that?"

"I think it was easier because it was a big school," she said. "I got a forged student ID, then a driver's license. Those were easy—there was a kid in the Jester dorm who made his tuition money that way—well, that, and selling weed. Social Security and the passport were tougher. I saved up and had them done by a professional he introduced me to. Halfway through my first semester, Dorothy Sinclair just disappeared. I was already Helen Bryant to the few people who knew me. I just finally had the paperwork to back it up."

She was impressed Henry and Ella had been able to track her.

"So," she looked at Henry whimsically, nodding toward her journal, "you found out the real truth about my affair with Mr. Bryant?"

"I read every word," he said. "You were an amazing writer, even then."

She brought them up to the present. In her first year as a teaching assistant in Nebraska, she'd met a music professor named Charles Porter, and they'd gotten married. They moved to UVic together, had two children, a boy and a girl, and built a nice life. Both of the kids were grown now. Her husband had died of cancer the previous fall.

"I'm so sorry," Ella said, reaching out for her hand. "So, what are your plans now?"

"Well, I was going to just stay here and write essays, maybe poetry, see if there was something worth reading in this old gray head," she said. "Now . . . I don't know."

"You could really help us tie up some loose ends back in Thurston," Ella said.

Helen shook her head. "I don't know," she said. "It's been so long."

"Honestly, Thurston has dried up," Henry said. "Evelyn is about the only person left. But . . . she and Arnie both acted really strange when I mentioned the basement. Maybe they buried that girl down there, and spent the last fifty years thinking it was you."

"Poor Sherry," Helen said. "She's my Christ figure, you know? She died in my place."

"Wow," Henry breathed.

"... and her death set me free. My life has been completely different because of her."

"You have an opportunity to set Evelyn and Arnie free, if you're willing," Ella said. "It sounds like it really was an accident. You're the only witness."

Helen sat, silent, blinking, her mind obviously racing.

"You're the only one who can set it straight, Helen," Henry said. "Dottie."

She looked at him, then Ella, took a deep breath, then let it out slowly.

"You know, you run and run and run, your whole life," she said. "Finally, you start to believe no one is chasing you anymore. Then, one day..." she smiled, "there they are!

"Maybe you're right," she said. "Maybe it's time we all had a little closure."

After another pause, she smiled.

"It's been a long time since I had any good Texas barbecue."

* * *

**Thurston**

Arnie didn't know what to do next. He knew he wasn't going to just go to Fort Worth, find Ella and Henry, and gun them down. That was a fantasy.

Grudgingly, he admitted his mother was probably right. Leave it alone and they will lose interest. It was a hobby for them, a game.

But if they came back to Thurston, he would be ready for them. He knew they were suspicious about what had happened to Dottie, and their attention had been drawn to the C&C building's basement. He couldn't afford for anyone to go snooping down there. He began to work on a new plan, just in case.

His mom went to Loganville every Tuesday to run errands and see her lawyer, and once a month, she went to the Rotary Club. He picked Rotary day, parked nearby, waited until she was gone, then let himself in and headed straight down the basement stairs. He stepped into the darkness and turned on his flashlight.

Arnie was not prepared for the moment.

The basement was just as he'd left it, almost fifty years earlier: dirt floor punctuated by orderly brick piers, holding the giant steel beams that supported the building. The low ceiling was the floor of Abbott's. In the ghostly quiet, he could almost hear the music, shoppers browsing overhead, the ringing of cash registers. Throughout the basement, surplus bricks were stacked here and there, extras no one had bothered to haul away. And off to one side, a bucket, half-full of dried ancient mortar. Looking past it, up under the side wall, he could see a section walled in with hastily laid bricks. Tears filled his eyes.

Arnie had come to plot an ambush. He'd forgotten he was visiting a tomb.

Suddenly he was a teenage boy again, tenderly carrying the broken body of the only girl he would ever love, laying her on that ledge, then walling it closed forever. He would give everything he had if he could just run the clock back and keep that from happening.

He bowed his head for a moment, then gathered himself, walked over, and raised the dock door. It took him four trips to carry in an arsenal of loaded guns, along with tarps, sacks of mortar, a few bricklaying tools, and a bucket of water. This time, he was ready.

If anyone decided to profane this holy place, there would be a couple more burials.

* * *

Dottie insisted they call her Helen, the name she'd gone by most of her adult life. After an evening of questions and answers, she decided she could trust Henry and Ella. She would fly back to Fort Worth with them. Natalie wouldn't be home for a few weeks, so she could stay with Ella. If their plan worked, it would give Evelyn and Arnie closure, provide a decent burial for Sherry, and furnish Helen with an ending—a happy one, she hoped—for the implausible autobiography she was now determined to write.

Driving home from the airport, they began to talk strategy.

"I don't think Evelyn will be willing to meet with us again," Ella said. "And if we give her a heads-up, Arnie is probably going to be there, too, waiting for us."

"And it'll be more than just threats this time," Henry said. "That guy's seriously scary."

"We're going to have to surprise Evelyn somehow," Ella said.

Helen was quiet in the back seat. Finally, she spoke. "You know, Arnie was fine right up to our senior year. He had just gotten so big, and he was a football star, and it's like it went to his head. That's when he started to get scary. Before then, he was just a big puppy."

"Well, that puppy did two tours in Vietnam, then some prison time," Ella said. "His rap sheet is as long as your arm. When he starts scowling and growling, you've got a problem."

"He did have a temper," Helen said.

"You wrote about it!" Henry said. "And we've seen it, too, close-up."

Henry took the exit for the Cultural District. They gave Helen a driving tour of Fort Worth, a city she hadn't seen since the 1960s, through the Cultural District, Sundance Square and the Bass Performance Hall, then up North Main to the Stockyards.

"Might as well go ahead and hit Riscky's," he said, looking at Helen in the rearview mirror. "That barbecue itch isn't going to scratch itself!"

Later that evening, they sat around Ella's living room, drinking coffee and brainstorming. Suddenly Ella stood up and pointed at Henry. "What about your newspaper buddy?"

"Viv?" Henry asked.

"Yeah, Viv," she said. "Evelyn hasn't connected us with Viv yet, has she?" She looked at Helen. "This is the lady who runs the newspaper office in Loganville. She gave Henry some good information. They bonded, you know, that 'printers-ink-in-the-veins' thing. She was the one who gave us your old subscription card, for Helen Bryant."

"That's what led us to Chadron," Henry said.

"Wow," Helen said. "I'd forgotten about that. I did subscribe for a few years, just to keep tabs on my mom. It got depressing after a while, school closings and hard times and obituaries. One night, I finally just called her."

"You called your mom?" Ella asked.

"I wanted to put her mind at ease, let her know I was alive and didn't hold anything against her," Helen said. "I asked her not to, but I'm pretty sure she told Evelyn."

". . . who obviously didn't believe her," Henry said.

Helen shrugged. "Who knows? Maybe she wanted to, but couldn't. Not long after that, I saw my mother's obituary. It was really short. I was the only survivor listed. I didn't renew the subscription. A year or so later we both got jobs at UVic where I could teach and finish my Ph.D."

It had been a long day, and they knew Helen must be worn out from both the travel and the emotion of the last twenty-four hours. Henry and Ella were still technically on vacation, so they decided to go see Viv the next day and ask her to arrange a surprise meeting with Evelyn.

One thing was certain: It needed to be in a public place.

* * *

By Friday evening, everything was set. Viv called Evelyn and invited her to a small reception the Rotary Club was holding for a district governor. As the oldest member, with all those years of perfect attendance, she told Evelyn he had specifically requested she be there.

"Okay," Evelyn said. "But I don't remember anything about this at the last meeting."

"It's short notice," Viv said. "A lot of members won't be able to come."

Evelyn was silent for a moment. "Viv, they aren't trying to give me some kind of award, are they? Is this some kind of surprise party? 'Cause if it is, I'm not interested."

"No!" she said. "Evelyn! You know me better than that! You deserve an award, but that's not it. It's just what I said: the district governor wants to meet our most distinguished member."

"Humph," she said. "Extinguished is more like it. But I guess I'll come. What time is it?"

"Seven o'clock," Viv said. The line clicked.

It was six when Henry, Ella, and Helen got into town and parked on a back street. They walked around the corner and tapped on the glass. Viv let them in quickly and locked the door behind them.

"Y'all step into the publisher's office," she said. "He retired ten years ago, but he still comes down and reads the papers a couple mornings a week. Most of the time, it's empty."

She closed the door and turned to face Helen, putting out her hand. "You must be Dottie," she said. "Wow. After all these years, you've come back home. What a story!"

"I'm Helen now," she said. "That's been my name for almost fifty years, so that's what I answer to. And if it's okay, let's hold off on any stories in the newspaper."

"Your call!" Viv said, laughing. "It would make a great human-interest feature, though. I thought I would snap a few pictures of you and Evelyn, when y'all get together."

Henry and Ellen looked at each other, and at Helen.

"We're not sure how that's going to go over, Viv," Henry said.

"What do you mean? Evelyn's not shy. She's been on TV, for cryin' out loud."

Ella finally spoke. "We're pretty sure Evelyn thinks Dottie is dead."

Viv looked puzzled. "How could she think that? She's the one who set up the trust. Shoot, she wrote the obit and listed Dottie as a survivor. She was best friends with Dottie's mother."

Henry and Ella looked at each other. It was Henry's turn.

"We believe she thinks Dottie's dead because she and Arnie

thought they buried her in the basement of their building," he said.

"What?" Viv had to sit down. She looked at Helen, then at Ella and Henry. "I think I missed something here. Dottie—Helen—is sitting right here. What makes Evelyn think she's dead and buried in the basement?"

Helen took over, recounting the graduation night story, fighting with her mother, getting in with Arnie, falling from the mesa—and the girl who jumped and tumbled all the way down.

"So, who was it?" Viv asked.

"We're pretty sure it was a girl named Sherry who had a crush on Arnie," Helen said. "On graduation night, she was dressed exactly like me. She'd even dyed her hair blonde. What she was doing in the back of Arnie's truck, I have no idea. But just as I fell out, she jumped."

"She jumped? Like, committed suicide?" Viv was transfixed.

Helen nodded. "We must have come out at exactly the same moment. A mesquite tree stopped my fall, but she jumped beyond me. Arnie thought I was the girl who fell all the way down the mesa. But I was right there, watching the whole, awful thing.

"What's really sad is that . . ." She paused before continuing.

"Well, there's a lot that's really sad. But it's especially sad that no one missed Sherry. And that Evelyn and Arnie have spent their whole lives thinking I was dead and buried in their basement, carrying that guilt around, all those years."

"That's . . . quite a story," Viv said. "I guess Evelyn . . ." Her voice trailed off. "So, how's Evelyn going to take this? How do you tell someone the body they buried wasn't who they thought it was? Is this gonna be good news or bad news?"

"We have no idea," Henry said.

Just then there was a tap at the glass. It was Evelyn.

Viv shut the office door behind her and went to the front to let Evelyn in.

"So, where is everybody?" she fumed. "Where's this out-of-town bigshot who just has to see me?" She glared at Viv, her eyes fierce. "Viv Cooper, if this is some kind of surprise party, I'm about to ruin it, because I'm going to turn right around and walk out of here."

She waved her arms. "Okay, everybody! You can come out now!" she yelled. "The old lady is leaving!"

"No!" Viv said. "Evelyn . . . have a seat. It's not a party, but . . ." she looked nervously over her shoulder, "it is a surprise. A really, really big surprise."

Just then, Henry and Ella stepped out of the publisher's office. Evelyn stood up.

"What are they doing here? I'm not talking to these people!" she said angrily. "They lied to me, and I'll bet they lied to you, just to get me down here. Those—"

"Evelyn," Henry said. She turned to face him, and everyone held their breath. "We lured you down here under false pretenses. But there's something you need to know."

She glared at him.

"We found Dottie," he said. "She's alive."

The old woman's face registered hope, disbelief, and rage, all at the same time.

"You—" she cut herself off, shaking her head, dismissing the idea. "No, you didn't. You may think you did, but you didn't."

"We did," Ella said. "She's here."

She turned around as Helen stepped into the office doorway.

"Hi, Miss Chitwood," Helen said.

Evelyn took a step back, then sat down, missed the chair, and went straight to the floor. Henry and Viv both sprang to help her, but she waved them away angrily. She looked up at Helen, shaking her head in disbelief. She covered her mouth but could not stifle her sobs. She pulled up to a kneeling position, never taking her eyes off of Helen's face.

"It is you, isn't it?" she gasped.

"Yes," Helen said. "It's me, Dorothy Sinclair. For the last fifty years or so, it's been Helen Bryant, then Helen Porter. But I'm Dottie. My mother, Mary, was your best, truest friend—and you were hers."

Evelyn began trying to stand. Henry again reached to take her elbow, but she shook him off and struggled to her feet by herself. She walked over to Helen and looked her over, head to toe, then stared intently into her face.

"But how did you . . . what happened?" she stammered. "Who did we—"

"It was Sherry," Helen said, anticipating the question. "She must have been hiding in the back of Arnie's pickup and jumped at the same time I fell. I latched onto a tree, but she went all the way down."

Through tears, Evelyn looked down at her hands. "I didn't even look," she said. "Arnie said it was you."

"Apparently the fall left her unrecognizable," Henry said.

"And she had dressed exactly like Dottie that night," Ella added. "She even dyed her hair blonde. She had a big crush on Arnie."

Evelyn sank back to the floor, shaking. "All these years," she muttered. "All these years."

Viv reached down, and Evelyn let her take her arm and help her up.

"Why don't y'all come sit in the office, where it's nicer?" she said. "I know you have lots of questions, and Dottie—Helen—does, too. Y'all can take as long as you want."

They had just clicked the office door shut when a pickup screeched to a stop out front. Ella looked at Henry, and as if in slow motion, they dove to the floor.

In the next instant, the front glass window was shattered by the blast of a shotgun.

* * *

Arnold Chitwood stepped through the shattered window, avoiding the jagged icicles of glass as he cranked another shell into the chamber of his .12-gauge shotgun. Henry moved in front of Ella as they looked down its barrel.

"I don't know what's goin' on or how you got my mom down here, but this little scavenger hunt of yours is over," he said. "We're goin' to Thurston."

Inside the publisher's office, Viv motioned for Helen and Evelyn to keep still and quiet as she dialed 9-1-1 on the office phone. She whispered for help to come quick, then laid the phone on the desk, cracked the door and peered out.

"Arnie!" she yelled. "This is Vivian. Lay that gun down! I've already called 9-1-1. The police will be here any second."

"They better get here damn quick, 'cause we ain't stayin'!" he yelled back. "These two amateur detectives wanted to see the basement over there at the C&C, and I'm about to show it to 'em. In fact, I've got a couple of spots down there with their names on 'em! Come on out here, Viv!" he yelled. "I could use a little help."

Viv stepped out as he motioned Henry and Ella to their feet. Ella tried to reason with him.

"Think this through, man," she said. "All you've done so far is vandalism. That's a little jail time. You take us at gunpoint, that's armed kidnapping. That's the rest of your life in pr—"

"SHUT UP!" he screamed. "You need to worry about the rest of YOUR life, because it's not gonna be very long. Now turn around! Both of you!"

He pulled a package of plastic zip ties out of his pocket and gave it to Viv, ordering her to secure Henry's and Ella's wrists behind them while he continued holding the gun on them. She started with Henry.

"TIGHT!" Arnie barked, and she complied. As she reached to do Ella's, a voice came from the office door. He looked, and there stood his mother.

"Arnie!" Evelyn yelled. "Drop that shotgun and let those people go! You're making a bad mistake a whole lot worse!"

"Shut up, Ma!" he shouted, pointing the shotgun at her. "I told you before, I'm done talkin' to you!" He motioned for Henry and Ella to step out through the broken window. They could hear sirens in the distance. Arnie stepped through and opened the back door of his truck.

"Both of you, get in!" he ordered, waving the gun. "Legs in the floorboard, faces to the rear. Nobody's gonna be no hero, okay?" The sirens were getting louder. "Move!" he yelled.

Henry and Ella moved, but too slowly for Arnie's liking. He pointed the shotgun straight up and fired another blast into the night sky. "I said MOVE! I can kill you here as easy as I can over there!" He pumped another shell into the chamber and pointed the gun at them.

Ella started to get in, with Henry behind her.

"Arnie, you're not going to get away with this," Evelyn yelled, stepping out of the publisher's office. "This is a bad plan."

He stepped over in front the window and pointed the shotgun at her. "Maybe so, Ma, but it's my plan. And I told you to shut up! I've got plenty of room and plenty of bricks—I'd just as soon bury my whole past down there!" he yelled, veins popping out on his forehead.

Henry saw his chance. Even though his hands were shackled behind him, his legs were free. He took a step back, then bolted forward and jumped, hurling himself into Arnie's back.

The big man outweighed Henry by more than a hundred pounds, but his legs were right up against the low wall in front of the window, and Henry brought enough force to push him off balance. His shins hit the wall and momentum carried him forward through the opening to face-plant on the floor. The shotgun discharged as he fell, blowing a hole in the office ceiling. He let go as he landed, and it skittered across the floor to Viv's feet. She quickly reached to pick it up. Just then, four Loganville police officers appeared in the window, guns drawn.

"Stay down!" one of them barked at Arnie, stepping through the window and planting a knee between his shoulders. "Ms. Cooper, just put that shotgun back on the floor. Everybody keep your hands in plain sight until we get this all sorted out."

When the officer rolled Arnie over, the big man was looking into the barrels of three pistols. Still lying flat, he slowly stretched his hands above his head and clenched his eyes shut, as if by not looking he could remove himself from the scene. Two of the officers holstered their guns and took him by his burly arms, helping him up and handcuffing him at the same time.

Ella, still outside, moved her hands and realized Viv had not tightened her zip-ties. She wiggled free, then noticed that after bouncing off of Arnie, Henry had fallen on the low wall of jagged glass, rolled off, and was not moving. Looking closer, she saw blood pooling beneath him.

"Looks like I got one of 'em!" Arnold grinned, then he looked at Ella. "Uh-oh, lawyer-lady—I don't think your boyfriend's gonna make it!"

One of the officers immediately called for an ambulance. Ella was quicker. She stepped through the window and rolled Henry over, quickly found the wound on his arm, and applied pressure to stop the bleeding. She leaned down and whispered softly to Henry, and he smiled through the pain.

Arnie wasn't grinning when Ella looked up at him.

"I think he *is* going to make it," she said. "You should probably worry about your own future, Mr. Chitwood." She looked at Evelyn, then back at Arnie. "I'm pretty sure Mom's lawyer isn't going to get you out of this one."

One of the police officers opened the door and was about to lead Arnie out when another voice came from the direction of the office.

"Arnie," Helen said quietly. "I'm sorry it all came down to this."

He turned, saw who was speaking, and looked like he had seen a ghost.

"Dottie?" he gasped. "Dottie? How . . . You're alive?"

"Yes," she said.

"But you . . . up on the mesa—Dottie, you fell! You died! I picked you up," he said, shaking his head back and forth in denial. "I carried you. You were dead! We buried you!"

"That was Sherry," Helen said. "She must have been hiding in the pickup bed. She—"

"Sherry?" His mind went back to that night. "She got out at the liquor store. I told her . . . if she didn't want to party . . . Then when I came back, she was gone. I guess she crawled back there. But why?"

"She loved you, Arnie," Helen said. "That's why she kept trying to be like me—so you'd pay attention to her. The way she dressed, her hair—that was all for you. She thought if she could just be me, you'd love her, too.

"And when she heard you say you'd never love anyone else, she jumped—at the exact same moment that I fell."

In spite of the two officers holding his arms, Arnie sank to his knees, moaning. He stayed there, head bowed, as the paramedics brought a stretcher and quickly loaded Henry onto it. Ella went with them. Soon the ambulance's siren diminished, and Arnie spoke again.

"Dottie, I'm sorry," he said. "I . . ."

"I'm sorry, too, Arnie," she said. Then she looked at Evelyn. "I owe you an apology too, Miss Chitwood. I was a coward. I ran away from Thurston, away from my mom and away from y'all, and everybody. You all had to live with the mess I left behind.

"I can't set it right now, I know. It's been too long. It's too late."

Evelyn took a deep breath. Her mind was racing, her heart pounding. Helen reminded her so much of Mary.

"Honey, we're all sorry for a lot of things," she said, her voice shaking. "None of this is your fault. We all could have done better, made better choices. I'm just so grateful you called your mother. I wish you could have seen her face—it meant everything to her. You coming back now—this means a lot, too. You didn't have to, I know."

The officers led Arnie to a police car and sped away. Evelyn reached out to Viv for a hug and both of them quickly dissolved into tears. Helen walked up and laid her hands on both their shoulders, and they admitted her into their embrace.

It was the least they could do.

**Epilogue**

The next day, the police, the Logan County Sheriff's Department, and the Tarrant County Medical Examiner's office conducted a search in the basement of the C&C building in Thurston. They found a cache of guns and ammunition, along with sacks of mortar, bricklaying tools, and water. At Evelyn's direction, they broke through a small, hastily installed brick wall up under the building's edge and found the mummified corpse of a young white female wrapped in what was left of a blue plastic tarp.

In the left front pocket of her cutoff jeans, the coroner found Arnold Chitwood's senior ring from the class of 1969. They identified her as Sherry Statzenberger and noted seventeen broken and dislocated bones, including a fractured skull and broken neck, all consistent with a devastating fall. The cause of death was listed as accidental. No next-of-kin were found, so she was buried in Thurston Memorial Park, with Evelyn Chitwood covering the entire expense.

No charges were filed against Evelyn or Arnie for failing to report a death or mishandling a corpse. The statute of limitations had run out decades earlier.

Arnold Chitwood was charged with possession of a firearm and destruction of property for the incident at the *Loganville Ledger*. His parole was revoked, and he was sentenced to serve out the remaining two-and-a-half years on his DWI sentence.

He was still in the Logan County Jail, awaiting transfer, when Evelyn made her first visit, bringing Dottie, aka Helen Bryant Porter. She forgave him and asked again for their forgiveness. She said she would write to him and share a copy of her book when it came out. She told Evelyn she would always be grateful for her friendship to her mother. Evelyn told her Mary's friendship was one of the great honors of her life.

Henry Palmer got two units of A negative blood and twelve stitches in the ER at Logan County Memorial Hospital. He was not admitted, but went home that night with Ella and Helen and slept, hard, while they sat up talking most of the night. The next day, he went to Haltom's Jewelry and bought a ring, and when he got back to Ella's place, he took a knee and asked her to marry him. She said yes.

They were married at the First Methodist Church in Fort Worth, having persuaded Helen to stick around long enough to be part of the simple outdoor ceremony. Evelyn insisted on hosting the reception. Two weeks later, Henry was honored as a hero by the Loganville Police and the Logan County Sheriff's Office for his actions in ending the standoff at the *Ledger*.

Helen went home to Victoria, British Columbia, with a check for just over $220,000—the proceeds of her mother's estate, held in trust for her since her mother's death. She immediately began work on her autobiography titled *My Life in Exile*. It would become a *New York Times* bestseller.

After a honeymoon in Victoria, Ella returned to her job as corporate counsel for the Penwell Architecture Firm in Fort Worth. Henry kept his job, too, but cut back to thirty hours a week so he could start on a book highlighting turn-of-the-century architecture in Texas. The C&C building in Thurston was prominently featured, and the book sold modestly well as part of the TCU Press catalogue, where it was hailed as an important contribution to the state's history.

Evelyn Chitwood continued to live in her penthouse apartment in the C&C building, and paid her taxes to purchase it back from Logan County. She installed lights in the basement and started a nonprofit organization to build and operate a museum in the old Abbott's Department Store on the ground floor. Lovingly restored, with many of the old fixtures still in place and a trove of ladies' dresses, hats, and shoes for the mannequins, the store was decked out for Christmas year-round. It became a tourist attraction and drew a steady stream of visitors off the highway, breathing life back into the old ghost town.

Evelyn also commissioned a sculpture to go up on the mesa overlooking Thurston. The unusual design incorporates her old pickup, mounted at a precarious angle on the edge of the cliff, anchored by a forty-foot steel cross emerging from the bed and thrusting straight up into the Texas sky. Thousands of drivers see it daily as they pass by. Those who visit the museum can get a copy of Helen's book and learn the story behind it.

Henry and Ella donated the sewing machine and other items from the original Abbott's store back to the museum. They sold the rolltop desk, the dining table and chairs, the vintage pistol, and a few other items, recovering slightly more than their initial $675 investment.

They still go to storage unit auctions occasionally, just for fun.

They do not bid.

The End.

**About the Author**

Bob Buckel grew up in Lamesa, Texas, and spent most of his working life in the community newspaper business as a sportswriter, editor, and publisher. Since 1987, he and his wife, Krisan, have lived in Azle, where they raised three children and two foster children. She is a retired bilingual educator who volunteers as an ESL teacher for refugees, asylees, and other immigrants. They are active in church and community, and Bob spends his nonwriting time gardening, making compost, tinkering in the shop, and playing guitar.

www.ingramcontent.com/pod-product-compliance
Lightning Source LLC
LaVergne TN
LVHW091144230926
848584LV00025B/185
* 9 7 8 0 8 7 5 6 5 9 8 2 4 *